A Literary Christmas

A Literary Christmas

GREAT CONTEMPORARY CHRISTMAS STORIES

Edited and with an Introduction by
Lilly Golden

THE ATLANTIC MONTHLY PRESS
NEW YORK

Published simultaneously in Canada
Printed in the United States of America

Library of Congress Cataloging-in-Publication Data

A Literary Christmas: great contemporary Christmas stories / edited by
Lilly Golden.
1. Christmas stories. 2. Christmas—Fiction. 3. Short stories.
I. Golden, Lilly.
PR6120.95.C6L58   1992
808.83'10833—dc20   92-10703

ISBN 0-87113-583-3 (pbk.)

Design by Laura Hough

The Atlantic Monthly Press
841 Broadway
New York, NY 10003

1   3   5   7   9   10   8   6   4   2

Contents

CONTENTS

CONTENTS

CONTENTS

A Literary Christmas

LILLY GOLDEN

Introduction

When we consider the notion of the literary Christmas story, writers like Charles Dickens and O. Henry, who have given us definitive classics of the genre, immediately come to mind. The paradigm of the "Christmas story" as received from the old masters conjures up images of dimly lit, snow-covered cobblestone streets, peopled with bonneted women and top-hatted men scurrying home to warm their feet by a fire. Meanwhile, we, the reader, sit ensconced in our living room and, if we're lucky enough, nestled by our own hearth, holding on our lap a leather-bound tome, sipping eggnog, basking in the Christmas spirit. Outside, though, we hear not the clatter of horse-drawn carriages but the roar of cars speeding down the freeway. Indeed, Christmas in the late twentieth century is a far cry from Yuletide in Mr. Dickens's day, but what about the Christmas story? How has the literary form evolved compared to its subject?

What type of Christmas vision would be inspired by some of the most acclaimed writers of *our* time? Skeptics may find it contradictory to employ the contemporary short story set in the age of strip malls and elevator music to articulate something as time-honored and baroque as the Christmas spirit. Or, conversely, it may seem incongruous to use the highly developed and self-reflexive modern short story to depict the commercialized farce that some feel the Christmas season has become. Paul Auster begins his tale by voicing his misgivings when asked to write a Christmas story:

"The very phrase 'Christmas story' had unpleasant associations for me, evoking dreadful outpourings of hypocritical mush and treacle. Even at their best, Christmas stories were no more than wish-fulfillment dreams, fairy tales for adults, and I'd be damned if I'd ever allowed myself to write something like that. And yet, how could anyone write an unsentimental Christmas story? It was a contradiction in terms, an impossibility, an out-and-out conundrum. One might just as well try to imagine a racehorse without legs, or a sparrow without wings. . . ."

But, as you will see, Paul Auster and the others featured in this anthology lay such doubt to rest. In fact, the marriage between the season and the literary form is as sound as it ever was. For mistletoe and ho-ho-ho aside, what is Christmas if not a time when the nuances of our lives are magnified, when our worlds are illuminated and laid bare? And what is a short story if not a revelation of some truth about ourselves, some insight into the human heart? At its best, the short story will lead us to moments of clarity, to epiphany. And Christmas at its spiritual root is, after all, the celebration of a miracle.

Regardless of the manner in which Christmas is observed, ranging from deep religious sentiment to overextended credit cards, a universal aspect of the season is its emphasis on communion in a secular sense. Christmas is a season of convergence. People unite with friends and family or, in contrast, feel their loneliness acutely. It is a time when people look about themselves, take stock of their lives, and feel either grateful or denied, when joys are celebrated and the painful truths of life become evident, when love seems sweeter and losses more bitter.

It is for their wise and beautiful renderings of such confluences that the stories in this collection were selected. Gathered here are the works of some of the best contemporary writers from all over the world. Their stories are widely varied in setting, plot, character, culture, and religion, and though they share the subject of Christmas, whether as a central theme or as subtext, each explores the season and its psychological and emotional (and even political) reverberations from its unique perspective.

So settle back into your favorite chair and enjoy *A Literary Christmas*'s harvest from the modern masters of the art of fiction. You will find in each of these marvelous stories—some uplifting, some deeply melancholy—a Christmas gem, a gift, a bit of magic and grace.

FRANK O'CONNOR

Christmas Morning

I never really liked my brother, Sonny. From the time he was a baby he was always the mother's pet and always chasing her to tell her what mischief I was up to. Mind you, I was usually up to something. Until I was nine or ten I was never much good at school, and I really believe it was to spite me that he was so smart at his books. He seemed to know by instinct that this was what Mother had set her heart on, and you might almost say he spelled himself into her favor.

"Mummy," he'd say, "will I call Larry in to his t-e-a?" or: "Mummy, the k-e-t-e-l is boiling," and, of course, when he was wrong she'd correct him, and next time he'd have it right and there would be no standing him. "Mummy," he'd say, "aren't I a good speller?" Cripes, we could all be good spellers if we went on like that!

Mind you, it wasn't that I was stupid. Far from it. I was just restless and not able to fix my mind for long on any one thing. I'd do the lessons for the year before, or the lessons for the year after: what I couldn't stand were the lessons we were supposed to be doing at the time. In the evenings I used to go out and play with the Doherty gang. Not, again, that I was rough, but I liked the excitement, and for the life of me I couldn't see what attracted Mother about education.

"Can't you do your lessons first and play after?" she'd say, getting white with indignation. "You ought to be ashamed of yourself that your baby brother can read better than you."

She didn't seem to understand that I wasn't, because there didn't seem to me to be anything particularly praiseworthy about reading, and it struck me as an occupation better suited to a sissy kid like Sonny.

"The dear knows what will become of you," she'd say. "If only you'd stick to your books you might be something good like a clerk or an engineer."

"I'll be a clerk, Mummy," Sonny would say smugly.

"Who wants to be an old clerk?" I'd say, just to annoy him. "I'm going to be a soldier."

"The dear knows, I'm afraid that's all you'll ever be fit for," she would add with a sigh.

I couldn't help feeling at times that she wasn't all there. As if there was anything better a fellow could be!

Coming on to Christmas, with the days getting shorter and the shopping crowds bigger, I began to think of all the things I might get from Santa Claus. The Dohertys said there was no Santa Claus, only what your father and mother gave you, but the Dohertys were a rough class of children you wouldn't expect Santa to come to anyway. I was rooting round for whatever information I could pick up about him, but there didn't seem to be much. I was no hand with a pen, but if a letter would do any good I was ready to chance writing to him. I had plenty of initiative and was always writing off for free samples and prospectuses.

"Ah, I don't know will he come at all this year," Mother said with a worried air. "He has enough to do looking after steady boys who mind their lessons without bothering about the rest."

"He only comes to good spellers, Mummy," said Sonny. "Isn't that right?"

"He comes to any little boy who does his best, whether he's a good speller or not," Mother said firmly.

Well, I did my best. God knows I did! It wasn't my fault if, four days before the holidays, Flogger Dawley gave us sums we couldn't do, and Peter Doherty and myself had to go on the lang. It wasn't for love of it, for, take it from me, December is no month for mitching, and we spent most of our time sheltering from the rain in a store on the quays. The only mistake we

5

made was imagining we could keep it up till the holidays without being spotted. That showed real lack of foresight.

Of course, Flogger Dawley noticed and sent home word to know what was keeping me. When I came in on the third day the mother gave me a look I'll never forget, and said: "Your dinner is there." She was too full to talk. When I tried to explain to her about Flogger Dawley and the sums she brushed it aside and said: "You have no word." I saw then it wasn't the langing she minded but the lies, though I still didn't see how you could lang without lying. She didn't speak to me for days. And even then I couldn't make out what she saw in education, or why she wouldn't let me grow up naturally like anyone else.

To make things worse, it stuffed Sonny up more than ever. He had the air of one saying: "I don't know what they'd do without me in this blooming house." He stood at the front door, leaning against the jamb with his hands in his trouser pockets, trying to make himself look like Father, and shouted to the other kids so that he could be heard all over the road.

"Larry isn't left go out. He went on the lang with Peter Doherty and me mother isn't talking to him."

And at night, when we were in bed, he kept it up.

"Santa Claus won't bring you anything this year, aha!"

"Of course he will," I said.

"How do you know?"

"Why wouldn't he?"

"Because you went on the lang with Doherty. I wouldn't play with them Doherty fellows."

"You wouldn't be left."

"I wouldn't play with them. They're no class. They had the bobbies up at the house."

"And how would Santa know I was on the lang with Peter Doherty?" I growled, losing patience with the little prig.

"Of course he'd know. Mummy would tell him."

"And how could Mummy tell him and he up at the North Pole? Poor Ireland, she's rearing them yet! 'Tis easy seen you're only an old baby."

"I'm not a baby, and I can spell better than you, and Santa won't bring you anything."

"We'll see whether he will or not," I said sarcastically, doing the old man on him.

But, to tell the God's truth, the old man was only bluff. You could never tell what powers these superhuman chaps would have of knowing what you were up to. And I had a bad conscience about the langing because I'd never before seen the mother like that.

That was the night I decided that the only sensible thing to do was to see Santa myself and explain to him. Being a man, he'd probably understand. In those days I was a good-looking kid and had a way with me when I liked. I had only to smile nicely at one old gent on the North Mall to get a penny from him, and I felt if only I could get Santa by himself I could do the same with him and maybe get something worthwhile from him. I wanted a model railway: I was sick of Ludo and Snakes-and-Ladders.

I started to practice lying awake, counting five hundred and then a thousand, and trying to hear first eleven, then midnight, from Shandon. I felt sure Santa would be round by midnight, seeing that he'd be coming from the north, and would have the whole of the South Side to do afterward. In some ways I was very farsighted. The only trouble was the things I was farsighted about.

I was so wrapped up in my own calculations that I had little attention to spare for Mother's difficulties. Sonny and I used to go to town with her, and while she was shopping we stood outside a toy shop in the North Main Street, arguing about what we'd like for Christmas.

On Christmas Eve when Father came home from work and gave her the housekeeping money, she stood looking at it doubtfully while her face grew white.

"Well?" he snapped, getting angry. "What's wrong with that?"

"What's wrong with it?" she muttered. "On Christmas Eve!"

"Well," he asked truculently, sticking his hands in his trouser pockets as though to guard what was left, "do you think I get more because it's Christmas?"

7

"Lord God," she muttered distractedly. "And not a bit of cake in the house, nor a candle, nor anything!"

"All right," he shouted, beginning to stamp. "How much will the candle be?"

"Ah, for pity's sake," she cried, "will you give me the money and not argue like that before the children? Do you think I'll leave them with nothing on the one day of the year?"

"Bad luck to you and your children!" he snarled. "Am I to be slaving from one year's end to another for you to be throwing it away on toys? Here," he added, tossing two half crowns on the table, "that's all you're going to get, so make the most of it."

"I suppose the publicans will get the rest," she said bitterly.

Later she went into town, but did not bring us with her, and returned with a lot of parcels, including the Christmas candle. We waited for Father to come home to his tea, but he didn't, so we had our own tea and a slice of Christmas cake each, and then Mother put Sonny on a chair with the holy water stoup to sprinkle the candle, and when he lighted it she said: "The light of Heaven to our souls." I could see she was upset because Father wasn't in—it should be the oldest and youngest. When we hung up our stockings at bedtime he was still out.

Then began the hardest couple of hours I ever put in. I was mad with sleep but afraid of losing the model railway, so I lay for a while, making up things to say to Santa when he came. They varied in tone from frivolous to grave, for some old gents like kids to be modest and well-spoken, while others prefer them with spirit. When I had rehearsed them all I tried to wake Sonny to keep me company, but that kid slept like the dead.

Eleven struck from Shandon, and soon after I heard the latch, but it was only Father coming home.

"Hello, little girl," he said, letting on to be surprised at finding Mother waiting up for him, and then broke into a self-conscious giggle. "What have you up so late?"

"Do you want your supper?" she asked shortly.

"Ah, no, no," he replied. "I had a bit of pig's cheek at Daneen's on my way up." (Daneen was my uncle.) "I'm very fond of a bit of pig's cheek. . . . My goodness, is it that late?" he exclaimed, letting on to be astonished. "If I knew that I'd have gone to the North Chapel for midnight Mass. I'd like to hear the *Adeste* again. That's a hymn I'm very fond of—a most touching hymn."

Then he began to hum it falsetto.

> "*Adeste fideles*
> *Solus domus dagus.*"

Father was very fond of Latin hymns, particularly when he had a drop in, but as he had no notion of the words he made them up as he went along, and this always drove Mother mad.

"Ah, you disgust me!" she said in a scalded voice, and closed the room door behind her. Father laughed as if he thought it a great joke; and he struck a match to light his pipe and for a while puffed at it noisily. The light under the door dimmed and went out but he continued to sing emotionally.

> "*Dixie medearo*
> *Tutum tonum tantum*
> *Venite adoremus.*"

He had it all wrong but the effect was the same on me. To save my life I couldn't keep awake.

Coming on to dawn, I woke with the feeling that something dreadful had happened. The whole house was quiet, and the little bedroom that looked out on the foot and a half of backyard was pitch-dark. It was only when I glanced at the window that I saw how all the silver had drained out of the sky. I jumped out of bed to feel my stocking, well knowing that the worst had happened. Santa had come while I was asleep, and gone away with an entirely false impression of me, because all he had left me was some sort of book, folded up, a pen and pencil, and a tuppenny bag of sweets. Not even Snakes-and-Ladders! For a while I was too stunned even to think. A fellow who was able to drive over rooftops and climb down chimneys without getting stuck—God, wouldn't you think he'd know better?

Then I began to wonder what that foxy boy, Sonny, had. I went to his side of the bed and felt his stocking. For all his spelling and sucking up he hadn't done so much better, because, apart from a bag of sweets like mine, all Santa had left him was a popgun, one that fired a cork on a piece of string and which you could get in any huckster's shop for sixpence.

All the same, the fact remained that it was a gun, and a gun was better than a book any day of the week. The Dohertys had a gang, and the gang fought the Strawberry Lane kids who tried to play football on our road. That gun would be very useful to me in many ways, while it would be lost on Sonny who wouldn't be let play with the gang, even if he wanted to.

Then I got the inspiration, as it seemed to me, direct from Heaven. Suppose I took the gun and gave Sonny the book! Sonny would never be any good in the gang: he was fond of spelling, and a studious child like him could learn a lot of spellings from a book like mine. As he hadn't seen Santa any more than I had, what he hadn't seen wouldn't grieve him. I was doing no harm to anyone; in fact, if Sonny only knew, I was doing him a good turn which he might have cause to thank me for later. That was one thing I was always keen on; doing good turns. Perhaps this was Santa's intention the whole time and he had merely become confused between us. It was a mistake that might happen to anyone. So I put the book, the pencil, and the pen into Sonny's stocking and the popgun in my own and returned to bed and slept again. As I say, in those days I had plenty of initiative.

It was Sonny who woke me, shaking me to tell me that Santa had come and left me a gun. I let on to be surprised and rather disappointed in the gun, and to divert his mind from it made him show me his picture book, and cracked it up to the skies.

As I knew, that kid was prepared to believe anything, and nothing would do him then but to take the presents in to show Father and Mother. This was a bad moment for me. After the way she had behaved about the langing, I distrusted Mother, though I had the consolation of believing that the only person who could contradict me was now somewhere up by the North Pole. That gave me a certain confidence, so Sonny and I burst in with our presents, shouting: "Look what Santa Claus brought!"

Father and Mother woke, and Mother smiled, but only for an instant. As she looked at me her face changed. I knew that look; I knew it only too well. It was the same she had worn the day I came home from langing, when she said I had no word.

"Larry," she said in a low voice, "where did you get the gun?"

"Santa left it in my stocking, Mummy," I said, trying to put on an injured air, though it baffled me how she guessed that he hadn't. "He did, honest."

"You stole it from that poor child's stocking while he was asleep," she said, her voice quivering with indignation. "Larry, Larry, how could you be so mean?"

"Now, now, now," Father said deprecatingly, " 'tis Christmas morning."

"Ah," she said with real passion, "it's easy it comes to you. Do you think I want my son to grow up a liar and a thief?"

"Ah, what thief, woman?" he said testily. "Have sense, can't you?" He was as cross if you interrupted him in his benevolent moods as if they were of the other sort, and this one was probably exacerbated by a feeling of guilt for his behavior of the night before. "Here, Larry," he said, reaching out for the money on the bedside table, "here's sixpence for you and one for Sonny. Mind you don't lose it now!"

But I looked at Mother and saw what was in her eyes. I burst out crying, threw the popgun on the floor, and ran bawling out of the house before anyone on the road was awake. I rushed up the lane behind the house and threw myself on the wet grass.

I understood it all, and it was almost more than I could bear; that there was no Santa Claus, as the Dohertys said, only Mother trying to scrape together a few coppers from the housekeeping; that Father was mean and common and a drunkard, and that she had been relying on me to raise her out of the misery of the life she was leading. And I knew that the look in her eyes was the fear that, like my father, I should turn out to be mean and common and a drunkard.

PAUL AUSTER

Auggie Wren's Christmas Story

I heard this story from Auggie Wren. Since Auggie doesn't come off too well in it, at least not as well as he'd like to, he's asked me not to use his real name. Other than that, the whole business about the lost wallet and the blind woman and the Christmas dinner is just as he told it to me.

Auggie and I have known each other for close to eleven years now. He works behind the counter of a cigar store on Court Street in downtown Brooklyn, and since it's the only store that carries the little Dutch cigars I like to smoke, I go in there fairly often. For a long time, I didn't give much thought to Auggie Wren. He was the strange little man who wore a hooded blue sweatshirt and sold me cigars and magazines, the impish, wisecracking character who always had something funny to say about the weather or the Mets or the politicians in Washington, and that was the extent of it.

But then one day several years ago he happened to be looking through a magazine in the store, and he stumbled across a review of one of my books. He knew it was me because a photograph accompanied the review, and after that things changed between us. I was no longer just another customer to Auggie, I had become a distinguished person. Most people couldn't care less about books and writers, but it turned out that Auggie considered himself an artist. Now that he had cracked the secret of who I was, he embraced me as an ally, a confidant, a brother-in-arms. To tell the truth, I found it rather embarrassing. Then, almost inevitably, a moment came when he asked if I would be willing to look at his photographs. Given his enthusiasm and good will, there didn't seem to be any way I could turn him down.

God knows what I was expecting. At the very least, it wasn't what Auggie showed me the next day. In a small, windowless room at the back of the store, he opened a cardboard box and pulled out twelve identical black photo albums. This was his life's work, he said, and it didn't take him more than five minutes a day to do it. Every morning for the past twelve years, he had stood at the corner of Atlantic Avenue and Clinton Street at precisely seven o'clock and had taken a single color photograph of precisely the same view. The project now ran to more than four thousand photographs. Each album represented a different year, and all the pictures were laid out in sequence, from January 1 to December 31, with the dates carefully recorded under each one.

As I flipped through the albums and began to study Auggie's work, I didn't know what to think. My first impression was that it was the oddest, most bewildering thing I had ever seen. All the pictures were the same. The whole project was a numbing onslaught of repetition, the same street and the same buildings over and over again, an unrelenting delirium of redundant images. I couldn't think of anything to say to Auggie, so I continued turning pages, nodding my head in feigned appreciation. Auggie himself seemed unperturbed, watching me with a broad smile on his face, but after I'd been at it for several minutes, he suddenly interrupted me and said, "You're going too fast. You'll never get it if you don't slow down."

He was right, of course. If you don't take the time to look, you'll never manage to see anything. I picked up another album and forced myself to go more deliberately. I paid closer attention to details, took note of shifts in the weather, watched for the changing angles of light as the seasons advanced. Eventually, I was able to detect subtle differences in the traffic flow, to anticipate the rhythm of the different days (the commotion of workday mornings, the relative stillness of weekends, the contrast between Saturdays and Sundays). And then, little by little, I began to recognize the faces of the people in the background, the passersby on their way to work, the same people in the same spot every morning, living an instant of their lives in the field of Auggie's camera.

Once I got to know them, I began to study their postures, the way they carried themselves from one morning to the next, trying to discover their moods from these surface indications, as if I could imagine stories for them, as if I could penetrate the invisible dramas locked inside their bodies. I picked up another album. I was no longer bored, no longer puzzled as I had been at first. Auggie was photographing time, I realized, both natural time and human time, and he was doing it by planting himself in one tiny corner of the world and willing it to be his own, by standing guard in the space he had chosen for himself. As he watched me pore over his work, Auggie continued to smile with pleasure. Then, almost as if he had been reading my thoughts, he began to recite a line from Shakespeare. "Tomorrow and tomorrow and tomorrow," he muttered under his breath, "time creeps on its petty pace." I understood then that he knew exactly what he was doing.

That was more than two thousand pictures ago. Since that day, Auggie and I have discussed his work many times, but it was only last week that I learned how he acquired his camera and started taking pictures in the first place. That was the subject of the story he told me, and I'm still struggling to make sense of it.

Earlier that same week, a man from the *New York Times* called me and asked if I would be willing to write a short story that would appear in the paper on Christmas morning. My first impulse was to say no, but the man was very charming and persistent, and by the end of the conversation I told him I would give it a try. The moment I hung up the phone, however, I fell into a deep panic. What did I know about Christmas? I asked myself. What did I know about writing short stories on commission?

I spent the next several days in despair, warring with the ghosts of Dickens, O. Henry and other masters of the Yuletide spirit. The very phrase "Christmas story" had unpleasant associations for me, evoking dreadful outpourings of hypocritical mush and treacle. Even at their best, Christmas stories were no more than wish-fulfillment dreams, fairy tales for adults,

15

and I'd be damned if I'd ever allowed myself to write something like that. And yet, how could anyone propose to write an unsentimental Christmas story? It was a contradiction in terms, an impossibility, an out-and-out conundrum. One might just as well try to imagine a racehorse without legs, or a sparrow without wings.

I got nowhere. On Thursday I went out for a long walk, hoping the air would clear my head. Just past noon, I stopped in at the cigar store to replenish my supply, and there was Auggie, standing behind the counter as always. He asked me how I was. Without really meaning to, I found myself unburdening my troubles to him. "A Christmas story?" he said after I had finished. "Is that all? If you buy me lunch, my friend, I'll tell you the best Christmas story you ever heard. And I guarantee that every word of it is true."

We walked down the block to Jack's, a cramped and boisterous delicatessen with good pastrami sandwiches and photographs of old Dodger teams hanging on the walls. We found a table at the back, ordered our food, and then Auggie launched into his story.

"It was the summer of '72," he said. "A kid came in one morning and started stealing things from the store. He must have been about nineteen or twenty, and I don't think I've ever seen a more pathetic shoplifter in my life. He's standing by the rack of paperbacks along the far wall and stuffing books into the pockets of his raincoat. It was crowded around the counter just then, so I didn't see him at first. But once I noticed what he was up to, I started to shout. He took off like a jackrabbit, and by the time I managed to get out from behind the counter, he was already tearing down Atlantic Avenue. I chased after him for about half a block, and then I gave up. He'd dropped something along the way, and since I didn't feel like running anymore, I bent down to see what it was.

"It turned out to be his wallet. There wasn't any money inside, but his driver's license was there along with three or four snapshots. I suppose I could have called the cops and had him arrested. I had his name and address from the license, but I felt kind of sorry for him. He was just a measly little punk, and once I looked at those pictures in his wallet, I couldn't bring myself to feel very angry at him. Robert Goodwin. That was his name. In one of the pictures, I remember, he was standing with his arm around his mother or grandmother. In another one, he was sitting there at age nine or ten dressed in a baseball uniform with a big smile on his face. I just didn't have the heart. He was probably on dope now, I figured. A poor kid from Brooklyn without much going for him, and who cared about a couple of trashy paperbacks anyway?

"So I held onto the wallet. Every once in a while I'd get a little urge to send it back to him, but I kept delaying and never did anything about it. Then Christmas rolls around and I'm stuck with nothing to do. The boss usually invites me over to his house to spend the day, but that year he and his family were down in Florida visiting relatives. So I'm sitting in my apartment that morning feeling a little sorry for myself, and then I see Robert Goodwin's wallet lying on a shelf in the kitchen. I figure what the hell, why not do something nice for once, and I put on my coat and go out to return the wallet in person.

"The address was over in Boerum Hill, somewhere in the projects. It was freezing out that day, and I remember getting lost a few times trying to find the right building. Everything looks the same in that place, and you keep going over the same ground thinking you're somewhere else. Anyway, I finally get to the apartment I'm looking for and ring the bell. Nothing happens. I assume no one's there, but I try again just to make sure. I wait a little longer, and just when I'm about to give up, I hear someone shuffling to the door. An old woman's voice asks who's there, and I say I'm looking for Robert Goodwin. 'Is that you, Robert?' the old woman says, and then she undoes about fifteen locks and opens the door.

"She has to be at least eighty, maybe ninety years old, and the first thing I notice about her is that she's blind. 'I knew you'd come, Robert,' she says. 'I knew you wouldn't forget your Granny Ethel on Christmas.' And then she opens her arms as if she's about to hug me.

"I didn't have much time to think, you understand. I had to say something real fast, and before I knew what was happening, I could hear the words coming out of my mouth. 'That's right, Granny Ethel,' I said. 'I came back to see you on Christmas.' Don't ask me why I did it. I don't have any idea. Maybe I didn't want to disappoint her or something, I don't know. It just came out that way, and then this old woman was suddenly hugging me there in front of the door, and I was hugging her back.

"I didn't exactly say that I was her grandson. Not in so many words, at least, but that was the implication. I wasn't trying to trick her, though. It was like a game we'd both decided to play—without having to discuss the rules. I mean, that woman *knew* I wasn't her grandson Robert. She was old and dotty, but she wasn't so far gone that she couldn't tell the difference between a stranger and her own flesh and blood. But it made her happy to pretend, and since I had nothing better to do anyway, I was happy to go along with her.

"So we went into the apartment and spent the day together. The place was a real dump, I might add, but what else can you expect from a blind woman who does her own housekeeping? Every time she asked me a question about how I was, I would lie to her. I told her I'd found a good job working in a cigar store, I told her I was about to get married, I told her a hundred pretty stories, and she made like she believed every one of them. 'That's fine, Robert,' she would say, nodding her head and smiling. 'I always knew things would work out for you.'

"After a while, I started getting pretty hungry. There didn't seem to be much food in the house, so I went out to a store in the neighborhood and brought back a mess of stuff. A precooked chicken, vegetable soup, a bucket of potato salad, a chocolate cake, all kinds of things. Ethel had a couple of bottles of wine stashed in her bedroom, and so between us we managed to put together a fairly decent Christmas dinner. We both got a little tipsy from the wine, I remember, and after the meal was over we went out to sit in the living room, where the chairs were more comfortable. I had to take a pee, so I excused myself and went to the bathroom down the hall. That's where things took yet another turn. It was ditsy enough doing my little jig as Ethel's grandson, but what I did next was positively crazy, and I've never forgiven myself for it.

* * *

"I go into the bathroom, and stacked up against the wall next to the shower, I see a pile of six or seven cameras. Brand-new thirty-five-millimeter cameras, still in their boxes, top-quality merchandise. I figure this is the work of the real Robert, a storage place for one of his recent hauls. I've never taken a picture in my life, and I've certainly never stolen anything, but the moment I see those cameras sitting in the bathroom, I decide I want one of them for myself. Just like that. And without even stopping to think about it, I tuck one of the boxes under my arm and go back to the living room.

"I couldn't have been gone for more than three minutes, but in that time Granny Ethel had fallen asleep in her chair. Too much Chianti, I suppose. I went into the kitchen to wash the dishes, and she slept on through the whole racket, snoring like a baby. There didn't seem to be any point in disturbing her, so I decided to leave. I couldn't even write a note to say good-bye, seeing that she was blind and all, and so I just left. I put her grandson's wallet on the table, picked up the camera again, and walked out of the apartment. And that's the end of the story."

"Did you ever go back to see her?" I asked.

"Once," he said. "About three or four months later. I felt so bad about stealing the camera, I hadn't even used it yet. I finally made up my mind to return it, but Ethel wasn't there anymore. I don't know what happened to her, but someone else had moved into the apartment, and he couldn't tell me where she was."

"She probably died."

"Yeah, probably."

"Which means that she spent her last Christmas with you."

"I guess so. I never thought of it that way."

"It was a good deed, Auggie. It was a nice thing you did for her."

"I lied to her, and then I stole from her. I don't see how you can call that a good deed."

"You made her happy. And the camera was stolen anyway. It's not as if the person you took it from really owned it."

"Anything for art, eh Paul?"

"I wouldn't say that. But at least you've put the camera to good use."

"And now you've got your Christmas story, don't you?"

"Yes," I said. "I suppose I do."

I paused for a moment, studying Auggie as a wicked grin spread across his face. I couldn't be sure, but the look in his eyes at that moment was so mysterious, so fraught with the glow of some inner delight, that it suddenly occurred to me that he had made the whole thing up. I was about to ask him if he'd been putting me on, but then I realized he would never tell. I had been tricked into believing him, and that was the only thing that mattered. As long as there's one person to believe it, there's no story that can't be true.

"You're an ace, Auggie," I said. "Thanks for being so helpful."

"Any time," he answered, still looking at me with that maniacal light in his eyes. "After all, if you can't share your secrets with your friends, what kind of a friend are you?"

"I guess I owe you one."

"No you don't. Just put it down the way I told it to you, and you don't owe me a thing."

"Except the lunch."

"That's right. Except the lunch."

I returned Auggie's smile with a smile of my own, and then I called out to the waiter and asked for the check.

TOBIAS WOLFF

Champagne

My stepfather Dwight said that he had once seen Lawrence Welk in the dining car of a train. Dwight said that he'd walked right up to him and told him that he was his favorite conductor, and he probably did, for it was true that he loved the champagne music of Lawrence Welk better than any other music. Dwight had a large collection of Lawrence Welk records. When "The Lawrence Welk Show" came on TV we were expected to watch it with him, and be quiet, and get up only during commercials. Dwight pulled his chair up close to the set. He leaned forward as the bubbles rose over the Champagne Orchestra and Lawrence Welk came onstage salaaming in every direction, crying out declarations of humility in his unctuous, brain-scalding Swedish kazoo of a voice.

Dwight's eyes widened at the virtuosity of Big Tiny Little Junior, who played ragtime piano while looking over his shoulder at the camera. He gazed with chaste ardor at the Lovely Champagne Lady Alice Lon, who smiled the same tremulous smile through every note of every song until she got canned and replaced by the Lovely Champagne Lady Norma Zimmer. He gloated over the Lovely Little Lennon Sisters as if they were his own daughters, and laughed out loud at the cruel jokes Lawrence Welk made at the expense of his slobbering Irish tenor, Joe Feeney. Joe Feeney was the latest addition to the Champagne Ensemble and obviously felt himself on pretty shaky ground, especially after the Lovely Champagne Lady Alice Lon was sent packing and then the Ragtime Piano Virtuoso Big Tiny Little Junior got replaced by the Ragtime Piano Virtuoso Jo Ann Castle, who pummeled the keys like a butcher tenderizing meat. When Joe Feeney sang he held nothing back. He worked himself up to the point of tears, and flecks of saliva flew off his wet lips. You had the feeling that Joe Feeney was singing for his life.

About halfway through the show, Dwight would take out his old Conn saxophone and finger the stops in time to the music. Sometimes, when he got really carried away, he would forget himself and blow on it, and a squawk would come out.

After Dwight's daughter Norma graduated from Concrete High she moved down to Seattle. She worked in an office where she met a man named Kenneth who took her for long drives in his Austin Healey sports car and tried to talk her into getting married. Norma called my mother all the time and asked for advice. What should she do? She still loved Bobby Crow, but Bobby wasn't going anywhere. He didn't even have a job. Kenneth was ambitious. On the other hand, nobody liked him. He had very strong opinions about everything and was also a Seventh-Day Adventist. But that wasn't it, exactly. Kenneth just didn't have a very good personality.

Then Norma called up and said she'd decided to marry Kenneth. She refused to explain her decision, but insisted it was final. Naturally, she wanted to invite Kenneth to Chinook to meet the family, and it was finally settled that he should come up during Christmas, when her brother Skipper would also be home.

Dwight got the spirit that year. He made a wreath for the door and hung pine boughs all over the living room. A couple of weeks before Christmas he and I drove up into the mountains to get a tree. It was early afternoon, a cold light rain falling. Dwight drank from a pint bottle as we scouted the woods. We found a fine blue spruce growing all by itself in the middle of a clearing, and Dwight let me cut it down while he took nips off his bottle and squinted up at the misty peaks all around us. Once I got the tree down we started wrestling it through the dense growth, back toward the fire road where we'd left the car. We had walked a good distance and the going was rough. I could hear Dwight laboring for breath and muttering when he stumbled. I kept waiting for him to bark at me, but he never did. He was that pleased about Norma coming home.

After dinner that night Dwight went into the living room with a can of spray paint and began to shake it. He was very thorough when it came to painting, and if he was using spray paint he always followed the directions to the letter and shook the can well. The agitator rattled loudly as he swung the can back and forth. Pearl, my other stepsister, and I were doing our homework at the dining room table. We pretended not to watch. My mother was out somewhere or else she would've asked him what he thought he was doing, and possibly even stopped him.

When he finished shaking the can, Dwight pulled the tree into the middle of the living room and walked around it two or three times. Then, starting at the top and working his way down, he proceeded to spray it with white paint. I thought he meant to put a few splashes here and there to suggest snow, but he sprayed the whole thing—trunk and all. The needles drank up the paint and turned faintly blue again. Dwight put on another coat. It took him three cans before he was done, but the tree stayed white.

By the next day, when we decorated the tree, the needles had already begun to drop off. Every time you touched a limb it set off a little cascade of them. No one said anything. My mother hung a few balls, then sat down and stared at the tree.

The needles kept falling, pattering softly down on the white crepe paper spread around the trunk. By the time Norma and Skipper arrived the tree was half-bare. They had driven up together from Seattle; Kenneth had to work, but he was all set to join us the following day.

Norma must have told Bobby Crow she was coming. He showed up just after dinner that night, restless and grim, silent when Skipper tried to banter with him. He took Norma somewhere, then drove her back a couple of hours later. But she didn't get out of the car. The rest of us sat around in the living room, and watched the lights blink on the tree, and talked about anything but the fact that Norma was still outside with Bobby Crow. The lights didn't blink at different times like twinkling stars but all at once, flashing on and off like a neon sign outside a roadhouse.

I was in bed when Norma finally came inside and ran to her room, giving long ululating cries that appalled me and made me cringe in anticipation. I heard Pearl try to soothe her, then my mother joined them and I heard her voice too, lower than Pearl's, the two of them speaking sometimes in turn and sometimes together so that their voices formed one murmurous braid of sound. Skipper shifted in his bed but slept on, and in time, as Norma's keening subsided, I lay back and went to sleep myself.

Kenneth pulled up the next afternoon and by dinnertime we all hated him. He knew it, and relished it, even sought it out. As soon as he stepped out of his Austin Healey, he started complaining about the remoteness of the camp and the discomfort of the drive and the imprecision of the directions Norma had left behind for him. He had a fussy, aggrieved voice and thin disappointed lips. He wore a golf cap and perforated leather gloves that snapped across the wrist. He removed one of his gloves as he complained, tugging delicately at each finger, then going on to the next until the glove came free. He took off the other just as slowly and carefully, then turned to Norma. "Don't I get a kiss?"

She bent forward to peck him on the cheek but he seized her face between his hands and kissed her long and full on the lips. It was obvious that he was French-kissing her. We stood watching this and smiling the same foolish smiles we had brought outside to welcome him with.

After Kenneth had wolfed down a sandwich, Dwight made the mistake of offering him a drink. "Oh, boy," Kenneth said. "I guess you don't know much about me." He said that he believed he had a duty to lay his cards on the table, and so he did.

"I don't know," Dwight said. "I don't see the harm in a drink now and then."

"I'm sure you don't," Kenneth said. "I'm sure the drug fiend doesn't see the harm in a needle now and then."

This led to an exchange of words. My mother stepped in and acted jolly and moved us from the kitchen into the living room, where she must have hoped that the presence of the tree and the gifts would remind us why we were together, and call us to our better selves. But Kenneth started laying more cards on the table. There truly was no end of them. Skipper finally said, "Look, Kenneth . . . why don't you lay off?"

"What are you afraid of, Skipper?"

"Afraid?" Skipper's eyelids fluttered as if he were trying to confirm some improbable image.

"I only tell you this because I love you," Kenneth said, "but you are very frightened people. Very frightened. But hey, there's no need to be—the news is good!"

"Just who the hell do you think you are?" Dwight said.

Kenneth smiled. "Go on. I can take it."

Norma tried to change the subject but Kenneth could take any comment and find something in it to deplore. Argument was the only kind of sound he knew how to make. And if you didn't give in to him he smirked and offered you his pity for being so ignorant and misled. He wasn't reluctant to get personal. Soon enough Dwight and Skipper got personal back, and then Pearl and I put our oars in. Insulting this man was a profound pleasure, and a pleasure not only for us; a flush of excitement came into his pallid face as the words got meaner and harder to take back. He kept our blood up by saying, "If you think that bothers me, you're sadly mistaken," and "Sorry, try again," and "I've had worse than that."

This went on for some time. As we baited him Kenneth smiled in a secretive way and sucked on an empty Yellow-Bole pipe with which, he later told me, he strengthened his willpower by tempting himself to smoke.

Norma was mute. She sat next to Kenneth on the sofa and stared at the floor while he absently rubbed his hand up and down her back. Every time he touched her I felt despair. At last my mother came in from the kitchen and suggested that Norma take Kenneth out and show him around Chinook. Norma nodded and stood up, but Kenneth said he didn't want to leave now, just when things were getting interesting.

Norma implored him with her eyes.

Finally he left with her. In the wake of his going we exchanged looks of exultation and shame. A fidgety silence came upon us. One by one we drifted away to other parts of the house.

But at dinner it started up again. Kenneth couldn't stop himself. Even when he was quiet you could feel him preparing his next charge. The only thing that could shut him up was the TV. When the TV came on Kenneth went silent, staring and still as an owl in a tree.

Over the next couple of days my mother talked each of us into spending some time alone with him so we could get to know one another as individuals. This proved a mistake. Some people are better left unknown. Our walks and drives with Kenneth ended early and culminated in shouts and slamming doors. Years later my mother told me he'd made a pass at her.

We could all see that Norma didn't love Kenneth. But she stayed next to him, and submitted to his demonstrations of passion, and refused to say a word against him. She even, in the end, married him. But not before Dwight had nearly killed himself trying to stop her. He drove down to Seattle almost every weekend, sometimes bringing us along, more often by himself, always with some new scheme for luring her away from Kenneth. Nothing worked. He returned late Sunday night or early Monday morning, eyes bloodshot from the long drive, too tired and baffled even to quarrel.

Norma married Kenneth, and had their baby, and they moved into a duplex near Bothell. When we came down for visits she acted happy and never complained about anything. But she was pale and angular, all her lazy lushness gone. Her green eyes blazed in the starkness of her face. She had taken up smoking—out on their little patio where Kenneth wouldn't smell it when he got home—and she continuously excused herself during our visits to go outside and puff greedily on a cigarette, tapping her feet and looking up at the sky, now and then glancing back at us through the sliding glass door.

I saw Bobby Crow in Concrete a year or so later, just after I'd started high school there. He was standing beside a truck with some other men, most of them Indians. Bobby still had a measure of renown for his gridiron magic, and I thought I would impress the two boys I was with by a show of familiarity. As we walked past the truck I said, "Hey, Bobo, how's it going?" The men fell quiet and looked over at us. Bobby fixed me with a stare. "Who the hell are you talking to?" he said. His eyes were full of murder.

We watched TV most of Christmas Eve. When it got dark, Dwight left the house lights off so we could get the full effect of the lights on the tree. We broke to eat, then went back to the set. By the time "The Lawrence Welk Christmas Special" came on we were glassy-eyed and slack-jawed, stunned with viewing. The Champagne Orchestra played a medley of Christmas favorites, the sacred and profane mixed effervescently together, and then someone wearing knee breeches and a tricornered hat acted the part of Franz Gruber while Lawrence Welk intoned the narrative: "It was Christmas Eve in the little town of Oberndorf, and snow was falling as the organist Franz Gruber made his weary way to the little church that was soon to become famous throughout the world. . . ." The Gruber character paused on the church steps, looked up suddenly with the fire of inspiration in his eyes, then dashed inside and plunked out "Silent Night." He had to change a couple of notes here and there, but after he got it right the orchestra segued in and subsumed it into their own champagne arrangement, with Joe Feeney sobbing out a verse a cappella at the very end.

The scene shifted. We found ourselves in an elegant room where, under a shimmering tree, the Lovely Little Lennon Sisters began to sing a medley of their own. Firelight gleamed on their faces. Snow fell slowly past the window behind them, a glockenspiel chimed in accompaniment. They were singing "Chestnuts Roasting on an Open Fire" when Dwight nudged me and motioned me to follow him. He looked pleased with himself. "It's about time we got some use out of those chestnuts," he said.

The chestnuts. Almost two years had passed since I'd shucked them and stored them away. In all that time no one had said a word about them. They'd been forgotten by everyone but me, and I'd kept my mouth shut because I didn't want to remind Dwight to give me the job again.

We climbed up into the attic and worked our way down to where I'd put the boxes. It was cramped and musty. From below I could hear faint voices singing. Dwight led the way, probing the darkness with a flashlight. When he found the boxes he stopped and held the beam on them. Mold covered the cardboard sides and rose from the tops of the boxes like dough swelling out of a bread pan. Its surface, dark and solid-looking, gullied and creased like cauliflower, glistened in the light. Dwight played the beam over the boxes, then turned it on the basin where the beaver, also forgotten these two years past, had been left to cure. Only a pulp remained. This too was covered with mold, but a different kind than the one that had gotten the chestnuts. This mold was white and transparent, a network of gossamer filaments that had flowered to a height of two feet or so above the basin. It was like cotton candy but more loosely spun. And as Dwight played the light over it I saw something strange. The mold had no features, of course, but its outline somehow suggested the shape of the beaver it had consumed: a vague cloud-picture of a beaver crouching in the air.

If Dwight noticed it he didn't say anything. I followed him back downstairs and into the living room. My mother had gone to bed, but everyone else was still watching TV. Dwight picked up his saxophone again and played silently along with the Champagne Orchestra. The tree blinked. Our faces darkened and flared, darkened and flared.

MARK RICHARD

The Birds for Christmas

We wanted *The Birds* for Christmas. We had seen the commercials for it on the television donated thirdhand by the Merchant Seamen's and Sailors' Rest Home, a big black-and-white Zenith of cracked plastic and no knobs, a dime stuck in the channel selector. You could adjust the picture and have no sound, or hi-fi sound and no picture. We just wanted the picture. We wanted to see *The Birds*.

The Old Head Nurse said not to get our hopes up. It was a "Late Show" after Lights Out the night before Christmas Eve. She said it would wake the babies and scare the Little Boys down on the far end of the ward. Besides, she said, she didn't think it was the type of movie we should be seeing Christmas week. She said she was certain there would be Rudolph and Frosty on. That would be more appropriate for us to watch on the night before Christmas Eve.

"*Fuck* Frosty," Michael Christian said to me. "I seen that a *hunrett* times. I want to see *The Birds*, man. I want to see those birds get all up *in* them people's hair. That's some real Christmas TV to me."

Michael Christian and I were some of the last Big Boys to be claimed for Christmas. We were certain *someone* would eventually come for us. We were not frightened yet. There were still some other Big Boys around—the Big Boy who ran away to a gas station every other night, the Human Skeleton who would bite you, and the guy locked away on the sun porch who the Young Doctors were taking apart an arm and a leg at a time.

The Young Doctors told Michael Christian that their Christmas gift to him would be that one day he would be able to do a split onstage like his idol, James Brown. There never seemed to be any doubt in Michael Christian's mind about that. For now, he just wanted to see *The Birds* while he pretended to be James Brown in the Hospital.

Pretending to be James Brown in the Hospital was not without its hazards for Michael Christian; he had to remember to keep his head lifted from his pillow so as not to *bedhead* his budding Afro. Once, when he was practicing his singing, the nurses rushed to his bed asking him where it hurt.

"I'm warming up 'I Feel Good,' stupid bitches," said Michael Christian. Then his bed was jerked from the wall and wheeled with great speed, pushed and pulled along by hissing nurses, jarring other bedsteads, Michael Christian's wrists hanging over the safety bed rails like jailhouse-window hands; he was on his way to spend a couple of solitary hours out in the long, dark, and empty hall, him rolling his eyes at me as he sped past, saying, "Aw, man, now I feel BAD!"

Bed wheeling into the hall was one of the few alternatives to corporal punishment the nurses had, most of them being reluctant to spank a child in traction for spitting an orange pip at his neighbor, or to beat a completely burned child for cursing. Bed wheeling into the hall was especially effective at Christmastime, when it carried the possibility of missing Christmas programs. A veteran of several Christmases in the hospital and well acquainted with the grim Christmas programs, Michael Christian scoffed at the treasures handed out by the church and state charities—the aging fruit, the surplus ballpoint pens, the occasional batches of recycled toys that didn't work, the games and puzzles with missing pieces. Michael Christian's Christmas Wish was as specific as mine. I wanted a miniature train set with batteries so I could lay out the track to run around on my bed over the covers. Not the big Lionel size or the HO size. I wanted the set you could see in magazines, where they show you the actual size of the railroad engine as being no larger than a walnut.

"You never get that, man," Michael Christian said, and he was right.

James Brown in the Hospital's Christmas Wish was for *The Birds* for Christmas. And, as Michael Christian's friend, I became an accomplice in his desire. In that way, "birds" became a code, the way words can among boys.

"Gimme some BIRDS!" Michael Christian would squawk when the society ladies on their annual Christmas visit asked us what we wanted.

"How about a nice hairbrush?" a society lady said, laying one for white people at the foot of Michael Christian's bed.

"I want a pick," Michael Christian told her.

"A pick? A shovel and a pick? To dig with?" asked the society lady.

"I think he wants a comb for his hair," I said. "For his Afro."

"That's right: a pick," said Michael Christian. "Tell this stupid white bitch something. *Squawk, squawk,*" he said, flapping his elbows like wings, as the nurses wheeled him out into the hall. "Gimme some BIRDS!" he shouted, and when they asked me, I said to give me some birds, too.

Michael Christian's boldness over the Christmas programs increased when Ben, the night porter, broke the television. Looking back, it may not be fair to say that Ben, the night porter, actually broke the television, but one evening it was soundlessly playing some kiddie Christmas show and Ben was standing near it mopping up a spilled urinal can when the screen and the hope of Michael Christian's getting his Christmas Wish blackened simultaneously. Apologetic at first, knowing what even a soundless television meant to children who had rarely seen any television at all, Ben then offered to "burn up your butt, Michael Christian, legs braces and all" when Michael Christian hissed "stupid nigger" at Ben, beneath the night nurse's hearing. It was a somber Lights Out.

The next night, a priest and some students from the seminary came by. Practice Preachers, Michael Christian said. While one of the students read the Christmas story from the Bible, Michael Christian pretended to peck his own eyes out with pinched fingers. When the story was finished, Michael Christian said, "Now, you say the sheepherding guys was so afraid, right?"

"*Sore* afraid," said the Practice Preacher. "The shepherds had never seen angels before, and they were *sore* afraid."

"Naw," said Michael Christian. "I'll tell you what—they saw these big

31

white things flapping down and they was big *birds*, man. I know *birds*, man, I know when you got bird *problems*, man!"

"They were *angels*," said the young seminary student.

"Naw," said Michael Christian. "They was big white birds, and the sheepherding guys were *so* afraid the big white birds was swooping down and getting all up in they *hair* and stuff! *Squawk, squawk!*" he said, flapping around in his bed.

"*Squawk, squawk!*" I answered, and two of the Practice Preachers assisted the nurses in wheeling Michael Christian into the hall and me into the linen cupboard.

One night in the week before Christmas, a man named Sammy came to visit. He had been a patient as a child, and his botched cleft-palate and harelip repairs were barely concealed by a weird line of blond mustache. Sammy owned a hauling company now, and he showed up blistering drunk, wearing a ratty Santa suit, and began handing out black-strapped Timex junior wristwatches. I still have mine, somewhere.

One by one we told Sammy what we wanted for Christmas, even though we were not sure, because of his speech defect, that that was what he was asking. Me, the walnut train; Michael Christian, *The Birds*. We answered without enthusiasm, without hope: it was all by rote. By the end of the visit, Sammy was a blubbering sentimental mess, reeking of alcohol and promises. Ben, the night porter, put him out.

It was Christmas Eve week. The boy who kept running away finally ran away for good. Before he left, he snatched the dime from the channel selector on our broken TV. We all saw him do it and we didn't care. We didn't even yell out to the night nurse, so he could get a better head start than usual.

It was Christmas Eve week, and Michael Christian lay listless in his bed. We watched the Big Boy ward empty. Somebody even came for one of the moaners, and the guy out on the sun porch was sent upstairs for a final visit to the Young Doctors so they could finish taking him apart.

On the night before Christmas Eve, Michael Christian and I heard street shoes clicking down the long corridor that led to where we lay. It was after Lights Out. We watched and waited and waited. It was just Sammy the Santa, except this time he was wearing a pale-blue leisure suit, his hair was oiled back, and his hands, holding a red-wrapped box, were clean.

What we did not want for Christmas were wristwatches. What we did not want for Christmas were bars of soap. We did not want any more candy canes, bookmarks, ballpoint pens, or somebody else's last year's broken toy. For Christmas we did not want plastic crosses, dot books, or fruit baskets. No more handshakes, head pats, or storybook times. It was the night before Christmas Eve, and Michael Christian had not mentioned *The Birds* in days, and I had given up on the walnut train. We did not want any more Christmas Wishes.

Sammy spoke with the night nurse, we heard him plead that it was Christmas, and she said all right, and by her flashlight she brought him to us. In the yellow spread of her weak batteries, we watched Michael Christian unwrap a portable television.

There was nothing to be done except plug the television into the wall. It was Christmas, Sammy coaxed the reluctant night nurse. They put the little TV on a chair, and we watched the end of an Andy Williams Christmas Special. We watched the eleven-o'clock news. Then the movie began: *The Birds*. It was Christmas, Sammy convinced the night nurse.

The night nurse wheeled her chair away from the chart table and rolled it to the television set. The volume was low, so as not to disturb the damaged babies at the Little Boy end of the ward—babies largely uncollected until after the holidays, if at all. Sammy sat on an empty bed. He patted it. Michael Christian and I watched *The Birds*.

During the commercials, the night nurse checked the hall for the supervisor. Sammy helped her turn any infant that cried out. The night nurse let Sammy have some extra pillows. Michael Christian spoke to me only once during the entire movie: quietly, during a commercial when we were alone, he said, "Those birds messing them people *up*."

When the movie was over, it was the first hours of Christmas Eve. The night nurse woke Sammy and let him out through the sun porch. She told us to go to sleep, and rolled her chair back to her chart table. In the emptiness you could hear the metal charts click and scratch, her folds of white starch rustle. Through a hole in the pony blanket I had pulled over my head I could see Michael Christian's bed. His precious Afro head was buried deep beneath his pillow.

At the dark end of the ward a baby cried in its sleep and then was still.

It was Christmas Eve, and we were sore afraid.

NTOZAKE SHANGE

Christmas for Sassafrass, Cypress & Indigo

Hilda Effania couldn't wait till Christmas. The Christ Child was born. Hallelujah. Hallelujah. The girls were home. The house was humming. Hilda Effania justa singing, cooking up a storm. Up before dawn. Santa's elves barely up the chimney. She chuckled. This was gonna be some mornin'. Yes, indeed. There was nothing too good for her girls. Matter of fact, what folks never dreamed of would only just about do. That's right, all her babies home for Christmas Day. Hilda Effania cooking up a storm. Little Jesus Child lyin' in his manger. Praise the Lord for all these gifts. Hilda Effania justa singin':

> Poor little Jesus Child, Born in a Manger
> Sweet little Jesus Child
> & they didn't know who you were.

BREAKFAST WITH HILDA EFFANIA & HER GIRLS ON CHRISTMAS MORNING

HILDA'S TURKEY HASH

1 pound diced cooked turkey
   meat (white & dark)
2 medium onions, diced
1 red sweet pepper, diced
1 full boiled potato, diced

1 tablespoon cornstarch
3 tablespoons butter
Salt to taste, pepper too
(A dash of corn liquor,
   optional)

35

In a heavy skillet, put your butter. Sauté your onions & red pepper. Add your turkey, once your onions are transparent. When the turkey's sizzling, add your potato. Stir. If consistency is not to your liking, add the cornstarch to thicken, the corn liquor to thin. Test to see how much salt & pepper you want, & don't forget your cayenne.

CATFISH/ THE WAY ALBERT LIKED IT

½ cup flour
½ cup cornmeal
Salt
Pepper
½ cup buttermilk

3 beaten eggs
Oil for cooking
Lemons
6 fresh catfish

Sift flour and cornmeal. Season with your salt & pepper. Mix the beaten eggs well with the buttermilk. Dip your fish in the egg & milk. Then roll your fish in the cornmeal-flour mix. Get your oil spitting hot in a heavy skillet. Fry your fish, not too long, on both sides. Your lemon wedges are for your table.

TRIO MARMALADE

1 tangerine
1 papaya
1 lemon

Sugar
Cold water

Delicately grate rinds of fruits. Make sure you have slender pieces of rind. Chop up your pulp, leaving the middle section of each fruit. Put the middles of the fruits and the seeds somewhere else in a cotton wrap. Add three times the amount of pulp & rind.

That's the measure for your water. Keep this sitting overnight. Get up the next day & boil this for a half hour. Drop your wrapped seed bag in there. Boil that, too. & mix in an exact equal of your seed bag with your sugar (white or brown). Leave it be for several hours. Come back. Get it boiling again. Don't stop stirring. You can test it & test it, but you'll know when it jells. Put on your table or in jars you seal while it's hot.

Now you have these with your hominy grits. (I know you know how to make hominy grits.) Fried eggs, sunny-side up. Ham-sliced bacon, butter rolls & Aunt Haydee's Red Pimiento Jam. I'd tell you that receipt, but Aunt Haydee never told nobody how it is you make that. I keep a jar in the pantry for special occasions. I get one come harvest.

Mama's breakfast simmering way downstairs drew the girls out of their sleep. Indigo ran to the kitchen. Sassafrass turned back over on her stomach to sleep a while longer, there was no House Mother ringing a cowbell. Heaven. Cypress brushed her hair, began her daily pliés & leg stretches. Hilda Effania sat at her kitchen table, drinking strong coffee with Magnolia Milk, wondering what the girls would think of her tree.

"Merry Christmas, Mama." Indigo gleamed. "May I please have some coffee with you? Nobody else is up yet. Then we can go see the tree, can't we, when they're all up. Should I go get 'em?" Indigo was making herself this coffee as quickly as she could, before Hilda Effania said "no." But Hilda was so happy Indigo could probably have had a shot of bourbon with her coffee.

"Only half a cup, Indigo. Just today." Hilda watched Indigo moving more like Cypress. Head erect, back stretched tall, with some of Sassafrass's easy coyness.

"So you had a wonderful time last night at your first party?"

"Oh, yes, Mama." Indigo paused. "But you know what?" Indigo sat down by her mother with her milk tinged with coffee. She stirred her morning treat, serious as possible. She looked her mother in the eyes. "Mama, I don't think boys are as much fun as everybody says."

"What do you mean, darling?"

"Well, they dance & I guess eventually you marry 'em. But I like my fiddle so much more. I even like my dolls better than boys. They're fun, but they can't talk about important things."

Hilda Effania giggled. Indigo was making her own path at her own pace. There'd be not one more boy-crazy, obsessed-with-romance child in her house. This last one made more sense out of the world than either of the other two. Alfred would have liked that. He liked independence.

"Good morning, Mama. Merry Christmas." Sassafrass was still tying her bathrobe as she kissed her mother.

"Merry Christmas, Indigo. I see Santa left you a cup of coffee."

"This is not my first cup of coffee. I had some on my birthday, too."

"Oh, pardon me. I didn't realize you were so grown. I've been away, you know?" Sassafrass was never very pleasant in the morning. Christmas was no exception. Indigo & her mother exchanged funny faces. Sassafrass wasn't goin' to spoil this day.

"Good morning. Good morning. Good morning, everyone." Cypress flew through the kitchen: *coupé jeté en tournant.*

"Merry Christmas, Cypress," the family shouted in unison.

"Oh, Mama, you musta been up half the night cooking what all I'm smelling." Cypress started lifting pot tops, pulling the oven door open.

"Cypress, you know I can't stand for nobody to be looking in my food till I serve it. Now, come on away from my stove."

Cypress turned to her mama, smiling. "Mama, let's go look at the tree."

"I haven't finished my coffee," Sassafrass yawned.

"You can bring it with you. That's what I'm gonna do," Indigo said with sweet authority.

The tree glistened by the front window of the parlor. Hilda Effania had covered it, of course, with cloth & straw. Satin ribbons of scarlet, lime, fuchsia, bright yellow, danced on the far limbs of the pine. Tiny straw angels of dried palm swung from the upper branches. Apples shining, next to candy canes & gingerbread men, brought shouts of joy & memory from the girls, who recognized their own handiwork. The black satin stars with appliqués of the Christ Child Cypress had made when she was ten. Sassafrass fingered the lyres she fashioned for the children singing praises of the little Jesus: little burlap children with lyres she'd been making since she could thread a needle, among the miniatures of Indigo's dolls. Hilda Effania had done something else special for this Christmas, though. In silk frames of varied pastels were the baby pictures of her girls & one of her wedding day: Hilda Effania & Alfred, November 30, 1946.

Commotion. Rustling papers. Glee & Surprise. Indigo got a very tiny laced brassiere from Cypress. Sassafrass had given her a tiny pair of earrings, dangling golden violins. Indigo had made for both her sisters dolls in their very own likenesses. Both five feet tall, with hips & bras. Indigo had dressed the dolls in the old clothes Cypress & Sassafrass had left at home.

"Look in their panties," Indigo blurted. Cypress felt down in her doll's panties. Sassafrass pulled her doll's drawers. They both found velvet sanitary napkins with their names embroidered cross the heart of silk.

"Oh, Indigo. You're kidding. You're not menstruating, are you?"

"Indigo, you got your period?"

"Yes, she did." Hilda Effania joined, trying to change the subject. She'd known Indigo was making dolls, but not that the dolls had their period.

"Well, what else did you all get?" Hilda asked provocatively.

Cypress pulled out an oddly shaped package wrapped entirely in gold sequins. "Mama, this is for you." The next box was embroidered continuously with Sassafrass's name. "Here, guess whose?" Cypress held Indigo's shoulders. Indigo had on her new bra over her nightgown. Waiting for her mother & sister to open their gifts, Cypress did *tendues*. "Hold still, Indigo. If you move, my alignment goes off."

"Oh, Cypress, this is just lovely." Hilda Effania didn't know what else to say. Cypress had given her a black silk negligee with a very revealing bed jacket. "I certainly have to think when I could wear this & you all won't be home to see it."

"Aw, Mama. Try it on," Cypress pleaded.

"Yeah, Mama. Put that on. It looks so nasty." Indigo squinched up her face, giggled.

"Oh, Cypress, these are so beautiful, I can hardly believe it." Sassafrass held the embroidered box open. In the box lined with beige raw silk were seven cherry-wood hand-carved crochet needles of different gauges.

"Bet not one white girl up to the Callahan School has ever in her white life laid eyes on needles like that!" Cypress hugged her sister, flexed her foot. "Indigo, you got to put that bra on under your clothes, not on top of 'em. Mama, would you look at this little girl?"

Hilda Effania had disappeared. "I'm trying on this scandalous thing, Cypress. You all look for your notes at the foot of the tree." She shouted from her bedroom, thinking she looked pretty good for a widow with three most grown girls.

Hilda Effania always left notes for the girls, explaining where their Christmas from Santa was. This practice began the first year Sassafrass had doubted that a fat white man came down her chimney to bring her anything. Hilda solved that problem by leaving notes from Santa Claus for all the children. That way they had to go search the house, high & low, for their gifts. Santa surely had to have been there. Once school chums & reality interfered with this myth, Hilda continued the practice of leaving her presents hidden away. She liked the idea that each child experienced her gift in privacy. The special relationship she nurtured with each was protected from rivalries, jokes & Christmas confusions. Hilda Effania loved thinking that she'd managed to give her daughters a moment of their own.

My Oldest Darling, Sassafrass,

In the back of the pantry is something from Santa. In a red box by the attic window is something your father would want you to have. Out by the shed in a bucket covered with straw is a gift from your Mama.

Love to you,

Mama

40

Darling Cypress,

Underneath my hat boxes in the 2nd floor closet is your present from Santa. Look behind the tomatoes I canned last year for what I got you in your Papa's name. My own choice for you is under your bed.

XOXOX,

Mama

Sweet Little Indigo,

This is going to be very simple. Santa left you something outside your violin. I left you a gift by the outdoor stove on the right-hand side. Put your coat on before you go out there. And the special something I got you from your Daddy is way up in the china cabinet. Please, be careful.

I love you so much,

Mama

In the back of the pantry between the flour & rice, Sassafrass found a necklace of porcelain roses. Up in the attic across from Indigo's mound of resting dolls, there was a red box all right, with a woven blanket of mohair, turquoise & silver. Yes, her father would have wanted her to have a warm place to sleep. Running out to the shed, Sassafrass knocked over the bucket filled with straw. There on the ground lay eight skeins of her mother's finest spun cotton, dyed so many colors. Sassafrass sat out in the air feeling her yarns.

Cypress wanted her mother's present first. Underneath her bed, she felt tarlatan. A tutu. Leave it to Mama. Once she gathered the whole thing out where she could see it, Cypress started to cry. A tutu *juponnage*, reaching to her ankles, rose & lavender. The waist was a wide sash with the most delicate needlework she'd ever seen. Tiny toe shoes in white & pink graced brown ankles tied with ribbons. Unbelievable. Cypress stayed in her room dancing in her tutu till lunchtime. Then she found *The Souls of Black Folk* by Du Bois near the tomatoes from her Papa's spirit. She was the only one who'd insisted on calling him Papa, instead of Daddy or Father. He didn't mind. So she guessed he wouldn't mind now. "Thank you so much, Mama & Papa." Cypress slowly went to the second-floor closet where she found Santa'd left her a pair of opal earrings. To thank her mother Cypress did a complete *port de bras*, in the Cecchetti manner, by her mother's vanity. The mirrors inspired her.

Indigo had been very concerned that anything was near her fiddle that she hadn't put there. Looking at her violin, she knew immediately what her gift from Santa was. A brand-new case. No secondhand battered thing from Uncle John. Indigo approached her instrument slowly. The case was of crocodile skin, lined with white velvet. Plus, Hilda Effania had bought new rosin, new strings. Even cushioned the fiddle with cleaned raw wool. Indigo carried her new case with her fiddle outside to the stove where she found a music stand holding *A Practical Method for Violin* by Nicolas Laoureux. "Oh, my. She's right about that. Mama would be real mad if I never learned to read music." Indigo looked through the pages, understanding nothing. Whenever she was dealing with something she didn't understand, she made it her business to learn. With great difficulty, she carried her fiddle, music stand & music book into the house. Up behind the wine glasses that Hilda Effania rarely used, but dusted regularly, was a garnet bracelet from the memory of her father. Indigo figured the bracelet weighed so little, she would definitely be able to wear it every time she played her fiddle. Actually, she could wear it while conversing with the Moon.

Hilda Effania decided to chance fate & spend the rest of the morning in her fancy garb from Cypress. The girls were silent when she entered the parlor in black lace. She looked like she did in those hazy photos from before they were born. Indigo rushed over to the easy chair & straightened the pillows.

"Mama, I have my present for you." Hilda Effania swallowed hard. There was no telling what Indigo might bring her.

"Well, Sweetheart. I'm eager for it. I'm excited, too."

Indigo opened her new violin case, took out her violin, made motions of tuning it (which she'd already done). In a terribly still moment, she began

42

"My Buddy," Hilda Effania's mother's favorite song. At the end, she bowed to her mother. Her sisters applauded.

Sassafrass gave her mother two things: a woven hanging of twined ikat using jute and raffia, called "You Know Where We Came From, Mama," & six amethysts with holes drilled through, for her mother's creative weaving.

"Mama, you've gotta promise me you won't have a bracelet or a ring or something made from them. Those are for your very own pieces." Sassafrass wanted her mother to experience weaving as an expression of herself, not as something the family did for Miz Fitzhugh. Hilda Effania was still trying to figure out where in the devil she could put this "hanging," as Sassafrass called it.

"Oh, no, dear. I wouldn't dream of doing anything with these stones but what you intended."

When the doorbell rang, Hilda Effania didn't know what to do with herself. Should she run upstairs? Sit calmly? Run get her house robe? She had no time to do any of that. Indigo opened the door.

"Merry Christmas, Miz Fitzhugh. Won't you come in?" Hilda sank back in the easy chair. Cypress casually threw her mother an afghan to cover herself. Miz Fitzhugh in red wool suit, tailored green satin shirt, red tam, all Hilda's design, and those plain brown pumps white women like, wished everyone a "Merry Christmas." She said Mathew, her butler, would bring some sweetbreads & venison over later, more toward the dinner hour. Miz Fitzhugh liked Sassafrass the best of the girls. That's why she'd sponsored her at the Callahan School. The other two, the one with the gall to want to be a ballerina & the headstrong one with the fiddle, were much too much for Miz Fitzhugh. They didn't even wanta be weavers. What was becoming of the Negro, refusing to ply an honorable trade.

Nevertheless, Miz Fitzhugh hugged each one with her frail blue-veined arms, gave them their yearly checks for their savings accounts she'd established when each was born. There be no talk that her Negroes were destitute. What she didn't know was that Hilda Effania let the girls use that money as they pleased. Hilda believed every family needed only one mother. She was the mother to her girls. That white lady was mighty generous, but she wasn't her daughters' mama or manna from Heaven. If somebody needed taking care of, Hilda Effania determined that was her responsibility; knowing in her heart that white folks were just peculiar.

"Why, Miz Fitzhugh, that's right kindly of you," Hilda honeyed.

"Why, Hilda, you know I feel like the girls were my very own," Miz Fitzhugh confided. Cypress began a series of violent *ronds de jambe*. Sassafrass picked up all the wrapping papers as if it were the most important thing in the world. Indigo felt some huge anger coming over her. Next thing she knew, Miz Fitzhugh couldn't keep her hat on. There was a wind justa pushing, blowing Miz Fitzhugh out the door. Because she had blue blood or blue veins, whichever, Indigo knew Miz Fitzhugh would never act like anything strange was going on. She'd let herself be blown right out the door with her white kid gloves, red tailored suit & all. Waving good-bye, shouting, "Merry Christmas," Miz Fitzhugh vanished as demurely as her station demanded.

Sucha raucous laughing & carrying on rarely came out of Hilda Effania's house like it did after Miz Fitzhugh'd been blown away. Hilda Effania did an imitation of her, hugging the girls.

"But Miz Fitzhugh, do the other white folks know you touch your Negroes?" Hilda responded, "Oh, I don't tell anyone!"

Eventually they all went to their rooms, to their private fantasies & preoccupations. Hilda was in the kitchen working the fat off her goose, fiddling with the chestnut stuffing, wondering how she would handle the house when it was really empty again. It would be empty; not even Indigo would be home come January.

"Yes, Alfred. I think I'm doing right by 'em. Sassafrass is in that fine school with rich white children. Cypress is studying classical ballet with Effie in New York City. Imagine that? I'm sending Indigo out to Difuskie with Aunt Haydee. Miz Fitzhugh's promised me a tutor for her. She doesn't want the child involved in all this violence 'bout the white & the colored going to school together, the integration. I know you know what I mean, 'less up there's segregated too.

"No, Alfred, I'm not blaspheming. I just can't imagine another world. I'm trying to, though. I want the girls to live the good life. Like what we planned. Nice husbands. Big houses. Children. Trips to Paris & London. Going to the opera. Knowing nice people for friends. Remember we used to say we were the nicest, most interesting folks we'd ever met? Well, I don't want it to be that way for our girls. You know, I'm sort of scared of being here by myself. I can always talk to you, though. Can't I?

"I'ma tell Miz Fitzhugh that if she wants Indigo in Difuskie, that tutor will have to be a violin teacher. Oh, Alfred, you wouldn't believe what she can do on that fiddle. If you could only see how Cypress dances. Sassafrass's weavings. I wish you were here sometimes, so we could tell the world to look at what all we, Hilda Effania & Alfred, brought to this world."

Once her Christmas supper was organized in the oven, the frigerator, the sideboard, Hilda Effania slept in her new negligee, Alfred's WWII portrait close to her bosom.

IVAN KLÍMA

A Christmas Conspiracy Tale

On Wednesday morning, the day before Christmas, I got up at a quarter past four. Although I had set the alarm for five o'clock, the thought of having to get up so damnably early had kept me awake since three. I shuffled off to the dining room, which had a north-facing window on whose frame was mounted a thermometer. Pointing my flashlight at the scale, I saw that it registered only a fraction above freezing. Cold enough for me not to relish the prospect of spending eight or nine hours out in the open, standing up and with my hands forever immersed in cold water. Still, it wasn't too bad for the time of year, so I should not really bewail my fate—it could have been much colder.

The kids were asleep, my wife too, and so I made my own breakfast and ate it in the kitchen. Then I put on two pullovers, a windcheater, and three pairs of socks. After yesterday's experience I would have preferred four, but my boots were too small for that.

I had been inveigled into this whole business by Peter, a former colleague of mine from the faculty. Peter was a lecturer in aesthetics, a literary critic and philologist. These past three years, however, he had been earning a living first as a night watchman in the warehouse of some building firm, and then as a stoker. During that time he had spent all his savings and, having discovered that it was impossible to keep body and soul together by honest toil, had decided to chuck it in and seek a more lucrative way of life.

I had not heard from him for at least half a year, and then he phoned

46

me a week ago; after the usual questions about my health and work came a matter-of-fact query: "How would you like to sell fish?"

"How would I like *what. . .?*"

"Sell carp for Christmas," he explained. "You can earn a heap of money doing that."

"Oh but I . . ." The proposal was so unexpected that I completely missed my opportunity to refuse. "Well, I must say that's something I've never thought of doing."

"Of course you haven't," he said reassuringly. "Who would have? But you're a writer—you should try your hand at everything."

"I'm not the kind of writer who has to try everything," I countered.

"Sure you are!" he replied, his voice tinged with the authority of his former calling. "Anyway, you'll make a lot of money. You're not going to tell me you couldn't use it, now that Christmas is coming."

"But look, I've never killed a carp in my life. I just couldn't do it," I added, hoping that this would be the end of the matter.

"Oh, don't worry about that side of it," he said. "Leave *that* to me. And that apart, it's child's play. Two or three days, that's all, and you can expect to take home at least two thou."

An hour later he was at my apartment, to continue his enthusiastic depiction of the job he wanted me to undertake. Last year, one of his former students had sold carp outside the White Swan department store, and in four days had earned ten thousand, tax-free. And even if we did not manage to get as good a venue—because that would obviously cost us—we'd still be sure to make two or three thousand at the very least. Of course, he explained, if we wanted a decent spot we would first have to grease somebody's palm.

At last I realized what he was after. He had a splendid idea, he was willing to put in some hard work himself and even to slaughter the carp, but he needed a partner with some capital.

"How much?" I asked him.

Peter had a squint. Now, too, each of his eyes was looking in a different direction. What I found suspicious was that neither was looking at me.

"Well . . . how much?"

"Say five hundred for the spot," he replied, "a hundred for the fish warden, and a bottle of brandy for the manager of the supermarket in front of which we'll do the selling."

"That's quite an investment," I pointed out.

"The more we put in, the more we'll make," he assured me. "And I've found a fantastic spot in Strašnice."

"What's that with the fish warden?"

He explained that if you wanted to make a profit you had to have decent fish. That former student of his—who had made enough money selling carp outside the White Swan to pay for a trip to India—had told him about some fellow who had ignored the fish warden. The fish warden had then simply called out, "Fish for Mr. Scrooge!" and the soldiers opened a different tank, out of which came carp that looked more like minnows.

"Soldiers?" I asked, puzzled by this new element in the transaction. "*What* soldiers?"

"Why, those manning the fish tanks, of course," he replied somewhat uncertainly. "They tell me there are soldiers there. So what."

I did not share his confidence where the soldiers were concerned, but if the truth were told, it wasn't the eight hundred crowns he was asking that put me off. I simply did not fancy the idea of standing there in the street from morning till night next to a tank full of carp. In any case, I didn't particularly need the money; I had enough to live on and a little in the savings bank. Things being as they were I could hardly expect to be earning more. So I was not really interested in this extra cash; I wouldn't know what to do with it, unless I donated it to somebody. If you are willing to hand money out, you can never have enough. But for *that* purpose two thousand was a ridiculous amount.

True, a number of my friends were in jail, all of them dangerous subversives and conspirators, if you were to believe the indictment. That they should be cooling their heels in prison while we others were enjoying a degree of freedom which even allowed us to choose whether we wished to sell carp was all part of the Russian roulette that fate had been playing with us for some thirty years.

One of those in prison had been a colleague of mine in the editorial office of a literary magazine in the days when these were still being published in this country. Christmas would be just the right time to pay his wife a visit and bring her a little money.

I lent Peter that eight hundred. He left in high spirits, promising to see to everything, fish included.

At a quarter to five I was ready. I had washed, shaved, breakfasted, put on three pairs of socks and a pair of boots. Now I tried reading the sports page of yesterday's newspaper, but there is not much in the way of sports going on around Christmas, and we all know that there is nothing of interest in the rest of the paper at any time of year.

At five I emerged into the frosty morning. The thin mist smelled of smoke, sulfur, and bad humor. Soon we'll all choke and become extinct, just as we have poisoned the fish in most of our rivers. All we are left with are some bemused carp in a few select ponds.

Yesterday was our first day as fish salesmen. We reached the agreed spot in complete darkness. The carp, which Peter had procured the day before, filled a huge tank standing in front of the dimly lighted supermarket; its manager, a portly, graying, elegantly attired fellow, gave us a friendly greeting, his friendship having previously been secured with a bottle of brandy. He gave us a hand with the wooden counter we brought out of the storeroom, and then he dragged out an ancient-looking pair of scales. For a while he looked on, amused, as we attempted to align the scales on this complicated contraption, then he pushed us out of the way and, after making some fine adjustments, jovially assured us that it could now be relied on to give us five percent extra per kilogram. He further instructed us never to fail throwing the fish on the scales with the maximum quantity of water—"tip the water out only if the customer has looked at the scales beforehand"—then snatch the carp away as soon as the indicator reaches the highest point, making sure at the same time that the scales should not ever show a whole, easily read weight such as one or one and a half kilos. We listened most attentively, which encouraged him to give us some more useful hints. Naturally, it went without saying that we had to round the price up to the nearest whole number, if possible to the number nine, which was the best of all whole numbers. Then throw in a few odd pence on top, as that made it look more convincing. By way of example the manager thrust his hand in the tank, fished out a carp and threw it on to the recently adjusted scales. One kilogram nineteen crowns, then add a few pence for the sake of appearances—say, nineteen crowns sixty. Customers as a rule pay with a large denomination note and don't expect any small change. That gives us an acceptable price of twenty crowns. However, the manager continued our initiation with evident glee, it can happen that a somewhat absentminded customer enables you to quote an even higher price, like twenty crowns twenty. In that case always demand your change back. If this proves difficult, you can show magnanimity by saying, "Never mind, you keep the change—I'll collect it next Christmas!" Not only does that look good, the customer will usually demur and tip you a crown or two extra, *on top* of the twenty. You can thus make three or four crowns on a seventeen-crown carp, taking into account what you already gained on the scales.

Noticing the astonished expression on my face, the manager obviously concluded that I was scared, and so he turned to me and assured me there was nothing to be afraid of. Most of the customers were women, who hardly ever noticed what the weight was, much less were able to calculate the price. But of course it was up to me to be skillful and to use psychology: to sum up the customer, chat her up a bit so that she forgets she is out shopping but feels she is making a date. And therefore, men, beware of men! All this, the manager imparted to us with a faint smile on his lips, as if he were not being serious but just joking, merely playacting for our benefit.

"However, as soon as you mention the price you have to be serious again. Sometimes it helps to apologize and say you've got it wrong, correcting the price in the customer's favor."

He pointed to the scales, with the seventeen-crown carp still writhing on top of them, giving us a graphic demonstration of what he had in mind.

"That'll be twenty-three sixty, madam," he said, picking up the writhing fish and turning toward me, carp in hand. "Oh, I *beg* your pardon! Just one moment, please." He threw the carp back on the scales, only to snatch it off again, his face assuming so penitent an expression that to harbor any doubt about the sincerity of his apology or to defile that moment of truth by indulging in something as base as addition or subtraction would have been to offend his integrity as a salesman and his dignity as a human being. "There," he cried, "I almost cheated you, madam. It's only twenty-two crowns ten." And with these words the manager hurled the unfortunate carp back into the tank, packed with its fellow victims which kept opening their stupid mouths, as Nature intended, oblivious to the coins clinking in their throats for the sake of which they would shortly be fished out, slaughtered, fraudulently overpriced, and eventually eaten.

I got off the half-empty bus. It was only half-past five, which meant I had added an extra thirty minutes to the inevitable eight hours of freezing. The street was deserted, except for a few sleepy, obviously irritable pedestrians. From afar I could see our tank. The day before had not been a raging success, businesswise. Although women had trooped into the supermarket by the dozen, buying up everything from sugar to soap powder as if bereft of reason, to our dismay they appeared to be in no hurry to purchase their Christmas carp, perhaps because they had no room left in their bulging shopping bags; and so we froze outside the store for nothing. It was not till almost lunchtime that a few old-age pensioners and housewives took any interest in what we had to offer. I did the weighing and collected the money while Peter doubled as fisherman-murderer. He handed me the still seemingly live bodies, which I would cautiously place on the scales. The old ladies looked on trustingly, while the younger women exchanged a few sentences, some even flirted with me a little, so that I all but forgot that I was there to sell fish and not to make assignations. While engaged in all this chatter, I had my work cut out just converting grams into crowns—as for any rounding up, I lacked the necessary gall, cynicism and mental agility.

The women left and we were alone again. And cold. Peter started telling me all about Hašek's materialism and anarchism but then—doubtless influenced by the tankful of animal life at our side—quickly switched to animal symbolism in the works of Franz Kafka. He pointed out that with Kafka, man could always change into an animal, but never the other way round. In his view, the animal is invariably something repulsive, foul, slimy—a mouse, a mole, a monkey, even an insect. Peter could not say whether this included fish.

We carried on this conversation for a while, but it was too elevated a topic for those freezing conditions. We therefore played at being conspirators and succeeded (exactly how and by what means we did not for the moment specify) in forcing the government to obey our instructions. We ordered the immediate release of all political prisoners and restricted police powers to such a degree that they became practically nonexistent. We agreed that we would not put anyone on trial, and thus do away, once and for all, with the unending cycle of retribution which only created new victims. And finally, how else, we set about drawing up editorial programs—naturally consisting entirely of banned authors. We ended up with some eighty titles, whereas the total of carp we had managed to sell was eight. Not nearly so encouraging as the outcome of our conspiratorial activity.

At two o'clock we "shut up shop" for thirty minutes, adjourning for a hot cup of tea with rum to the storeroom at the rear of the supermarket. It was prepared for us on the manager's orders by one of the three young shop assistants who answered to the somewhat exotic name of Daniela. Her face, though, was typically Slav, her small nose flattened Russian-style, her hair probably a little reddish but you could not tell because she had recently had it dyed yellow, no doubt with a view to the approach of Christmas.

We sipped our tea, Miss Daniela sipping with us. Holding the mug in her tiny flippers, she looked quite delectable. She was generous with the rum, and so we felt very cozy with her in that storeroom at the rear of the shop. My friend, in keeping with his former vocation, recounted stories about famous writers while I, when asked to contribute to the entertainment, told them about my meeting with a former president. I don't think his name meant anything to the young lady from the supermarket, but she seemed quite thrilled to be rubbing shoulders with someone who had, in his turn, rubbed shoulders with a president. She kept eyeing me with what she no doubt considered provocative glances.

Arriving at our stall next day, the first thing I saw was the enormous pool of water licking the sides of the tank. I waded through it on tiptoe and, fearing the worst, looked inside.

Countless open fish mouths gaped at me from among the mass of carp bodies in that waterless container, some of the expiring bodies still twitching in their death throes.

I was seized with panic. There must have been a good eight thousand crowns' worth of fish in there. In all his calculations, Peter had never made any mention of the possibility of their total extinction. Quick as a flash I wondered if I had in any way been responsible for the catastrophe, but I could not think of anything I had done wrong or neglected to do. Then, stripping off my windcheater and rolling up the sleeves of both my pullovers—and doing my best to overcome my revulsion—I thrust my arm into the welter of twitching bodies. It did not take me long to locate the aperture through which the water had escaped, but it was at least another quarter of an hour (or so it seemed to me) before I found the plug. At last I did discover it under that mountain of fish and wedged it into the opening with all the strength I could muster. Any water that might still have remained in the tank would now no longer run out.

The trouble was, I had no means of filling the tank up again. Finding a paper cup in the waste bin I tried to scoop up some water from the pool on the pavement, but it was hopeless.

I threw away the cup and ran into the building that housed our supermarket. At this hour, naturally, it was closed. I crept past the doors of the apartments, trying to detect signs of life inside.

With the exception of the postman delivering a telegram, only *they* can ring a stranger's doorbell at 6:00 A.M. when they come to make an arrest. Only now did it occur to me that anyone in that line of work had to be quite shameless and thick-skinned.

I ran down to the cellar in the hope of finding a laundry room.

I did find a laundry room. From behind the locked door I could even hear a tap dripping. Taking my bunch of keys from my pocket I tried in vain to open the door. The thought of those dying carp lent me courage and I lunged at the door with my shoulder, kicking it several times for good measure.

The sound of footsteps up above startled me. I had enough to contend with already without being accused of hooliganism.

As I made my way backstairs I saw yellow-haired Daniela tripping toward the tank with a bucket of water in her hand. "These rotten tanks," she said by way of explanation. "Everything around here is rotten. Our freezers go on the blink at least once a month, usually on a Sunday. Come Monday morning we've got ice-cream pastries and spinach running all over the floors. The burglar alarm goes off if somebody just *walks* past the shop window in the evening and it'll ring like mad, fit to wake the dead. Then the cops turn up and get the manager out of bed to check if anything's been taken."

We kept bringing bucketfuls of water to the tank, Daniela complaining all the while about the rotten supermarket where a person could not earn a penny on the side because all the goods came already packaged and weighed. Coffee was the only commodity you could make a *little* profit on, but for that you again had to have empty bags. She recalled her predecessor, who got hold of some Tuzex bags, which she filled with the coffee that was left under the grinder; she patiently filled the black Tuzex Special bags and took these all the way to Vršovice, where she sold them door-to-door, both for Czech crowns and for Tuzex coupons. With her coupons she bought genuine Scotch, which she then sold here at the store, making some two hundred crowns per bottle. In the end someone had ratted on her and she had to go, being posted to a pharmacy in Hostivař. Instead of coffee, she now had plaster of Paris to weigh, and instead of whiskey she sold genuine South Bohemian wine.

By the time my friend and the cause of all my misfortune turned up, there was enough water in the tank for some of the fish bodies to turn their bellies heavenward and so demonstrate their pitiful demise.

We dumped all the corpses into a bucket, and as soon as the manager arrived went to ask him what to do with them so as not to infringe any hygiene regulations.

He glanced inside the bucket without the least sign of surprise, as if it had been he himself who had taken the plug out during the night. "How many?" he asked.

"Sixteen, I'd say," replied my friend. (Actually there were twenty, but I suppose Peter thought that by quoting a lower figure he would minimize our fiasco.)

"You'd *say?*" the manager repeated mockingly. "And now you'll want to throw them out, no doubt?"

"Well, what else?"

Astonishment at last showed in the manager's face. "What else? What *else?*" Why, we'll gut them, cut them up into portions, and sell them at a higher price, of course."

And so I found myself in the warm and intimate atmosphere of the storeroom. With an apron, a butcher's knife, and the yellow-haired Daniela to help me, I stood over a much-used bench right at the back, hidden from the eyes of the world behind boxes full of sunflower-oil bottles, to put the dead fish to good use.

It was a large storeroom, which smelled of spice and soap powder. In the corner opposite, a huge wooden crate with a hinged top attracted my attention. I had no idea what kind of merchandise it could be used for.

Miss Daniela squeezed between me and the wall of boxes. Lightly brushing against my back with her breasts, she gave a delighted giggle and said wasn't it a scream to be given such a cushy job for a change.

I had never gutted a fish in my life, and so I watched attentively as her gentle fingers grasped the knife, cut open the gray body of the carp, and carefully extracted the innards.

"What do you do normally?" she asked. "Last Christmas we had a bunch of students here—but you're not a student, are you?"

"No, it's many years since *I* was a student."

"What you said yesterday about the president, remember? That was a lot of codswallop, wasn't it?"

"No."

"No?"

"No."

"Cross your heart?"

"No really!"

"Would you believe it!" She threw the portions of fish into a tin bowl. "What do they call you?"

"Ivan."

"That's not much of a name, is it?"

"Well, I suppose they didn't think so when they gave it to me."

"Not that I think much of *my* name," she admitted.

"What name would you prefer, then?"

"Lucia. Isn't that a lovely name? Lucia Masopustová," she replied in a dreamy voice.

"Otherwise you're happy?"

"What do you mean, otherwise?"

"With your lot."

The word *lot* seemed to amuse her. "Go on with you," she said, going over to the washbasin to rinse her hands. Then she pulled a chair across, sat down, and took a packet of cigarettes from her coat pocket. She offered me one, but I refused it, saying I didn't smoke. "Well, you can at least sit down, can't you." She took a wooden box down from the pile and placed it opposite her chair. "I don't have to tell you I'd much rather work in a greengrocer's or a gas station." She crossed her legs, shortening the distance between us. Although our legs did not touch, a mouse could not have squeezed through the space between them. It was obviously up to me to eliminate the space altogether. "Go on," I said. "Wouldn't you mind the fumes?"

"Mind? Have you any idea how much you can make in a month?"

"No," I confessed.

"Ten thousand, if it's a halfway decent pump. Eight at the very least."

"You're kidding," I said in disbelief. "Anyway, what would you do with all that money?"

"Lord Almighty!" she exclaimed, "You'd be surprised."

"All right, then why *don't* you work at a gas station?"

"Are you being funny?" She gave me a look full of contempt. Just then I heard a door squeak and then the voice of the manager. "Dana!" he shouted. "What's with those fish? Let's have some portions over here!"

Miss Daniela leapt from her chair, put out her cigarette, grabbed the tin bowl with six halves of carp, and made for the door.

I got up, picked up the next deceased and cut his belly open. I was itching to find out how Peter was doing outside, but I did not fancy leaving my warm haven. I would have to go out there before too long, though—it was hardly fair to leave a friend to freeze out in the street while I chatted up the shop assistant.

Daniela came back. "He says we'd better get a move on. There's a bunch of old ladies waiting."

"I'm doing all I can."

"That's all right," she said. "Fuck 'em."

And with this she resumed our previous conversation. "If it was that easy, everybody would be working at the gas stations. D'ya know how much I'd have to cough up? Twenty-five thousand at least—and *then* they'd put me in the storeroom for a year, where I'd earn bugger-all. And what if after that they give me the boot? Or if the boss whose palm I'd greased gets the elbow? I'd have to pay up all over again."

"So what about the greengrocer's?" I asked.

"It's all the same," she said dejectedly, cutting open another corpse. "You didn't get *here* for nothing, did you?"

She looked up at me.

"No, I didn't."

"What do you do for a living?"

"Guess!"

"How should I know. You're not a student, and you don't work with your hands. Maybe you've been in the jug?"

I shrugged.

"I see," she said, nodding to show she understood.

"What charge would you say?"

"Charge? You mean why they put you inside?"

"That's right."

"Black market?" she ventured.

"No."

"Embezzlement?"

"No."

"Or did you open your mouth in the pub and say something you shouldn't have?"

"Well . . ." I said noncommittally. I don't like telling lies.

"What did they give you?"

"Doesn't matter," I said, closing the subject with a wave of my hand.

"I know," she said. "My elder sister got two years hard labor. She used to work at a railway station. And she didn't do nothing, either. Just because she knew about the pilfering that went on. My dad did six years, but I don't remember nothing about that, I had only just been born. *He* did time because he had owned a shop. When he came out he said to us: 'I never stole a bean in my life, and let me tell you, I was a damned fool!' "

"What does your father do now?"

"He's retired," she said. "Before that he was in charge of a canteen. But he never learned the ropes. My parents just didn't know the score." She threw another gutted fish in the bowl and went on: "You know who *does* know the ropes? Him over there," she pointed toward the shop. "Our manager. F'r instance he used to transport the meat from the slaughterhouse in Budějovice. They always dropped off a quarter of the load for themselves and delivered the rest. But then the others got greedy and wanted to split it half and half. Well, our boss knows better than that, he knows when it's better to call it a day. So he moved, while his chums carried on for another year, and then went mad and started buying houses and posh foreign cars and they all landed up behind bars. By that time our manager was here in Prague, delivering beer in cahoots with a guy at the brewery, but again he wouldn't dream of taking too much, he was too clever for that. Just a few cases from each truckload. But that was enough to give them each a hundred a day. And then he got fed up driving all the time and got the job here in the supermarket. He's been here five years now and d'ya think he's had a deficit in all that time? Not on your life!'' She raised her forefinger to emphasize the absence of a deficit under her boss's management. "He's got everybody bribed up at head office, and so he always knows a week in advance when a stocktaking is due, so they can never catch him by surprise. *And* he keeps in with us, too,'' she concluded her eulogy.

"Want some more tea?'' she asked. "I guess your friend might like some, too.''

On her way to the stove she again had to pass between me and the boxes that formed a high wall behind my back. I leaned backward and felt her soft body trapped in the narrow space.

"Oh, Mr. Ivan!'' I heard her protest softly. "What're you up to?''

Now I suppose I should have turned swiftly and kissed her. But what then? And in any case my hands were covered in carp blood, and for some reason it seemed inappropriate to wipe them on my apron as a prelude to an amorous gambit. Before I could decide what to do, much less do it, I felt her moist girlish breath on my face and heard her whisper: "Not now! If you want, I'll wait for you at six, when the shop shuts.''

At that moment we heard loud voices coming from the shop. They grew louder and louder. I quickly stepped forward, Daniela put the kettle down on the bench, and both of us ran into the supermarket.

There, between the shelves, stood an ugly wizened old man wearing ludicrously large, baggy trousers. In one white hand he held a metal cane, in the other a carp, his ruddy face aflame with fury. He was yelling at the top of his voice, and I gathered that he had bought a carp from us a little earlier and when he got home and weighed it had discovered that he had been cheated. By at least two crowns.

I was petrified, feeling as if I had just been caught out in some million-crown swindle.

The manager, on the other hand, was his usual calm, smiling self. He offered to weigh the fish again and exchange it for another or refund any money the old gentleman might have been overcharged; no one was infallible, but he could honestly not remember when they had last had any complaint of this nature. But the old man would not part with the corpus delicti, perhaps he was not even interested in getting his money back but just wanted to yell at us and make a scene. The manager—and I was amazed to find how much I admired his cool—took the old gent by the elbow and propelled him delicately past the checkouts and out of the shop, soft-soaping him all the time as he did so. He asked him to keep calm, urged him to take into account his, the manager's unblemished reputation, and again suggested that the customer have the carp reweighed, either here or else-where if he did not trust us.

"You're damned right, I don't trust you!" shouted the old man. "And I *will* get it weighed somewhere else." And with this he shuffled off.

Daniela's yellow head leaned closer to me and I again felt her breath as she explained that the crusty old man was Mr. Vondráček, who weighed everything he brought home on his scales, even the content of tins, and then returned to raise hell in the shop. All the staff knew him and would usually give him more than he was entitled to but he never came back to *return* anything. Now of course he would go and have the carp weighed, but I wasn't to worry, the only scale he trusted anywhere in the vicinity was at the butcher's, and Mr. Koňas, the butcher, would take care of it. Winking at me, she said that Mr. Koňas had little magnetic bits of metal which, if need be, he would attach to the bottom of his scales where they could not be seen. When he took the meat off the scales he would unobtrusively remove the bits of metal so that the customer was no wiser and thought he was getting the proper weight.

Less than an hour later—I was by this time again out in the cold, weighing and wrapping up the carp we had resuscitated so that they could be murdered for profit—a broad-shouldered, red-cheeked man in a white apron turned up, and I was sure this had to be Mr. Koňas the butcher. As he approached, Mr. Koňas informed us at the top of his voice that we owed him a hefty carp. "You see lads," he exclaimed joyfully, "I weighed the fish for the old duffer and told him that you *had* made a mistake of twenty pence in the price—but in his favor! *And* I explained that a fish isn't a lump of cheese, that it loses weight fast as the water drains away from inside. He gaped at me just like a fish, his mouth wide open, and I bet you he won't bother you again for a month at least."

The butcher was still speaking when the manager hauled a plump, two-kilo carp out of the tank, killed it with a blow to the head with a heavy screwdriver, wrapped it up and handed it to Mr. Koňas. And just then it came to me that in this world of ours there existed real conspirators, that there was a far-reaching conspiracy of those who had seen through the futility of all ideals and the deadly ambiguity of all human illusions, a resolute brotherhood of true materialists who knew that the only things that mattered were those you could hold in your hand or put in your pocket, that money could buy anything and that anyone could be bribed—except Death, which they preferred to ignore, and a few foolish individuals who could be locked up in prison, exiled out of the country or at the very least into subterranean boiler rooms, there to stoke furnaces and think their wayward thoughts. While I on the whole was one of the fools, at this moment I happened to be with the others, having been invited into their midst. Yes, now both Peter and I were one of *them*, enjoying their protection and solidarity. God help me, I almost wallowed in the warm feeling which comes of *belonging*. We carried on selling carp all that afternoon. More and more customers showed up, most of them women, until they formed a long line. The weather had turned a little warmer, and there was a touch of spring in the faint breeze. How much more pleasant it would have been out in the country, taking a long walk among the meadows—for me as well as for all these people waiting their turn in the line. But they had decided that they must have a carp, on top of the mountain of pork and beef and smoked meats, the potato salad, apple strudel, brawn and ice cream and bowls full of Christmas sweetmeats they had baked these past few days.

I realized that I was beginning to hate this multitude, to despise all these people, and that this was the first part of my initiation into the general conspiracy.

Fortunately, at quarter past five we did away with our last victim. Then we had to clean the tank, put the wooden counter back in the storeroom, return the miraculous scales with our thanks, and count our takings. Peter took charge of the money while I went out again to sweep the pavement. And, since there was less litter than cash, I finished first. Going back to the storeroom, where that morning Daniela and I had cut up the dead carp, I sat down on a chair and closed my eyes. The air was warm and moist, the place was filled with assorted aromas, and hot water bubbled in the kettle. I reflected for a while longer about the general conspiracy. Not that I thought of it as some kind of Mafia; none, or at least certainly not the majority, of its members had any criminal intent, nor were they intentionally dishonest. They were, rather, ordinary, average people who had not been offered a single idea, a single worthwhile goal that would have given meaning to their life, and they themselves had not found the strength of character to discover them on their own. This is how a whole community of the defeated had come into being, bringing together a motley crew of butchers, greengrocers, party secretaries and factory managers, bribed supervisors and coal men and corrupt newspapermen and, no doubt, also those who had been appointed to uncover and smash this conspiracy.

My reverie was interrupted by the sound of soft footsteps, and looking up I saw the yellow-haired Miss Daniela, now without her white coat and dressed only in a blue skirt and white blouse. "Mr. Ivan," she whispered, "do you still want to . . . ?" And she beckoned me to follow her, leading the way to the opposite corner where the big crate stood behind all those shelves. Seeing it at close quarters I noticed that it had handles on each side, like a cabin trunk. "Here," whispered Daniela, lifting the lid of the mammoth coffin. Inside, I could see, everything was ready: blankets and two pillows.

Daniela quickly unbuttoned her blouse, while I made a start by hurriedly shedding my boots. Then we both squeezed into the crate. As I was lowering myself down next to her I saw that there was yet another handle on the inside of the lid, and I raised myself up again to pull it shut over us.

It was now almost completely dark inside the crate, just a gleam of light seeming to come from her yellow hair. Perhaps it was the peroxide—how should I know?

"Darling," I said emitting the customary sigh, and embraced her half-naked body.

"Be quiet, Mr. Ivan," she whispered. "You have to be quiet as a mouse, they'll be here in a minute." I felt her pushing my palms away from her body, then her flipper slipping inside my trousers.

"Mr. Ivan," she whispered hotly. "I saw straightaway you weren't just any old student come to earn a little pocket money before Christmas, and I didn't believe you'd been inside, neither. Your friend told me what you do, that you write plays for TV and earn heaps of money. Oh, Mr. Ivan," she was by now agitating my penis with both hands, "what's twenty thousand to you. I've saved up the rest and I know about a service station where we'd get it back in six months and anything we earned after that would be ours to keep."

"You mean you want me to come in with you?" I asked, astonished.

"I'll marry you and I'll be faithful to you for the rest of my life," whispered Miss Daniela passionately. "That station is right by the highway, all the truck drivers use it and lots of those that go abroad, too. In a couple of years we'll make enough to buy a house, and you can have a brand-new car and we'll go on holiday to the seaside. We'll have a marvelous life, what do you say?"

I heard someone calling my name outside, and, still bemused by Miss Daniela's loving touch, I quickly threw the lid open. Jumping onto the concrete floor, I ran outside to join Peter in my bare feet—or rather in my three pairs of woolen socks.

"I just don't understand how this could've happened," Peter said, standing there with several bundles of bank notes in his hand. He was so shocked that he failed to notice the disordered state of my attire.

"What's wrong?"

"That scale was fixed," Peter lamented, "and we sold twenty carp in portions for almost twice their proper price, *and* you charged the customers the way the manager showed us."

"Well, I did the best I could," I said, suddenly feeling that I had to stand up for myself. "Did we make a loss?"

He nodded but did not reply.

"How much?"

"Eight hundred."

"You mean we've lost what we put in?"

He shook his head. "No, over and above that." He looked as if he were about to burst into tears.

"Oh, to hell with it," I said. "To hell with all the money."

The savings banks would still be open tomorrow morning. I would take out two thousand and take it to the wife of my colleague who was locked up because he refused to join the great conspiracy.

"I just can't understand how it could've happened," said Peter plaintively. "All those fish, and we must've made at least two crowns on each one of them."

I shrugged. In my mind's eye I could see all those conspirators, stealthily advancing on our fish tank under cover of the frosty night: our manager leading the way, followed by Mr. Koňas the butcher and the yellow-haired Daniela and all the greengrocers and party secretaries, factory managers and bribed supervisors, coal merchants and corrupt newspapermen. . . . Each and every one of them thrusting greedy hands into our tank and scuttling away with our carp. . . .

"All I can say is that next time you want to sell carp you'd better spend the night with them."

"You think so?" His eyes seemed to light up as he got the message, but all he did was shrug his shoulders.

Well, I guess he was right, at that. It would have been no use. *They* would always find a way to cheat us; we just didn't belong.

SEAN O'FAOLAIN

Two of a Kind

Maxer Creedon was not drunk, but he was melancholy-drunk, and he knew it and he was afraid of it.

At first he had loved being there in the jammed streets, with everybody who passed him carrying parcels wrapped in green or gold, tied with big red ribbons and fixed with berried holly sprigs. Whenever he bumped into someone, parcels toppled and they both cried "Ooops!" or "Sorree!" and laughed at one another. A star of snow sank nestling into a woman's hair. He smelled pine and balsam. He saw twelve golden angels blaring silently from twelve golden trumpets in Rockefeller Plaza. He pointed out to a cop that when the traffic lights down Park Avenue changed from red to green the row of white Christmas trees away down the line changed color by reflection. The cop was very grateful to him. The haze of light on the tops of the buildings made a halo over Fifth Avenue. It was all just the way he knew it would be, and he slopping down from Halifax in that damned old tanker. Then, suddenly, he swung his right arm in a wild arc of disgust.

"To hell with 'em! To hell with everybody!"

"Ooops! Hoho, there! Sorree!"

He refused to laugh back.

"Poor Creedon!" he said to himself. "All alone in New York, on Christmas-bloody-well-Eve, with nobody to talk to, and nowhere to go only back to the bloody old ship. New York all lit up. Everybody all lit up. Except poor old Creedon.'

He began to cry for poor old Creedon. Crying, he reeled through the

65

passing feet. The next thing he knew he was sitting up at the counter of an Eighth Avenue drugstore sucking black coffee, with one eye screwed up to look out at the changing traffic lights, chuckling happily over a yarn his mother used to tell him long ago about a place called Ballyroche. He had been there only once, nine years ago, for her funeral. Beaming into his coffee cup, or looking out at the changing traffic lights, he went through his favorite yarn about Poor Lily:

"Ah, wisha! Poor Lily! I wonder where is she atall, atall now. Is she dead or alive. It all happened through an Italian who used to be going from one farm to another selling painted statues. Bandello his name was, a handsome black divil o' hell! I never in all my born days saw a more handsome divil. Well, one wet, wild, windy October morning what did she do but creep out of her bed and we all sound asleep and go off with him. Often and often I heard my father say that the last seen of her was standing under the big tree at Ballyroche Cross, sheltering from the rain, at about eight o'clock in the morning. It was Mikey Clancy the postman saw her. 'Yerrah, Lily girl,' says he, 'what are you doing here at this hour of the morning?' 'I'm waiting,' says she, 'for to go into Fareens on the milk cart.' And from that day to this not a sight nor a sound of her no more than if the earth had swallowed her. Except for the one letter from a priest in America to say she was happily married in Brooklyn, New York."

Maxer chuckled again. The yarn always ended up with the count of the years. The last time he heard it the count had reached forty-one. By this year it would have been fifty.

Maxer put down his cup. For the first time in his life it came to him that the yarn was a true story about a real woman. For as long as four traffic-light changes he fumbled with this fact. Then, like a man hearing a fog signal come again and again from an approaching ship, and at last hearing it close at hand, and then seeing an actual if dim shape, wrapped in a cocoon of haze, the great idea revealed itself.

He lumbered down from his stool and went over to the telephones. His lumpish finger began to trace its way down the gray pages among the Brooklyn Ban's. His finger stopped. He read the name aloud. *Bandello, Mrs.*

Lily. He found a dime, tinkled it home, and dialed the number slowly. On the third ring he heard an old woman's voice. Knowing that she would be very old and might be deaf, he said very loudly and with the extrameticulous enunciation of all drunks:

"My name is Matthew Creedon. Only my friends all call me Maxer. I come from Limerick, Ireland. My mother came from the townland of Ballyroche. Are you by any chance my Auntie Lily?"

Her reply was a bark:

"What do you want?"

"Nothing at all! Only I thought, if you are the lady in question, that we might have a bit of an ould gosther. I'm a sailor. Docked this morning in the Hudson."

The voice was still hard and cold:

"Did somebody tell you to call me?"

He began to get cross with her.

"Naw! Just by a fluke I happened to look up your name in the directory. I often heard my mother talking about you. I just felt I'd like to talk to somebody. Being Christmas and all to that. And knowing nobody in New York. But if you don't like the idea, it's OK with me. I don't want to butt in on anybody. Good-bye."

"Wait! You're sure nobody sent you?"

"Inspiration sent me! Father Christmas sent me!" (She could take that any way she bloody well liked!) "Look! It seems to me I'm buttin' in. Let's skip it."

"No. Why don't you come over and see me?"

Suspiciously he said:

"This minute?"

"Right away!"

At the sudden welcome of her voice all his annoyance vanished.

"Sure, Auntie Lily! I'll be right over. But, listen, I sincerely hope you're not thinking I'm buttin' in. Because if you are . . ."

"It was very nice of you to call me, Matty, very nice indeed. I'll be glad to see you."

He hung up, grinning. She was just like his mother—the same old Limerick accent. After fifty years. And the same bossy voice. If she was a day she'd be seventy. She'd be tall, and thin, and handsome, and the real lawdy-daw, doing the grand lady, and under it all she'd be as soft as mountain moss. She'd be tidying the house now like a divil. And giving jaw to ould Bandello. If he was still alive.

He got lost on the subway, so that when he came up it was dark. He paused to have another black coffee. Then he paused to buy a bottle of Jamaica rum as a present for her. And then he had to walk five blocks before he found the house where she lived. The automobiles parked under the lights were all snow-covered. She lived in a brownstone house with high steps. Six other families had rooms in it.

The minute he saw her on top of the not brightly lighted landing, looking down at him, he saw something he had completely forgotten. She had his mother's height, and slimness, and her wide mouth, but he had forgotten the pale, liquid blue of the eyes and they stopped him dead on the stairs, his hand tight on the banister. At the sight of them he heard the soft wind sighing over the level Limerick plain and his whole body shivered. For miles and miles not a sound but that soughing wind that makes the meadows and the wheat fields flow like water. All over that plain, where a crossroads is an event, where a little, sleepy lake is an excitement. Where their streams are rivers to them. Where their villages are towns. The resting cows look at you out of owls' eyes over the greasy tips of the buttercups. The meadow grass is up to their bellies. Those two pale eyes looking down at him were bits of the pale albino sky stretched tightly over the Shannon plain.

Slowly he climbed up to meet her, but even when they stood side by side she was still able to look down at him, searching his face with her pallid eyes. He knew what she was looking for, and he knew she had found it when she threw her bony arms around his neck and broke into a low, soft wailing just like that Shannon wind.

"Auntie! You're the living image of her!"

On the click of a finger she became bossy and cross with him, hauling him by his two hands into her room:

"You've been drinking! And what delayed you? And I suppose not a scrap of solid food in your stomach since morning?"

He smiled humbly.

"I'm sorry, Auntie. 'Twas just on account of being all alone, you know. And everybody else making whoopee." He hauled out the peace offering of the rum. "Let's have a drink!"

She was fussing all over him immediately.

"You gotta eat something first. Drinking like that all day, I'm ashamed of you! Sit down, boy. Take off your jacket. I got coffee, and cookies, and hamburgers, and a pie. I always lay in a stock for Christmas. All of the neighbors visit me. Everybody knows that Lily Bandello keeps an open house for Christmas, nobody is ever going to say Lily Bandello didn't have a welcome for all her friends and relations at Christmastime. . . ."

She bustled in and out of the kitchenette, talking back to him without stop.

It was a big, dusky room, himself looking at himself out of a tall, mirrored wardrobe piled on top with cardboard boxes. There was a divan in one corner as high as a bed, and he guessed that there was a washbasin behind the old peacock screen. A single bulb hung in the center of the ceiling, in a fluted glass bell with pink frilly edges. The pope over the bed was Leo XIII. The snowflakes kept touching the bare windowpanes like kittens' paws trying to get in. When she began on the questions, he wished he had not come.

"How's Bid?" she called out from the kitchen.

"Bid? My mother? Oh, well, of course, I mean to say . . . My mother? Oh, she's grand, Auntie! Never better. For her age, of course, that is. Fine, fine out! Just like yourself. Only for the touch of the old rheumatism now and again."

"Go on, tell me about all all of them. How's Uncle Matty? And how's Cis? When were you down in Ballyroche last? But, sure, it's all changed now

I suppose, with electric light and everything up-to-date? And I suppose the old pony and trap is gone years ago? It was only last night I was thinking of Mikey Clancy the postman." She came in, planking down the plates, an iced Christmas cake, the coffeepot: "Go on! You're telling me nothing."

She stood over him, waiting, her pale eyes wide, her mouth stretched. He said:

"My Uncle Matty? Oh well, of course, now, he's not as young as he was. But I saw him there last year. He was looking fine. Fine out. I'd be inclined to say he'd be a bit stooped. But in great form. For his age, that is."

"Sit in. Eat up. Eat up. Don't mind me. He has a big family now, no doubt?"

"A family? Naturally! There's Tom. And there's Kitty, that's my Aunt Kitty, it *is* Kitty, isn't it, yes, my Auntie Kitty. And . . . God, I can't remember the half of them."

She shoved the hamburgers toward him. She made him pour the coffee and tell her if he liked it. She told him he was a bad reporter.

"Tell me all about the old place!"

He stuffed his mouth to give him time to think.

"They have twenty-one cows. Holsteins. The black-and-white chaps. And a red barn. And a shelter belt of pines. 'Tis lovely there now to see the wind in the trees, and when the night falls the way the lighthouse starts winking at you, and . . ."

"What lighthouse?" She glared at him. She drew back from him. "Are ye daft? What are you dreaming about? Is it a lighthouse in the middle of the County Limerick?"

"There is a lighthouse! I saw it in the harbor!"

But he suddenly remembered that where he had seen it was in a toy shop on Eighth Avenue, with a farm beyond it and a red barn and small cows, and a train going round and round it all.

"Harbor, Matty? Are ye out of your senses?"

"I saw it with my own two eyes."

Her eyes were like marbles. Suddenly she leaned over like a willow— just the way his mother used to lean over—and laughed and laughed.

"I know what you're talking about now. The lighthouse on the Shannon! Lord save us, how many times did I see it at night from the hill of Ballingarry! But there's no harbor, Matty."

"There's the harbor at Foynes!"

"Oh, for God's sake!" she cried. "That's miles and miles and miles away. 'Tis and twenty miles away! And where could you see any train, day or night, from anywhere at all near Ballyroche?"

They argued it hither and over until she suddenly found that the coffee was gone cold and rushed away with the pot to the kitchen. Even there she kept up the argument, calling out that certainly, you could see Moneygay Castle, and the turn of the River Deel on a fine day, but no train, and then she went on about the stepping-stones over the river, and came back babbling about Normoyle's bull that chased them across the dry river, one hot summer's day. . . .

He said:

"Auntie! Why the hell did you never write home?"

"Not even once?" she said, with a crooked smile like a bold child.

"Not a sight nor a sound of you from the day you left Ballyroche, as my mother used to say, no more than if the earth swallowed you. You're a nice one!"

"Eat up!" she commanded him, with a little laugh and a tap on his wrist.

"Did you always live here, Auntie Lily?"

She sat down and put her face between her palms with her elbows on the table and looked at him.

"Here? Well, no . . . That is to say, no! My husband and me had a house of our very own over in East Fifty-eighth. He did very well for himself. He was quite a rich man when he died. A big jeweler. When he was killed in an airplane crash five years ago he left me very well off. But sure I didn't need a house of my own and I had lots of friends in Brooklyn, so I came to live here."

"Fine! What more do you want, that is for a lone woman! No family?"

"I have my son. But he's married, to a Pole, they'll be over here first thing tomorrow morning to take me off to spend Christmas with them. They have an apartment on Riverside Drive. He is the manager of a big department store, Macy's on Flatbush Avenue. But tell me about Bid's children. You must have lots of brothers and sisters. Where are you going from here? Back to Ireland? To Limerick? To Ballyroche?''

He laughed.

"Where else would I go? Our next trip we hit the port of London. I'll be back like an arrow to Ballyroche. They'll be delighted to hear I met you. They'll be asking me all sorts of questions about you. Tell me more about your son, Auntie. Has he a family?''

"My son? Well, my son's name is Thomas. His wife's name is Catherine. She is very beautiful. She has means of her own. They are very happy. He is very well off. He's in charge of a big store, Sears, Roebuck on Bedford Avenue. Oh, a fine boy. Fine out! As you say. Fine out. He has three children. There's Cissy, and Matty. And . . .''

Her voice faltered. When she closed her eyes he saw how old she was. She rose and from the bottom drawer of a chest of drawers she pulled out a photograph album. She laid it in front of him and sat back opposite him.

"That is my boy.''

When he said he was like her she said he was very like his father. Maxer said that he often heard that her husband was a most handsome man.

"Have you a picture of him?''

She drew the picture of her son toward her and looked down at it.

"Tell me more about Ballyroche,'' she cried.

As he started into a long description of a harvest home he saw her eyes close again, and her breath came more heavily and he felt that she was not hearing a word he said. Then, suddenly, her palm slapped down on the picture of the young man, and he knew that she was not heeding him any more than if he weren't there. Her fingers closed on the pasteboard. She shied it wildly across the room, where it struck the glass of the window flat on, hesitated and slid to the ground. Maxer saw snowflakes melting as often as they touched the pane. When he looked back at her she was leaning across the table, one white lock down over one eye, her yellow teeth bared.

"You spy!" she spat at him. "You came from *them!* To spy on me!"

"I came from friendliness."

"Or was it for a ha'porth of look-about? Well, you can go back to Ballyroche and tell 'em whatever you like. Tell 'em I'm starving if that'll please 'em, the mean, miserable, lousy set that never gave a damn about me from the day I left 'em. For forty years my own sister, your mother, never wrote one line to say . . ."

"You know damn well she'd have done anything for you if she only knew where you were. Her heart was stuck in you. The two of you were inside one another's pockets. My God, she was forever talking and talking about you. Morning noon and night . . ."

She shouted at him across the table.

"I wrote six letters. . . ."

"She never got them."

"I registered two of them."

"Nobody ever got a line from you, or about you, only for the one letter from the priest that married you to say you were well and happy."

"What he wrote was that I was down and out. I saw the letter. I let him send it. That Wop left me flat in this city with my baby. I wrote to everybody—my mother, my father, to Bid after she was your mother and had a home of her own. I had to work every day of my life. I worked today. I'll work tomorrow. If you want to know what I do I clean out offices. I worked to bring up my son, and what did he do? Walked out on me with that Polack of his and that was the last I saw of him, or her, or any human being belonging to me until I saw you. Tell them every word of it. They'll love it!"

Maxer got up and went over slowly to the bed for his jacket. As he buttoned it he looked at her glaring at him across the table. Then he looked away from her at the snowflakes feeling the windowpane and dying there. He said, quietly:

"They're all dead. As for Limerick—I haven't been back to Ireland for eight years. When my mum died my father got married again. I ran away to sea when I was sixteen."

He took his cap. When he was at the door he heard a chair fall and then she was at his side, holding his arm, whispering gently to him:

"Don't go away, Matty." Her pallid eyes were flooded. "For God's sake, don't leave me alone with *them* on Christmas Eve!"

Maxer stared at her. Her lips were wavering as if a wind were blowing over them. She had the face of a frightened girl. He threw his cap on the bed and went over and sat down beside it. While he sat there like a big baboon, with his hands between his knees, looking at the snowflakes, she raced into the kitchen to put on the kettle for rum punch. It was a long while before she brought in the two big glasses of punch, with orange sliced in them, and brown sugar like drowned sand at the base of them. When she held them out to him he looked first at them, and then at her, so timid, so pleading, and he began to laugh and laugh—a laugh that he choked by covering his eyes with his hands.

"Damn ye!" he groaned into his hands. "I was better off drunk."

She sat beside him on the bed. He looked up. He took one of the glasses and touched hers with it.

"Here's to poor Lily!" he smiled.

She fondled his free hand.

"Lovie, tell me this one thing and tell me true. Did she really and truly talk about me? Or was that all lies too?"

"She'd be crying rain down when she'd be talking about you. She was always and ever talking about you. She was mad about you."

She sighed a long sigh.

"For years I couldn't understand it. But when my boy left me for that Polack I understood it. I guess Bid had a tough time bringing you all up. And there's no one more hard in all the world than a mother when she's thinking of her own. I'm glad she talked about me. It's better than nothing."

They sat there on the bed talking and talking. She made more punch, and then more, and in the end they finished the bottle between them, talking about everybody either of them had known in or within miles of the County Limerick. They fixed to spend Christmas Day together, and have Christmas dinner downtown, and maybe go to a picture and then come back and talk some more.

Every time Maxer comes to New York he rings her number. He can hardly breathe until he hears her voice saying, "Hello, Matty." They go on the town then and have dinner, always at some place with an Irish name, or a green neon shamrock above the door, and then they go to a movie or a show, and then come back to her room to have a drink and a talk about his last voyage, or the picture postcards he sent her, his latest bits and scraps of news about the Shannon shore. They always get first-class service in restaurants, although Maxer never noticed it until the night a waiter said, "And what's mom having?" at which she gave him a slow wink out of her pale Limerick eyes and a slow, lover's smile.

MICHEL TOURNIER

Jesu, Joy of Man's Desiring

A Christmas story
For Danny Cowl, this invented story,
which will remind him of a real one

Can you make a career as a great international concert pianist when your name is Gammon? By calling their son Raphael, thus placing him under the tutelage of the most ethereal and melodious of all the archangels, the Gammons may have been unconsciously taking up this challenge. In any case, the child soon showed signs of being gifted with an intelligence and sensitivity that sanctioned all their hopes. They put him at the piano as soon as he was old enough to sit on a stool. His progress was remarkable. Blond, blue-eyed, pale, aristocratic, he was every whit a Raphael, and in no way a Gammon.

At ten, he was already famous as a child prodigy and much fought over by the organizers of fashionable soirees. The ladies went into ecstasies when he leaned his delicate, transparent face over the keyboard and, enveloped, so it seemed, in the blue shadow of the wings of the invisible archangel, sent the notes of Johann Sebastian Bach's chorale "Jesu, Joy of Man's Desiring" floating up to the heavens like a mystical love song.

But the child paid dearly for these exceptional moments. Each year saw an increase in the number of hours a day he was made to practice. At twelve, he was already working six hours a day, and he found himself envying the fate of boys who were blessed with neither talent nor genius, nor with the promise of a brilliant career. It sometimes brought tears to his eyes when, on a fine day, relentlessly chained to his instrument, he heard the merry cries of his schoolmates enjoying themselves outdoors.

Came his sixteenth year. His talent was flowering with incomparable abundance. He was the star pupil of the Paris Conservatoire. On the other hand, when adolescence succeeded childhood, it did not seem to wish to retain the slightest trace of his former angelic visage. It seemed as if the wicked fairy Puberty had waved her magic wand over him and was determined to devastate the romantic angel that he had been. His bony, asymmetrical face, his protruding eyes, his receding chin, the thick glasses he had to wear because of his galloping myopia, none of this would really have mattered if it hadn't been for his permanent expression of stubborn amazement—which was much more likely to raise a laugh than to set people dreaming. In his appearance, at least, "Gammon" seemed to have completely triumphed over "Raphael."

Young Bénédicte Prieur, who was two years younger than he, seemed to be impervious to this lack of charm. A pupil at the conservatoire, she simply saw him, no doubt, as the great virtuoso he was in the process of becoming. In any case, she lived only in and for music, and the parents of the two children wondered in amazement whether their relationship would ever go beyond the ecstatic intimacy they reached when playing duets.

Raphael came out top in the conservatoire examination at a record age and began to pick up a few pupils to make his modest ends meet. Bénédicte and he were engaged, but they had decided to put off their marriage until times were better. They lived on love, music, and hope, and experienced some years of divine happiness. When they were lost in a concert which each dedicated to the other, Raphael, drunk with exaltation and gratitude, brought the evening to a close by playing once again Johann Sebastian Bach's chorale "Jesu, Joy of Man's Desiring." For him, this was not only a tribute to the greatest composer of all time, but also an ardent prayer to God, to ask him to safeguard so pure and ardent a union. And so the notes that floated up from his fingers at the piano rippled with celestial laughter, with the divine hilarity that was none other than the Creator's benediction of his own created being.

But destiny was to put such an exquisite equilibrium to the test. Raphael had a friend, like him a graduate of the conservatoire, who earned his living by accompanying a chansonnier in a nightclub. As he was a violinist, he didn't feel he was compromising his integrity by pounding away on an old upright piano to punctuate the inept couplets the chansonnier was mouthing downstage. Now, this Henri Durieu was about to leave for his first tour of the provinces, and he asked Raphael to stand in for him for four weeks so as not to jeopardize this invaluable pay packet.

Raphael hesitated. It would have been bad enough to have to sit for a couple of hours in that somber, badly ventilated place and listen to someone talking rubbish. But to have to go there every evening and, even worse, play a piano in such ignoble conditions . . . The fee, which for a single evening was the equivalent of a good dozen private lessons, was no compensation for this sacrilegious ordeal.

He was just about to refuse when, to his great surprise, Bénédicte asked him to think again. They had been engaged for a very long time. Raphael's career as an infant prodigy had been forgotten years ago, and no one knew how long he would have to wait until he became famous. But these few evenings might provide them with the extra income they needed to enable them to get a home together. Was it too much of a sacrifice, then? Could Raphael go on putting off their marriage simply because of the image—certainly worthy of respect, but nevertheless rather abstract—he had of his art? He agreed.

The chansonnier he had to accompany was called Gabbler. Enormous, flabby and flaccid, he trundled from one extremity of the stage to the other, relating in a whining voice all the sorrows and misfortunes that life never stopped heaping on him. The whole secret of his burlesque lay in this very simple observation: if you are the victim of a misadventure, you interest people; of two misadventures, you inspire them to pity; of a hundred misadventures, you make them laugh. Hence, you only have to exaggerate the pathetic and calamitous side of a character to get the audience roaring with laughter at him.

The very first evening, Raphael assessed the quality of the laughter. Sadism, spite, and a taste for the contemptible were cynically flaunted in it. In exhibiting his misery, Gabbler hit the audience below the belt and reduced it to its lowest common denominator. He turned these decent bourgeois, who were neither better nor worse than any others, into the vilest of criminals. His entire act was based on the infectious force of the ignoble, on the contagion of evil. In the bursts of laughter that hit the walls of the little theater Raphael recognized the laughter of the Devil himself, the triumphal roar, in other words, that is the breeding ground of hatred, cowardice, and stupidity.

And it was this ignoble merchandise that he was supposed to accompany at the piano, and not only accompany, but underline, amplify, exacerbate. At the piano; hence, with the aid of the sacred instrument on which he played Johann Sebastian Bach's chorales! Throughout his childhood and adolescence he had known evil only in its negative forms: discouragement, laziness, boredom, indifference. Now, for the first time, he was meeting it in a growling, grimacing, positive incarnation—that of the infamous Gabbler, whose active accomplice he was becoming.

What was his surprise, then, one evening when he was on his way to his daily hell, to see on the bill posted on the door of the café-theater a sticker adding, underneath the name Gabbler:

ACCOMPANIED AT THE PIANO BY GAMMON

He rushed into the manager's office, where he was received with open arms. Yes, the manager had felt obliged to include his name on the bill. It was only fair. His performance at the piano escaped none of the spectators and enormously enriched poor Gabbler's number—which, it was true, was a little threadbare. And in any case, the two names were just made for each other: Gammon and Gabbler. No one could have dreamed up a more sonorous, a more typical combination, or anything more delightfully daffy. And naturally his fee would be increased. Substantially.

Raphael had gone to the office to protest. He came out thanking the manager, and inwardly cursing his own timidity and feebleness.

That evening, he described the scene to Bénédicte. Very far from sharing his indignation, she congratulated him on his success and was delighted at the increase in their finances. After all, since the whole point of the operation was that it should be lucrative, wasn't it better for it to bring in as much money as possible? Raphael felt he was the victim of a general conspiracy.

Gabbler's attitude toward him, on the other hand, became very much cooler. Up till then he had treated him with patronizing condescension. Raphael was his accompanist, an unobtrusive, useful, but inglorious role which called for no more than abnegation and tact. But he was now attracting some of the audience's attention, hence some of their applause, and it had got to the point where even the manager had noticed it.

"Don't overdo it, old man, don't overdo it," he told Raphael, who could bear no more.

The situation would certainly have become aggravated if Durieu's return hadn't put an end to it. Relieved, Raphael went back to his lessons with the feeling of having fulfilled his duty, and with the memory of an experience that was all the more instructive in that it had been so harsh. Shortly afterward, he married Bénédicte.

Marriage didn't change Raphael's life much, but it gave him a sense of his responsibilities which he had so far been able to ignore. He had to share his young wife's worries, for she had great trouble in making ends meet, especially since every month they had to pay the installments on the apartment, the car, the television set, and the washing machine, all bought on credit. Their evenings were now more frequently spent in adding up figures than in communing in the pure beauty of a Bach chorale.

Coming home a little late one day, he found Bénédicte all excited by a visit she had had a few minutes earlier. It was Raphael, of course, whom the manager of the café-theater had come to see, but in his absence he had told Bénédicte the reason for his visit. No, this time it wasn't a question of accompanying the lamentable Gabbler, whose contract in any case would not be renewed for the coming season. But perhaps Raphael would agree to play a few solo piano pieces between two comic numbers? This would create a pleasant diversion in the middle of the program. The audience could only be delighted by such a parenthesis of calm and beauty inserted in a program which, for the remaining portion, would be full of gusto and gaiety.

Raphael refused point-blank. Never again would he descend into that den of pestilence in which he had suffered for a whole month. He had endured the experience of evil in his own domain, that of music and public performance. That was a very good thing, but he had no more to learn from it.

Bénédicte waited for the storm to pass. Then, in the following days, she gently returned to the attack. What he was being offered had nothing in common with accompanying the pathetic Gabbler. He would be playing solos, and whatever he chose. In short, he was being given an opportunity to practice his profession as a soloist. Certainly this debut was modest, but you had to start somewhere. Had he any choice?

She returned to it every day, patiently, tirelessly. At the same time she started thinking about moving to a different district. She dreamed of an old, and more spacious, apartment in a residential district. But this improvement in their life-style would demand sacrifices.

He sacrificed himself, and signed an engagement for six months, which could be terminated by the payment of a substantial indemnity by whichever party took the initiative in breaking the contract.

From the very first evening he realized the terrible trap he had fallen into. The audience was still vibrant and tumultuous from the previous number, a grotesque tango performed by a female giant and a male dwarf. When Raphael appeared onstage, in the black suit that was both too tight and too short for him, with his stilted, hunted air, his seminarian's face rigid with fright behind his thick glasses, everything seemed precisely calculated to form a highly comic composition. He was greeted with howls of laughter. As ill luck would have it, his piano stool was too low. He swiveled the seat to raise it, but in his agitation he unscrewed it completely and found himself facing a hysterical audience with a stool in two halves, like a mushroom with its cap separated from its stalk. In any normal situation it would probably have taken him only a few seconds to put the seat back in place. But, assailed by the photographers' flashes, the coordination of his movements impaired by panic, he had the added misfortune to drop his glasses, without which he couldn't see a thing. When he started to look for them, groping around the floor on all fours, the audience's joy knew no bounds. Next, he had to struggle for several long minutes with the two halves of the stool before he was finally able to sit down at the piano with trembling hands, and with his memory put to rout. What did he play that evening? He wouldn't have been able to say. Every time he touched the instrument the howls of laughter, which had subsided, started up again with renewed vigor. When he reached the wings, he was dripping with sweat and overcome by shame.

The manager clasped him in his arms.

"My dear Gammon," he exclaimed, "you were admirable, do you hear me, ad-mi-ra-ble. You are the great revelation of the season. Your gift for comic improvisation is incomparable. And what a presence! You only have to appear for people to start laughing. The moment you touch the piano they go berserk. And in any case, I'd invited the press. I knew how it would be."

Behind him, modest and smiling, Bénédicte effaced herself under the avalanche of compliments. Raphael hung on to her image as a shipwrecked mariner clings to a rock. He looked her in the face with imploring insistence. She remained sleek, radiant, and unshakable, did young Bénédicte Prieur, who had this evening become Madame Gammon, the wife of the celebrated comic musician. Maybe she was thinking of her splendid residential apartment, from now on within her reach.

The press was indeed triumphal. It spoke of a new Buster Keaton. It extolled Raphael's sorrowful countenance, which resembled that of a frantic anthropoid ape, his catastrophic clumsiness, his grotesque manner of playing the piano. And the same photo appeared everywhere, the one that caught him on all fours, groping around for his glasses between the two halves of his stool.

They moved. Next, an impresario undertook to represent Gammon's interests. They had him make a film. Then a second film. With the third, they were able to move once again, and this time establish themselves in a mansion in the avenue de Madrid, in Neuilly.

One day, they received a visit. Henri Durieu had come to pay homage to the tremendous success of his former comrade. He walked diffidently around among the gilded paneling, the crystal candelabra, and the old masters. As second violin in the Alençon municipal orchestra, he couldn't get over so much magnificence. And yet he had nothing to complain about. In any case, he was no longer to be seen playing the piano in nightclubs, and that was the main thing, wasn't it? He could no longer bear to prostitute his art in that fashion, he stoutly declared.

They spoke of the years they had spent at the conservatoire together, of their hopes, their disappointments, and of the patience each had needed to find his own way. Durieu hadn't brought his violin with him. But Raphael sat down at the piano and played Mozart, Beethoven, and Chopin.

"What a career you could have made as a soloist!" Durieu exclaimed. "Though it's true that you were destined for other laurels. We all have to follow the dictates of our own vocation."

More than once the critics had mentioned the name of Grock apropos of Gammon, and declared that the legendary Swiss Auguste might well have finally found his successor.

Gammon did in fact make his circus debut in Urbino, one Christmas Eve. For a long time the locals had been looking for someone to play the supporting role of the whiteface clown. After a few inconclusive trials, Bénédicte surprised everyone by suggesting herself. Why not? Dressed in a tight, embroidered vest, and breeches, wearing silver slippers, her face made up with chalk, one eyebrow painted black over her forehead, where it formed a lofty, interrogative and mocking arc, and speaking in a high-and-mighty fashion, she did wonders, did young Bénédicte Prieur, who had henceforth become the partner and indispensable foil of the celebrated musician-clown, Gammon.

Wearing a pink cardboard cranium and a false nose shaped like a sweet potato, lost in a tailcoat with a celluloid shirtfront teetering around his neck, and pants corkscrewing down onto enormous clodhoppers, Gammon played the part of a failed artist, a naively pretentious ignoramus who had come to give a piano recital. But the most dreadful cacophony came from his clothes, from the swivel stool, and above all from the piano itself. The slightest touch on any key triggered off a booby trap or a catastrophe: a jet of water, a puff of smoke, a grotesque noise like a fart, a belch, a whistle. And the audience burst into peals of laughter, raised the roof from all the tiers, and crushed him under his own buffoonery.

Deafened by these joyous catcalls, Gammon sometimes used to think about poor Gabbler, who no doubt had never fallen so low. But what protected him was his myopia, for his makeup made it impossible for him to wear his glasses and he could therefore see practically nothing, merely big patches of colored lights. Even though thousands of torturers were driving him silly with their bestial laughter, at least he had the advantage of not seeing them.

Was there still some work to be done to perfect the diabolical piano number? Did a kind of miracle take place that evening under the big top in Urbino? The plan was that, in the finale, after struggling through a piece of music as best he could, the unfortunate Gammon should witness the explosion of his piano, which would vomit out into the ring a vast array of hams, custard pies, and strings of black and white sausages. But something quite different occurred.

The savage laughs died down at the sudden immobility of the clown. Then, when the most complete silence reigned, he began to play. With contemplative, meditative, fervent serenity he played "Jesu, Joy of Man's Desiring," the Bach chorale that had soothed his student years. And the poor old circus piano, for all its gimmicks and gadgets, obeyed his hands marvelously, and sent the divine melody floating up to the obscure heights of the big top, with its temporarily invisible trapezes and rope ladders. After the inferno of guffaws it was the hilarity of the heavens, tender and spiritual, which soared over a crowd in communion.

A long silence prolonged the last note, as if the chorale were continuing in the Beyond. Then, in the shimmering clouds of his myopia, the musician-clown saw the piano lid rising. It didn't explode. It didn't spew out sausages.

It opened slowly like a huge, somber flower, and released a beautiful archangel with wings of light, the archangel Raphael, the one who had been watching over him all his life and preventing him from quite becoming Gammon.

PAUL BOWLES

The Frozen Fields

The train was late because the hotbox under one of the coaches had caught fire in the middle of a great flat field covered with snow. They had stayed there about an hour. After the noise and rushing of the train, the sudden silence and the embarrassed stirring of people in their seats induced a general restlessness. At one point another train had shot by on the next track with a roar worse than thunder; in the wake of that, the nervousness of the passengers increased, and they began to talk fretfully in low voices.

Donald had started to scratch pictures with his fingernail in the ice that covered the lower part of the windowpane by his seat. His father had said: "Stop that." He knew better than to ask "Why?" but he thought it; he could not see what harm it would do, and he felt a little resentful toward his mother for not intervening. He could have arranged for her to object to the senseless prohibition, but experience had taught him that she could be counted on to come to his defense only a limited number of times during any given day, and it was imprudent to squander her reserve of goodwill.

The snow had been cleared from the station platform when they got out. It was bitter cold; a fat plume of steam trailed downward from the locomotive, partially enveloping the first coach. Donald's feet ached with the cold.

"There's Uncle Greg and Uncle Willis!" he cried, and he jumped up and down several times.

"You don't have to shout," said his father. "We see them. And stand still. Pick up your bag."

Uncle Willis wore a black bearskin coat that almost touched the ground. He put his hands under Donald's arms and lifted him up so that his head was at a level with his own, and kissed him hard on the mouth. Then he swung him over into Uncle Greg's arms, and Uncle Greg did the same thing. "How's the man, hey?" cried Uncle Greg as he set him down.

"Fine," said Donald, conscious of a feeling of triumph, because his father did not like to see boys being kissed. "Men shake hands," he had told him. "They don't kiss each other."

The sky was crystal clear, and although it was already turning lavender with the passing of afternoon, it still shone with an intense light, like the sky in one scene at the Russian Ballet. His mother had taken him a few weeks earlier because she wanted to see Pavlova; it was not the dancing that had excited him, but the sudden direct contact with the world of magic. This was a magic sky above him now, nothing like the one he was used to seeing above the streets of New York. Everything connected with the farm was imbued with magic. The house was the nucleus of an enchanted world more real than the world that other people knew about. During the long green summers he had spent there with his mother and the members of her family he had discovered that world and explored it, and none of them had ever noticed that he was living in it. But his father's presence here would constitute a grave danger, because it was next to impossible to conceal anything from him, and once aware of the existence of the other world he would spare no pains to destroy it. Donald was not yet sure whether all the entrances were safely guarded or effectively camouflaged.

They sat in the back of the sleigh with a brown buffalo robe tucked around them. The two big gray horses were breathing out steam through their wide nostrils. Silently the white countryside moved past, its frozen trees pink in the late light. Uncle Greg held the reins, and Uncle Willis, sitting beside him, was turned sideways in his seat, talking to Donald's mother.

"My feet hurt," said Donald.

"Well, God Almighty, boy!" cried Uncle Willis. "Haven't you got 'em on the bricks? There are five hot bricks down there. That's what they're there for." He bent over and lifted up part of the heavy lap robe. The bricks were wrapped in newspaper.

"My feet are like blocks of ice, too," said Donald's mother. "Here, take your shoes off and put your feet on these." She pushed two of the bricks toward Donald.

"He just wants attention," said Donald's father. But he did not forbid him to have the bricks.

"Is that better?" Uncle Willis asked a moment later.

"It feels good. How many miles is it to the farm?"

"Seven miles to The Corner, and a mile and a half from there."

"Oh, I know it's a mile and a half from The Corner," said Donald. He had walked it many times in the summer, and he knew the names of the farms along the road. "First you come to the Elders, then the Landons, then the Madisons—"

His father pushed him hard in the ribs with his elbow. "Just keep quiet for a while."

Uncle Willis pretended not to have heard this. "Well, well. You certainly have a good memory. How old are you now?"

Donald's throat had constricted; it was a familiar occurrence which did not at all mean that he was going to cry—merely that he felt like crying. He coughed and said in a stifled voice: "Six." Then he coughed again; ashamed, and fearful that Uncle Willis might have noticed something amiss, he added: "But I'll be seven the day after New Year's."

They were all silent after that; there were only the muffled rhythm of the horses' trot and the soft, sliding sound of the runners on the packed snow. The sky was now a little darker than the white meadows, and the woods on the hillside beyond, with their millions of bare branches, began to look frightening. Donald was glad to be sitting in the middle. He knew there were no wolves out there, and yet, could anybody be really certain? There had been wolves at one time—and bears as well—and simply because nobody had seen one in many years, they now said there weren't any. But that was no proof.

They came to The Corner, where the road to the farm turned off from the main road. Seven rusty mailboxes stood there in a crooked row, one for each house on the road.

"R.F.D. number 1," said Uncle Willis facetiously. This had always been a kind of joke among them, ever since they had bought the farm, because they were townspeople and thought the real farmers were very funny.

Now Donald felt he was on home ground, and it gave him the confidence to say: "Rural free delivery." He said the words carefully, since the first one sometimes gave him difficulty. But he pronounced it all right, and Uncle Greg, without turning round, shouted: "That's right! You go to school now?"

"Yes." He did not feel like saying more, because he was following the curves in the road, which he knew by heart. But everything looked so different from the way he remembered it that he found it hard to believe it was the same place. The land had lost its intimacy, become bare and unprotected. Even in the oncoming night he could see right through the leafless bushes that should have hidden the empty fields beyond. His feet were all right now, but his hands in their woolen mittens under the buffalo skin were numb with cold.

The farm came into view; in each downstairs window there was a lighted candle and a holly wreath. He bent over and put his shoes on. It was hard because his fingers ached. When he sat up again the sleigh had stopped. The kitchen door had opened; someone was coming out. Everyone was shouting "Hello!" and "Merry Christmas!" Between the sleigh and the kitchen he was aware only of being kissed and patted, lifted up and set down, and told that he had grown. His grandfather helped him take off his shoes again and removed a lid from the top of the stove so he could warm his hands over the flames. The kitchen smelled, as in summer, of woodsmoke, sour milk and kerosene.

It was always very exciting to be in the midst of many people. Each one was an added protection against the constant watchfulness of his mother and father. At home there were only he and they, so that mealtimes were periods of torture. Tonight there were eight at the supper table. They put an enormous old leather-bound dictionary in a chair so he would be high enough, and he sat between his grandmother and Aunt Emilie. She had dark brown eyes and was very pretty. Uncle Greg had married her a year ago, and Donald knew from many overheard conversations that none of the others really liked her.

Gramma was saying: "Louisa and Ivor couldn't get down till tomorrow. Mr. Gordon's driving them down as far as Portersville in his car. They'll all stay in the hotel tonight, and we've got to go in first thing in the morning and bring them out."

"Mr. Gordon, too, I suppose," said his mother.

"Oh, probably," Uncle Greg said. "He won't want to stay alone Christmas Day."

His mother looked annoyed. "It seems sort of unnecessary," she said. "Christmas is a *family* day, after all."

"Well, he's part of the family now," said Uncle Willis with a crooked smile.

His mother replied with great feeling: "I think it's terrible."

"He's pretty bad these days," put in Grampa, shaking his head.

"Still on the old firewater?" asked his father.

Uncle Greg raised his eyebrows. "That and worse. You know. . . . And Ivor too."

Donald knew they were being mysterious because of him. He pretended not to be listening, and busied himself making marks on the tablecloth with his napkin ring.

His father's mouth had fallen open with astonishment. "Where do they get it?" he demanded.

"Prescription," said Uncle Willis lightly. "Some crooked Polack doctor up there."

"Oh, honestly," cried his mother. "I don't see how Louisa *stands* it."

Aunt Emilie, who had been quiet until now, suddenly spoke. "Oh, I don't know," she said speculatively. "They're both very good to her. I think Mr. Gordon's very generous. *He* pays the rent on her apartment, you know, and gives her the use of the car and chauffeur most afternoons."

"You don't know anything about it," said Uncle Greg in a gruff, unpleasant voice which was meant to stop her from talking. But she went on, a bit shrilly, and even Donald could hear that they were in the habit of arguing.

"I *do* happen to know that Ivor's perfectly willing to give her a divorce any time she wants it, because she told me so herself."

There was silence at the table; Donald was certain that if he had not been there they would all have begun to talk at that point. Aunt Emilie had said something he was not supposed to hear.

"Well," said Uncle Willis heartily, "how about another piece of cake, Donald, old man?"

"How about bed, you mean," said his father. "It's time he went to bed."

His mother said nothing, helped him from his chair and took him upstairs.

The little panes of his bedroom window were completely covered with ice. Opening his mouth, he breathed on one pane until a round hole had been melted through and he could see blackness outside. "Don't do that, dear," said his mother. "Gramma'll have to clean the window. Now come on; into bed with you. There's a nice hot brick under the covers so your feet won't get cold." She tucked the blankets around him, kissed him, and took the lamp from the table. His father's voice, annoyed, came up from the foot of the stairs. "Hey, Laura! What's going on up there? Come on."

"Won't there be any light in my room at all?" Donald asked her.

"I'm coming," she called. She looked down at Donald. "You never have a light at home."

"I know, but home I can turn it on if I need it."

"Well, you're not going to need it tonight. Your father would have a fit if I left the lamp. You know that. Now just go to sleep."

"But I won't be able to sleep," he said miserably.

"Laura!" shouted his father.

"Just a *minute!*" she cried, vexed.

"Please, Mother. . . ?"

Her voice was adamant. "This cold air will put you to sleep in two shakes of a lamb's tail. Now go to sleep." She went to the doorway, the lamp in her hand, and disappeared through it, closing the door behind her.

There was a little china clock on the table that ticked very loud and fast. At infrequent intervals from below came a muffled burst of laughter which immediately subsided. His mother had said: "I'll open this window about an inch; that'll be enough." The room was growing colder by the minute. He pushed the sole of one foot against the heated brick in the middle of the bed and heard the crackle of the newspaper that enfolded it. There was nothing left to do but go to sleep. On his way through the borderlands of consciousness he had a fantasy. From the mountain behind the farm, running silently over the icy crust of the snow, leaping over the rocks and bushes, came a wolf. He was running toward the farm. When he got there he would look through the windows until he found the dining room where the grown-ups were sitting around the big table. Donald shuddered when he saw his eyes in the dark through the glass. And now, calculating every movement perfectly, the wolf sprang, smashing the panes, and seized Donald's father by the throat. In an instant, before anyone could move or cry out, he was gone again with his prey still between his jaws, his head turned sideways as he dragged the limp form swiftly over the surface of the snow.

The white light of dawn was in the room when he opened his eyes. Already there were bumpings in the bowels of the house: people were stirring. He heard a window slammed shut, and then the regular sound of someone splitting wood with a hatchet. Presently there were nearer noises, and he knew that his parents in the next room had gotten up. Then his door was flung open and his mother came in, wearing a thick brown flannel bathrobe, and with her hair falling loose down her back. "Merry Christmas!" she cried, holding up a gigantic red mesh stocking crammed with fruit and small packages. "Look what I found hanging by the fireplace!" He was disappointed because he had hoped to go and get his stocking himself. "I brought it up to you because the house is as cold as a barn," she told him. "You stay put right here in bed till it's warmed up a little."

"When'll we have the tree?" The important ritual was the tree: the most interesting presents were piled under it.

"You just hold your horses," she told him. "You've got your stocking. We can't have the tree till Aunt Louisa gets here. You wouldn't want her to miss it, would you?"

"Where's my present for Aunt Louisa and Uncle Ivor? Uncle Ivor's coming, too, isn't he?"

"Of course he's coming," she replied, with that faintly different way of speaking she used when she mentioned Uncle Ivor. "I've already put it under the tree with the other things. Now you just stay where you are, all covered up, and look at your stocking. I'm going to get dressed." She shivered and hurried back into her room.

The only person he had to thank at breakfast was his grandfather, for a box of colored pencils which had been jammed into the foot of the stocking. The other gifts had been tagged: "For Donald from Santa." Uncle Willis and Uncle Greg had eaten an early breakfast and gone in the sleigh to the hotel in Portersville to fetch Aunt Louisa and Uncle Ivor. When they got back, Donald ran to the window and saw that Mr. Gordon had come. Everyone had talked so mysteriously about Mr. Gordon that he was very eager to see him. But at that moment his mother called him upstairs to help her make the beds. "We all have to do as much as we can for Gramma," she told him. "Lord knows she's got all she can manage with the kitchen work."

But eventually he heard Aunt Louisa calling up the staircase. They went down: he was smothered in kisses, and Aunt Louisa asked him: "How's my boy? You're *my* boy, aren't you?" Then Uncle Ivor kissed him, and he shook hands with Mr. Gordon, who was already sitting in Grampa's armchair, where nobody else ever sat. He was plump and pale, and he wore two big diamond rings on one hand and an even bigger sapphire on the other. As he breathed he wheezed slightly; now and then he pulled an enormous yellow silk handkerchief out of his breast pocket and wiped his forehead with it. Donald sat down on the other side of the room and turned the pages of a magazine, from time to time looking up to observe him. He had called Donald "my lad," which sounded very strange, like someone talking in a book. At one point he noticed Donald's attention and beckoned to him. Donald went and stood beside the armchair while Mr. Gordon reached into his pocket and pulled out a fat watch with a little button, and tiny chimes struck inside the watch. A few minutes later he signaled to him afresh; Donald bounded over to him and pressed the button again. The next time, his mother told him to stop bothering Mr. Gordon.

"But he *asked* me to," objected Donald.

"Sit down right there. We're all going in and have our tree in a little while. Uncle Ivor's going to be Santa Claus."

Presently Uncle Willis came into the room. "Well, everybody, he said, rubbing his hands together, "I think the parlor's warm enough now. How about our tree?"

"It's about time," said Aunt Emilie. She was wearing a red taffeta dress which Donald had heard his mother discussing with his father earlier. "*Most* inappropriate," she had said. "The girl doesn't seem to realize she's living on a farm." Aunt Emilie reached down and took Donald's hand. "Would you care to accompany me, sir?" she said. They walked into the parlor holding hands. The fire in the fireplace roared and crackled.

"Where's Ivor?" said Uncle Greg. "Has everybody got a seat?"

"Here he is," said Uncle Ivor, coming in from the hallway. He had put on an old red knit skullcap and a red dressing gown, and he had a wreath of green fluted paper around his neck. "This is all Santa Claus could find," he announced.

Aunt Louisa began to laugh. "Look at your Uncle Ivor," she told Donald. "I am," said Donald. But he was really looking at the tree. It was a tall hemlock that reached to the ceiling, and underneath it was piled the most enormous assortment of packages he had ever seen. "Look at that!" they all cried.

"What *do* you suppose is in them all?" said Aunt Louisa.

"I don't know," he replied.

Uncle Ivor sat down on the floor as near the tree as he could get, and lifting up a large crate he passed it to Uncle Greg, who stood in the middle of the room. "Let's get this out of the way first," he said. Then Uncle Greg intoned: "To Donald from the folks at Rutland."

While Uncle Ivor went on passing out packages, Donald struggled with his box. He was vaguely aware of the little cries that were being uttered around him: "How lovely! But it's too much!" "Oh, you shouldn't have!" "Why did you do it?" as the others opened their gifts, but he was too preoccupied to notice that most of the exclamations were being addressed to Mr. Gordon, who sat in the window looking very pleased.

It was too good to believe: a fire engine three feet long, with rubber tires and a bell and a siren and three ladders that shot upward automatically when it stopped. Donald looked at it and for a moment was almost frightened by the power he knew it had to change his world.

"Oh . . . isn't . . . that . . . lovely!" said his mother, her annoyance giving a sharp edge to each word. "Louisa, why did you do it?" Donald glanced up quickly and saw Aunt Louisa indicate Mr. Gordon with a jerk of her head, as if she were saying: "Everything is his fault."

His mother moved along the floor toward the crate and fished out the greeting card. "I want you to keep each card in with the present it came with," she told Donald, "because you'll have a lot of thank-you notes to write tomorrow, and you don't want to get them mixed up. But you can thank Aunt Louisa and Uncle Ivor right now."

He hated to be told to thank a person in that person's presence, as though he were a baby. But he said the words bravely, facing Mr. Gordon: "Thank you so much for the beautiful fire engine."

"There's more there, my lad," beamed Mr. Gordon; the diamonds flashed in the sunlight.

Aunt Emilie was holding out her arm in front of her, looking at her new wristwatch. Grampa had put on a black silk dressing gown and was smoking a cigar. He looked perfectly content as he turned to Mr. Gordon and said:

"Well, you've spoiled us all." But Donald's mother interpreted his phrase as a reproach, and added in explanation: "We're not used to getting such *elaborate* gifts, Mr. Gordon."

Mr. Gordon laughed and turning to Donald, told him: "You've barely started, my lad. Tell your Uncle Ivor to get on with it."

Now it seemed as though nearly every package was for Donald. He opened them as fast as he could, and was freshly bewildered by the apparition of each new marvel. There were, of course, the handkerchiefs and books and mufflers from the family, but there was also a Swiss music box with little metal records that could be changed; there were roller skates, a large set of lead soldiers, a real accordion, and a toy village with a streetcar system that ran on a battery. As Donald opened each package, the little cries of admiration made by his parents came closer to sounding like groans. Finally his father said, in a voice loud enough for Mr. Gordon to hear him above the general conversation: "It's bad business for one kid to get so much."

Mr. Gordon had heard him. "You were young once yourself," he said airily.

Aunt Emilie was trying on a fur jacket that Uncle Greg had given her. Her face was flushed with excitement; she had just planted a big kiss on Uncle Greg's cheek.

"The little Astor baby got five thousand dollars' worth of toys on its last birthday," she said to Donald's father, running her hand back and forth along the fur.

Donald's father looked at her with narrowed eyes. "That," he said, enunciating very clearly, "is what might be called an *asinine* remark."

Save for the crackling of the fire there was silence for a moment in the room. Those who had not heard knew that something had happened. Uncle Greg looked quickly at Donald's father, and then at Aunt Emilie. Maybe there would be a quarrel, thought Donald, with everyone against his father. The idea delighted him; at the same time he felt guilty, as though it were his doing.

Uncle Ivor was handing him a package. Automatically he untied the ribbon and pulled out a tan cashmere sweater. "That's Mother and Daddy's present to you," his mother said quietly. "It's a little big for you now, but I got it big purposely so you could grow into it." The small crisis had passed; they all began to talk again. Donald was relieved and disappointed. "How about christening that bottle of brandy?" cried Uncle Willis.

"You menfolk sit here," Gramma told them. "We've got to get out into the kitchen."

"I'll bring yours out to you," said Uncle Ivor to Aunt Louisa as she got up.

On her way out of the room Donald's mother bent over and touched his shoulder. "I want you to put every present back into its box just the way it was. After that you carry them all up into our room and stack them carefully in the corner under the window. You hear me?"

She went out. Donald sat a moment; then he jumped up and ran after her to ask if he might save out just one thing—the fire engine, perhaps. She was saying to Gramma: ". . . quite uncalled for. Besides, I don't know how we're *ever* going to get it all back to New York. Owen can take the big things at least with him tomorrow, I suppose."

He stopped running and felt peace descend upon him. His father was leaving the farm. Then let him take everything with him, fire engine and all; it would not matter. He turned and went back into the parlor, where he meticulously packed the toys into their boxes, put the covers on, and tied them up with lengths of ribbon and string.

"What's all this?" exclaimed Mr. Gordon suddenly, noticing him. "What are you doing?"

"I have to take everything upstairs," said Donald.

His father joined the conversation. "I don't want to find those boxes lying all over the place up there, either. See that you pile 'em neatly. Understand?"

Donald continued to work without looking up.

After a moment Mr. Gordon said under his breath: "Well, I'll be damned." Then to Donald's father: "I've seen some well-behaved kids in my time, but I don't mind telling you I never saw one like *that*. Never."

"Discipline begins in the cradle," said his father shortly.

"It's sinister," murmured Mr. Gordon to himself.

Donald glanced up and saw his father looking at Mr. Gordon with hatred.

In the kitchen his grandmother, his aunts and his mother were busy preparing dinner. Donald sat by the window mashing potatoes. The blue of the sky had disappeared behind one curtain of cloud, uniformly white. "We'll have more snow before night," said Gramma, looking out of the window above the sink.

"Want to smell something good?" Donald's mother asked him. He ran across to the stove and she opened the oven door: the aroma of onions mingled with that of the roasting turkey. "He's coming along beautifully," she announced. She shut the oven door with a bang and hung the pot holders on their hooks. Then she went into the pantry. Donald followed her. It was very cold in here, and it smelled of pickles and spices. His mother was searching for something along the shelves, among the jars and tin boxes.

"Mother," he said.

"Hmm?" she replied distraughtly, without looking down at him.

"Why does Mr. Gordon live at Uncle Ivor's?"

Now she did look at him, and with an intensity that startled him. "What was that?" she demanded sharply. Then, before he could repeat his question, she went on in a suddenly matter-of-fact voice: "Dear, don't you know that Uncle Ivor's what they call a male nurse? Like Miss Oliver, you remember, who took care of you when you had influenza? Only a man. A man nurse."

"Is Mr. Gordon sick?"

"Yes, he is," she said, lowering her voice to little more than a whisper. "He's a very sick man, but we don't talk about it."

"What's he got?" He was conscious of being purposely childish at the moment, in the hope of learning more. But his mother was already saying: "I don't know, dear. You go back into the kitchen now. It's too cold for you in here. Scoot! Out with you!" He giggled, ran back into the kitchen, satisfied for having definitely established the existence of a mystery.

During dinner his father looked across at him with the particular kind of sternness he reserved for remarks which he knew were unwelcome, and said: "You haven't been outside yet today, young man. We'll take a walk down the road later."

Aunt Louisa had brought a large glass of brandy to the table with her and was sipping it along with her food. "It's too cold, Owen," she objected. "He'll catch his death o' cold." Donald knew she was trying to help him, but he wished she had kept quiet. If it became an issue, his father would certainly not forget about the walk.

"Too cold!" scoffed his father. "We have a few basic rules in *our* little family, and one of them is that he has to get some fresh air every day."

"Couldn't you make an exception for Christmas? Just for one day?" demanded Aunt Louisa.

Donald did not dare look up, for fear of seeing the expression on his father's face.

"Listen, Louisa," he said acidly. "I suggest you just stay on your side of the fence, and I'll stay on mine. We'll get along a lot better." Then as an afterthought he snapped: "That all right with you?"

Aunt Louisa leaned across Grampa's plate toward Donald's father and spoke very loud, so that everyone stopped eating. "No, it's not all right with me!" she cried. "All you do is pick on the child from morning till night. It's shameful! I won't sit by and watch my own flesh and blood plagued that way!"

Both Gramma and Donald's father began to speak at once. Gramma was saying, "Louisa," trying to soothe her. Donald's father shouted: "You've never *had* a kid. You don't know the first thing *about* raising kids."

"I know when a man's selfish and plain cussed," Aunt Louisa declared.

"Louisa!" cried Gramma in a tone of surprise and mild reproof. Donald continued to look at his plate.

"Have I ever come up to Rutland and stuck my nose in your affairs and criticized? Have I?" demanded Donald's father.

"Now come on," said Uncle Willis quickly. "Let's not spoil a beautiful Christmas."

"That's right," Grampa said. "We're all happy. Let's not say anything we'll be sorry for later."

But Aunt Louisa would not retreat. She took a fast gulp of brandy and almost choked on it. Then, still leaning toward Donald's father, she went on: "What do you mean, come to Rutland and criticize? What've you got to criticize in Rutland? Something wrong there?"

For an instant Donald's father did not reply. During that instant it was as though everyone felt the need to say something without being able to say it. The one who broke the short silence was Donald's father, using a peculiar, soft voice which Donald recognized immediately as a vicious imitation of Uncle Ivor. "Oh, *no!* There's nothing wrong in *Rut*land!"

Suddenly, with two simultaneous motions, Donald's mother slapped her napkin into her place and pushed her chair back violently. She rose and ran out of the room, slamming the door. No one said anything. Donald sat frozen, unable to look up, unable even to breathe. Then he realized that his father had got up, too, and was on his way out.

"Leave her alone, Owen," said Gramma.

"You keep out of this," his father said. His footsteps made the stairs creak as he went up. No one said anything until Gramma made as if to rise. "I'm going up," she declared.

"For God's sake, Abbie, sit still," Grampa told her. Gramma cleared her throat but did not get up.

Aunt Louisa looked very red, and the muscles of her face were twitching. "Hateful," she said in a choked voice. "Just hateful."

"I felt like slapping his face," confided Aunt Emilie. "Did you hear what he said to me when we were having our presents?"

At a glance from Uncle Greg, Aunt Emilie stopped. "Why, Donald!" she exclaimed brightly, "you've scarcely touched your dinner! Aren't you hungry?"

In his mind's eye he was seeing the bedroom upstairs, where his father was twisting his mother's arm and shaking her to make her look at him. When she wouldn't, he punched her, knocking her down, and kicked her as hard as he could, all over her body. Donald looked up. "Not very," he said.

Without warning Mr. Gordon began to talk, holding his glass in front of him and examining it as he turned it this way and that. "Family quarrels," he sighed. "Same old thing. Reminds me of my boyhood. When I look back on it, it seems to me we never got through a meal without a fight, but I suppose we must have once in a while." He set the glass down. "Well, they're all dead now, thank God."

Donald looked quickly across at Mr. Gordon as if he were seeing him for the first time.

"It's snowing!" cried Gramma triumphantly. "Look, it's snowing again. I knew we'd have more snow before dark." She did not want Mr. Gordon to go on talking.

Aunt Louisa sobbed once, got up, and went out into the kitchen. Uncle Ivor followed her.

"Why, Donald! You've got the wishbone!" cried Aunt Emilie. "Eat the meat off it and we'll hang it up over the stove to dry, and tomorrow we'll wish on it. Wouldn't that be fun?"

He picked it up in his fingers and began to chew on the strips of white meat that clung to it. When he had carefully cleaned it, he got down and went out into the kitchen with it.

The room was very quiet; the teakettle simmered on the stove. Outside the window the falling snowflakes looked dark against the whiteness beyond. Aunt Louisa was sitting on the high stool, doubled over, with a crumpled handkerchief in her hand, and Uncle Ivor was bending over her talking in a very low voice. Donald laid the wishbone on the sink shelf and started to tiptoe out, but Uncle Ivor saw him. "How'd you like to go up to the henhouse with me, Donald?" he said. "I've got to find us a dozen eggs to take back to Rutland."

"I'll get my coat," Donald told him, eager to go out before his father came back downstairs.

The path up the hill to the henhouse had been made not by clearing the snow away but by tramping it down. The new snow was drifting over the track; in some places it already had covered it. When Uncle Ivor went into the henhouse Donald stood still, bending his head back to catch some snowflakes in his mouth. "Come on in and shut the door. You'll let all the heat out," Uncle Ivor told him.

"I'm coming," said Donald. He stepped through the doorway and closed the door. The smell inside was very strong. As Uncle Ivor approached the hens, they set up a low, distrustful murmur.

"Tell me, Donald," said Uncle Ivor as he explored the straw with his hands.

"What?" said Donald.

"Does your mother often run to her room and shut the door, the way she did just now?"

"Sometimes."

"Why? Is your father mean to her?"

"Oh," said Donald vaguely, "they have fights." He felt uncomfortable.

"Yes. Well, it's a great pity your father ever got married. It would have been better for everybody if he'd stayed single."

"But then I wouldn't have been born at all," cried Donald, uncertain whether Uncle Ivor was serious or not.

"At least, we *hope* not!" said Uncle Ivor, rolling his eyes and looking silly. Now Donald knew it was a kind of joke, and he laughed. The door was flung open. "Donald!" roared his father.

"What is it?" he said, his voice very feeble.

"Come out here!"

He stumbled toward the door; his father was peering inside uncertainly. "What are you doing in there?" he demanded.

"Helping Uncle Ivor look for eggs."

"Hmmph!" Donald stepped out and his father shut the door.

They started to walk along the road in the direction of the Smithson farm. Presently his father fell in behind him and prodded him in the back, saying: "Keep your head up. Chest out! D'you want to get round-shouldered? Before you know it you'll have curvature of the spine."

When they had got out of sight of the house, in a place where the tangle of small trees came to the edge of the road on both sides, his father stopped walking. He looked around, reached down, picked up a handful of the new snow, and rolled it into a hard ball. Then he threw it at a fairly large tree, some distance from the road. It broke, leaving a white mark on the dark trunk. "Let's see you hit it," he told Donald.

A wolf could be waiting here, somewhere back in the still gloom of the woods. It was very important not to make him angry. If his father wanted to take a chance and throw snowballs into the woods, he could, but Donald would not. Then perhaps the wolf would understand that he, at least, was his friend.

"Go on," said his father.

"No. I don't want to."

With mock astonishment his father said: "Oh, you don't?" Then his face became dangerous and his voice cracked like a whip, "Are you going to do what I told you?"

"No." It was the first time he had openly defied him. His father turned very red.

"Listen here, you young whippersnapper!" he cried, his voice tight with anger. "You think you're going to get away with this?" Before Donald knew what was happening, his father had seized him with one hand while he bent over and with the other scooped up as much snow as he could. "We'll settle this little matter right now," he said through his teeth. Suddenly he was rubbing the snow violently over Donald's face, and at the same time that Donald gasped and squirmed, he pushed what was left of it down his neck. As he felt the wet, icy mass sliding down his back, he doubled over. His eyes were squeezed shut; he was certain his father was trying to kill him. With a desperate lunge he bounded free and fell face-downward into the snow.

"Get up," his father said disgustedly. He did not move. If he held his breath long enough he might die.

His father yanked him to his feet. "I've had just about enough of your monkeyshines," he said. Clutching him tightly with both hands, he forced him to hobble ahead of him, back through the twilight to the house.

Donald moved forward, looking at the white road in front of him, his mind empty of thoughts. An unfamiliar feeling had come to him: he was not sorry for himself for being wet and cold, or even resentful at having been mistreated. He felt detached; it was an agreeable, almost voluptuous sensation which he accepted without understanding or questioning it.

As they advanced down the long alley of maple trees in the dusk his father said: "Now you can go and cry in your mother's lap."

"I'm not crying," said Donald loudly, without expression. His father did not answer.

Fortunately the kitchen was empty. He could tell from the sound of the voices in the parlor that Aunt Louisa, Uncle Ivor and Mr. Gordon were getting ready to leave. He ran upstairs to his room and changed his clothes completely. The hole he had breathed in the ice on the windowpane had frozen over thickly again, but the round mark was still visible. As he finished dressing his mother called him. It was completely dark outside. He went downstairs. She was standing in the hallway.

"Oh, you've changed your clothes," she said. "Come out and say good-bye to Aunt Louisa and Uncle Ivor. They're in the kitchen." He looked quickly at her face to see if there were signs of her recent tears: her eyes were slightly bloodshot.

Together they went into the kitchen. "Donald wants to say good-bye to you" she told Mr. Gordon, steering Donald to Aunt Louisa. "You've given him a wonderful Christmas"—her voice became reproachful—"but it was *much* too much."

The thick beaver collar of Mr. Gordon's overcoat was turned up over his ears, and he had on enormous fur gloves. He smiled and clapped his hands together expectantly; it made a cushioned sound. "Oh, it was a lot of fun," he said. "He reminds me a little of myself, you know, when I was his age. I was a sort of shy and quiet lad, too." Donald felt his mother's hand tighten on his shoulder as she pushed him toward Aunt Louisa. "Mm," she

104

said. "Well, Auntie Louisa, here's somebody who wants to say good-bye to you."

Even in the excitement of watching Uncle Willis and Uncle Greg drive the others off in the sleigh, Donald did not miss the fact that his father had not appeared in the kitchen at all. When the sleigh had moved out of sight down the dark road, everyone went into the parlor and Grampa put another log on the fire.

"Where's Owen?" Gramma said in a low voice to Donald's mother.

"He must be upstairs. To tell the truth, I don't care very much where he is."

"Poor child," said Gramma. "Headache a little better?"

"A little." She sighed. "He certainly managed to take all the pleasure out of *my* Christmas."

"A mean shame," said Gramma.

"It was all I could do to look Ivor in the face just now. I meant it."

"I'm sure they all understood," said Gramma soothingly. "Just don't you fret about it. Anyway, Owen'll be gone tomorrow, and you can rest up."

Shortly after Uncle Willis and Uncle Greg got back, Donald's father came downstairs. Supper was eaten in almost complete silence; at no time did his father speak to him or pay him any attention. As soon as the meal was over his mother took him upstairs to bed.

When she had left him, he lay in the dark listening to the sound of the fine snow as the wind drove it against the panes. The wolf was out there in the night, running along paths that no one had ever seen, down the hill and across the meadow, stopping to drink at a deep place in the brook where the ice had not formed. The stiff hairs of his coat had caught the snow; he shook himself and climbed up the bank to where Donald sat waiting for him. Then he lay down beside him, putting his heavy head in Donald's lap. Donald leaned over and buried his face in the shaggy fur of his scruff. After a while they both got up and began to run together, faster and faster, across the fields.

ANNIE DILLARD

The World in a Bowl of Soup: A Christmas Story

Once there was a great feast held in a banquet hall of such enormous proportions that you could not believe men built such a thing. Two thousand chandeliers hung from the ceiling: lumber cut from all the world's forests made the walls and parti-color floor. Great loose areas of the hall were given to various activities: there were dances and many kinds of gaming; a corner was devoted to the sick and injured, and another to the weaving of cloth. Children chanted rhymes wherever they gathered, and young men sought pretty girls in greenhouses or behind the damask hangings of booths and stalls.

The feast lasted all night long. Guests sat at a table as long as a river that stretched down the middle of the hall. No one cloth could cover such a table, nor could one centerpiece suffice. So the table was decorated in hundreds of different themes, with different combinations of colors and kinds of tableware, with various carved figures and various drinks, and with lively musicians in costume playing to each set of guests a special music.

There was only a single course served to the guests, but that was a soup made of so many ingredients it seemed to contain all other dishes. The soup was served continuously, all night long, and there were so many guests that all the places at the table were always taken, and the benches always full, when the servants ladled the soup into the endlessly decorated array of metal, glass, wood, and pottery bowls.

* * *

Now, the host of this feast was a young man of tremendous wealth and power who stood behind a curtain on a balcony above the great hall and watched the guests as they ate and drank at the long table. He thought: "All night long people have been eating as much soup as they wanted and then coming back to the table for more. It is good that they enjoy themselves. But not one person has seen or really understood the excellence of that soup."

So the host parted the curtain a crack more and let his gaze fall. It fell directly on an old man who happened to be sitting at the table in his line of vision, looking about and thinking of nothing at all. At once the old man felt an overwhelming sense of power, an impact as if his spirit had been struck broadside and wakened to a flood of light. He bowed his head and saw, through charged eyes, his bowl of soup that had come alive and was filled to endless depths with wonderful things.

There were green fields in his soup bowl, with carrots growing, one by one, in slender rows. As he watched, transfixed, men and women in bright vests and scarves came and pulled the carrots, one by one, out of the soil, and carried them in baskets to shaded kitchens, where they scrubbed them with yellow brushes under running water. He saw white-faced cattle lowing and wading in rivers, with dust on the whorled and curly white hair between their ears. He saw tomatoes in kitchen gardens set out as seedlings by women in plaid shirts and by strong-handed men; and he watched the tomatoes as, before his eyes, the light from the sun blew each one up like a balloon. Cells on the root hairs of beans swelled and divided, and squashes grew spotted and striped in the fall. Wine aged in caves, and the barrel maker went home to his wife through sunlight and shade.

He saw the ocean, and he seemed to be in the ocean himself, swimming over orange crabs that looked like coral, or off the deep Atlantic banks where whitefish school. Or again he saw the tops of poplars and the whole sky brushed with clouds in pallid streaks, under which wild ducks flew with outstretched necks and called, one by one, and flew on.

All these things the old man saw in his soup. Scenes grew in depth and sunlit detail under his eyes and were replaced by ever more scenes, until, with the flight of wild ducks, the worlds resolved into one blue sky, now streaked, now clear, and, at last, into soup again, dark soup, fragrant in its bowl. The host had let the curtain fall shut.

The man blinked and moved his head from side to side. "I see now," he said to himself, "that this is truly an excellent soup, praise God." And he ate his bowlful and joined the dancers in a daze, a kind of very energetic daze.

THOMAS M. DISCH

Xmas

It was December 12 and the Christmas coming up looked like it was going to be the worst yet, a catastrophe. He began to get in more and more of a state about it. The Geritol jingle from the six-o'clock news formed a tape loop in his head and played itself over and over. Make every day count. Do what you really want to do. Every day every day every day.

Partly the problem was being stuck here in the heart of the woeful Midwest, the American Siberia. Because he was divorced, the company considered him more deployable than his married colleagues. He'd been posted to four branches in as many years. Each new posting represented a step up the ladder but even so. This time at least he was returning somewhere, and if it wasn't anywhere he'd have *chosen* to return to, he could take comfort that it wasn't as alien as Anchorage, which had been one of the alternatives. Here there were faces he could recognize, names he could remember, addresses still extant in his address book.

That was the other part of the problem. None of these names and faces bore thinking of. He had run out of friends. Not just here but everywhere, in the whole creation. Practically speaking he'd become a misanthrope. Certainly he'd never intended to, and he had no theory to back up his spontaneous dislike of the people he knew. It had just sneaked up on him gradually over the years, like baldness.

Last Christmas it had reached the point where he'd received only a single present that could be considered a gift of friendship, and in the ensuing year the friend who'd given it to him had totaled his new Buick and himself in a collision on the Santa Monica Freeway. This Christmas, therefore, there would be no booty under the tree, no stuffing in his stocking, nobody in the whole world to care. It was gross to make such reckonings, it was embarrassing, but it was true. Christmas was coming at him like the searchlight in pursuit of an escaped convict, ready to expose the mess he'd made of his life.

It wasn't fair. At almost any other time he was rather contented, not to say smug, with the shape that his life—meaning his career—had taken. He liked his work, he did it well, and he was making good money. But all through Advent his success had a distinct aftertaste of ashes. Better an underling and swaddled in love than a vice-president and alone for the holidays. If he'd wanted to build a crèche, it would have represented not the stable in Bethlehem but Herod's palace, with lots of little plaster statuettes of Herod's staff and secretaries.

It shouldn't have made such a difference. Other people in his position seemed to glide by Yuletide with just a few *bahs* and *humbugs*. It shouldn't but it did. He'd been the oldest child in a large family, and the drama of gathering the various branches and generations together for solemn unwrappings around the Christmas tree had been a major one. It wasn't just getting; it even transcended the slightly less suspect pleasure of giving, for he could be aroused by the wholly impersonal tableau of his cousin Dolly opening presents from people he'd never heard of. And then, the next morning, there'd been the ever-lovely fiction of presents from Santa, a pretense he'd maintained well into adolescence for the sake of his younger brothers. That golden age was gone, irretrievably. His parents had died, and his brothers had chosen to contest a will that had given him a firstborn's (or lion's) share, including the house. His lawyers had won the case, and he'd sold the house to a developer for a spitefully low price, with the result that there was no chance, now or ever, of flying back home to horn in on his brothers' festivities. The house had become a methadone clinic.

* * *

It was the twelfth and then the thirteenth and every store window in this frozen city's lamentable downtown reproached him for not being part of the human race. Santa's elves hammered with manic, unflagging industry in the windows of Evans & McDowell's, while in the rival department store across the street a ballerina performed a perpetual pirouette, touching with her gilded wand gift after gift after gift whose sweet mysteries he would never see unveiled. A pair of gloves? Stereo earphones? A deluxe edition of Monopoly? Whatever, they were not for him and he would never know.

He thought of buying presents for himself but that smacked too patently of self-pity and, what was worse, futility.

Still, there was one little charity he might perform that would not go unappreciated. He stopped at his liquor store on the way home and asked for a bottle of Chivas Regal and one of Cordon Bleu.

"I'm afraid we're out of Christmas boxes for the Chivas," the clerk said.

He assured him it would be all right, that he'd use his own gift wrap, and at the stationery shop next door he did buy a long tube of their most expensive gold-foil wrap and two big stick-on bows of simulated red ribbon.

At home he wrapped the two boxed bottles carefully and put them away in the hall closet. He meant to unwrap them and drink them on Christmas Eve.

On the fifteenth he bought a gigantic Scotch pine. Mrs. Lurkey, the super's wife, seeing him wrestle it into the elevator, thanked him for his check and wished him a merry Christmas.

"The same to you," he shouted, just as the doors chomped together on the lowest branches of his twenty-dollar pine.

He was up till after midnight decorating the thing. Balls, lights, garlands, tinsel, and an antique art deco angel on the top.

When he was done he sank back on his recliner and thought: "There, that does it. I've exorcised Christmas. *I'm* in control."

But he lay awake that night remembering past Christmases in obsessive detail—the presents he'd got and the presents he'd given, the different turkeys and the single underdone goose.

He was forty-three years old. Every day did *not* count. He did *not* do what he really wanted to. Every day every day every day.

Next morning on the way into the office and altogether against his principles he dropped ten dollars into a Salvation Army pot. He thought it might help.

His secretary had sorted his mail, as requested, into actual business and seasons greetings, of which there were twelve, eight from underlings, three from superiors, and one from his opposite number in the Cincinnati office. He read the texts that various employees of Hallmark and Norcross and UNICEF had written to print on the blank insides of their cards. Harley Krueger wished him:

A wonderful world of
good wishes for the
HOLIDAY SEASON.

Mrs. Palmer, of Accounting, offered this thought:

Every gift of love to our neighbors
is a gift of peace to our world.

And Ted and Vita Milstein saluted him with a multilingual:

Seasons Greetings
Meilleurs Voeux
Felices Fiestas
C HoBblm Toaom.

They all went into his attaché case, and that night he propped them up under the tree, a little paper fortress to guard him from his doom.

* * *

On the evening of the eighteenth, with Christmas only a week away, he began to imagine friends, friends who would (if they'd been real) have given him the presents he wasn't going to get, friends who cherished his good qualities and forgave his faults. This required, in order to formulate such friends with any exactness, that he ask himself what his good qualities and his faults were.

He couldn't think of any, in either category.

Wasn't it, he wondered, a fault in itself that he didn't like other people more than he did? In college he'd had lots of friends. He'd been a pre-med and palled around with other pre-meds. Then, in his senior year, someone, he never found out who, sabotaged a crucial organic chemistry experiment, and someone else (he suspected his roommate) had swiped all his notebooks a week before the finals. He didn't get into med school. (In fairness it must be said that even without treachery his would have been a borderline case.) After that, working at this job and that job, he'd formed a few tentative friendships, although he tended to think of Ralph and Bob and Terry even then more as "acquaintances" or at best "colleagues." He'd had a wife, and a mistress, sort of, both very beautiful and both rather limited intellectually, putting it kindly. Such love as he'd felt for them was of the obsessive, grabbing kind. He'd never thought of women as potential friends, understanding and understood, but rather as mysterious bosomy embodiments of Otherness.

He was lonely. Of course. But he'd come to think of loneliness as a necessary attribute of manhood, the moral corollary of being clearheaded. Being clearheaded, he couldn't help being aware that the people he knew were shits. There might be people elsewhere in the world who were not. He had no theoretical reason for supposing that there weren't. But he had yet to meet them.

As to the propriety or sanity of inventing his own alternatives, that gave him no concern. From his earliest years, when he had governed the complex fates of two families of multicolored bowling pins, his fantasy life had been hyperactive. In later years his unreal friends had usually been females who differed from each other chiefly with respect to their sexual proclivities, but at least he'd kept in practice, and even then he was capable of daydreaming long James Bondish adventures on which blond Trina or even raven-haired Rebecca would accompany him, adventures in which sex figured only peripherally. He had no qualms: it could be done.

The first friend to be hypothesized was John Bartram Hall, who was now seventy and living in retirement in Savannah, Georgia, with two Negro servants and a stamp collection of exceptional rarity. Hall would have been his first boss, assuming he'd gone to work at Meinhard-Commercial, as he'd seriously considered doing in his last weeks of grad school. His real-life bosses had been little more than rednecks in business suits, true believers in football, Goldwater, and flying saucers. Their only merit had been a coarseness of wit so genuine that they never knew till much too late when they'd been outmaneuvered in the brushes and skirmishes of middle-management politics. John Bartram Hall, by contrast, was a man of culture, a bon vivant, a gentleman. He was solicitous of his protégé in an avuncular way and anxious to remedy the defects of his false-genteel suburban upbringing and an education top-heavy with science and math. He selected his shoes and censored his ties and helped him get an American Express card when his first application had been refused. He bullied him into reading grown-up books and made him sit down and listen to the three M's—Mozart, Monteverdi, and Mahler. They talked about important things. They were friends. Once (to mark his retirement) Hall took him on a four-day holiday to Las Vegas, where he proceeded to lose a bundle with the most gentlemanly aplomb.

There was something uneasy-making about this first friendship, a distinct undercurrent of something latent and unmentionable, that prompted him to fashion, perhaps too hastily, an Eve for his Adam. He called her Weena Jessel, after Weena of *Green Mansions* and Mary Jessel, whom he'd lusted after uselessly all through eleventh grade. Weena was an ex–call girl who now worked as a beautician and dealt dope. He'd first met her, or would have, late in '68, as his marriage was breaking up. Weena was Venus the goddess of love, manic and languorous, all-accommodating yet fiercely independent, a centerfold come to life. Through her he'd discovered his own deepest feelings. Through him she'd found the strength to leave her life of degradation. Basically, Weena was Jane Fonda in *Klute*, minus the dialogue. It wasn't so much that she was stupid (though she would accuse herself of that from time to time) but rather that she was overprotective of her tenuous, never-entirely-expressible thoughts. Occasionally, in an odd remark or in one of the sad little watercolors she painted of doll-faced modistes and pink ballerinas, he could glimpse the possibility of a finer Weena trapped inside this one, a Weena, alas, lost forever in a haze of drugs.

He became fascinated with the way his fantasy, like a hooked fish invisible beneath his boat, seemed to have a life of its own. Deliberately he let it run with his line. Weena (it developed) was really rather dull! It was all very well to respect her potentialities but in the here and now, except when they had sex, Weena was about as interesting as a dead TV screen. Trying to carry on a conversation with her was like trying to talk to seaweed. It was like being married all over again.

One night, the nineteenth of December, he arranged to meet her at the diner across from the beauty shop where she worked. He never showed up. Weena waited two hours and then slowly, sadly, walked home through the snow.

It's hard to make friends, even imaginary friends, and harder still to keep them. Something, his reality principle or his death wish, kept intruding, like a vengeful witch cursing each newly fledged friend with warts and foibles and fatal flaws of character. Lolah Silverberg was his most painful disappointment in this respect, for she had seemed at first the most promising of his creations, virtually a new direction for his hopes to move in, a grail to go off in quest of.

Lolah was the polar opposite of Weena. She was homely, but homely, like George Eliot or Virginia Woolf, in a manner associated with abundance of character. Not Venus but gray-eyed Athena. Not only could you talk to her, you could listen. She had ideas, beliefs, a sense of humor. What's more, she could cope. After years of teaching she was now an assistant principal in one of the city's toughest junior high schools. Like himself, she was divorced. By mutual unspoken agreement they never discussed their exes. She lived with her two teenage daughters, Alice and Emma, in the same apartment building on a higher floor. Often he'd go up the fire stairs late at night to play long, guilty games of Monopoly with them, till two or three in the morning. They were happy just being together. He began to wonder (in his fantasy) if he were in love.

If so, that love was not returned, for suddenly Lolah began to avoid him, suddenly she was always in a hurry somewhere else. Once, on Adams Street, she'd seen him approaching from the opposite direction and—obviously to avoid the chance encounter—had stooped down, pretending to lace a shoe. (That had happened to him in real life, in Omaha.) Her daughters would answer the phone and say that Lolah wasn't there and could they take a message. He knew they were lying and that they were under orders to. What had he done to deserve it? Was it because he'd criticized her for letting Alice and Emma subscribe to an astrology magazine? Because he made jokes about her affecting to be part Cherokee? Could she be so petty? In any case he'd sent her an imaginary letter apologizing for these slights. It was more basic: he had begun to bore her. No, it was something still worse and more serious, something rooted in his nature, something he couldn't imagine.

He'd known from the very start that the last of his friends, Peter Snyder, was a son of a bitch. A thin, red-haired parrot of a man, vain as a mirror, Peter considered himself a kind of count of Monte Cristo with a score to settle against the world at large. He wrote (this much was a fact) the movie reviews for the *Evening Star-Courier*, as intemperate and mean-spirited a column as one could find this side of John Simon. Through all of 1975 the only movie he had anything good to say about was *Jaws*. There were people (he was one) who took the *Star-Courier* just for the spectacle of Snyder's savage tongue. He was also a sponge: of food, of booze, of books, of whatever he could wangle. He would even make jokes about it, as though to show that he was on your side, after all.

They'd met at a party that Lolah had taken him to, and over the next weeks he'd graduated from being one of the admiring throng to the status of an old pal thanks to an apparently ungrudging willingness to provide all the flattery and the free drinks that Snyder required. The quid for this quo was that he got to be a witness to the man's kamikaze assaults on other subjects than the movies. Watergate, naturally, had been his heyday, but with half a bottle of B & L under his belt (Snyder was not, bless him, picky about labels) there was nothing that wasn't grist for his mill. He would assassinate the characters of his friends or complain about the weather or ridicule the pretensions of the restaurant he was being taken to, all with an equanimity that was equal to his eloquence.

He was not such a fool as to suppose that Peter Snyder *liked* him, or that he liked Snyder. He thought of him rather as a cell mate in the world's prison, one who made the time pass better than most, but a criminal essentially, a person not to be trusted.

If there was anything worse than being Peter Snyder, it was being Peter Snyder's sycophant, and that's what he'd become.

At this point he stopped inventing imaginary friends.

It was the night before Christmas. Besides the liquor and the Christmas cards there were four presents under the tree: a present from John Bartram Hall, a present from Weena Jessel, a present from Lolah Silverberg, and a present from Peter Snyder. They were wrapped in gold foil paper but they lacked bows. Weena's was the smallest, about the size of a box of Anacin, and Peter's the largest, the size of a brick.

Not yet, he told himself. Later.

He broke out the Chivas and put on a record from his album of Handel's *Messiah*. "Oh, we like sheep!" the chorus announced cheerily. "Oh, we like sheep!" He'd made a mistake. Instead of the opening Nativity section he'd hit the Crucifixion. But it sounded pretty in a tinkly way that suited the occasion just as well, even when the chorus was laughing Christ to scorn. "Oh, we like sheep! Oh, we like sheep!" The lights on the tree seemed to blink on and off in time to the music. He drank a toast to George Frideric Handel.

The phone rang.

He turned down the volume and answered it by the third ring. A woman wished him a merry Christmas. Her name was Janet, and she'd dialed a wrong number. He tried to keep her on the phone with small talk but she grew uneasy. He proposed marriage and hung up.

When he turned the volume back up, the tenor was just starting the recitative that goes, "He was cut off out of the land of the living. . . ." And even that Handel made to seem halfway cheerful.

The record played over and over. He'd neglected to lower the arm of the changer.

At midnight he thought, "Now's the time to open the presents."

But next morning they were still intact underneath the big red wool stocking hanging limply from the arm of the recliner. Oddly, he did not feel hung over. He'd only dozed off for four hours, so maybe he was still drunk. Half of the brandy was left and a smidgen of Scotch. He put off opening the presents till later and watched a nondenominational church service while he soaked in the tub. Children in red choir robes walked about with candles, singing shrill carols.

He made a very simple stuffing for the turkey, nothing but bread crumbs, butter, celery, onion, and seasonings. It weighed twelve pounds and it went into the oven at ten thirty. That meant, according to Fannie Farmer, that it should come out at two thirty or three.

The pie came from a local bakery. He could pop it in the oven when the bird came out. Nothing else required much in the way of preparation. There would be instant mashed potatoes, yams from a can, and frozen peas, all of which could be done at the last minute. Simple but sufficient. The important thing was to uphold tradition.

There was nothing but dreck on the television, and he still didn't feel like opening the presents, so he occupied the time by doing his next year's taxes.

All the while it had cooked it had smelled terrific, but now, sitting there on the table, and sitting there himself before it, he had no appetite at all. He'd put on the *Messiah* again, careful this time to start with side 1. He just sat there like a marble allegory of Abundance all through "Comfort ye my people (saith your God)" without lifting the carving knife or looking up from the poinsettias on his paper napkin.

He felt iniquitous and utterly cast down.

Was there no way to combat Christmas? Must it make him wretched over and over all through his life?

Or, as the countertenor put it, rather more pointedly: "Who may abide the day of His coming? Who shall stand when He appeareth?"

Slowly and reverently, in strict time to the contralto's joyful air ("O thou that tellest good tidings to Zion"), he began to stab the golden turkey in its moist, plump breast.

Later, after he'd cleaned up most of the mess, and feeling cleansed himself and radiant and free, he fed the scraps of his sacrifice into the incinerator. Along with it went the presents from his four imaginary friends. He'd never opened them and he would never know how they had meant to surprise him.

PETER MATTHIESSEN

The Centerpiece

In 1941 Grandmother Hartlingen, Madrina to the family, was considerably older than anyone I had ever known, "too old for Christmas presents," as she said. She had given way gently to her years, lowering the window upon her past as on a too-early snow, yet thoughtfully aware of its delicate weight on the high eaves of her household.

None of her family lived beneath her roof, nor even in the township of Concord, but they were present nevertheless, in neat smiling ranks upon her bedroom tables, ones and twos and threes, and in various postures of memory throughout the rooms. Most of them would gather for her German Christmas, and the rest had preceded her into the ground. These she had long ago forgiven, they lost no favor on the bedroom tables, represented only a certain unsatisfactory transience, like gypsies or violets.

In the dark December of 1941, I alone among Madrina's descendants suffered no misgivings about her festival. To a boy of fourteen, German Christmas meant receiving presents twelve hours in advance and Christmas Day free to enjoy them and had nothing whatever to do with Germany.

The relation of Christmas to war seemed as tenuous to Madrina as to myself. She had visited Germany but twice in her lifetime and did not intend to visit there again. At the same time, although she was born in New York City, a heritage of Christmas in Bavaria was imprinted in the first pages of her mind, not only of the Hartlingen gathering itself but of the beauty of this tradition to all Germans, at home or abroad. For Madrina,

120

like a fountain sinking back into its well, had returned unconsciously to her source as she grew older and had long since astounded her countrymen of Concord by referring to herself as High German. No shell threatened the household of habit her universe had become, and although she crocheted for the soldiers and was offended by the Red Cross refusal of her offer of blood—good German blood, she assured them—she saw no grounds whatsoever for renouncing her German Christmas. It never occurred to her, in fact. Those of the family to whom it did occur awaited in vain the reprieve from Concord and finally, not daring open rebellion, forgathered uneasily on Christmas Eve. It was the last German Christmas ever celebrated in our family, for Madrina died late in the following year.

Everybody forgathered, that is, except Cousin Millicent, aged fifteen, who refused to leave the car.

My cousin was known in school as Silly Milly, and, as cousins are apt to be, she was ill-favored and even a little distempered. She contributed to family gatherings her own special brand of lackluster silence, as if life in general were a personal affront and no stratagem on the part of others would make her a party to it. Milly was the last descendant Madrina would have suspected as the viper, and Milly's parents, Uncle Charles and Aunt Alice, were as startled as the rest of us. Milly's teacher in school, her one friend in the world, had lost a brother at Pearl Harbor, and Milly's awareness of the forces of good and evil was far keener than my own. After all, I told her, Madrina isn't celebrating a *Japanese* Christmas.

We had gone to sing Christmas carols in the country church. When the tramping of boots had died in the hallway and the family, the snow still white on their heads, had picked their way into the living room and paid homage to Madrina, there was a moment of silence for the mutineer.

"Good," Madrina said, taking the census through her lorgnette, attached by a wisp of chain to her collar. I can remember how struck I was by this large matriarchal woman with a full-featured serenity of visage entirely absent in the generations grouped before her. "Good," she repeated, "you've come at last. And where is Millicent?"

"Silly Milly," I remarked, from behind the Christmas tree. I had winnowed my presents from a heap which cornucopiaed from the base of the spruce to the shoulder of the hearth, and was engaged in arraying them in good order for opening. The face of the tree was splendid in red candles, with fine antique ornaments, gilt and silver, garnet and emerald, and Bohemian crystal of the sort Madrina said was no longer made. "Silly Milly," I said, "won't come to German Christmas."

Uncle Charles requested my silence, and Aunt Alice stepped forward. "It's nothing, Madrina," she said and smiled.

"What? What's nothing? Don't smile at me that way, Alice. Are you ill?"

"Milly's taking a stand," Uncle Charles announced, and I saw my father wince. "I'm sure she'll be in in a while, Madrina."

"Taking a stand? What on earth is he saying?" Madrina seized her lorgnette again and peered at her elder son as at an impostor. "The child is far too young to take a stand on *anything*."

She pronounced "take-a-stand" all in a word, as if Milly, in conspiracy with Uncle Charles, were doing something unheard-of, even a trifle indecent.

"What is it, Charles? Have her come in this instant."

"In a few minutes, Madrina," my father said. "She's being very silly about it."

"Silly Milly," I repeated, vindicated, and was promptly admonished by my sister Polly, the eldest of the younger generation and its unofficial keeper. Madrina's attention was thereby drawn to me.

"Wolfgang," she said, "come out from behind that tree and fetch a candy to your cousin."

"My name's not Wolfgang," I objected, but out I came. Madrina had taken to calling me Wolfgang quite arbitrarily, since my given name is Wendell and my popular title is Sandy. I think Wolfgang satisfied a curious humor of Madrina's devoted to the nettling of my parents. "What candy?" I said.

"What candy, *Madrina*," Polly said. Polly was very tiresome as a child.

"It doesn't matter what candy," my mother said. "Do as you're told, Wendell."

"Sandy," I said. I ran into the dining room to look for candy and greet the servants but was arrested, as I had been every year, by the wondrous centerpiece on the table. It was five feet long, Saint Nicholas and the rein-deer before a hostelry, hand-wrought of mahogany and bone, and restaged each year with cotton-and-mica snow. After a long service in Germany, a century of Hartlingen Christmases, it had been delivered into Madrina's hands and now symbolized to all of us not only Christmas but the past. It was girded round with pine fronds and holly, the orbit of a vast oval of silverware and banquet oddments, muscat raisins, mints, almonds, wine, cranberry jelly, and butterballs. Madrina had beautiful silver, ancient and heavy with Hartlingen history, the epochs of pigs with apples in their mouths and wine from golden goblets.

I secured a thin mint for Milly, but it deteriorated in transit, and Madrina instructed me to throw it into the fire. "Take one of those," she said and pointed out a gleaming coffer on a side table, guarded by dancing Dresden figurines, ivory burgomasters, and a peevish dachshund named Bismark V, decaying on a period chair.

"I hope they're not *German* candies," I said.

"You'd be in luck if they were," Madrina told me and laughed so oddly that I turned to stare at her. The reason for Milly's stand had obviously been explained, and now my grandmother regarded the family, fourteen strong about the room, with an abstracted gaze, as if they could not be her family after all.

Uncomfortable, I selected the biggest item from the box and hastened through the snow to Milly. Milly had her nose pressed to the rear window of the car, and although she ducked back at my appearance, I knew she was happy someone had come.

"Here, silly," I said.

She struck the candy from my hand.

"Oh-h!" Milly gasped. "That old German thing! I don't love *her* any-more."

"Can I have your candy, then?" I said, picking it up.

"No!" Milly said and, snatching it from me, burst into tears. Now she was uglier than ever, and I had neither the age nor wisdom to be sorry for her. "And I won't come in. I won't!" Her knee, in stamping, knocked the candy into the snow.

"All right," I said, seizing it, "but you're spoiling everything." I ran back up the path, my mission a delightful failure.

The wreathed light from the windows gave body to the darkness, breathing tracery into the slow arras of snow. It gave the house a snug, enchanted air, like some magic sanctuary of childhood deep in a wood. The holly berries on the door wreath, round red as picture peasants' cheeks, and the deep green halo of ground pine itself were as fresh as our New World winter. Inside, the voices traveled on pine-scented air, safe from the future and from Millicent's war.

"Silly Milly lost the candy in the snow and won't come in," I reported, swallowing the last of it.

There was a pause, and eyes turned to Madrina for her dictum.

Madrina said, "How very foolish."

She rang for Clara, who presently appeared with a copper caldron of brandy and milk and nutmeg and a set of silver mugs. There was a fine bowl of nuts by the fire, black walnuts, butternuts, and hazelnuts, and seated in warmth, one eye cast luxuriously on my presents, I indulged myself in contempt for Milly and pity for Madrina, undone by the rude granddaughter outside.

Seated in her flowered chair as still and enduring as the dry cattails and bittersweet in the vase behind her, Madrina told us a tale of another Christmas, another century, her face alive with soft expressive rhythms, like a moment of birds in a winter tree.

Her German cousin Ernst was traveling with his mother to a Hartlingen Christmas of long ago, and as the carriage was to pass the region of the Black Forest, the coachman advised his passengers of the danger of brigands, then very numerous in the byways. The brigands were captained by a well-mannered man of noble extraction, so it was said, who treated his victims with great courtesy so long as they offered no resistance, but dealt very harshly with objectors. Madrina's cousin Ernst was just the sort to object: he had no sense of humor in such matters, and his mother cautioned him strongly against rash actions in the event of trouble. No sooner had she spoken than the carriage halted, and she was handed down by an enormous bearded gentleman, who relieved her discreetly of all jewelry but a family brooch, of the sentimental value of which she had managed to persuade him. At this moment Ernst sprang from the carriage, brandishing a pistol, and was on the point of *taking a stand* on the matter, Madrina said tartly, when his head, parted from his shoulders by the sword of a mounted henchman, rolled ignominiously under the carriage. Very regrettable, the chieftain remarked, and seized the brooch.

Madrina's aunt was inconsolable. She bent and peered under the carriage, where, catching the eye of her son, she shouted at him: "I told you, Ernst! I told you, you blockhead!"

Madrina peered from one descendant to the next, as if seeking a successor by the gauge of laughter. But her own smile faltered, then disappeared entirely. "We shall go to dinner," she whispered. The family stared toward the hallway, where not Milly but Clara, her hands prim on her apron, leaned sepulchrally into the room. "We will start without Miss Millicent, Clara," Madrina said, less to Clara than to Milly herself, as if she had said, I told you, Ernst, I told you!

Marching past the faded tapestries and bronze-green urns from the halls of her forebears, artifacts far too ponderous for the houses of her children, Madrina entered the dining room, touching the oaken chairs fondly as she journeyed to her place.

"She will come in a minute, Madrina," Aunt Alice said.

"She will do as she pleases," said Madrina.

From my position, far away below the salt, the centerpiece stretched eternally between the two lines of heads which converged on the white face of Madrina. She gave a whispered benediction, and afterward the family toasted her, holding high the glasses of Rhenish wine. Against the candlelight and the chandelier, the red wine glowed like liquid rubies, and for the last time in my life I was wholly in the past again, a baron at a medieval board, drunk on the wine of my betters.

When, late in the second course, the centerpiece ignited from a fallen candle, the flame ran a furious circle in the snow before an uncle had the wit to dash his wine at it. The inn was tinder in the molten cotton, and the whalebone reindeer pranced proudly on the table, freed forever of Saint Nicholas, who perished in his sleigh.

In the chaos of motion and voices I saw Madrina, the only person still seated, observing the destruction as if the ruin of this antiquated treasure was somehow fitting, as if she sensed that, like the tapestries and urns, it was far too venerable and vast to serve the New World Hartlingens again.

She did not respond to the condolences addressed to her, but sat in silence, her hands folded on her lap. When at last she could be heard, she said: "Milly . . . I would like to see Milly."

And as if the girl had been poised on the threshold, the door flew open and Milly appeared, in a flurry of snow and tears, stumbling forward to Madrina. Milly cried very loudly in Madrina's embrace, and Madrina was crying, too, a harsh unwilling sputter which her glaring eyes denied.

"It's all my fault," Milly was saying, "it's all my fault."

And Madrina, looking over Milly's shoulder at the black Saint Nicholas, said: "How foolish, my dear. I am as American as you are. We are simply celebrating Christmas Eve."

ITALO CALVINO

Santa's Children

No period of the year is more gentle and good, for the world of industry and commerce, than Christmas and the weeks preceding it. From the streets rises the tremulous sound of the mountaineers' bagpipes; and the big companies, till yesterday coldly concerned with calculating gross product and dividends, open their hearts to human affections and to smiles. The sole thought of boards of directors now is to give joy to their fellowman, sending gifts accompanied by messages of goodwill both to other companies and to private individuals; every firm feels obliged to buy a great stock of products from a second firm to serve as presents to third firms; and those firms, for their part, buy from yet another firm further stocks of presents for the others; the office windows remain aglow till late, especially those of the shipping department, where the personnel work overtime wrapping packages and boxes; beyond the misted panes, on the sidewalks covered by a crust of ice, the pipers advance. Having descended from the dark mysterious mountains, they stand at the downtown intersections, a bit dazzled by the excessive lights, by the excessively rich shop windows; and heads bowed, they blow into their instruments; at that sound among the businessmen the heavy conflicts of interest are placated and give way to a new rivalry: to see who can present the most conspicuous and original gift in the most attractive way.

At Sbav and Co. that year the Public Relations Office suggested that the Christmas presents for the most important persons should be delivered at home by a man dressed as Santa Claus.

The idea won the unanimous approval of the top executives. A complete Santa Claus outfit was bought: white beard, red cap and tunic edged in white fur, big boots. They had the various delivery men try it on, to see whom it fitted best, but one man was too short and the beard touched the ground; another was too stout and couldn't get into the tunic; another was too young; yet another was too old and it wasn't worth wasting makeup on him.

While the head of the Personnel Office was sending for other possible Santas from the various departments, the assembled executives sought to develop the idea: the Human Relations Office wanted the employees' Christmas packages also to be distributed by Santa Claus, at a collective ceremony; the Sales Office wanted Santa to make a round of the shops as well; the Advertising Office was worried about the prominence of the firm's name, suggesting that perhaps they should tie four balloons to a string with the letters S-B-A-V.

All were caught up in the lively and cordial atmosphere spreading through the festive, productive city; nothing is more beautiful than the sensation of material goods flowing on all sides and, with it, the goodwill each feels toward the others; for this, this above all, as the skirling sound of the pipes reminds us, is what really counts.

In the shipping department, goods—material and spiritual—passed through Marcovaldo's hands, since it represented merchandise to load and unload. And it was not only through loading and unloading that he shared in the general festivity, but also by thinking that at the end of that labyrinth of hundreds of thousands of packages there waited a package belonging to him alone, prepared by the Human Relations Office, and even more, by figuring how much was due him at the end of the month, counting the Christmas bonus and his overtime hours. With that money, he too would be able to rush to the shops and buy, buy, buy, to give presents, presents, presents, as his most sincere feelings and the general interests of industry and commerce decreed.

The head of the Personnel Office came into the shipping department with a fake beard in his hand. "Hey, you!" he said to Marcovaldo. "See how this beard looks on you. Perfect! You're Santa then. Come upstairs. Get moving. You'll be given a special bonus if you make fifty home deliveries per day."

Got up as Santa Claus, Marcovaldo rode through the city on the saddle of the motorbike-truck laden with packages wrapped in varicolored paper, tied with pretty ribbons, and decorated with twigs of mistletoe and holly. The white cotton beard tickled him a little but it protected his throat from the cold air.

His first trip was to his own home, because he couldn't resist the temptation of giving his children a surprise. At first, he thought, they won't recognize me. Then I bet they'll laugh!

The children were playing on the stairs. They barely looked up. "Hi, Papà."

Marcovaldo was let down. "Hmph . . . Don't you see how I'm dressed?"

"How are you supposed to be dressed?" Pietruccio said. "Like Santa Claus, right?"

"And you recognized me first thing?"

"Easy! We recognized Signor Sigismondo, too; and he was disguised better than you!"

"And the janitor's brother-in-law!"

"And the father of the twins across the street!"

"And the uncle of Ernestina—the girl with the braids!"

"All dressed like Santa Claus?" Marcovaldo asked, and the disappointment in his voice wasn't due only to the failure of the family surprise, but also because he felt that the company's prestige had somehow been impaired.

"Of course. Just like you," the children answered. "Like Santa Claus. With a fake beard, as usual." And turning their backs on him, the children became absorbed again in their games.

It so happened that the public relations offices of many firms had had the same idea at the same time; and they had recruited a great number of people, jobless for the most part, pensioners, street vendors, and had dressed them in the red tunic, with the cotton wool beard. The children, the first few times, had been amused, recognizing acquaintances under that disguise, neighborhood figures, but after a while they were jaded and paid no further attention.

The game they were involved in seemed to absorb them entirely. They had gathered on a landing and were seated in a circle. "May I ask what you're plotting?" Marcovaldo inquired.

"Leave us alone, Papà; we have to fix our presents."

"Presents for who?"

"For a poor child. We have to find a poor child and give him presents."

"Who said so?"

"It's in our school reader."

Marcovaldo was about to say: "You're poor children yourselves!" But during this past week he had become so convinced that he was an inhabitant of the Land of Plenty, where all purchased and enjoyed themselves and exchanged presents, that it seemed bad manners to mention poverty; and he preferred to declare: "Poor children don't exist any more!"

Michelino stood up and asked: "Is that why you don't bring us presents, Papà?"

Marcovaldo felt a pang at his heart. "I have to earn some overtime now," he said hastily, "and then I'll bring you some."

"How do you earn it?"

"Delivering presents," Marcovaldo said.

"To us?"

"No, to other people."

"Why not to us? It'd be quicker."

Marcovaldo tried to explain. "Because I'm not the Human Relations Santa Claus, after all; I'm the Public Relations Santa Claus. You understand?"

"No."

"Never mind." But since he wanted somehow to apologize for coming home empty-handed, he thought he might take Michelino with him, on his round of deliveries. "If you're good, you can come and watch your Papà

"Him? What kind of a present could you give him?"

"Oh, we fixed them up very nice, . . . three presents, all wrapped in silver paper."

The younger boys spoke up: "We all went together to take them to him! You should have seen how happy he was!"

"I'll bet!" Marcovaldo said. "That was just what he needed to make him happy: your presents!"

"Yes, ours! . . . He ran over right away to tear off the paper and see what they were. . . ."

"And what were they?"

"The first was a hammer: that big round hammer, the wooden kind. . . ."

"What did he do then?"

"He was jumping with joy! He grabbed it and began to use it!"

"How?"

"He broke all the toys! And all the glassware! Then he took the second present. . . ."

"What was that?"

"A slingshot. You should have seen him. He was so happy! He hit all the glass balls on the Christmas tree. Then he started on the chandeliers. . . ."

"That's enough. I don't want to hear anymore! And the . . . third present?"

"We didn't have anything left to give, so we took some silver paper and wrapped up a box of kitchen matches. That was the present that made him happiest of all. He said: "They never let me touch matches!" He began to strike them, and . . ."

"And?"

". . . and he set fire to everything!"

Marcovaldo was tearing his hair. "I'm ruined!"

The next day, turning up at work, he felt the storm brewing. He dressed again as Santa Claus, in great haste, loaded the presents to be delivered onto the truck, already amazed that no one had said anything to him, and then he saw, coming toward him, the three section chiefs: the one from public relations, the one from advertising, and the one from sales.

"Stop!" they said to him. "Unload everything. At once!"

This is it, Marcovaldo said to himself and could already picture himself fired.

"Hurry up! We have to change all the packages!" the three section chiefs said. "The Society for the Implementation of Christmas Consumption has launched a campaign to push the Destructive Gift!"

"On the spur of the moment like this," one of the men remarked. "They might have thought of it sooner. . . ."

"It was a sudden inspiration the president had," another chief explained. "It seems his little boy was given some ultramodern gift articles, Japanese, I believe, and for the first time the child was obviously enjoying himself. . . ."

"The important thing," the third added, "is that the Destructive Gift serves to destroy articles of every sort: just what's needed to speed up the pace of consumption and give the market a boost. . . . All in minimum time and within a child's capacities. . . . The president of the society sees a whole new horizon opening out. He's in seventh heaven, he's so enthusiastic. . . ."

"But this child . . ." Marcovaldo asked, in a faint voice: "did he really destroy much stuff?"

"It's hard to make an estimate, even a hazy one, because the house was burned down. . . ."

Marcovaldo went back to the street, illuminated as if it were night, crowded with mammas and children and uncles and grannies and packages and balloons and rocking horses and Christmas trees and Santa Clauses and chickens and turkeys and fruitcakes and bottles and bagpipers and chimney sweeps and chestnut vendors shaking pans of chestnuts over round, glowing black stoves.

And the city seemed smaller, collected in a luminous vessel, buried in the dark heart of a forest, among the age-old trunks of the chestnut trees and an endless cloak of snow. Somewhere in the darkness the howl of the wolf was heard; the hares had a hole buried in the snow, in the warm red earth under a layer of chestnut burrs.

A jack hare came out, white, onto the snow; he twitched his ears, ran beneath the moon, but he was white and couldn't be seen, as if he weren't there. Only his little paws left a light print on the snow, like little clover leaves. Nor could the wolf be seen, for he was black and stayed in the black darkness of the forest. Only if he opened his mouth, his teeth were visible, white and sharp.

There was a line where the forest, all black, ended and the snow began, all white. The hare ran on this side, and the wolf on that.

The wolf saw the hare's prints on the snow and followed them, always keeping in the black, so as not to be seen. At the point where the prints ended there should be the hare, and the wolf came out of the black, opened wide his red maw and his sharp teeth, and bit the wind.

The hare was a bit farther on, invisible; he scratched one ear with his paw and escaped, hopping away.

Is he here? There? Is he a bit farther on?

Only the expanse of snow could be seen, white as this page.

PATRICIA HIGHSMITH

A Clock Ticks at Christmas

"Have you got a spare franc, madame?"

That was how it began.

Michèle looked down over her armfuls of boxes and plastic bags at a small boy in a loose tweed coat and tweed cap that hung over his ears. He had big dark eyes and an appealing smile. "Yes!" She managed to drop two francs which were still in her fingers after paying the taxi.

"*Merci*, madame!"

"And this," said Michèle, suddenly remembering that she had stuck a ten-franc note into her coat pocket a moment ago.

The boy's mouth fell open. "Oh, madame! *Merci!*"

One slippery shopping bag had fallen. The boy picked it up.

Michèle smiled, secured the bag handle with one finger, and pressed the door button with an elbow. The heavy door clicked open, and she stepped over a raised threshold. A shove of her shoulder closed the door, and she crossed the courtyard of her apartment house. Bamboo trees stood like slender sentinels on left and right, and laurels and ferns grew on either side of the cobbled path she took to Court E. Charles would be home, as it was nearly six. What would he say to all the packages, the more than three thousand francs she had spent today? Well, she had done most of their Christmas shopping, and one of the presents was for Charles to give his family—he could hardly complain about that—and the rest of the presents were for Charles himself and her parents, and only one thing was for her, a Hermès belt that she hadn't been able to resist.

"Father Christmas!" Charles said as Michèle came in. "Or Mother Christmas?"

She had let the packages fall to the floor in the hall. "Whew! Yes, a good day! A lot done, I mean. Really!"

"So it seems." Charles helped her to gather the boxes and bags.

Michèle had taken off her coat and slipped out of her shoes. They tossed the parcels on the big double bed in their bedroom, Michèle talking all the while. She told him about the pretty white tablecloth for his parents, and about the little boy downstairs who had asked her for a franc. "A franc—after all I bought today! Such a sweet little boy about ten years old. And so poor-looking—his clothes. Just like the old stories about Christmas, I thought. You know? When someone with less asks for such a little bit." Michèle was smiling broadly, happily.

Charles nodded. Michèle's was a rich family. Charles Clement had worked his way up from apprentice mason at sixteen to become the head of his company, Athenas Construction, at twenty-eight. At thirty, he had met Michèle, the daughter of one of his clients, and married her. Sometimes Charles felt dazzled by his success in his work and in his marriage, because he adored Michèle and she was lovely. But he realized that he could more easily imagine himself as the small boy asking for a franc, which he would never have done, than he could imagine himself as Michèle's brother, for instance, dispensing largesse with her particular attitude, at once superior and kindly. He had seen that attitude before in Michèle.

"Only one franc?" Charles said finally, smiling.

Michèle laughed. "No, I gave him a ten-franc note. I had it loose in my pocket—and after all it's Christmas."

Charles chuckled. "That little boy will be back."

Michèle was facing her closet, whose sliding doors she had opened. "What should I wear tonight? That light purple dress you like or—the yellow? The yellow one's newer."

Charles circled her waist with his arm. The row of dresses and blouses, long skirts, looked like a tangible rainbow: shimmering gold, velvety blue, beige and green, satin and silk. He could not even see the light purple in all of it, but he said, "The light purple, yes. Is that all right with you?"

"Of course, dear."

They were going out to dinner at the apartment of some friends. Charles went back into the living room and resumed his newspaper, while Michèle showered and changed her clothes. Charles wore his house slippers—the habit of an old man, he thought, though he was only thirty-two. At any rate, it was a habit he had had since his teens, when he had been living with his parents in the Clichy area. Half the time he had come home with his shoes and socks damp from standing in mud or water on a construction lot, and woolen house slippers had felt good. Otherwise Charles was dressed for the evening in a dark blue suit, a shirt with cuff links, a silk tie knotted but not yet tightened at the collar. Charles lighted his pipe—Michèle would be a long while yet—and surveyed his handsome living room, thinking of Christmas. Its first sign was the dark green wreath some thirty centimeters in diameter, which Michèle must have bought that morning, and which leaned against the fruit bowl on the dining table. Michèle would put it on the knocker of the apartment door, he knew. The brass fixtures by the fireplace gleamed as usual, poker and tongs, polished by Geneviève, their *femme de ménage*. Four of the six or seven oil paintings on the walls were of Michèle's ancestors, two of them in white ruffled lace collars. Charles poured himself a small Glenfiddich whiskey and sipped it straight. The best whiskey in the world, in his opinion. Yes, fate had been good to him. He had luxury and comfort, everywhere he looked. He stepped out of his clumsy house slippers and carried them into the bedroom, where he put on his shoes for the evening with the aid of a silver shoehorn. Michèle was still in the bathroom, humming, doing her makeup.

Two days later Michèle again encountered the small boy to whom she had given the ten-franc note. She was nearly at her house door before she saw him, because she had been concentrating on a white poodle that she had just bought. She had dismissed her taxi at the corner of the street and was carefully leading the puppy on his new black and gold leash along the curb. The puppy did not know in which direction to go, unless Michèle tugged throb went through her, akin to a sense of personal embarrassment, as if she were responsible for the theft, which was only a possibility, not yet a fact. But Michèle felt guilt as she glanced at her husband's slightly troubled face. He was opening a letter with his thumbnail.

"What did you do today, darling?" asked Charles, smiling once more, putting his letter away in a business folder.

Michèle told him she had argued with the telephone company about their last bill and won, this on Charles's behalf as he had queried a long-distance call, had looked in at the hairdresser's but only for an hour, and had aired Zeke three times, and she thought the puppy was learning fast. She did not tell Charles about buying two pairs of shoes for the boy called Paul, or about the visit of Paul and his sister to the apartment.

"And I hung the wreath on the door," said Michèle. "Not a lot of work, I know, but didn't you notice?"

"Of course. How could I have missed it?" He embraced her and kissed her cheek. "Very pretty, darling, the wreath."

That was Saturday. On Sunday Charles worked for a few hours in his office alone, as he often did. Michèle bought a small Christmas tree with an X-shaped base and spent part of the afternoon decorating it, having put it on the dining table finally, instead of the floor, because the puppy refused to stop playing with the ornaments. Michèle did not look forward to the obligatory visit to Charles's parents—who never had a tree, and even Charles considered Christmas trees a silly import from England—on Christmas Eve Monday at 5:00 P.M. They lived in a big old walk-up apartment house in the eighteenth *arrondissement*. Here they would exchange presents and drink hot red wine that always made Michèle feel sickish. The rest of the evening would be jollier at her parents' apartment in Neuilly. They would have a cold midnight supper with champagne and watch color TV of Christmas breaking all over the world. She told this to Zeke.

"Your first Christmas, Zeke! And you'll have—a *turkey* leg!"

The puppy seemed to understand her and galloped around the living room with a lolling tongue and mischievous black eyes. And Paul and Marie-Jeanne? Were they smiling now? Maybe Paul was, with his two pairs

143

of shoes. And maybe there was time for her to buy a shirt, a blouse for Marie-Jeanne, a cake for the other brother and sister, before Christmas Day. She could do that Monday, and maybe she'd see Paul and be able to give him the presents. Christmas meant giving, sharing, communicating with friends and neighbors and even with strangers. With Paul, she had begun.

"Oo-woo-woo," said the puppy, crouching.

"One second, Zeke, darling!" Michèle hurried to get his leash.

She flung on a fur jacket, and she and Zeke went out.

Zeke at once made for the gutter, and Michèle gave him a word of praise. The fancy grocery store across the street was open, and Michèle bought a box of candy—a beautiful tin box costing over a hundred francs—because the red ribbon on it had caught her eye.

"Madame—*bonjour!*"

Once more Michèle looked down at Paul's upturned face. His nose was bright pink with cold.

"Happy Christmas again, madame!" Paul said, smiling, stamping his feet. He wore the brown pair of new shoes. His hands were rammed into his pockets.

"Would you like a hot chocolate?" Michèle asked. A *bar-tabac* was just a few meters distant.

"*Non, merci.*" Paul twisted his neck shyly.

"Or soup!" Michèle said with inspiration. "Come up with me!"

"My sister is with me." Paul turned quickly, stiff with cold, and at that moment Marie-Jeanne dashed out of the *bar-tabac*.

"Ah, *bonjour*, madame!" Marie-Jeanne was grinning, carrying a blue straw shopping bag which looked empty, but she opened it to show her brother. "Two packs. That's right?—Cigarettes for my father," she said to Michèle.

"Would you like to come up for a few minutes and see my Christmas tree?" Michèle's hospitality still glowed strongly. What was wrong with giving these two a bowl of hot soup and some candy?

They came. In the apartment, Michèle switched on the radio to London, which was giving out with carols. Just the thing! Marie-Jeanne squatted in front of the Christmas tree and chattered to her brother about the pretty packages amassed at the base, the decorations, the little presents perched in the branches. Michèle was heating a tin of split pea soup to which she had added an equal amount of milk. Good nourishing food! The English choir-boys sang a French carol, and they all joined in:

> *Il est né le divin enfant . . .*
> *Chantez hautbois, résonnez musettes . . .*

Then as before they were gone all too suddenly—their laughter and chatter—Zeke barked as if to call them back, and Michèle was left with the empty soup bowls and crumpled chocolate papers to clear away. Impulsively Michèle had given them the pretty cookie box to take home. And Charles was due in a few minutes. Michèle had tidied the kitchen and was walking into the living room when she heard the click of the lift door and Charles's step in the hall, and at the same time noticed a gap on the mantel. The clock! Charles's ormolu clock! It couldn't be gone. But it *was* gone.

A key was fitted into the lock, and the door opened.

Michèle seized a box—yellow-wrapped; house slippers for Charles—and set it where the clock had been.

"Hello, darling!" Charles said, kissing her.

Charles wanted a cup of tea: the temperature was dropping and he had nearly caught a chill waiting for a taxi just now. Michèle made tea for both of them and tried to seat herself so that Charles would take a chair that put his back to the fireplace, but this didn't work, as Charles took a different armchair from the one Michèle had intended.

"What's the idea of a present up there?" Charles asked, meaning the yellow package.

Charles had an eye for order. Smiling, still in a good mood, he left his first cup of tea and went to the mantel. He took the package, turned toward the Christmas tree, then looked back at the mantel. "And where's the clock? You took it away?"

Michèle clenched her teeth, longing to lie, to say, yes, she'd put it in

145

a cupboard in order to have room for Christmas decorations on the mantel, but would that make sense? "No, I—"

"Something the matter with the clock?" Charles's face had grown serious, as if he were inquiring about the health of a member of the family whom he loved.

"I don't know where it is," Michèle said.

Charles's brows came down and his body tensed. He tossed the light-weight package down on the table where the tree stood. "Did you see that boy again?—Did you invite him up?"

"Yes, Charles. Yes—I know I—"

"And today was perhaps the second time he was here?"

Michèle nodded. "Yes."

"For God's sake, Michèle! You know that's where my letter opener went too, don't you? But the clock! My God, it's one hell of a lot more important! Where does this kid live?"

"I don't know."

Charles made a move toward the telephone and stopped. "When was he here? This afternoon?"

"Yes, less than an hour ago. Charles, I really am sorry!"

"He can't live far from here.—How *could* he have done it with you here with him?"

"His sister was here too." Michèle had showed her where the bathroom was. Of course Paul had taken the clock, then, put it in that blue shopping bag.

Charles understood and nodded grimly. "Well, they'll have a nice Christmas, pawning that. And I'll bet we won't see either of them around here for the next many days—if ever. How could you bring such hoodlums into the *house?*"

Michèle hesitated, shocked by Charles's wrath. It was wrath turned against her. "They were cold and they were hungry—and poor." She looked her husband in the eyes.

"So was my father," Charles said slowly, "when he acquired that clock."

Michèle knew. The ormolu clock had been the Clement family's pride and joy since Charles had been twelve or so. The clock had been the one handsome item in their working class household. It had caught Michèle's eye the first time she had visited the Clements, because the rest of the furnishings were dreadful *style rustique,* all varnish and Formica. And Charles's father had given the clock to them as a wedding present.

"Filthy swine," Charles murmured, drawing on a cigarette, looking at the gap on the mantel. "You don't know such people perhaps, my dear Michèle, but I do. I grew up with them."

"Then you might be more sympathetic! If we can't get the clock back, Charles, I'll buy another for us, as near like it as possible. I can remember exactly how that clock looked."

Charles shook his head, squeezed his eyes shut and turned away.

Michèle left the room, taking the tea things with her. It was the first time she had seen Charles near tears.

Charles did not want to go to the dinner party to which they were invited that evening. He suggested that Michèle go alone and make some excuse for him, and Michèle at first said she would stay at home too, then changed her mind and got dressed.

"I don't see what's the matter with my idea of buying another clock," Michèle said. "I don't see—"

"Maybe you'll never see," Charles said.

Michèle had known Bernard and Yvonne Petit a long time. Both had been friends of Michèle's before she and Charles were married. Michèle wanted very much to tell Yvonne the story about the clock, but it was not a story one could tell at a dinner table of eight, and by coffee time Michèle had decided it was best not to tell it at all: Charles was seriously upset, and the mistake was her own. But Yvonne, as Michèle was leaving, asked her if something was on her mind, and Michèle was relieved to admit there was. She and Yvonne went into a library much like the one in Michèle's apartment, and Michèle told the story quickly.

"We've got just the clock you need *here!*" said Yvonne. "Bernard doesn't even much like it. Ha! That's a terrible thing to say, isn't it? But the clock's right here, darling Michèle. Look!'' Yvonne pushed aside some invitation cards, so that the clock on the library mantel showed plainly on its splayed base: black hands, its round face crowned with a tiara of gilded knobs and curlicues.

The clock was indeed very like the one that had been stolen. While Michèle hesitated, Yvonne found newspaper and a plastic bag in the kitchen and wrapped the clock securely. She pressed it into Michèle's hands. "A Christmas present!"

"But it's the principle of the thing. I know Charles. So do you, Yvonne. If the clock that was stolen were from my family, if I'd known it all my life, even, I know it wouldn't matter to me so much."

"I know, I know."

"It's the fact that these kids were poor—and that it's Christmas. I asked them in, Paul first, by himself. Just to see their faces light up was so wonderful for me. They were so grateful for a bowl of soup. Paul told me they live in a basement somewhere."

Yvonne listened, though it was the second time Michèle had told her all this. "Just put the clock on the mantel where the clock was—and hope for the best." Yvonne spoke with a confident smile.

When Michèle got home by taxi, Charles was in bed reading. Michèle unwrapped the clock in the kitchen and set it on the mantel. Amazing how much it did look like the other clock! Charles, behind his newspaper, said that he had taken Zeke out for a walk half an hour ago. Otherwise Charles was silent, and Michèle did not try to talk to him.

The next morning, Christmas Eve, Charles spotted the new clock on the mantel as he walked into the living room from the kitchen, where he and Michèle had just breakfasted. Charles turned to Michèle with a shocked look in his eyes. "All right, Michèle. That's enough."

"Yvonne gave it to me. To us. I thought—just for *Christmas*—" What had she thought? How had she meant to finish that sentence?

"You do *not* understand," he said firmly. "I gave the police a description of that clock last night. I went to the police station, and I intend to get that clock back! I also informed them of the boy aged 'about ten' and his sister who live somewhere in the neighborhood in a basement."

Charles spoke as if he had declared war on a formidable enemy. To Michèle it was absurd. Then as Charles talked on in his tone of barely repressed fury about dishonesty, handouts to the irresponsible, to those who had not earned them or even tried to, about hooligans' disrespect for private property, Michèle began to understand. Charles felt that his castle had been invaded, that the enemy had been admitted by his own wife—and that she was on their side. Are you a Communist, Charles might have asked, but he didn't. Michèle didn't consider herself a Communist, never had.

"I simply think the rich ought to share," she interrupted.

"Since when are we rich, really rich, I mean?" Charles replied. "Well, I know. Your family, they *are* rich and you're used to it. You inherited it. That's not your fault."

Why on earth should it be her fault, Michèle wondered and began to feel on surer ground. She had read often enough in newspapers and books that wealth had to be shared in this century, or else. "Well—and as for these kids, I'd do the same thing again," she said.

Charles's cheeks shook with exasperation. "They insulted us! This was thievery!"

Michèle's face grew warm. She left the room, as furious as Charles. But Michèle felt that she had a point. More than that, that she was right. She should put it into words, organize her argument. Her heart was beating fast. She glanced at the open bedroom door, expecting Charles's figure, expecting his voice, asking her to come back. There was silence.

Charles went off to his office half an hour later and said he would probably not be back before three thirty. They were to go to his parents' house between four and five. Michèle rang up Yvonne, and in the course of their conversation Michèle's thoughts became clearer, and her trickle of tears stopped.

"I think Charles's attitude is wrong," Michèle said.

"But you mustn't say that to a man, dear Michèle. You be careful."

That afternoon at four, Michèle began tactfully with Charles. She asked him if he liked the wrapping of the present for his mother. The package contained the white tablecloth, which she had shown Charles.

"I'm not going. I can't." He went on, over Michèle's protestations. "Do you think I can face my parents—admit to them that the clock's been stolen?"

Why mention the clock, unless he wanted to ruin Christmas, Michèle thought. She knew it was useless to try to persuade him to come, so she gave it up. "I'll go—and take their presents." So she did, and left Charles at home to sulk, and to wait for a possible telephone call from the police, he had said.

Michèle had gone out laden with Charles's parents' presents as well as those for her own parents. Charles had said he would turn up at her parents' Neuilly apartment at 8:00 P.M. or so. But he did not. Michèle's parents suggested that she telephone Charles: maybe he had fallen asleep or was working and had lost track of time, but Michèle did not telephone him. Everything was so cheerful and beautiful at her parents' house—their tree, the champagne buckets, her nice presents, one a travel umbrella in a leather case. Charles and the clock story loomed like an ugly black shadow in the golden glow of her parents' living room, and Michèle again blurted out the events.

Her father chuckled. "I remember that clock—I think. Nothing so great about it. It wasn't made by Cellini after all."

"It's the sentiment, however, Edouard," said Michèle's mother. "A pity it had to happen just at Christmas. And it was careless of you, Michèle. But—I have to agree with you, yes, they were simply little urchins of the *street*, and they were tempted."

Michèle felt further strengthened.

"Not the end of the world," Edouard murmured, pouring more champagne.

Michèle remembered her father's words the next day, Christmas Day, and on the day after. It was not the end of the world, but the end of something. The police had not found the clock, but Charles believed they would. He had spoken to them with some determination, he assured Michèle, and had brought them a colored drawing of the clock which Charles had made at the age of fourteen.

"Naturally the thieves wouldn't pawn it so soon," Charles said to Michèle, "but they're not going to drop it in the Seine either. They'll try to get cash for it sooner or later, and then we'll nail them."

"Frankly, I find your attitude unchristian and even cruel," said Michèle.

"And I find your attitude—silly."

It was not the end of the world, but it was the end of their marriage. No later words, no embrace if it ever came, could compensate Michèle for that remark from her husband. And, just as vital, she felt a deep dislike, a real aversion to her within Charles's heart and mind. And she for him? Was it not a similar feeling? Charles had lost something that Michèle considered human—if he had ever had it. With his poorer, less privileged background, Charles should have had more compassion than she, Michèle thought. What was wrong? And what was right? She felt muddled, as she sometimes did when she tried to ponder the phrases of carols, or of some poems, which could be interpreted in a couple of ways, and yet the heart, or sentiment always seemed to seek and find a path of its own, as hers had done, and wasn't this right? Wasn't it right to be forgiving, especially at this time of year?

Their friends, their parents counseled patience. They should separate for a week or so. Christmas always made people nervous. Michèle could come and stay at Yvonne and Bernard's apartment, which she did. Then she and Charles could talk again, which they did. But nothing really changed, not at all.

Michèle and Charles were divorced within four months. And the police never found the clock.

HARPER LEE

Christmas

"You can just take that back, boy!"

This order, given by me to Cecil Jacobs, was the beginning of a rather thin time for Jem and me. My fists were clenched and I was ready to let fly. Atticus had promised me he would wear me out if he ever heard of me fighting any more; I was far too old and too big for such childish things, and the sooner I learned to hold in, the better off everybody would be. I soon forgot.

Cecil Jacobs made me forget. He had announced in the school yard the day before that Scout Finch's daddy defended niggers. I denied it but told Jem.

"What'd he mean sayin' that?" I asked.

"Nothing," Jem said. "Ask Atticus, he'll tell you."

"Do you defend niggers, Atticus?" I asked him that evening.

"Of course I do. Don't say nigger, Scout. That's common."

" 'S what everybody at school says."

"From now on it'll be everybody less one—"

"Well if you don't want me to grow up talkin' that way, why do you send me to school?"

My father looked at me mildly, amusement in his eyes. Despite our compromise, my campaign to avoid school had continued in one form or another since my first day's dose of it: the beginning of last September had brought on sinking spells, dizziness, and mild gastric complaints. I went so far as to pay a nickel for the privilege of rubbing my head against the head of Miss Rachel's cook's son, who was afflicted with a tremendous ring-worm. It didn't take.

But I was worrying another bone. "Do all lawyers defend n-Negroes, Atticus?"

"Of course they do, Scout."

"Then why did Cecil say you defended niggers? He made it sound like you were runnin' a still."

Atticus sighed. "I'm simply defending a Negro—his name's Tom Rob-inson. He lives in that little settlement beyond the town dump. He's a member of Calpurnia's church, and Cal knows his family well. She says they're clean-living folks. Scout, you aren't old enough to understand some things yet, but there's been some high talk around town to the effect that I shouldn't do much about defending this man. It's a peculiar case—it won't come to trial until summer session. John Taylor was kind enough to give us a postponement. . . ."

"If you shouldn't be defendin' him, then why are you doin' it?"

"For a number of reasons," said Atticus. "The main one is, if I didn't I couldn't hold up my head in town, I couldn't represent this county in the legislature, I couldn't even tell you or Jem not to do something again."

"You mean if you didn't defend that man, Jem and me wouldn't have to mind you anymore?"

"That's about right."

"Why?"

"Because I could never ask you to mind me again. Scout, simply by the nature of the work, every lawyer gets at least one case in his lifetime that affects him personally. This one's mine, I guess. You might hear some ugly talk about it at school, but do one thing for me if you will: you just hold your head high and keep those fists down. No matter what anybody says to you, don't you let 'em get your goat. Try fighting with your head for a change, . . . it's a good one, even if it does resist learning."

"Atticus, are we going to win it?"

"No, honey."

"Then why—"

"Simply because we were licked a hundred years before we started is no reason for us not to try to win," Atticus said.

"You sound like Cousin Ike Finch," I said. Cousin Ike Finch was Maycomb County's sole surviving Confederate veteran. He wore a General Hood–type beard of which he was inordinately vain. At least once a year Atticus, Jem and I called on him, and I would have to kiss him. It was horrible. Jem and I would listen respectfully to Atticus and Cousin Ike rehash the war. "Tell you, Atticus," Cousin Ike would say, "the Missouri Compromise was what licked us, but if I had to go through it agin I'd walk every step of the way there an' every step back jist like I did before an' furthermore we'd whip 'em this time; . . . now in 1864, when Stonewall Jackson came around by—I beg your pardon, young folks. Ol' Blue Light was in heaven then, God rest his saintly brow. . . ."

"Come here, Scout," said Atticus. I crawled into his lap and tucked my head under his chin. He put his arms around me and rocked me gently. "It's different this time," he said. "This time we aren't fighting the Yankees, we're fighting our friends. But remember this, no matter how bitter things get, they're still our friends and this is still our home."

With this in mind, I faced Cecil Jacobs in the school yard next day: "You gonna take that back, boy?"

"You gotta make me first!" he yelled. "My folks said your daddy was a disgrace an' that nigger oughta hang from the water tank!"

I drew a bead on him, remembered what Atticus had said, then dropped my fists and walked away, "Scout's a cow—ward!" ringing in my ears. It was the first time I ever walked away from a fight.

Somehow, if I fought Cecil I would let Atticus down. Atticus so rarely asked Jem and me to do something for him, I could take being called a coward for him. I felt extremely noble for having remembered, and remained noble for three weeks. Then Christmas came and disaster struck.

Jem and I viewed Christmas with mixed feelings. The good side was the tree and Uncle Jack Finch. Every Christmas Eve day we met Uncle Jack at Maycomb Junction, and he would spend a week with us.

A flip of the coin revealed the uncompromising lineaments of Aunt Alexandra and Francis.

I suppose I should include Uncle Jimmy, Aunt Alexandra's husband, but as he never spoke a word to me in my life except to say, "Get off the fence," once, I never saw any reason to take notice of him. Neither did Aunt Alexandra. Long ago, in a burst of friendliness, Aunty and Uncle Jimmy produced a son named Henry, who left home as soon as was humanly possible, married, and produced Francis. Henry and his wife deposited Francis at his grandparents' every Christmas, then pursued their own pleasures.

No amount of sighing could induce Atticus to let us spend Christmas Day at home. We went to Finch's Landing every Christmas in my memory. The fact that Aunty was a good cook was some compensation for being forced to spend a religious holiday with Francis Hancock. He was a year older than I, and I avoided him on principle: he enjoyed everything I disapproved of and disliked my ingenuous diversions.

Aunt Alexandra was Atticus's sister, but when Jem told me about changelings and siblings, I decided that she had been swapped at birth, that my grandparents had perhaps received a Crawford instead of a Finch. Had I ever harbored the mystical notions about mountains that seem to obsess lawyers and judges, Aunt Alexandra would have been analogous to Mount Everest: throughout my early life, she was cold and there.

When Uncle Jack jumped down from the train Christmas Eve day, we had to wait for the porter to hand him two long packages. Jem and I always thought it funny when Uncle Jack pecked Atticus on the cheek; they were the only two men we ever saw kiss each other. Uncle Jack shook hands with Jem and swung me high, but not high enough: Uncle Jack was a head shorter than Atticus; the baby of the family, he was younger than Aunt Alexandra. He and Aunty looked alike, but Uncle Jack made better use of his face: we were never wary of his sharp nose and chin.

He was one of the few men of science who never terrified me, probably because he never behaved like a doctor. Whenever he performed a minor service for Jem and me, as removing a splinter from a foot, he would tell us exactly what he was going to do, give us an estimation of how much it would hurt, and explain the use of any tongs he employed. One Christmas I lurked in corners nursing a twisted splinter in my foot, permitting no one to come near me. When Uncle Jack caught me, he kept me laughing about a preacher who hated going to church so much that every day he stood at his gate in his dressing gown, smoking a hookah and delivering five-minute sermons to any passersby who desired spiritual comfort. I interrupted to make Uncle Jack let me know when he would pull it out, but he held up a bloody splinter in a pair of tweezers and said he yanked it while I was laughing, that was what was known as relativity.

"What's in those packages?" I asked him, pointing to the long thin parcels the porter had given him.

"None of your business," he said.

Jem said, "How's Rose Aylmer?"

Rose Aylmer was Uncle Jack's cat. She was a beautiful yellow female Uncle Jack said was one of the few women he could stand permanently. He reached into his coat pocket and brought out some snapshots. We admired them.

"She's gettin' fat," I said.

"I should think so. She eats all the leftover fingers and ears from the hospital."

"Aw, that's a damn story," I said.

"I beg your pardon?"

Atticus said, "Don't pay any attention to her, Jack. She's trying you out. Cal says she's been cussing fluently for a week, now."

Uncle Jack raised his eyebrows and said nothing. I was proceeding on the dim theory, aside from the innate attractiveness of such words, that if Atticus discovered I had picked them up at school he wouldn't make me go.

But at supper that evening when I asked him to pass the damn ham, please, Uncle Jack pointed at me. "See me afterward, young lady," he said.

When supper was over, Uncle Jack went to the living room and sat down. He slapped his thighs for me to come sit on his lap. I liked to smell him: he was like a bottle of alcohol and something pleasantly sweet. He pushed back my bangs and looked at me. "You're more like Atticus than your mother," he said. "You're also growing out of your pants a little."

"I reckon they fit all right."

"You like words like *damn* and *hell* now, don't you?"

I said I reckoned so.

"Well I don't," said Uncle Jack, "not unless there's extreme provocation connected with 'em. I'll be here a week, and I don't want to hear any words like that while I'm here. Scout, you'll get in trouble if you go around saying things like that. You want to grow up to be a lady, don't you?"

I said not particularly.

"Of course you do. Now let's get to the tree."

We decorated the tree until bedtime, and that night I dreamed of the two long packages for Jem and me. Next morning Jem and I dived for them: they were from Atticus, who had written Uncle Jack to get them for us, and they were what we had asked for.

"Don't point them in the house," said Atticus when Jem aimed at a picture on the wall.

"You'll have to teach 'em to shoot," said Uncle Jack.

"That's your job," said Atticus. "I merely bowed to the inevitable."

It took Atticus's courtroom voice to drag us away from the tree. He declined to let us take our air rifles to the Landing (I had already begun to think of shooting Francis) and said if we made one false move he'd take them away from us for good.

Finch's Landing consisted of 366 steps down a high bluff and ending in a jetty. Farther downstream, beyond the bluff, were traces of an old cotton landing, where Finch Negroes had loaded bales and produce, unloaded blocks of ice, flour and sugar, farm equipment, and feminine apparel. A two-rut road ran from the riverside and vanished among dark trees. At the end of the road was a two-story white house with porches circling it upstairs and downstairs. In his old age, our ancestor Simon Finch had built it to please his nagging wife; but with the porches all resemblance to ordinary houses of its era ended. The internal arrangements of the Finch house were indicative of Simon's guilelessness and the absolute trust with which he regarded his offspring.

There were six bedrooms upstairs, four for the eight female children, one for Welcome Finch, the sole son, and one for visiting relatives. Simple enough; but the daughters' rooms could be reached only by one staircase, Welcome's room and the guest room only by another. The daughters' staircase was in the ground floor bedroom of their parents, so Simon always knew the hours of his daughters' nocturnal comings and goings.

There was a kitchen separate from the rest of the house, tacked onto it by a wooden catwalk; in the backyard was a rusty bell on a pole, used to summon field hands or as a distress signal; a widow's walk was on the roof, but no widows walked there—from it, Simon oversaw his overseer, watched the riverboats, and gazed into the lives of surrounding landholders.

There went with the house the usual legend about the Yankees: one Finch female, recently engaged, donned her complete trousseau to save it from raiders in the neighborhood; she became stuck in the door to the daughters' staircase but was doused with water and finally pushed through. When we arrived at the Landing, Aunt Alexandra kissed Uncle Jack, Francis kissed Uncle Jack, Uncle Jimmy shook hands silently with Uncle Jack, Jem and I gave our presents to Francis, who gave us a present. Jem felt his age and gravitated to the adults, leaving me to entertain our cousin. Francis was eight and slicked back his hair.

"What'd you get for Christmas?" I asked politely.

"Just what I asked for," he said. Francis had requested a pair of knee pants, a red leather book sack, five shirts and an untied bow tie.

"That's nice," I lied. "Jem and me got air rifles, and Jem got a chemistry set—"

"A toy one, I reckon."

"No, a real one. He's gonna make me some invisible ink, and I'm gonna write to Dill in it."

Francis asked what was the use of that.

"Well, can't you just see his face when he gets a letter from me with nothing in it? It'll drive him nuts."

Talking to Francis gave me the sensation of settling slowly to the bottom of the ocean. He was the most boring child I ever met. As he lived in Mobile, he could not inform on me to school authorities, but he managed to tell everything he knew to Aunt Alexandra, who in turn unburdened herself to Atticus, who either forgot it or gave me hell, whichever struck his fancy. But the only time I ever heard Atticus speak sharply to anyone was when I once heard him say, "Sister, I do the best I can with them!" It had something to do with my going around in overalls.

Aunt Alexandra was fanatical on the subject of my attire. I could not possibly hope to be a lady if I wore breeches; when I said I could do nothing in a dress, she said I wasn't supposed to be doing things that required pants. Aunt Alexandra's vision of my deportment involved playing with small stoves, tea sets, and wearing the Add-a-Pearl necklace she gave me when I was born; furthermore, I should be a ray of sunshine in my father's lonely life. I suggested that one could be a ray of sunshine in pants just as well, but Aunty said that one had to behave like a sunbeam, that I was born good but had grown progressively worse every year. She hurt my feelings and set my teeth permanently on edge, but when I asked Atticus about it, he said there were already enough sunbeams in the family and to go on about my business, he didn't mind me much the way I was.

At Christmas dinner, I sat at the little table in the dining room; Jem and Francis sat with the adults at the dining table. Aunty had continued to isolate me long after Jem and Francis graduated to the big table. I often wondered what she thought I'd do, get up and throw something? I sometimes thought of asking her if she would let me sit at the big table with the rest of them just once, I would prove to her how civilized I could be; after all, I ate at home every day with no major mishaps. When I begged Atticus to use his influence, he said he had none—we were guests, and we sat where she told us to sit. He also said Aunt Alexandra didn't understand girls much, she'd never had one.

But her cooking made up for everything: three kinds of meat, summer vegetables from her pantry shelves; peach pickles, two kinds of cake and ambrosia constituted a modest Christmas dinner. Afterward, the adults made for the living room and sat around in a dazed condition. Jem lay on the floor, and I went to the backyard. "Put on your coat," said Atticus dreamily, so I didn't hear him.

Francis sat beside me on the back steps. "That was the best yet," I said.

"Grandma's a wonderful cook," said Francis. "She's gonna teach me how."

"Boys don't cook." I giggled at the thought of Jem in an apron.

"Grandma says all men should learn to cook, that men oughta be careful with their wives and wait on 'em when they don't feel good," said my cousin.

"I don't want Dill waitin' on me," I said. "I'd rather wait on him."

"Dill?"

"Yeah. Don't say anything about it yet, but we're gonna get married as soon as we're big enough. He asked me last summer."

Francis hooted.

"What's the matter with him?" I asked. "Ain't anything the matter with him."

"You mean that little runt Grandma says stays with Miss Rachel every summer?"

"That's exactly who I mean."

"I know all about him," said Francis.

"What about him?"

"Grandma says he hasn't got a home—"

"Has too, he lives in Meridian."

"—he just gets passed around from relative to relative, and Miss Rachel keeps him every summer."

"Francis, that's not so!"

Francis grinned at me. "You're mighty dumb sometimes, Jean Louise. Guess you don't know any better, though."

"What do you mean?"

"If Uncle Atticus lets you run around with stray dogs, that's his own business, like Grandma says, so it ain't your fault. I guess it ain't your fault if Uncle Atticus is a nigger lover besides, but I'm here to tell you it certainly does mortify the rest of the family—"

"Francis, what the hell do you mean?"

"Just what I said. Grandma says it's bad enough he lets you all run wild, but now he's turned out a nigger lover we'll never be able to walk the streets of Maycomb agin. He's ruinin' the family, that's what he's doin'."

Francis rose and sprinted down the catwalk to the old kitchen. At a safe distance he called, "He's nothin' but a nigger lover!"

"He is not!" I roared. "I don't know what you're talkin' about, but you better cut it out this red-hot minute!"

I leapt off the steps and ran down the catwalk. It was easy to collar Francis. I said take it back quick.

Francis jerked loose and sped into the old kitchen. "Nigger lover!" he yelled.

When stalking one's prey, it is best to take one's time. Say nothing, and as sure as eggs he will become curious and emerge. Francis appeared at the kitchen door. "You still mad, Jean Louise?" he asked tentatively.

"Nothing to speak of," I said.

Francis came out on the catwalk.

"You gonna take it back, Fra—ancis?" But I was too quick on the draw. Francis shot back into the kitchen, so I retired to the steps. I could wait patiently. I had sat there perhaps five minutes when I heard Aunt Alexandra speak: "Where's Francis?"

"He's out yonder in the kitchen."

"He knows he's not supposed to play in there."

Francis came to the door and yelled, "Grandma, she's got me in here and she won't let me out!"

"What is all this, Jean Louise?"

I looked up at Aunt Alexandra. "I haven't got him in there, Aunty, I ain't holdin' him."

161

"Yes she is," shouted Francis, "she won't let me out!"

"Have you all been fussing?"

"Jean Louise got mad at me, Grandma," called Francis.

"Francis, come out of there! Jean Louise, if I hear another word out of you I'll tell your father. Did I hear you say *hell* a while ago?"

"Nome."

"I thought I did. I'd better not hear it again."

Aunt Alexandra was a back-porch listener. The moment she was out of sight Francis came out head up and grinning. "Don't you fool with me," he said.

He jumped into the yard and kept his distance, kicking tufts of grass, turning around occasionally to smile at me. Jem appeared on the porch, looked at us, and went away. Francis climbed the mimosa tree, came down, put his hands in his pockets and strolled around the yard. "Hah!" he said. I asked him who he thought he was, Uncle Jack? Francis said he reckoned I got told, for me to just sit there and leave him alone.

"I ain't botherin' you," I said.

Francis looked at me carefully, concluded that I had been sufficiently subdued, and crooned softly, "Nigger lover . . ."

This time, I split my knuckle to the bone on his front teeth. My left impaired, I sailed in with my right, but not for long. Uncle Jack pinned my arms to my sides and said, "Stand still!"

Aunt Alexandra ministered to Francis, wiping his tears away with her handkerchief, rubbing his hair, patting his cheek. Atticus, Jem, and Uncle Jimmy had come to the back porch when Francis started yelling.

"Who started this?" said Uncle Jack.

Francis and I pointed at each other. "Grandma," he bawled, "she called me a whore lady and jumped on me!"

"Is that true, Scout?" said Uncle Jack.

"I reckon so."

When Uncle Jack looked down at me, his features were like Aunt Alexandra's. "You know I told you you'd get in trouble if you used words like that? I told you, didn't I?"

"Yes sir, but—"

"Well, you're in trouble now. Stay there."

I was debating whether to stand there or run, and tarried in indecision a moment too long: I turned to flee but Uncle Jack was quicker. I found myself suddenly looking at a tiny ant struggling with a bread crumb in the grass.

"I'll never speak to you again as long as I live! I hate you an' despise you an' hope you die tomorrow!" A statement that seemed to encourage Uncle Jack, more than anything. I ran to Atticus for comfort, but he said I had it coming and it was high time we went home. I climbed into the backseat of the car without saying good-bye to anyone, and at home I ran to my room and slammed the door. Jem tried to say something nice, but I wouldn't let him.

When I surveyed the damage there were only seven or eight red marks, and I was reflecting upon relativity when someone knocked on the door. I asked who it was; Uncle Jack answered.

"Go away!"

Uncle Jack said if I talked like that he'd lick me again, so I was quiet. When he entered the room I retreated to a corner and turned my back on him. "Scout," he said, "do you still hate me?"

"Go on, please sir."

"Why, I didn't think you'd hold it against me," he said. "I'm disappointed in you—you had that coming and you know it."

"Didn't either."

"Honey, you can't go around calling people—"

"You ain't fair," I said, "you ain't fair."

Uncle Jack's eyebrows went up. "Not fair? How not?"

"You're real nice, Uncle Jack, an' I reckon I love you even after what you did, but you don't understand children much."

Uncle Jack put his hands on his hips and looked down at me. "And why do I not understand children, Miss Jean Louise? Such conduct as yours required little understanding. It was obstreperous, disorderly, and abusive—"

"You gonna give me a chance to tell you? I don't mean to sass you, I'm just tryin' to tell you."

Uncle Jack sat down on the bed. His eyebrows came together, and he peered up at me from under them. "Proceed," he said.

I took a deep breath. "Well, in the first place you never stopped to gimme a chance to tell you my side of it—you just lit right into me. When Jem an' I fuss Atticus doesn't ever just listen to Jem's side of it, he hears mine too, an' in the second place you told me never to use words like that except in ex—extreme provocation, and Francis provocated me enough to knock his block off—"

Uncle Jack scratched his head. "What was your side of it, Scout?"

"Francis called Atticus somethin', an' I wasn't about to take it off him."

"What did Francis call him?"

"A nigger lover. I ain't very sure what it means, but the way Francis said it—tell you one thing right now, Uncle Jack, I'll be—I swear before God if I'll sit there and let him say somethin' about Atticus."

"He called Atticus that?"

"Yes sir, he did, an' a lot more. Said Atticus'd be the ruination of the family an' he let Jem an' me run wild. . . ."

From the look on Uncle Jack's face, I thought I was in for it again. When he said, "We'll see about this," I knew Francis was in for it. "I've a good mind to go out there tonight."

"Please sir, just let it go. Please."

"I've no intention of letting it go," he said. "Alexandra should know about this. The idea of—wait'll I get my hands on that boy. . . ."

"Uncle Jack, please promise me somethin', please sir. Promise you won't tell Atticus about this. He—he asked me one time not to let anything I heard about him make me mad, an' I'd ruther him think we were fightin' about somethin' else instead. Please promise . . ."

"But I don't like Francis getting away with something like that—"

"He didn't. You reckon you could tie up my hand? It's still bleedin' some."

"Of course I will, baby. I know of no hand I would be more delighted to tie up. Will you come this way?"

Uncle Jack gallantly bowed me to the bathroom. While he cleaned and bandaged my knuckles, he entertained me with a tale about a funny near-sighted old gentleman who had a cat named Hodge, and who counted all the cracks in the sidewalk when he went to town. "There now," he said. "You'll have a very unladylike scar on your wedding ring finger."

"Thank you sir. Uncle Jack?"

"Ma'am?"

"What's a whore lady?"

Uncle Jack plunged into another long tale about an old prime minister who sat in the House of Commons and blew feathers in the air and tried to keep them there when all about him men were losing their heads. I guess he was trying to answer my question, but he made no sense whatsoever.

Later, when I was supposed to be in bed, I went down the hall for a drink of water and heard Atticus and Uncle Jack in the living room:

"I shall never marry, Atticus."

"Why?"

"I might have children."

Atticus said, "You've a lot to learn, Jack."

"I know. Your daughter gave me my first lessons this afternoon. She said I didn't understand children much and told me why. She was quite right. Atticus, she told me how I should have treated her—oh dear, I'm so sorry I romped on her."

Atticus chuckled. "She earned it, so don't feel too remorseful."

I waited, on tenterhooks, for Uncle Jack to tell Atticus my side of it. But he didn't. He simply murmured, "Her use of bathroom invective leaves nothing to the imagination. But she doesn't know the meaning of half she says—she asked me what a whore lady was. . . ."

"Did you tell her?"

"No, I told her about Lord Melbourne."

"Jack! When a child asks you something, answer him, for goodness' sake. But don't make a production of it. Children are children, but they can

165

spot an evasion quicker than adults, and evasion simply muddles 'em. No," my father mused, "you had the right answer this afternoon, but the wrong reasons. Bad language is a stage all children go through, and it dies with time when they learn they're not attracting attention with it. Hotheadedness isn't. Scout's got to learn to keep her head and learn soon, with what's in store for her these next few months. She's coming along, though. Jem's getting older and she follows his example a good bit now. All she needs is assistance sometimes."

"Atticus, you've never laid a hand on her."

"I admit that. So far I've been able to get by with threats. Jack, she minds me as well as she can. Doesn't come up to scratch half the time, but she tries."

"That's not the answer," said Uncle Jack.

"No, the answer is she knows I know she tries. That's what makes the difference. What bothers me is that she and Jem will have to absorb some ugly things pretty soon. I'm not worried about Jem keeping his head, but Scout'd just as soon jump on someone as look at him if her pride's at stake. . . ."

I waited for Uncle Jack to break his promise. He still didn't.

"Atticus, how bad is this going to be? You haven't had too much chance to discuss it."

"It couldn't be worse, Jack. The only thing we've got is a black man's word against the Ewells'. The evidence boils down to you-did–I-didn't. The jury couldn't possibly be expected to take Tom Robinson's word against the Ewells'—are you acquainted with the Ewells?"

Uncle Jack said yes, he remembered them. He described them to Atticus, but Atticus said, "You're a generation off. The present ones are the same, though."

"What are you going to do, then?"

"Before I'm through, I intend to jar the jury a bit—I think we'll have a reasonable chance on appeal, though. I really can't tell at this stage, Jack. You know, I'd hoped to get through life without a case of this kind, but John Taylor pointed at me and said, 'You're It.' "

"Let this cup pass from you, eh?"

"Right. But do you think I could face my children otherwise? You know what's going to happen as well as I do, Jack, and I hope and pray I can get Jem and Scout through it without bitterness, and most of all, without catching Maycomb's usual disease. Why reasonable people go stark raving mad when anything involving a Negro comes up, is something I don't pretend to understand. . . . I just hope that Jem and Scout come to me for their answers instead of listening to the town. I hope they trust me enough. . . . Jean Louise?"

My scalp jumped. I stuck my head around the corner. "Sir?"

"Go to bed."

I scurried to my room and went to bed. Uncle Jack was a prince of a fellow not to let me down. But I never figured out how Atticus knew I was listening, and it was not until many years later that I realized he wanted me to hear every word he said.

GRACE PALEY

The Loudest Voice

There is a certain place where dumb-waiters boom, doors slam, dishes crash; every window is a mother's mouth bidding the street shut up, go skate somewhere else, come home. My voice is the loudest.

There, my own mother is still as full of breathing as me and the grocer stands up to speak to her. "Mrs. Abramowitz," he says, "people should not be afraid of their children."

"Ah, Mr. Bialik," my mother replies, "if you say to her or her father 'Ssh,' they say, 'In the grave it will be quiet.' "

"From Coney Island to the cemetery," says my papa. "It's the same subway; it's the same fare."

I am right next to the pickle barrel. My pinky is making tiny whirlpools in the brine. I stop a moment to announce: "Campbell's tomato soup. Campbell's vegetable beef soup. Campbell's S-c-otch broth . . ."

"Be quiet," the grocer says, "the labels are coming off."

"Please, Shirley, be a little quiet," my mother begs me.

In that place the whole street groans: Be quiet! Be quiet! but steals from the happy chorus of my inside self not a tittle or a jot.

There, too, but just around the corner, is a red brick building that has been old for many years. Every morning the children stand before it in double lines which must be straight. They are not insulted. They are waiting anyway.

I am usually among them. I am, in fact, the first, since I begin with "A."

One cold morning the monitor tapped me on the shoulder. "Go to room 409, Shirley Abramowitz," he said. I did as I was told. I went in a hurry up a down staircase to room 409, which contained sixth-graders. I had to wait at the desk without wiggling until Mr. Hilton, their teacher, had time to speak.

After five minutes he said, "Shirley?"

"What?" I whispered.

He said, "My! My! Shirley Abramowitz! They told me you had a particularly loud, clear voice and read with lots of expression. Could that be true?"

"Oh yes," I whispered.

"In that case, don't be silly; I might very well be your teacher someday. Speak up, speak up."

"Yes," I shouted.

"More like it," he said. "Now, Shirley, can you put a ribbon in your hair or a bobby pin? It's too messy."

"Yes!" I bawled.

"Now, now, calm down." He turned to the class. "Children, not a sound. Open at page 39. Read till 52. When you finish, start again." He looked me over once more. "Now, Shirley, you know, I suppose, that Christmas is coming. We are preparing a beautiful play. Most of the parts have been given out. But I still need a child with a strong voice, lots of stamina. Do you know what stamina is? You do? Smart kid. You know, I heard you read 'The Lord is my shepherd' in assembly yesterday. I was very impressed. Wonderful delivery. Mrs. Jordan, your teacher, speaks highly of you. Now listen to me, Shirley Abramowitz, if you want to take the part and be in the play, repeat after me, 'I swear to work harder than I ever did before.'"

I looked to heaven and said at once, "Oh, I swear." I kissed my pinky and looked at God.

"That is an actor's life, my dear," he explained. "Like a soldier's, never tardy or disobedient to his general, the director. Everything," he said, "absolutely everything will depend on you."

That afternoon, all over the building, children scraped and scrubbed the turkeys and the sheaves of corn off the schoolroom windows. Good-bye Thanksgiving. The next morning a monitor brought red paper and green paper from the office. We made new shapes and hung them on the walls and glued them to the doors.

The teachers became happier and happier. Their heads were ringing like the bells of childhood. My best friend, Evie, was prone to evil, but she did not get a single demerit for whispering. We learned "Holy Night" without an error. "How wonderful!" said Miss Glacé, the student teacher. "To think that some of you don't even speak the language!" We learned "Deck the Halls" and "Hark! The Herald Angels." . . . They weren't ashamed and we weren't embarrassed.

Oh, but when my mother heard about it all, she said to my father: "Misha, you don't know what's going on there. Cramer is the head of the Tickets Committee."

"Who?" asked my father. "Cramer? Oh yes, an active woman."

"Active? Active has to have a reason. Listen," she said sadly, "I'm surprised to see my neighbors making tra-la-la for Christmas."

My father couldn't think of what to say to that. Then he decided: "You're in America! Clara, you wanted to come here. In Palestine the Arabs would be eating you alive. Europe you had pogroms. Argentina is full of Indians. Here you got Christmas. . . . Some joke, ha?"

"Very funny, Misha. What is becoming of you? If we came to a new country a long time ago to run away from tyrants, and instead we fall into a creeping pogrom, that our children learn a lot of lies, so what's the joke? Ach, Misha, your idealism is going away."

"So is your sense of humor."

"That I never had, but idealism you had a lot of."

"I'm the same Misha Abramovitch, I didn't change an iota. Ask anyone."

"Only ask me," says my mama, may she rest in peace. "I got the answer."

Meanwhile the neighbors had to think of what to say too.

Marty's father said: "You know, he has a very important part, my boy."

"Mine also," said Mr. Sauerfeld.

"Not my boy!" said Mrs. Klieg. "I said to him no. The answer is no. When I say no! I mean no!"

The rabbi's wife said, "It's disgusting!" But no one listened to her. Under the narrow sky of God's great wisdom she wore a strawberry blonde wig.

Every day was noisy and full of experience. I was Right-Hand Man. Mr. Hilton said: "How could I get along without you, Shirley?"

He said: "Your mother and father ought to get down on their knees every night and thank God for giving them a child like you."

He also said: "You're absolutely a pleasure to work with, my dear, dear child."

Sometimes he said: "For God's sakes, what did I do with the script? Shirley! Shirley! Find it."

Then I answered quietly: "Here it is, Mr. Hilton."

Once in a while, when he was very tired, he would cry out: "Shirley, I'm just tired of screaming at those kids. Will you tell Ira Pushkov not to come in till Lester points to that star the second time?"

Then I roared: "Ira Pushkov, what's the matter with you? Dope! Mr. Hilton told you five times already, don't come in till Lester points to that star the second time."

"Ach, Clara," my father asked, "what does she do there till six o'clock she can't even put the plates on the table?"

"Christmas," said my mother coldly.

"Ho! Ho!" my father said. "Christmas. What's the harm? After all, history teaches everyone. We learn from reading this is a holiday from pagan times also, candles, lights, even Chanukah. So we learn it's not altogether Christian. So if they think it's a private holiday, they're only ignorant, not patriotic. What belongs to history, belongs to all men. You want to go back to the Middle Ages? Is it better to shave your head with a secondhand razor? Does it hurt Shirley to learn to speak up? It does not. So maybe someday she won't live between the kitchen and the shop. She's not a fool.''

I thank you, Papa, for your kindness. It is true about me to this day. I am foolish but I am not a fool.

That night my father kissed me and said with great interest in my career, "Shirley, tomorrow's your big day. Congrats.''

"Save it," my mother said. Then she shut all the windows in order to prevent tonsillitis.

In the morning it snowed. On the street corner a tree had been decorated for us by a kind city administration. In order to miss its chilly shadow our neighbors walked three blocks east to buy a loaf of bread. The butcher pulled down black window shades to keep the colored lights from shining on his chickens. Oh, not me. On the way to school, with both my hands I tossed it a kiss of tolerance. Poor thing, it was a stranger in Egypt.

I walked straight into the auditorium past the staring children. "Go ahead, Shirley!" said the monitors. Four boys, big for their age, had already started work as propmen and stagehands.

Mr. Hilton was very nervous. He was not even happy. Whatever he started to say ended in a sideward look of sadness. He sat slumped in the middle of the first row and asked me to help Miss Glacé. I did this, although she thought my voice too resonant and said, "Show off!"

Parents began to arrive long before we were ready. They wanted to make a good impression. From among the yards of drapes I peeked out at the audience. I saw my embarrassed mother.

Ira, Lester, and Meyer were pasted to their beards by Miss Glacé. She almost forgot to thread the star on its wire, but I reminded her. I coughed a few times to clear my throat. Miss Glacé looked around and saw that everyone was in costume and on line waiting to play his part. She whispered, "All right . . ." Then:

Jackie Sauerfeld, the prettiest boy in first grade, parted the curtains with his skinny elbow and in a high voice sang out:

> *Parents dear*
> *We are here*
> *To make a Christmas play in time.*
> *It we give*
> *In narrative*
> *And illustrate with pantomime.*

He disappeared.

My voice burst immediately from the wings to the great shock of Ira, Lester, and Meyer, who were waiting for it but were surprised all the same.

"I remember, I remember, the house where I was born. . . ."

Miss Glacé yanked the curtain open and there it was, the house—an old hayloft, where Celia Kornbluh lay in the straw with Cindy Lou, her favorite doll. Ira, Lester, and Meyer moved slowly from the wings toward her, sometimes pointing to a moving star and sometimes ahead to Cindy Lou.

It was a long story and it was a sad story. I carefully pronounced all the words about my lonesome childhood, while little Eddie Braunstein wandered upstage and down with his shepherd's stick, looking for sheep. I brought up lonesomeness again, and not being understood at all except by some women everybody hated. Eddie was too small for that and Marty Groff took his place, wearing his father's prayer shawl. I announced twelve friends, and half the boys in the fourth grade gathered round Marty, who stood on an orange crate while my voice harangued. Sorrowful and loud, I declaimed about love and God and man, but because of the terrible deceit of Abie Stock we came suddenly to a famous moment. Marty, whose remembering tongue I was, waited at the foot of the cross. He stared desperately at the audience. I groaned, "My God, my God, why hast thou forsaken me?" The soldiers who were sheikhs grabbed poor Marty to pin him up to die, but he wrenched free, turned again to the audience, and spread his arms aloft to show despair and the end. I murmured at the top of my voice, "The rest is silence, but as everyone in this room, in this city—in this world—now knows, I shall have life eternal."

That night Mrs. Kornbluh visited our kitchen for a glass of tea.

"How's the Virgin?" asked my father with a look of concern.

"For a man with a daughter, you got a fresh mouth, Abramovitch."

"Here," said my father kindly, "have some lemon, it'll sweeten your disposition."

They debated a little in Yiddish, then fell in a puddle of Russian and Polish. What I understood next was my father, who said, "Still and all, it was certainly a beautiful affair, you have to admit, introducing us to the beliefs of a different culture."

"Well, yes," said Mrs. Kornbluh. "The only thing . . . you know Charlie Turner—that cute boy in Celia's class—a couple others? They got very small parts or no part at all. In very bad taste, it seemed to me. After all, it's their religion."

"Ach," explained my mother, "what could Mr. Hilton do? They got very small voices; after all, why should they holler? The English language they know from the beginning by heart. They're blond like angels. You think it's so important they should get in the play? Christmas . . . the whole piece of goods . . . they own it."

I listened and listened until I couldn't listen anymore. Too sleepy, I climbed out of bed and kneeled. I made a little church of my hands and said, "Hear, O Israel . . ." Then I called out in Yiddish, "Please, good night, good night. Ssh." My father said, "Ssh yourself," and slammed the kitchen door.

I was happy. I fell asleep at once. I had prayed for everybody: my talking family, cousins far away, passersby, and all the lonesome Christians. I expected to be heard. My voice was certainly the loudest.

EDNA O'BRIEN

The Doll

Every Christmas there came a present of a doll from a lady I scarcely knew. She was a friend of my mother's, and though they only met rarely, or accidentally at a funeral, she kept up the miraculous habit of sending me a doll. It would come on the evening bus shortly before Christmas, and it added to the hectic glow of those days when everything was charged with bustle and excitement. We made potato stuffing, we made mince pies, we made bowls of trifle, we decorated the windowsills with holly and with tinsel, and it was as if untoward happiness was about to befall us.

Each year's doll seemed to be more beautiful, more bewitching, and more sumptuously clad than the previous year's. They were of both sexes. There was a jockey in bright red and saffron, there was a Dutch drummer boy in maroon velvet, there was a sleeping doll in a crinoline, a creature of such fragile beauty that I used to fear for her when my sisters picked her up clumsily or tried to make her flutter her eyelashes. Her eyes were suggestive of beads and small blue flowers, having the haunting color of one and the smooth glaze of the other. She was named Rosalind.

My sisters, of course, were jealous and riled against the unfairness of my getting a doll, whereas they only got the usual dull flannel sock with tiny things in it, necessary things such as pencils, copybooks, plus some toffees and a licorice pipe. Each of my dolls was given a name, and a place of rest, in a corner or on a whatnot, or in an empty biscuit tin, and each had special conversations allotted to them, special endearments, and if necessary special chastisements. They had special times for fresh air—a doll would be brought out and splayed on a windowsill, or sunk down in the high grass and apparently abandoned. I had no favorites until the seventh doll came, and she was to me the living representation of a princess. She too was a sleeping doll, but a sizable one, and she was dressed in a pale-blue dress, with a gauze overdress, a pale-blue bonnet, and white kid button shoes. My sisters—who were older—were as smitten with her as I. She was uncanny. We all agreed that she was almost lifelike and that with coaxing she might speak. Her flaxen hair was like a feather to finger, her little wrists moved on a swivel, her eyelashes were black and sleek and the gaze in her eyes so fetching that we often thought she was not an inanimate creature, that she had a soul and a sense of us. Conversations with her were the most intense and the most incriminating of all.

It so happened that the teacher at school harbored a dislike for me and this for unfathomable reasons. I loved lessons, was first with my homework, always early for class, then always lighted the school fire, raked the ashes, and had a basket full of turf and wood when she arrived. In fact, my very diligence was what annoyed her and she would taunt me about it and proclaim what a "goody-goody" I was. She made jokes about my cardigan or my shoelaces or the slide in my hair, and to make the other girls laugh, she referred to me as "It." She would say, "It has a hole in its sock," or "It hasn't got a proper blazer," or "It has a daub on its copybook." I believe she hated me. If in an examination I came first—and I usually did—she would read out everyone's marks, leave mine until last, and say, "We know who swotted the most," as if I were in disgrace. If at cookery classes I made pancakes and offered her one, she would make a face as if I had offered her tripe or strychnine. She once got a big girl to give me fruit laxatives, pretending that they were sweets, and made great fun when I had to go in and out to the closets all day. It was a cruel cross to bear. When the inspector came and praised me, she said that I was brainy but that I lacked versatility. In direct contrast she was lovely to my sisters and would ask them occasionally how my mother was, and when was she going to send over a nice pot of homemade jam or a slab cake. I used to pray and make novenas that one day she would examine her conscience and think about how she wronged me and repent.

One day my prayers seemed on the point of being answered. It was November and already the girls were saving up for Christmas, and we knew that soon there would be the turkey market and soon after hams and candied peel in the grocery shop window. She said that since we'd all done so well in the catechism exam, she was going to get the infants to act in the school play and that we would build a crib and stack it with fresh hay and statues. Somebody said that my doll would make a most beautiful Virgin. Several girls had come home with me to see the doll and had been allowed to peep in at her in her box, which was lined with silver chaff. I brought her next day, and every head in the classroom craned as the teacher lifted the lid of the black lacquered box and looked in.

"She's passable," she said and told one of the girls to put the doll in the cookery cupboard until such time as she was needed. I grieved at being parted from her, but I was proud of the fact that she would be in the school play and be the cynosure of all. I had made her a cloak, a flowing blue cloak with a sheath of net over it and a little diamanté clasp. She was like a creature of moonlight, shimmering, even on dark wet days. The cookery cupboard was not a fit abode for her, but what could I do?

The play did not pass off without incident. The teacher's cousin Milo was drunk, belligerent, and offensive. He called girls up to the fire to pretend to talk to them and then touched the calves of their legs and tickled the backs of their knees. He called me up and asked would I click. He was an auctioneer from the city and unmarried. The teacher's two sons also came to look at the performance, but one of them left in the middle. He was strange and would laugh for no reason, and although over twenty he called the teacher "Mammy." He had very bright red hair and a peculiar stare in his eyes. For the most part, the infants forgot their lines, lost their heads, and the prompter was always late, so that the wrong girls picked up her cues. She was behind a curtain but could be heard out on the street. The whole thing was a fiasco. My doll was the star of the occasion and everyone raved about her.

Afterward there was tea and scones, and the teacher talked to those few mothers who had come. My mother had not come because at that time she was unable to confront crowds and even dreaded going to Mass on Sundays but believed that God would preserve her from the dizziness and suffocations that she was suffering from. After they had all left and a few of us had done the washing up, I went to the teacher and to my delight she gave me a wide genial smile. She thanked me for the doll, said that there was no denying but that the doll saved the play, and then, as I reached out, she staved my hand with a ruler and laughed heartily.

"You don't think I'm going to let you have her now, I've got quite fond of her . . . the little mite," she said, and gave the china cheek a tap. At home I was berserk. My mother said the teacher was probably teasing and that she would return the doll in a day or two. My father said that if she didn't she would have to answer to him, or else get a hammering. The days passed and the holidays came, and not only did she not give me my doll, but she took it to her own home and put it in the china cabinet along with cups and ornaments. Passing by their window, I would look in. I could not see her because the china cabinet was in a corner, but I knew where she was, as the maid Lizzie told me. I would press my forehead to the window and call to the doll and say that I was thinking of her and that rescue was being hatched.

Everyone agreed that it was monstrous, but no one talked to the teacher, no one tackled her. The truth is, they were afraid of her. She had a bitter tongue, and also, being superstitious, they felt that she could give us children brains or take them away, as a witch might. It was as if she could lift the brains out of us with a forceps and pickle them in brine. No one did anything, and in time I became reconciled to it. I asked once in a fit of bravura and the teacher said wasn't I becoming impudent. No longer did I halt to look in the window of her house but rather crossed the road, and I did not talk to Lizzie in case she should tell me something upsetting.

Once, I was sent to the teacher's house with a loin of pork and found her by the fire with her queer son, both of them with their stockings down, warming themselves. There were zigzags of heat on their shins. She asked if I wanted to go in and see the doll, but I declined. By then I was preparing to go away to boarding school and I knew that I would be free of her forever, that I would forget her, that I would forget the doll, forget most of what happened, or at least remember it without a quiver.

The years go by and everything and everyone gets replaced. Those we knew, though absent, are yet merged inextricably into new folk, so that each person is to us a sum of many others and the effect is of opening box after box in which the original is forever hidden.

The teacher dies a slow death, wastes to a thread through cancer, yet strives against it and says she is not ready. I hear the amount of money she left and her pitiable last words, but I feel nothing. I feel none of the rage and none of the despair. She does not matter to me anymore. I am on the run from them. I have fled. I live in a city. I am cosmopolitan. People come to my house, all sorts of people, and they do feats like dancing, or jesting, or singing, inventing a sort of private theater where we all play a part. I too play a part. My part is to receive them and disarm them, ply them with food and drink, and secretly be wary of them, be distanced from them. Like them I smile, and drift; like them I smoke or drink to induce a feverishness or a pleasant wandering hallucination. It was not something I cultivated. It developed of its own accord, like a spore that breathes in the darkness. So I am far from those I am with, and far from those I have left. At night I enjoy the farness. In the morning I touch a table or a teacup to make sure that it is a table or a teacup, and I talk to it, and I water the flowers and I talk to them, and I think how tender flowers are, and woods and woodsmoke and possibly how tender are my new friends, but that like me they are intent on concealment. None of us ever says where we come from or what haunts us. Perhaps we are bewildered or ashamed.

I go back. Duty hauls me back to see the remaining relatives, and I play the expected part. I had to call on the teacher's son. He was the undertaker and was in charge of my aunt's burial. I went to pay him, to "fix up," as it is called. His wife, whom I knew to be a bit scattered, admitted me amid peals of laughter. She said she always thought I had jet black hair, as she ran down the hall calling his name. His name is Denis. He shakes hands with me very formally, asks what kind of wreath I want and if it should be heart-shaped, circular, or in the form of a cross. I leave it all to him. There in the overstuffed china cabinet is my confiscated doll, and if dolls can age, it certainly had. Gray and moldy, the dress and cloak are as a shroud, and I thought, If I was to pick her up she would disintegrate.

"God, my mother was fond of her," he said, as if he were trying to tell me that she had been fond of me, too. Had he said so, I might have challenged. I was older now and it was clear to me that she had kept the doll out of perversity, out of pique and jealousy. In some way she had divined that I would have a life far away from them and adventures such as she herself would never taste. Sensing my chill, he boasted that he had not let his own children play with the doll, thereby implying that she was a sacred object, a treasured souvenir. He hauled out a brandy bottle and winked, expecting me to say yes. I declined.

A sickness had come over me, a sort of nausea for having cared so much about the doll, for having let them maltreat me, and now for no longer caring at all. My abrupt departure puzzled him. He did something unto-ward. He tried to kiss me. He thought perhaps that in my world it was the expected thing. Except that the kiss was proffered as a sympathy kiss, a kiss of condolence over my aunt's death. His face had the sour smell of a towel that he must have dried himself on, just before he came to welcome me. The kiss was clumsiness personified. I pitied him, but I could not stay, and I could not reminisce, and I could not pretend to be the fast kiss-easy woman he imagined me to be.

Walking down the street, where I walk in memory, morning noon and night, I could not tell what it was, precisely, that reduced me to such wretchedness. Indeed, it was not death but rather the gnawing conviction of not having yet lived. All I could tell was that the stars were as singular and as wondrous as I remembered them and that they still seemed like a link, an enticement to the great heavens, and that one day I would reach them and be absorbed into their glory, and pass from a world that, at that moment, I found to be rife with cruelty and stupidity, a world that had forgotten how to give.

Tomorrow . . . I thought. Tomorrow I shall be gone, and realized that I had not lost the desire to escape or the strenuous habit of hoping.

BOBBIE ANN MASON

Drawing Names

On Christmas Day, Carolyn Sisson went early to her parents' house to help her mother with the dinner. Carolyn had been divorced two years before, and last Christmas, coming alone, she had felt uncomfortable. This year she had invited her lover, Kent Ballard, to join the family gathering. She had even brought him a present to put under the tree, so he wouldn't feel left out. Kent was planning to drive over from Kentucky Lake by noon. He had gone there to inspect his boat because of an ice storm earlier in the week. He felt compelled to visit his boat on the holiday, Carolyn thought, as if it were a sad old relative in a retirement home.

"We're having baked ham instead of turkey," Mom said. "Your daddy never did like ham baked, but whoever heard of fried ham on Christmas? We have that all year round and I'm burned out on it."

"I love baked ham," said Carolyn.

"Does Kent like it baked?"

"I'm sure he does." Carolyn placed her gifts under the tree. The number of packages seemed unusually small.

"It don't seem like Christmas with drawed names," said Mom.

"Your star's about to fall off." Carolyn straightened the silver ornament at the tip of the tree.

"I didn't decorate as much as I wanted to. I'm slowing down. Getting old, I guess." Mom had not combed her hair, and she was wearing a work shirt and tennis shoes.

"You always try to do too much on Christmas, Mom."

Carolyn knew the agreement to draw names had bothered her mother. But the four daughters were grown, and two had children. Sixteen people were expected today. Carolyn herself could not afford to buy fifteen presents on her salary as a clerk at J. C. Penney's, and her parents' small farm had not been profitable in years.

Carolyn's father appeared in the kitchen, and he hugged her so tightly she squealed in protest.

"That's all I can afford this year," he said, laughing. As he took a piece of candy from a dish on the counter, Carolyn teased him. "You'd better watch your calories today."

"Oh, not on Christmas!"

It made Carolyn sad to see her handsome father getting older. He was a shy man, awkward with his daughters, and Carolyn knew he had been deeply disappointed over her failed marriage, although he had never said so. Now he asked, "Who bought these 'toes'?"

He would no longer say "nigger toes," his old name for the chocolate-covered creams.

"Hattie Smoot brought those over," said Mom. "I made a pants suit for her last week," she said to Carolyn. "She's the woman that had stomach bypass?"

"When PeeWee McClain had that, it didn't work and they had to fix him back like he was," said Dad. He offered Carolyn a piece of candy, but she shook her head no.

Mom said, "I made Hattie a dress back last spring for her boy's graduation, and she couldn't even find a pattern big enough. I had to 'low a foot. But after that bypass, she's down to a size twenty."

"I think we'll all need a stomach bypass after we eat this feast you're fixing," said Carolyn.

"Where's Kent?" Dad asked abruptly.

"He went to see about his boat. He said he'd be here."

Carolyn looked at the clock. She felt uneasy about inviting Kent. Everyone would be scrutinizing him, as if he were some new character on a soap opera. Kent, who drove a truck for the Kentucky Loose-Leaf Floor, was a part-time student at Murray State. He was majoring in accounting. When Carolyn had started going with him, early in the summer, they had gone sailing on his boat, which had "Joyce" painted on it. Later, he painted over the name, insisting he didn't love Joyce anymore, but he had never said he loved Carolyn. She did not know if she loved him. Each seemed to be waiting for the other to say it first.

While Carolyn helped her mother in the kitchen, Dad went to get her grandfather, her mother's father. Pappy, who had been disabled by a stroke, was cared for by a live-in housekeeper who had gone home to her own family for the day. Carolyn diced apples and pears for fruit salad while her mother shaped sweet-potato balls with marshmallow centers and rolled them in crushed cornflakes. On TV in the living room, "Days of Our Lives" was beginning, but the Christmas tree blocked their view of the television set.

"Whose name did you draw, Mom?" Carolyn asked, as she began seeding the grapes.

"Jim's."

"You put Jim's name in the hat?"

Mom nodded. Jim Walsh was the man Carolyn's younger sister, Laura Jean, was living with in St. Louis. Laura Jean was going to an interior-decorating school, and Jim was a textiles salesman she had met in a class. "I made him a shirt," Mom said.

"I'm surprised at you."

"Well, what was I to do?"

"I'm just surprised." Carolyn ate a grape and spit out the seeds. "Emily Post says the couple should be offered the same room when they visit."

"You know we'd never stand for that. I don't think your dad's ever got over her stacking up with that guy."

"You mean shacking up."

"Same thing." Mom dropped the potato masher, and the metal rattled on the floor. "Oh, I'm in such a tizzy," she said.

* * *

As the family began to arrive, the noise of the TV played against the greetings, the slam of the storm door, the outside wind rushing in. Carolyn's older sisters, Peggy and Iris, with their husbands and children, were arriving all at once, and suddenly the house seemed small. Peggy's children Stevie and Cheryl, without even removing their jackets, became involved in a basketball game on TV. In his lap, Stevie had a Merlin electronic toy, which beeped randomly. Iris and Ray's children, Deedee and Jonathan, went outside to look for cats.

In the living room, Peggy jiggled her baby, Lisa, on her hip and said, "You need you one of these, Carolyn."

"Where can I get one?" said Carolyn rather sharply.

Peggy grinned. "At the gittin' place, I reckon."

Peggy's critical tone was familiar. She was the only sister who had had a real wedding. Her husband, Cecil, had a Gulf franchise, and they owned a motor-cruiser, a pickup truck, a camper, a station wagon, and a new brick colonial home. Whenever Carolyn went to visit Peggy, she felt apologetic for not having a man who would buy her all these things, but she never seemed to be attracted to anyone steady or ambitious. She had been wondering how Kent would get along with the men of the family. Cecil and Ray were standing in a corner talking about gas mileage. Cecil, who was shorter than Peggy and was going bald, always worked on Dad's truck for free, and Ray usually agreed with Dad on politics to avoid an argument. Ray had an impressive government job in Frankfort. He had coordinated a ribbon-cutting ceremony when the toll road opened. What would Kent have to say to them? She could imagine him insisting that everyone go outside later to watch the sunset. Her father would think that was ridiculous. No one ever did that on a farm, but it was the sort of thing Kent would think of. Yet she knew that spontaneity was what she liked in him.

Deedee and Jonathan, who were ten and six, came inside then and immediately began shaking the presents under the tree. All the children were wearing new jeans and cowboy shirts, Carolyn noticed.

"Why are y'all so quiet?" she asked. "I thought kids whooped and hollered on Christmas."

"They've been up since *four*," said Iris. She took a cigarette from her purse and accepted a light from Cecil. Exhaling smoke, she said to Carolyn, "We heard Kent was coming." Before Carolyn could reply, Iris scolded the children for shaking the packages. She seemed nervous.

"He's supposed to be here by noon," said Carolyn.

"There's somebody now. I hear a car."

"It might be Dad, with Pappy."

It was Laura Jean, showing off Jim Walsh as though he were a splendid Christmas gift she had just received.

"Let me kiss everybody!" she cried, as the women rushed toward her. Laura Jean had not been home in four months.

"Merry Christmas!" Jim said in a booming, official-sounding voice, something like a TV announcer, Carolyn thought. He embraced all the women and then, with a theatrical gesture, he handed Mom a bottle of Rebel Yell bourbon and a carton of boiled custard, which he took from a shopping bag. The bourbon was in a decorative Christmas box.

Mom threw up her hands. "Oh, no, I'm afraid I'll be a alky-holic."

"Oh, that's ridiculous, Mom," said Laura Jean, taking Jim's coat. "A couple of drinks a day are good for your heart."

Jim insisted on getting coffee cups from a kitchen cabinet and mixing some boiled custard and bourbon. When he handed a cup to Mom, she puckered up her face.

"Law, don't let the preacher in," she said, taking a sip. "Boy, that sends my blood pressure up."

Carolyn waved away the drink that Jim offered her. "I don't start this early in the day," she said, feeling confused.

Jim was a large, dark-haired man with a neat little beard, like a bird's nest cupped on his chin. He had a northern accent. When he hugged her, Carolyn caught a whiff of cologne, something sweet, like chocolate syrup. Last summer, when Laura Jean had brought him home for the first time, she had made a point of kissing and hugging him in front of everyone. Dad had virtually ignored him. Now Carolyn saw that Jim was telling Cecil that he always bought Gulf gas. Red-faced, Ray accepted a cup of boiled custard.

Carolyn fled to the kitchen and began grating cheese for potatoes au gratin. She dreaded Kent's arrival.

When Dad arrived with Pappy, Cecil and Jim helped set up the wheelchair in a corner. Afterward, Dad and Jim shook hands, and Dad refused Jim's offer of bourbon. From the kitchen, Carolyn could see Dad hugging Laura Jean, not letting go. She went into the living room to greet her grandfather.

"They roll me in this buggy too fast," he said when she kissed his forehead.

Carolyn hoped he wouldn't notice the bottle of bourbon, but she knew he never missed anything. He was so deaf people had given up talking to him. Now the children tiptoed around him, looking at him with awe. Somehow, Carolyn expected the children to notice that she was alone, like Pappy.

At ten minutes of one, the telephone rang. Peggy answered and handed the receiver to Carolyn. "It's Kent," she said.

Kent had not left the lake yet. "I just got here an hour ago," he told Carolyn. "I had to take my sister over to my mother's."

"Is the boat OK?"

"Yeah. Just a little scraped paint. I'll be ready to go in a little while." He hesitated, as though waiting for assurance that the invitation was real.

"This whole gang's ready to eat," Carolyn said. "Can't you hurry?" She should have remembered the way he tended to get sidetracked. Once it took them three hours to get to Paducah, because he kept stopping at antique shops.

After she hung up the telephone, her mother asked, "Should I put the rolls in to brown yet?"

"Wait just a little. He's just now leaving the lake."

"When's this Kent feller coming?" asked Dad impatiently, as he peered into the kitchen. "It's time to eat."

"He's on his way," said Carolyn.

"Did you tell him we don't wait for stragglers?"

"No."

"When the plate rattles, we eat."

"I know."

"Did you tell him that?"

"No, I didn't!" cried Carolyn, irritated.

When they were alone in the kitchen, Carolyn's mother said to her, "Your dad's not hisself today. He's fit to be tied about Laura Jean bringing that guy down here again. And him bringing that whiskey."

"That was uncalled for," Carolyn agreed. She had noticed that Mom had set her cup of eggnog in the refrigerator.

"Besides, he's not too happy about that Kent Ballard you're running around with."

"What's it to him?"

"You know how he always was. He don't think anybody's good enough for one of his little girls, and he's afraid you'll get mistreated again. He don't think Kent's very dependable."

"I guess Kent's proving Dad's point."

Carolyn's sister Iris had dark brown eyes, unique in the family. When Carolyn was small, she tried to say "Iris's eyes" once and called them "Irish eyes," confusing them with a song their mother sometimes sang, "When Irish Eyes Are Smiling." Thereafter, they always teased Iris about her smiling Irish eyes. Today Iris was not smiling. Carolyn found her in a bedroom smoking, holding an ashtray in her hand.

"I drew your name," Carolyn told her. "I got you something I wanted myself."

"Well, if I don't want it, I guess I'll have to give it to you."

"What's wrong with you today?"

"Ray and me's getting a separation," said Iris.

"Really?" Carolyn was startled by the note of glee in her response. Actually, she told herself later, it was because she was glad her sister, whom she saw infrequently, had confided in her.

"The thing of it is, I had to beg him to come today, for Mom and Dad's sake. It'll kill them. Don't let on, will you?"

"I won't. What are you going to do?"

"I don't know. He's already moved out."

"Are you going to stay in Frankfort?"

"I don't know. I have to work things out."

Mom stuck her head in the door. "Well, is Kent coming or not?"

"He *said* he'd be here," said Carolyn.

"Your dad's about to have a duck with a rubber tail. He can't stand to wait on a meal."

"Well, let's go ahead then. Kent can eat when he gets here."

When Mom left, Iris said, "Aren't you and Kent getting along?"

"I don't know. He said he'd come today, but I have a feeling he doesn't really want to."

"To hell with men." Iris laughed and stubbed out her cigarette. "Just look at us—didn't we turn out awful? First your divorce. Now me. And Laura Jean bringing that guy down. Daddy can't stand him. Did you see the look he gave him?"

"Laura Jean's got a lot more nerve than I've got," said Carolyn, nodding. "I could wring Kent's neck for being late. Well, none of us can do anything right—except Peggy."

"Daddy's precious little angel," said Iris mockingly. "Come on, we'd better get in there and help."

While Mom went to change her blouse and put on lipstick, the sisters brought the food into the dining room. Two tables had been put together. Peggy cut the ham with an electric knife, and Carolyn filled the iced-tea glasses.

"Pappy gets buttermilk and Stevie gets Coke," Peggy directed her.

"I know," said Carolyn, almost snapping.

As the family sat down, Carolyn realized that no one ever asked Pappy to "turn thanks" anymore at holiday dinners. He was sitting there expectantly, as if waiting to be asked. Mom cut up his ham into small bits. Carolyn waited for a car to drive up, the phone to ring. The TV was still on.

"Y'all dig in," said Mom. "Jim? Make sure you try some of these dressed eggs like I fix."

"I thought your new boyfriend was coming," said Cecil to Carolyn.

"So did I!" said Laura Jean. "That's what you wrote me."

Everyone looked at Carolyn as she explained. She looked away.

"You're looking at that pitiful tree," Mom said to her. "I just know it don't show up good from the road."

"No, it looks fine." No one had really noticed the tree. Carolyn seemed to be seeing it for the first time in years—broken red-plastic reindeer, Styrofoam snowmen with crumbling top hats, silver walnuts, which she remembered painting when she was about twelve.

Dad began telling a joke about some monks who had taken a vow of silence. At each Christmas dinner, he said, one monk was allowed to speak.

"Looks like your vocal cords would rust out," said Cheryl.

"Shut up, Cheryl. Granddaddy's trying to tell something," said Cecil.

"So the first year it was the first monk's turn to talk, and you know what he said? He said, 'These taters is lumpy.' "

When several people laughed, Stevie asked, "Is that the joke?"

Carolyn was baffled. Her father had never told a joke at the table in his life. He sat at the head of the table, looking out past the family at the cornfield through the picture window.

"Pay attention, now," he said. "The second year Christmas rolled around again and it was the second monk's turn to say something. He said, 'You know, I think you're right. The taters *is* lumpy.' "

Laura Jean and Jim laughed loudly.

"Reach me some light bread," said Pappy. Mom passed the dish around the table to him.

"And so the third year," Dad continued, "the third monk got to say something. What he said—" Dad was suddenly overcome with mirth— "what he said was, 'If y'all don't shut up arguing about them taters, I'm going to leave this place!' "

After the laughter died, Mom said, "Can you imagine anybody not atalking all year long?"

"That's the way monks are, Mom," said Laura Jean. "Monks are economical with everything. They're not wasteful, not even with words."

"The Trappist monks are really an outstanding group," said Jim. "And they make excellent bread. No preservatives."

Cecil and Peggy stared at Jim.

"You're not eating, Dad," said Carolyn. She was sitting between him and the place set for Kent. The effort at telling the joke seemed to have taken her father's appetite.

"He ruined his dinner on nigger toes," said Mom.

"Dottie Barlow got a Barbie doll for Christmas and it's black," Cheryl said.

"Dottie Barlow ain't black, is she?" asked Cecil.

"No."

"That's funny," said Peggy. "Why would they give her a black Barbie doll?"

"She just wanted it."

Abruptly, Dad left the table, pushing back his plate. He sat down in the recliner chair in front of the TV. The Blue-Gray game was beginning, and Cecil and Ray were hurriedly finishing in order to join him. Carolyn took out second helpings of ham and Jell-O salad, feeling as though she was eating for Kent in his absence. Jim was taking seconds of everything, complimenting Mom. Mom apologized for not having fancy napkins. Then Laura Jean described a photography course she had taken. She had been photographing close-ups of car parts—fenders, headlights, mud flaps.

"That sounds goofy," said one of the children, Deedee.

Suddenly Pappy spoke. "Use to, the menfolks would eat first, and the children separate. The womenfolks would eat last, in the kitchen."

"You know what I could do with you all, don't you?" said Mom, shaking her fist at him. "I could set up a plank out in the field for y'all to eat on." She laughed.

"Times are different now, Pappy," said Iris loudly. "We're just as good as the men."

"She gets that from television," said Ray, with an apologetic laugh.

Carolyn noticed Ray's glance at Iris. Just then Iris matter-of-factly plucked an eyelash from Ray's cheek. It was as though she had momentarily forgotten about the separation.

Later, after the gifts were opened, Jim helped clear the tables. Kent still had not come. The baby slept, and Laura Jean, Jim, Peggy, and Mom played a *Star Trek* board game at the dining room table, while Carolyn and Iris played "Battlestar Galactica" with Cheryl and Deedee. The other men were quietly engrossed in a football game, a blur of sounds. No one had mentioned Kent's absence, but after the children had distributed the gifts, Carolyn refused to tell them what was in the lone package left under the tree. It was the most extravagantly wrapped of all the presents, with an immense ribbon, not a stick-on bow. An icicle had dropped on it, and it reminded Carolyn of an abandoned float from a parade.

At a quarter to three, Kent telephoned. He was still at the lake. "The gas stations are all closed," he said. "I couldn't get any gas."

"We already ate and opened the presents," said Carolyn.

"Here I am, stranded. Not a thing I can do about it."

Kent's voice was shaky and muffled, and Carolyn suspected he had been drinking. She did not know what to say, in front of the family. She chattered idly, while she played with a ribbon from a package. The baby was awake, turning dials and knobs on a Busy Box. On TV, the Blues picked up six yards on an end sweep. Carolyn fixed her eyes on the tilted star at the top of the tree. Kent was saying something about Santa Claus.

"They wanted me to play Santy at Mama's house for the littl'uns. I said—you know what I said? 'Bah, humbug!' Did I ever tell you what I've got against Christmas?"

"Maybe not." Carolyn's back stiffened against the wall.

"When I was little bitty, Santa Claus came to town. I was about five. I was all fired up to go see Santy, and Mama took me, but we were late, and he was about to leave. I had to run across the courthouse square to get to him. He was giving away suckers, so I ran as hard as I could. He was climbing up on the fire engine—are you listening?"

"Unh-huh." Carolyn was watching her mother, who was folding Christmas paper to save for next year.

Kent said, "I reached up and pulled at his old red pants leg, and he looked down at me, and you know what he said?"

"No, what?"

"He said, 'Piss off, kid.' "

"Really?"

"Would I lie to you?"

"I don't know."

"Do you want to hear the rest of my hard-luck story?"

"Not now."

"Oh, I forgot this was long-distance. I'll call you tomorrow. Maybe I'll go paint the boat. That's what I'll do! I'll go paint it right this minute."

After Carolyn hung up the telephone, her mother said, "I think my Oriental casserole was a failure. I used the wrong kind of mushroom soup. It called for cream of mushroom and I used golden mushroom."

"Won't you *ever* learn, Mom?" cried Carolyn. "You always cook too much. You make *such* a big deal—"

Mom said, "What happened with Kent this time?"

"He couldn't get gas. He forgot the gas stations were closed."

"Jim and Laura Jean didn't have any trouble getting gas," said Peggy, looking up from the game.

"We tanked up yesterday," said Laura Jean.

"Of course you did," said Carolyn distractedly. "You always think ahead."

"It's your time," Cheryl said, handing Carolyn the "Battlestar Galactica" toy. "I did lousy."

"Not as lousy as I did," said Iris.

Carolyn tried to concentrate on shooting enemy missiles raining through space. Her sisters seemed far away, like the spaceships. She was aware of the men watching football, their hands in action as they followed an exciting play. Even though Pappy had fallen asleep, with his blanket in his lap he looked like a king on a throne. Carolyn thought of the quiet accommodation her father had made to his father-in-law, just as Cecil and Ray had done with Dad, and her ex-husband had tried to do once. But Cecil had bought his way in, and now Ray was getting out. Kent had stayed away. Jim, the newcomer, was with the women, playing *Star Trek* as if his life depended upon it. Carolyn was glad now that Kent had not come. The story he had told made her angry, and his pity for his childhood make her think of something Pappy had often said—"Christmas is for children." Earlier, she had listened in amazement while Cheryl listed on her fingers the gifts she had received that morning: a watch, a stereo, a nightgown, hot curls, perfume, candles, a sweater, a calculator, a jewelry box, a ring. Now Carolyn saw Kent's boat as his toy, more important to him than the family obligations of the holiday.

Mom was saying, "I wanted to make a Christmas tablecloth out of red checks with green fringe. You wouldn't think knit would do for a tablecloth, but Hattie Smoot has the prettiest one."

"You can do incredible things with knit," said Jim with sudden enthusiasm. The shirt Mom had made him was bonded knit.

"Who's Hattie Smoot?" asked Laura Jean. She was caressing the back of Jim's neck, as though soothing his nerves.

Carolyn laughed when her mother began telling Jim and Laura Jean about Hattie Smoot's operation. Jim listened attentively, leaning forward with his elbows on the table, and asked eager questions, his eyes as alert as Pappy's.

"Is she telling a joke?" Cheryl asked Carolyn.

"No. I'm not laughing at you, Mom," Carolyn said, touching her mother's hand. She felt relieved that the anticipation of Christmas had ended. Still laughing, she said, "Pour me some of that Rebel Yell, Jim. It's time."

"I'm with you," Jim said, jumping up.

In the kitchen, Carolyn located a clean spoon while Jim washed some cups. Carolyn couldn't find the cup Mom had left in the refrigerator. As she took out the carton of boiled custard, Jim said, "It must be a very difficult day for you."

Carolyn was startled. His tone was unexpectedly kind, genuine. She was struck suddenly by what he must know about her, because of his intimacy with her sister. She knew nothing about him. When he smiled, she saw a gold cap on a molar, shining like a Christmas ornament. She managed to say, "It can't be any picnic for you, either. Kent didn't want to put up with us."

"Too bad he couldn't get gas."

"I don't think he wanted to get gas."

"Then you're better off without him." When Jim looked at her, Carolyn felt that he must be examining her resemblance to Laura Jean. He said, "I think your family's great."

Carolyn laughed nervously. "We're hard on you. God, you're brave to come down here like this."

"Well, Laura Jean's worth it."

They took the boiled custard and cups into the dining room. As Carolyn sat down, her nephew Jonathan begged her to tell what was in the gift left under the tree.

"I can't tell," she said.

"Why not?"

"I'm saving it till next year, in case I draw some man's name."

"I hope it's mine," said Jonathan.

Jim stirred bourbon into three cups of boiled custard, and gave one to Carolyn and one to Laura Jean. The others had declined. Then he leaned back in his chair—more relaxed now—and squeezed Laura Jean's hand. Carolyn wondered what they said to each other when they were alone, in St. Louis. She knew with certainty that they would not be economical with words, like the monks in the story. She longed to be with them, to hear what they would say. She noticed her mother picking at a hangnail, quietly ignoring the bourbon. Looking at the bottle's gift box, which showed an old-fashioned scene, children on sleds in the snow, Carolyn thought of

Kent's boat again. She felt she was in that snowy scene now with Laura Jean and Jim, sailing in Kent's boat into the winter breeze, into falling snow. She thought of how silent it was out on the lake, as though the whiteness of the snow were the absence of sound.

"Cheers!" she said to Jim, lifting her cup.

ANN BEATTIE

Where You'll Find Me

Friends keep calling my broken arm a broken wing. It's the left arm, now folded against my chest and kept in place with a blue scarf sling that is knotted behind my neck, and it weighs too much ever to have been winglike. The accident happened when I ran for a bus. I tried to stop it from pulling away by shaking my shopping bags like maracas in the air, and that's when I slipped on the ice and went down.

So I took the train from New York City to Saratoga yesterday, instead of driving. I had the perfect excuse not to go to Saratoga to visit my brother at all, but once I had geared up for it I decided to go through with the trip and avoid guilt. It isn't Howard I mind but his wife's two children—a girl of eleven and a boy of three. Becky either pays no attention to her brother Todd or else she tortures him. Last winter she used to taunt him by stalking around the house on his heels, clomping close behind him wherever he went, which made him run and scream at the same time. Kate did not intervene until both children became hysterical and we could no longer shout over their voices. "I think I like it that they're physical," she said. "Maybe if they enact some of their hostility like this, they won't grow up with the habit of getting what they want by playing mind games with other people." It seems to me that they will not ever grow up but will burn out like meteors.

Howard has finally found what he wants: the opposite of domestic tranquillity. For six years, he lived in Oregon with a pale, passive woman. On the rebound, he married an even paler pre-med student named Francine.

197

That marriage lasted less than a year, and then, on a blind date in Los Angeles, he met Kate, whose husband was away on a business trip to Denmark just then. In no time, Kate and her daughter and infant son moved in with him, to the studio apartment in Laguna Beach he was sharing with a screenwriter. The two men had been working on a script about Medgar Evers, but when Kate and the children moved in they switched to writing a screenplay about what happens when a man meets a married woman with two children on a blind date and the three of them move in with him and his friend. Then Howard's collaborator got engaged and moved out, and the screenplay was abandoned. Howard accepted a last-minute invitation to teach writing at an upstate college in New York, and within a week they were all ensconced in a drafty Victorian house in Saratoga. Kate's husband had begun divorce proceedings before she moved in with Howard, but eventually he agreed not to sue for custody of Becky and Todd in exchange for child-support payments that were less than half of what his lawyer thought he would have to pay. Now he sends the children enormous stuffed animals that they have little or no interest in, with notes that say, "Put this in Mom's zoo." A stuffed toy every month or so—giraffes, a life-size German shepherd, an overstuffed standing bear—and, every time, the same note.

The bear stands in one corner of the kitchen, and people have gotten in the habit of pinning notes to it—reminders to buy milk or get the oil changed in the car. Wraparound sunglasses have been added. Scarves and jackets are sometimes draped on its arms. Sometimes the stuffed German shepherd is brought over and propped up with its paws placed on the bear's haunch, imploring it.

Right now, I'm in the kitchen with the bear. I've just turned up the thermostat—the first one up in the morning is supposed to do that—and am dunking a tea bag in a mug of hot water. For some reason, it's impossible for me to make tea with loose tea and the tea ball unless I have help. The only tea bag I could find was Emperor's Choice.

I sit in one of the kitchen chairs to drink the tea. The chair seems to stick to me, even though I have on thermal long johns and a long flannel nightgown. The chairs are plastic, very nineteen-fifties, patterned with shapes that look sometimes geometric, sometimes almost human. Little things like malformed hands reach out toward triangles and squares. I asked. Howard and Kate got the kitchen set at an auction, for thirty dollars. They thought it was funny. The house itself is not funny. It has four fireplaces, wide-board floors, and high, dusty ceilings. They bought it with his share of an inheritance that came to us when our grandfather died. Kate's contribution to restoring the house has been transforming the baseboards into *faux marbre*. How effective this is has to do with how stoned she is when she starts. Sometimes the baseboards look like clotted versions of the kitchen-chair pattern, instead of marble. Kate considers what she calls "parenting" to be a full-time job. When they first moved to Saratoga, she used to give piano lessons. Now she ignores the children and paints the baseboards.

And who am I to stand in judgment? I am a thirty-eight-year-old woman, out of a job, on tenuous enough footing with her sometime lover that she can imagine crashing emotionally as easily as she did on the ice. It may be true, as my lover, Frank, says, that having money is not good for the soul. Money that is given to you, that is. He is a lawyer who also has money, but it is money he earned and parlayed into more money by investing in real estate. An herb farm is part of this real estate. Boxes of herbs keep turning up at Frank's office—herbs in foil, herbs in plastic bags, dried herbs wrapped in cones of newspaper. He crumbles them over omelets, roasts, vegetables. He is opposed to salt. He insists herbs are more healthful.

And who am I to claim to love a man when I am skeptical even about his use of herbs? I am embarrassed to be unemployed. I am insecure enough to stay with someone because of the look that sometimes comes into his eyes when he makes love to me. I am a person who secretly shakes on salt in the kitchen, then comes out with her plate, smiling, as basil is crumbled over the tomatoes.

Sometimes, in our bed, his fingers smell of rosemary or tarragon. Strong smells. Sour smells. Whatever Shakespeare says, or whatever is written in *Culpeper's Complete Herbal*, I cannot imagine that herbs have anything to do with love. But many brides-to-be come to the herb farm and buy branches of herbs to stick in their bouquets. They anoint their wrists with herbal extracts, to smell mysterious. They believe that herbs bring them luck. These days, they want tubs of rosemary in their houses, not ficus trees. "I got in right on the cusp of the new world," Frank says. He isn't kidding.

For the Christmas party tonight, there are cherry tomatoes halved and stuffed with peaks of cheese, mushrooms stuffed with pureed tomatoes, tomatoes stuffed with chopped mushrooms, and mushrooms stuffed with cheese. Kate is laughing in the kitchen. "No one's going to notice," she mutters. "No one's going to say anything."

"Why don't we put out some nuts?" Howard says.

"Nuts are so conventional. This is funny," Kate says, squirting more soft cheese out of a pastry tube.

"Last year we had mistletoe and mulled cider."

"Last year we lost our sense of humor. What happened that we got all hyped up? We even ran out on Christmas Eve to cut a tree—"

"The kids," Howard says.

"That's right," she says. "The kids were crying. They were feeling competitive with the other kids, or something."

"Becky was crying. Todd was too young to cry about that," Howard says.

"Why are we talking about tears?" Kate says. "We can talk about tears when it's not the season to be jolly. Everybody's going to come in tonight and love the wreaths on the picture hooks and think this food is so *festive*."

"We invited a new Indian guy from the Philosophy Department," Howard says. "American Indian—not an Indian from India."

"If we want, we can watch the tapes of *Jewel in the Crown*," Kate says.

"I'm feeling really depressed," Howard says, backing up to the counter and sliding down until he rests on his elbows. His tennis shoes are wet. He never takes off his wet shoes, and he never gets colds.

"Try one of those mushrooms," Kate says. "They'll be better when they're cooked, though."

"What's wrong with me?" Howard says. It's almost the first time he's looked at me since I arrived. I've been trying not to register my boredom and my frustration with Kate's prattle.

"Maybe we should get a tree," I say.

"I don't think it's Christmas that's making me feel this way," Howard says.

"Well, snap out of it," Kate says. "You can open one of your presents early, if you want to."

"No, no," Howard says, "it isn't Christmas." He hands a plate to Kate, who has begun to stack the dishwasher. "I've been worrying that you're in a lot of pain and you just aren't saying so," he says to me.

"It's just uncomfortable," I say.

"I know, but do you keep going over what happened, in your mind? When you fell, or in the emergency room, or anything?"

"I had a dream last night about the ballerinas at Victoria Pool," I say. "It was like Victoria Pool was a stage set instead of a real place, and tall, thin ballerinas kept parading in and twirling and pirouetting. I was envying their being able to touch their fingertips together over their heads."

Howard opens the top level of the dishwasher and Kate begins to hand him the rinsed glasses.

"You just told a little story," Howard says. "You didn't really answer the question."

"I don't keep going over it in my mind," I say.

"So you're repressing it," he says.

"Mom," Becky says, walking into the kitchen, "is it OK if Deirdre comes to the party tonight if her dad doesn't drive here to pick her up this weekend?"

"I thought her father was in the hospital," Kate says.

"Yeah, he was. But he got out. He called and said that it was going to snow up north, though, so he wasn't sure if he could come."

"Of course she can come," Kate says.

"And you know what?" Becky says.

"Say hello to people when you come into a room," Kate says. "At least make eye contact or smile or something."

"I'm not Miss America on the runway, Mom. I'm just walking into the kitchen."

"You have to acknowledge people's existence," Kate says. "Haven't we talked about this?"

"Oh, hel-*lo*," Becky says, curtsying by pulling out the sides of an imaginary skirt. She has on purple sweatpants. She turns toward me and pulls the fabric away from her hipbones. "Oh, hello, as if we've never met," she says.

"Your aunt here doesn't want to be in the middle of this," Howard says. "She's got enough trouble."

"Get back on track," Kate says to Becky. "What did you want to say to me?"

"You know what you do, Mom?" Becky says. "You make an issue of something and then it's like when I speak it's a big thing. Everybody's listening to me."

Kate closes the door to the dishwasher.

"Did you want to speak to me privately?" she says.

"Nooo," Becky says, sitting in the chair across from me and sighing. "I was just going to say—and now it's a big deal—I was going to say that Deirdre just found out that that guy she was writing all year is in *prison*. He was in prison all the time, but she didn't know what the P.O. box meant."

"What's she going to do?" Howard says.

"She's going to write and ask him all about prison," Becky says.

"That's good," Howard says. "That cheers me up to hear that. The guy probably agonized about whether to tell her or not. He probably thought she'd hot-potato him."

"Lots of decent people go to prison," Becky says.

"That's ridiculous," Kate says. "You can't generalize about convicts any more than you can generalize about the rest of humanity."

"So?" Becky says. "If somebody in the rest of humanity had something to hide, he'd hide it, too, wouldn't he?"

"Let's go get a tree," Howard says. "We'll get a tree."

"Somebody got hit on the highway carrying a tree home," Becky says. "Really."

"You really do have your ear to the ground in this town," Kate says. "You kids could be the town crier. I know everything before the paper comes."

"It happened yesterday," Becky says.

"Christ," Howard says. "We're talking about crying, we're talking about death." He is leaning against the counter again.

"We are not," Kate says, walking in front of him to open the refrigerator door. She puts a plate of stuffed tomatoes inside. "In your typical fashion, you've singled out two observations out of a lot that have been made, and—"

"I woke up thinking about Dennis Bidou last night," Howard says to me. "Remember Dennis Bidou, who used to taunt you? Dad put me up to having it out with him, and he backed down after that. But I was always afraid he'd come after me. I went around for years pretending not to cringe when he came near me. And then, you know, one time I was out on a date and we ran out of gas, and as I was walking to get a can of gas a car pulled up alongside me and Dennis Bidou leaned out the window. He was surprised that it was me and I was surprised that it was him. He asked me what happened and I said I ran out of gas. He said, 'Tough shit, I guess,' but a girl was driving and she gave him a hard time. She stopped the car and insisted that I get in the back and they'd take me to the gas station. He didn't say one word to me the whole way there. I remembered the way he looked in the car when I found out he was killed in Nam—the back of his head on that ramrod-straight body, and a black collar or some dark-colored collar pulled up to his hairline." Howard makes a horizontal motion with four fingers, thumb folded under, in the air beside his ear.

"Now you're trying to depress everybody," Kate says.

"I'm willing to cheer up. I'm going to cheer up before tonight. I'm going up to that Lions Club lot on Main Street and get a tree. Anybody coming with me?"

"I'm going over to Deirdre's," Becky says.

"I'll come with you, if you think my advice is needed," I say.

"For fun," Howard says, bouncing on his toes. "For fun—not advice."

He gets my red winter coat out of the closet, and I back into it, putting in my good arm. Then he takes a diaper pin off the lapel and pins the other side of the coat to the top of my shoulder, easing the pin through my sweater. Then he puts Kate's poncho over my head. This is the system, because I am always cold. Actually, Kate devised the system. I stand there while Howard puts on his leather jacket. I feel like a bird with a cloth draped over its cage for the night. This makes me feel sorry for myself, and then I *do* think of my arm as a broken wing, and suddenly everything seems so sad that I feel my eyes well up with tears. I sniff a couple of times. And Howard faced down Dennis Bidou, for my sake! My brother! But he really did it because my father told him to. Whatever my father told him to do he did. He drew the line only at smothering my father in the hospital when he asked him to. That is the only time I know of that he ignored my father's wishes.

"Get one that's tall enough," Kate says. "And don't get one of those trees that look like a cactus. Get one with long needles that swoops."

"Swoops?" Howard says, turning in the hallway.

"Something with some fluidity," she says, bending her knees and making a sweeping motion with her arm. "You know—something beautiful."

Before the guests arrive, a neighbor woman has brought Todd back from his play group and he is ready for bed, and the tree has been decorated with a few dozen Christmas balls and some stars cut out of typing paper, with paper-clip hangers stuck through one point. The smaller animals in the stuffed-toy menagerie—certainly not the bear—are under the tree, approximating the animals at the manger. The manger is a roasting pan, with a green dinosaur inside.

"How many of these people who're coming do I know?" I say.

"You know . . . you know . . ." Howard is gnawing his lip. He takes another sip of wine, looks puzzled. "Well, you know Koenig," he says. "Koenig got married. You'll like his wife. They're coming separately, because he's coming straight from work. You know the Miners. You know—you'll really like Lightfoot, the new guy in the Philosophy Department. Don't rush to tell him that you're tied up with somebody. He's a nice guy, and he deserves a chance."

"I don't think I'm tied up with anybody," I say.

"Have a drink—you'll feel better," Howard says. "Honest to God. I was getting depressed this afternoon. When the light starts to sink so early, I never can figure out what I'm responding to. I gray over, like the afternoon, you know?"

"OK, I'll have a drink," I say.

"The very fat man who's coming is in A.A.," Howard says, taking a glass off the bookshelf and pouring some wine into it. "These were just washed yesterday," he says. He hands me the glass of wine. "The fat guy's name is Dwight Kule. The Jansons, who are also coming, introduced us to him. He's a bachelor. Used to live in the Apple. Mystery man. Nobody knows. He's got a computer terminal in his house that's hooked up to some mysterious office in New York. Tells funny jokes. They come at him all day over the computer."

"Who are the Jansons?"

"You met her. The woman whose lover broke into the house and did caricatures of her and her husband all over the walls after she broke off with him. One amazing artist, from what I heard. You know about that, right?"

"No," I say, smiling. "What does she look like?"

"You met her at the races with us. Tall. Red hair."

"Oh, that woman. Why didn't you say so?"

"I told you about the lover, right?"

"I didn't know she had a lover."

"Well, fortunately she *had* told her husband, and they'd decided to patch it up, so when they came home and saw the walls—I mean, I get the idea that it was rather graphic. Not like stumbling upon hieroglyphics in a cave or something. Husband told it as a story on himself: going down to the paint store and buying the darkest can of blue paint they had to do the painting-over, because he wanted it done with—none of this three-coats stuff." Howard has another sip of wine. "You haven't met her husband," he says. "He's an anesthesiologist."

"What did her lover do?"

"He ran the music store. He left town."

"Where did he go?"

"Montpelier."

"How do you find all this stuff out?"

"Ask. Get told," Howard says. "Then he was cleaning his gun in Montpelier the other day, and it went off and he shot himself in the foot. Didn't do any real damage, though."

"It's hard to think of anything like that as poetic justice," I say. "So are the Jansons happy again?"

"I don't know. We don't see much of them," Howard says. "We're not really involved in any social whirl, you know. You only visit during the holidays, and that's when we give the annual party."

"Oh, hel-*lo*," Becky says, sweeping into the living room from the front door, bringing the cold and her girlfriend Deirdre in with her. Deirdre is giggling, head averted. "My friends! My wonderful friends!" Becky says, trotting past, hand waving madly. She stops in the doorway, and Deirdre collides with her. Deirdre puts her hand up to her mouth to muffle a yelp, then bolts past Becky into the kitchen.

"I can remember being that age," I say.

"I don't think I was ever that stupid," Howard says.

"A different thing happens with girls. Boys don't talk to each other all the time in quite the same intense way, do they? I mean, I can remember when it seemed that I never talked but that I was always *confiding* something."

"Confide something in me," Howard says, coming back from flipping the Bach on the stereo.

"Girls just talk that way to other girls," I say, realizing he's serious.

"Gidon Kremer," Howard says, clamping his hand over his heart. "God—tell me that isn't beautiful."

"How did you find out so much about classical music?" I say. "By asking and getting told?"

"In New York," he says. "Before I moved here. Before L.A., even. I just started buying records and asking around. Half the city is an unofficial guide to classical music. You can find out a lot in New York." He pours more wine into his glass. "Come on," he says. "Confide something in me."

In the kitchen, one of the girls turns on the radio, and rock and roll, played low, crosses paths with Bach's violin. The music goes lower still. Deirdre and Becky are laughing.

I take a drink, sigh, and nod at Howard. "When I was in San Francisco last June to see my friend Susan, I got in a night before I said I would, and she wasn't in town," I say. "I was going to surprise her, and she was the one who surprised me. It was no big deal. I was tired from the flight and by the time I got there I was happy to have the excuse to check into a hotel, because if she'd been there we'd have talked all night. Acting like Becky with Deirdre, right?"

Howard rolls his eyes and nods.

"So I went to a hotel and checked in and took a bath, and suddenly I got my second wind and I thought what the hell, why not go to the restaurant right next to the hotel—or in the hotel, I guess it was—and have a great dinner, since it was supposed to be such a great place."

"What restaurant?"

"L'Étoile."

"Yeah," he says. "What happened?"

"I'm telling you what happened. You have to be patient. Girls always know to be patient with other girls."

He nods yes again.

"They were very nice to me. It was about three-quarters full. They put me at a table, and the minute I sat down I looked up and there was a man on a banquette across the room from me. He was looking at me, and I was looking at him, and it was almost impossible not to keep eye contact. It just hit both of us, obviously. And almost on the other side of the curve of the banquette was a woman, who wasn't terribly attractive. She had on a wedding ring. He didn't. They were eating in silence. I had to force myself to look somewhere else, but when I did look up he'd look up, or he'd already be looking up. At some point he left the table. I saw that in my peripheral vision, when I had my head turned to hear a conversation on my right and I was chewing my food. Then after a while he paid the check and the two of them left. She walked ahead of him, and he didn't seem to be with her. I mean, he walked quite far behind her. But naturally he didn't turn his head. And after they left I thought, That's amazing. It was really like kinetic energy. Just wham. So I had coffee, and then I paid my check, and when I was leaving I was walking up the steep steps to the street and the waiter came up behind me and said, 'Excuse me. I don't know what I should do, but I didn't want to embarrass you in the restaurant. The gentleman left this for you on his way out.' And he handed me an envelope. I was pretty taken aback, but I just said, 'Thank you,' and continued up the steps, and when I got outside I looked around. He wasn't there, naturally. So I opened the envelope, and his business card was inside. He was one of the partners in a law firm. And underneath his name he had written, 'Who are you? Please call.' "

Howard is smiling.

"So I put it in my purse and I walked for a few blocks, and I thought, Well, what for, really? Some man in San Francisco? For what? A one-night stand? I went back to the hotel, and when I walked in the man behind the desk stood up and said, 'Excuse me. Were you just eating dinner?' and I said, 'A few minutes ago,' and he said, 'Someone left this for you.' It was a hotel envelope. In the elevator on the way to my room, I opened it, and it was the same business card, with 'Please call' written on it."

"I hope you called," Howard says.

"I decided to sleep on it. And in the morning I decided not to. But I kept the card. And then at the end of August I was walking in the East Village, and a couple obviously from out of town were walking in front of me, and a punk kid got up off the stoop where he was sitting and said to them, 'Hey—I want my picture taken with you.' I went into a store, and when I came out the couple and the punk kid were all laughing together, holding these Polaroid snaps that another punk had taken. It was a joke, not a scam. The man gave the kid a dollar for one of the pictures, and they walked off, and the punk sat back down on the stoop. So I walked back to where he was sitting, and I said, 'Could you do me a real favor? Could I have my picture taken with you, too?' "

"What?" Howard says. The violin is soaring. He gets up and turns the music down a notch. He looks over his shoulder. "Yeah?" he says.

"The kid wanted to know why I wanted it, and I told him because it would upset my boyfriend. So he said yeah—his face lit up when I said that—but that he really would appreciate two bucks for more film. So I gave it to him, and then he put his arm around me and really mugged for the camera. He was like a human boa constrictor around my neck, and he did a Mick Jagger pout. I couldn't believe how well the picture came out. And that night, on the white part on the bottom I wrote, 'I'm somebody whose name you still don't know. Are you going to find me?' and I put it in an envelope and mailed it to him in San Francisco. I don't know why I did it. I mean, it doesn't seem like something I'd ever do, you know?"

"But how will he find you?" Howard says.

"I've still got his card," I say, shrugging my good shoulder toward my purse on the floor.

"You don't know what you're going to do?" Howard says.

"I haven't thought about it in months."

"How is that possible?"

"How is it possible that somebody can go into a restaurant and be hit by lightning and the other person is, too? It's like a bad movie or something."

"Of course it can happen," Howard says. "Seriously, what are you going to do?"

"Let some time pass. Maybe send him something he can follow up on if he still wants to."

"That's an amazing story," Howard says.

"Sometimes—well, I hadn't thought about it in a while, but at the end of summer, after I mailed the picture, I'd be walking along or doing whatever I was doing and this feeling would come over me that he was thinking about me."

Howard looks at me strangely. "He probably was," he says. "He doesn't know how to get in touch with you."

"You used to be a screenwriter. What should he do?"

"Couldn't he figure out from the background that it was the Village?"

"I'm not sure."

"If he could, he could put an ad in the *Voice*."

"I think it was just a car in the background."

"Then you've got to give him something else," Howard says.

"For what? You want your sister to have a one-night stand?"

"You make him sound awfully attractive," Howard says.

"Yeah, but what if he's a rat? It could be argued that he was just cocky, and that he was pretty sure that I'd respond. Don't you think?"

"I think you should get in touch with him. Do it in some amusing way if you want, but I wouldn't let him slip away."

"I never had him. And from the looks of it he has a wife."

"You don't know that."

"No," I say. "I guess I don't know."

"Do it," Howard says. "I think you need this," and when he speaks he whispers—just what a girl would do. He nods his head yes. "Do it," he whispers again. Then he turns his head abruptly, to see what I am staring at. It is Kate, wrapped in a towel after her bath, trailing the long cord of the extension phone with her.

"It's Frank," she whispers, her hand over the mouthpiece. "He says he's going to come to the party after all."

I look at her dumbly, surprised. I'd almost forgotten that Frank knew I was here. He's only been here once with me, and it was clear that he didn't like Howard and Kate. Why would he suddenly decide to come to the party?

She shrugs, hand still over the mouthpiece. "Come here," she whispers.

I get up and start toward the phone. "If it's not an awful imposition," she says, "maybe he could bring Deirdre's father with him. He lives just around the corner from you in the city."

"Deirdre's father?" I say.

"Here," she whispers. "He'll hang up."

"Hi, Frank," I say, talking into the phone. My voice sounds high, false.

"I miss you," Frank says. "I've got to get out of the city. I invited myself. I assume since it's an annual invitation it's all right, right?"

"Oh, of course," I say. "Can you just hold on for one second?"

"Sure," he says.

I cover the mouthpiece again. Kate is still standing next to me.

"I was talking to Deirdre's mother in the bathroom," Kate whispers. "She says that her ex-husband's not really able to drive yet, and that Deirdre has been crying all day. If he could just give him a lift, they could take the train back, but—"

"Frank? This is sort of crazy, and I don't quite understand the logistics, but I'm going to put Kate on. We need for you to do us a favor."

"Anything," he says. "As long as it's not about Mrs. Joan Wilde-Younge's revision of a revision of a revision of a spiteful will."

I hand the phone to Kate. "Frank?" she says. "You're about to make a new friend. Be very nice to him, because he just had his gallbladder out, and he's got about as much strength as seaweed. He lives on Seventy-ninth Street."

I am in the car with Howard, huddled in my coat and the poncho. We are on what seems like an ironic mission. We are going to the 7-Eleven to get ice. The moon is shining brightly, and patches of snow shine like stepping-stones in the field on my side of the car. Howard puts on his directional signal suddenly and turns, and I look over my shoulder to make sure we're not going to be hit from behind.

"Sorry," he says. "My mind was wandering. Not that it's the best-marked road to begin with."

Miles Davis is on the tape deck—the very quiet kind of Miles Davis.

"We've got a second for a detour," he says.

"Why are we detouring?"

"Just for a second," Howard says.

"It's freezing," I say, dropping my chin to speak the words so my throat will warm up for a second. I raise my head. My clavicle is colder.

"What you said about kinetic energy made me think about doing this," Howard says. "You can confide in me and I can confide in you, right?"

"What are you talking about?"

"This," he says, turning onto property marked NO TRESPASSING. The road is quite rutted where he turns onto it, but as it begins to weave up the hill it smooths out a little. He is driving with both hands gripping the wheel hard, sitting forward in the seat as if the extra inch, plus the brights, will help him see more clearly. The road levels off, and to our right is a pond. It is not frozen, but ice clings to the sides, like scum in an aquarium. Howard clicks out the tape, and we sit there in the cold and silence. He turns off the ignition.

"There was a dog here last week," he says.

I look at him.

"Lots of dogs in the country, right?" he says.

"What are we doing here?" I say, drawing up my knees.

"I fell in love with somebody," he says.

I had been looking at the water, but when he spoke I turned and looked at him again.

"I didn't think she'd be here," he says quietly. "I didn't even really think that the dog would be here. I just felt drawn to the place, I guess—that's all. I wanted to see if I could get some of that feeling back if I came here. You'd get it back if you called that man, or wrote him. It was real. I could tell when you were talking to me that it was real."

"Howard, did you say that you fell in love with somebody? When?"

"A few weeks ago. The semester's over. She's graduating. She's gone in January. A graduate student—like that? A twenty-two-year-old kid. One of my pal Lightfoot's philosophy students." Howard lets go of the wheel. When he turned the ignition off, he had continued to grip the wheel. Now his hands are on his thighs. We both seem to be examining his hands. At least, I am looking at his hands so I do not stare into his face, and he has dropped his eyes.

"It was all pretty crazy," he says. "There was so much passion, so fast. Maybe I'm kidding myself, but I don't think I let on to her how much I cared. She saw that I cared, but she . . . she didn't know my heart kept stopping, you know? We drove out here one day and had a picnic in the car—it would have been your nightmare picnic, it was so cold—and a dog came wandering up to the car. Big dog. Right over there."

I look out my window, almost expecting that the dog may still be there.

"There were three freezing picnics. This dog turned up at the last one. She liked the dog—it looked like a mutt, with maybe a lot of golden retriever mixed in. I thought it was inviting trouble for us to open the car door, because it didn't look like a particularly friendly dog. But she was right and I was wrong. Her name is Robin, by the way. The minute she opened the door, the dog wagged its tail. We took a walk with it." He juts his chin forward. "Up that path there," he says. "We threw rocks for it. A sure crowd pleaser with your average lost-in-the-woods American dog, right? I started kidding around, calling the dog Spot. When we were back at the car, Robin patted its head and closed the car door, and it backed off, looking very sad. Like we were really ruining its day, to leave. As I was pulling out, she rolled down the window and said, 'Good-bye, Rover,' and I swear its face came alive. I think his name really was Rover."

"What did you do?" I say.

"You mean about the dog, or about the two of us?"

I shake my head. I don't know which I mean.

"I backed out, and the dog let us go. It just stood there. I got to look at it in the rearview mirror until the road dipped and it was out of sight. Robin didn't look back."

"What are you going to do?"

"Get ice," he says, starting the ignition. "But that isn't what you meant, either, is it?"

He backs up, and as we swing around toward our own tire tracks I turn my head again, but there is no dog there, watching us in the moonlight.

Back at the house, as Howard goes in front of me up the flagstone pathway, I walk slower than I usually do in the cold, trying to give myself time to puzzle out what he makes me think of just then. It comes to me at the moment when my attention is diverted by a patch of ice I'm terrified of slipping on. He reminds me of that courthouse figure—I don't know what it's called—the statue of a blindfolded woman holding the scales of justice. Bag of ice in the left hand, bag of ice in the right—but there's no blindfold. The door is suddenly opened, and what Howard and I see before us is Koenig, his customary bandanna tied around his head, smiling welcome, and behind him, in the glare of the already-begun party, the woman with red hair holding Todd, who clutches his green dinosaur in one hand and rubs his sleepy, crying face with the other. Todd makes a lunge—not really toward his father but toward wider spaces—and I'm conscious, all at once, of the cigarette smoke swirling and of the heat of the house, there in the entranceway, that turn the bitter-cold outdoor air silver as it comes flooding in. *Messiah*—Kate's choice of perfect music for the occasion—isn't playing; someone has put on Judy Garland, and we walk in just as she is singing, "That's where you'll find me." The words hang in the air like smoke.

"Hello, hello, hello, hello," Becky calls, dangling one knee-socked leg over the balcony as Deirdre covers her face and hides behind her. "To both of you, just because you're here, from me to you: a million—a trillion—hellos."

RAYMOND CARVER

Put Yourself in My Shoes

The telephone rang while he was run-
ning the vacuum cleaner. He had worked his way through the apartment
and was doing the living room, using the nozzle attachment to get at the cat
hairs between the cushions. He stopped and listened and then switched off
the vacuum. He went to answer the telephone.

"Hello," he said. "Myers here."

"Myers," she said. "How are you? What are you doing?"

"Nothing," he said. "Hello, Paula."

"There's an office party this afternoon," she said. "You're invited.
Dick invited you."

"I don't think I can come," Myers said.

"Dick just this minute said get that old man of yours on the phone. Get
him down here for a drink. Get him out of his ivory tower and back into
the real world for a while. Dick's funny when he's drinking. Myers?"

"I heard you," Myers said.

Myers used to work for Dick. Dick always talked of going to Paris to
write a novel, and when Myers had quit to write a novel, Dick had said he
would watch for Myers's name on the best-seller list.

"I can't come now," Myers said.

"We found out some horrible news this morning," Paula continued,
as if she had not heard him. "You remember Larry Gudinas. He was still
here when you came to work. He helped out on science books for a while,
and then they put him in the field, and then they canned him? We heard this

215

morning he committed suicide. He shot himself in the mouth. Can you imagine? Myers?"

"I heard you," Myers said. He tried to remember Larry Gudinas and recalled a tall, stooped man with wire-frame glasses, bright ties, and a receding hairline. He could imagine the jolt, the head snapping back. "Jesus," Myers said. "Well, I'm sorry to hear that."

"Come down to the office, honey, all right?" Paula said. "Everybody is just talking and having some drinks and listening to Christmas music. Come down," she said.

Myers could hear it all at the other end of the line. "I don't want to come down," he said. "Paula?" A few snowflakes drifted past the window as he watched. He rubbed his fingers across the glass and then began to write his name on the glass as he waited.

"What? I heard," she said. "All right," Paula said. "Well, then, why don't we meet at Voyles for a drink? Myers?"

"OK," he said. "Voyles. All right."

"Everybody here will be disappointed you didn't come," she said. "Dick especially. Dick admires you, you know. He does. He's told me so. He admires your nerve. He said if he had your nerve he would have quit years ago. Dick said it takes nerve to do what you did. Myers?"

"I'm right here," Myers said. "I think I can get my car started. If I can't start it, I'll call you back."

"All right," she said. "I'll see you at Voyles. I'll leave here in five minutes if I don't hear from you."

"Say hello to Dick for me," Myers said.

"I will," Paula said. "He's talking about you."

Myers put the vacuum cleaner away. He walked down the two flights and went to his car, which was in the last stall and covered with snow. He got in, worked the pedal a number of times, and tried the starter. It turned over. He kept the pedal down.

As he drove, he looked at the people who hurried along the side-walks with shopping bags. He glanced at the gray sky, filled with flakes, and at the tall buildings with snow in the crevices and on the window ledges. He tried to see everything, save it for later. He was between stories, and he felt despicable. He found Voyles, a small bar on a corner next to a men's clothing store. He parked in back and went inside. He sat at the bar for a time and then carried a drink over to a little table near the door.

When Paula came in she said, "Merry Christmas," and he got up and gave her a kiss on the cheek. He held a chair for her.

He said, "Scotch?"

"Scotch," she said, then "Scotch over ice" to the girl who came for her order.

Paula picked up his drink and drained the glass.

"I'll have another one, too," Myers said to the girl. "I don't like this place," he said after the girl had moved away.

"What's wrong with this place?" Paula said. "We always come here."

"I just don't like it," he said. "Let's have a drink and then go someplace else."

"Whatever you want," she said.

The girl arrived with the drinks. Myers paid her, and he and Paula touched glasses.

Myers stared at her.

"Dick says hello," she said.

Myers nodded.

Paula sipped her drink. "How was your day today?"

Myers shrugged.

"What'd you do?" she said.

"Nothing," he said. "I vacuumed."

She touched his hand. "Everybody said to tell you hi."

They finished their drinks.

"I have an idea," she said. "Why don't we stop and visit the Morgans for a few minutes. We've never met them, for God's sake, and they've been back for months. We could just drop by and say hello, we're the Myerses. Besides, they sent us a card. They asked us to stop by during the holidays.

217

They *invited* us. I don't want to go home," she finally said and fished in her purse for a cigarette.

Myers recalled setting the furnace and turning out all the lights before he had left. And then he thought of the snow drifting past the window.

"What about that insulting letter they sent telling us they heard we were keeping a cat in the house?" he said.

"They've forgotten about that by now," she said. "That wasn't anything serious, anyway. Oh, let's do it, Myers! Let's go by."

"We should call first if we're going to do anything like that," he said.

"No," she said. "That's part of it. Let's not call. Let's just go knock on the door and say hello, we used to live here. All right? Myers?"

"I think we should call first," he said.

"It's the holidays," she said, getting up from her chair. "Come on, baby."

She took his arm and they went out into the snow. She suggested they take her car and pick up his car later. He opened the door for her and then went around to the passenger's side.

Something took him when he saw the lighted windows, saw snow on the roof, saw the station wagon in the driveway. The curtains were open and Christmas tree lights blinked at them from the window.

They got out of the car. He held her elbow as they stepped over a pile of snow and started up the walk to the front porch. They had gone a few steps when a large bushy dog hurtled around the corner of the garage and headed straight for Myers.

"Oh, God," he said, hunching, stepping back, bringing his hands up. He slipped on the walk, his coat flapped, and he fell onto the frozen grass with the dread certainty that the dog would go for his throat. The dog growled once and then began to sniff Myers's coat.

Paula picked up a handful of snow and threw it at the dog. The porch light came on, the door opened, and a man called, "Buzzy!" Myers got to his feet and brushed himself off.

"What's going on?" the man in the doorway said. "Who is it? Buzzy, come here, fellow. Come here!"

"We're the Myerses," Paula said. "We came to wish you a merry Christmas."

"The Myerses?" the man in the doorway said. "Get out! Get in the garage, Buzzy. Get, get! It's the Myerses," the man said to the woman who stood behind him trying to look past his shoulder.

"The Myerses," she said. "Well, ask them in, ask them in, for heaven's sake." She stepped onto the porch and said, "Come in, please, it's freezing. I'm Hilda Morgan and this is Edgar. We're happy to meet you. Please come in."

They all shook hands quickly on the front porch. Myers and Paula stepped inside and Edgar Morgan shut the door.

"Let me have your coats. Take off your coats," Edgar Morgan said. "You're all right?" he said to Myers, observing him closely, and Myers nodded. "I knew that dog was crazy, but he's never pulled anything like this. I saw it. I was looking out the window when it happened."

This remark seemed odd to Myers, and he looked at the man. Edgar Morgan was in his forties, nearly bald, and was dressed in slacks and a sweater and was wearing leather slippers.

"His name is Buzzy," Hilda Morgan announced and made a face. "It's Edgar's dog. I can't have an animal in the house myself, but Edgar bought this dog and promised to keep him outside."

"He sleeps in the garage," Edgar Morgan said. "He begs to come in the house, but we can't allow it, you know." Morgan chuckled. "But sit down, sit down, if you can find a place with this clutter. Hilda, dear, move some of those things off the couch so Mr. and Mrs. Myers can sit down."

Hilda Morgan cleared the couch of packages, wrapping paper, scissors, a box of ribbons, bows. She put everything on the floor.

Myers noticed Morgan staring at him again, not smiling now.

Paula said, "Myers, there's something in your hair, dearest."

Myers put a hand up to the back of his head and found a twig and put it in his pocket.

"That dog," Morgan said and chuckled again. "We were just having a hot drink and wrapping some last-minute gifts. Will you join us in a cup of holiday cheer? What would you like?"

"Anything is fine," Paula said.

"Anything," Myers said. "We wouldn't have interrupted."

"Nonsense," Morgan said. "We've been . . . very curious about the Myerses. You'll have a hot drink, sir?"

"That's fine," Myers said.

"Mrs. Myers?" Morgan said.

Paula nodded.

"Two hot drinks coming up," Morgan said. "Dear, I think we're ready too, aren't we?" he said to his wife. "This is certainly an occasion."

He took her cup and went out to the kitchen. Myers heard the cupboard door bang and heard a muffled word that sounded like a curse. Myers blinked. He looked at Hilda Morgan, who was settling herself into a chair at the end of the couch.

"Sit down over here, you two," Hilda Morgan said. She patted the arm of the couch. "Over here, by the fire. We'll have Mr. Morgan build it up again when he returns." They sat. Hilda Morgan clasped her hands in her lap and leaned forward slightly, examining Myers's face.

The living room was as he remembered it, except that on the wall behind Hilda Morgan's chair he saw three small framed prints. In one print a man in a vest and frock coat was tipping his hat to two ladies who held parasols. All this was happening on a broad concourse with horses and carriages.

"How was Germany?" Paula said. She sat on the edge of the cushion and held her purse on her knees.

"We loved Germany," Edgar Morgan said, coming in from the kitchen with a tray and four large cups. Myers recognized the cups.

"Have you been to Germany, Mrs. Myers?" Morgan asked.

"We want to go," Paula said. "Don't we, Myers? Maybe next year, next summer. Or else the year after. As soon as we can afford it. Maybe as soon as Myers sells something. Myers writes.''

"I should think a trip to Europe would be very beneficial to a writer," Edgar Morgan said. He put the cups into coasters. "Please help yourselves." He sat down in a chair across from his wife and gazed at Myers. "You said in your letter you were taking off work to write."

"That's true," Myers said and sipped his drink.

"He writes something almost every day," Paula said.

"Is that a fact?" Morgan said. "That's impressive. What did you write today, may I ask?"

"Nothing," Myers said.

"It's the holidays," Paula said.

"You must be proud of him, Mrs. Myers," Hilda Morgan said.

"I am," Paula said.

"I'm happy for you," Hilda Morgan said.

"I heard something the other day that might interest you," Edgar Morgan said. He took out some tobacco and began to fill a pipe. Myers lighted a cigarette and looked around for an ashtray, then dropped the match behind the couch.

"It's a horrible story, really. But maybe you could use it, Mr. Myers." Morgan struck a flame and drew on the pipe. "Grist for the mill, you know, and all that," Morgan said and laughed and shook the match. "This fellow was about my age or so. He was a colleague for a couple of years. We knew each other a little, and we had good friends in common. Then he moved out, accepted a position at the university down the way. Well, you know how these things go sometimes—the fellow had an affair with one of his students."

Mrs. Morgan made a disapproving noise with her tongue. She reached down for a small package that was wrapped in green paper and began to affix a red bow to the paper.

"According to all accounts, it was a torrid affair that lasted for some months," Morgan continued. "Right up until a short time ago, in fact. A week ago, to be exact. On that day—it was in the evening—he announced to his wife—they'd been married for twenty years—he announced to his wife that he wanted a divorce. You can imagine how the fool woman took it, coming out of the blue like that, so to speak. There was quite a row. The whole family got into it. She ordered him out of the house then and there. But just as the fellow was leaving, his son threw a can of tomato soup at him and hit him in the forehead. It caused a concussion that sent the man to the hospital. His condition is quite serious."

Morgan drew on his pipe and gazed at Myers.

"I've never heard such a story," Mrs. Morgan said. "Edgar, that's disgusting."

"Horrible," Paula said.

Myers grinned.

"Now *there's* a tale for you, Mr. Myers," Morgan said, catching the grin and narrowing his eyes. "Think of the story you'd have if you could get inside that man's head."

"Or her head," Mrs. Morgan said. "The wife's. Think of *her* story. To be betrayed in such fashion after twenty years. Think how she must feel."

"But imagine what the poor *boy* must be going through," Paula said. "Imagine, having almost killed his father."

"Yes, that's all true," Morgan said. "But here's something I don't think any of you has thought about. Think about *this* for a moment. Mr. Myers, are you listening? Tell me what you think of this. Put yourself in the shoes of that eighteen-year-old coed who fell in love with a married man. Think about *her* for a moment, and then you see the possibilities for your story."

Morgan nodded and leaned back in the chair with a satisfied expression.

"I'm afraid I don't have any sympathy for her," Mrs. Morgan said. "I can imagine the sort she is. We all know what she's like, that kind preys on older men. I don't have any sympathy for him, either—the man, the chaser, no, I don't. I'm afraid my sympathies in this case are entirely with the wife and son."

"It would take a Tolstoy to tell it and tell it *right*," Morgan said. "No less than a Tolstoy. Mr. Myers, the water is still hot."

222

"Time to go," Myers said.

He stood up and threw his cigarette into the fire.

"Stay," Mrs. Morgan said. "We haven't gotten acquainted yet. You don't know how we have . . . speculated about you. Now that we're together at last, stay a little while. It's such a pleasant surprise."

"We appreciated the card and your note," Paula said.

"The card?" Mrs. Morgan said.

Myers sat down.

"We decided not to mail any cards this year," Paula said. "I didn't get around to it when I should have, and it seemed futile to do it at the last minute."

"You'll have another one, Mrs. Myers?" Morgan said, standing in front of her now with his hand on her cup. "You'll set an example for your husband."

"It *was* good," Paula said. "It warms you."

"Right," Morgan said. "It warms you. That's right. Dear, did you hear Mrs. Myers? It warms you. That's very good. Mr. Myers?" Morgan said and waited. "You'll join us?"

"All right," Myers said and let Morgan take the cup.

The dog began to whine and scratch at the door.

"That dog. I don't know what's gotten into that dog," Morgan said. He went to the kitchen and this time Myers distinctly heard Morgan curse as he slammed the kettle onto a burner.

Mrs. Morgan began to hum. She picked up a half-wrapped package, cut a piece of tape, and began sealing the paper.

Myers lighted a cigarette. He dropped the match in his coaster. He looked at his watch.

Mrs. Morgan raised her head. "I believe I hear singing," she said. She listened. She rose from her chair and went to the front window. "It *is* singing. Edgar!" she called.

Myers and Paula went to the window.

"I haven't seen carolers in years," Mrs. Morgan said.

"What is it?" Morgan said. He had the tray and cups. "What is it? What's wrong?"

"Nothing's wrong, dear. It's carolers. There they are over there, across the street," Mrs. Morgan said.

"Mrs. Myers," Morgan said, extending the tray. "Mr. Myers. Dear."

"Thank you," Paula said.

"*Muchas gracias*," Myers said.

Morgan put the tray down and came back to the window with his cup. Young people were gathered on the walk in front of the house across the street, boys and girls with an older, taller boy who wore a muffler and a topcoat. Myers could see the faces at the window across the way—the Ardreys—and when the carolers had finished, Jack Ardrey came to the door and gave something to the older boy. The group moved on down the walk, flashlights bobbing, and stopped in front of another house.

"They won't come here," Mrs. Morgan said after a time.

"What? Why won't they come here?" Morgan said and turned to his wife. "What a goddamned silly thing to say! Why won't they come here?"

"I just know they won't," Mrs. Morgan said.

"And I say they will," Morgan said. "Mrs. Myers, are those carolers going to come here or not? What do you think? Will they return to bless this house? We'll leave it up to you."

Paula pressed closer to the window. But the carolers were far down the street now. She did not answer.

"Well, now that all the excitement is over," Morgan said and went over to his chair. He sat down, frowned, and began to fill his pipe.

Myers and Paula went back to the couch. Mrs. Morgan moved away from the window at last. She sat down. She smiled and gazed into her cup. Then she put the cup down and began to weep.

Morgan gave his handkerchief to his wife. He looked at Myers. Presently Morgan began to drum on the arm of his chair. Myers moved his feet. Paula looked into her purse for a cigarette. "See what you've caused?" Morgan said as he stared at something on the carpet near Myers's shoes.

Myers gathered himself to stand.

"Edgar, get them another drink," Mrs. Morgan said as she dabbed at her eyes. She used the handkerchief on her nose. "I want them to hear about Mrs. Attenborough. Mr. Myers writes. I think he might appreciate this. We'll wait until you come back before we begin the story."

Morgan collected the cups. He carried them into the kitchen. Myers heard dishes clatter, cupboard doors bang. Mrs. Morgan looked at Myers and smiled faintly.

"We have to go," Myers said. "We have to go. Paula, get your coat."

"No, no, we insist, Mr. Myers," Mrs. Morgan said. "We want you to hear about Mrs. Attenborough, poor Mrs. Attenborough. You might appreciate this story, too, Mrs. Myers. This is your chance to see how your husband's mind goes to work on raw material."

Morgan came back and passed out the hot drinks. He sat down quickly.

"Tell them about Mrs. Attenborough, dear," Mrs. Morgan said.

"That dog almost tore my leg off," Myers said and was at once surprised at his words. He put his cup down.

"Oh, come, it wasn't that bad," Morgan said. "I saw it."

"You know writers," Mrs. Morgan said to Paula. "They like to exaggerate."

"The power of the pen and all that," Morgan said.

"That's it," Mrs. Morgan said. "Bend your pen into a plowshare, Mr. Myers."

"We'll let Mrs. Morgan tell the story of Mrs. Attenborough," Morgan said, ignoring Myers, who stood up at that moment. "Mrs. Morgan was intimately connected with the affair. I've already told you of the fellow who was knocked for a loop by a can of soup." Morgan chuckled. "We'll let Mrs. Morgan tell this one."

"You tell it, dear. And Mr. Myers, you listen closely," Mrs. Morgan said.

"We have to go," Myers said. "Paula, let's go."

"Talk about honesty," Mrs. Morgan said.

"Let's talk about it," Myers said. Then he said, "Paula, are you coming?"

"I want you to hear this story," Morgan said, raising his voice. "You will insult Mrs. Morgan, you will insult us both, if you don't listen to this story." Morgan clenched his pipe.

"Myers, please," Paula said anxiously. "I want to hear it. Then we'll go. Myers? Please, honey, sit down for another minute."

Myers looked at her. She moved her fingers, as if signaling him. He hesitated, and then he sat next to her.

Mrs. Morgan began. "One afternoon in Munich, Edgar and I went to the Dortmunder Museum. There was a Bauhaus exhibit that fall, and Edgar said the heck with it, let's take a day off—he was doing his research, you see—the heck with it, let's take a day off. We caught a tram and rode across Munich to the museum. We spent several hours viewing the exhibit and revisiting some of the galleries to pay homage to a few of our favorites amongst the old masters. Just as we were to leave, I stepped into the ladies' room. I left my purse. In the purse was Edgar's monthly check from home that had come the day before and a hundred and twenty dollars cash that I was going to deposit along with the check. I also had my identification cards in the purse. I did not miss my purse until we arrived home. Edgar immediately telephoned the museum authorities. But while he was talking I saw a taxi out front. A well-dressed woman with white hair got out. She was a stout woman and she was carrying two purses. I called for Edgar and went to the door. The woman introduced herself as Mrs. Attenborough, gave me my purse, and explained that she too had visited the museum that afternoon and while in the ladies' room had noticed a purse in the trash can. She of course had opened the purse in an effort to trace the owner. There were the identification cards and such giving our local address. She immediately left the museum and took a taxi in order to deliver the purse herself. Edgar's check was there, but the money, the one hundred twenty dollars, was gone. Nevertheless, I was grateful the other things were intact. It was nearly four o'clock and we asked the woman to stay for tea. She sat down, and after a little while she began to tell us about herself. She had been born and reared in Australia, had married young, had had three children, all sons, been widowed, and still lived in Australia with two of her sons. They raised sheep and had more than twenty thousand acres of land for the sheep to run in, and many drovers and shearers and such who worked for them at certain times of the year. When she came to our home in Munich, she was then on her way to Australia from England, where she had been to visit her youngest son, who was a barrister. She was returning to Australia when we met her," Mrs. Morgan said. "She was seeing some of the world in the process. She had many places yet to visit on her itinerary."

"Come to the point, dear," Morgan said.

"Yes. Here is what happened, then. Mr. Myers, I'll go right to the climax, as you writers say. Suddenly, after we had had a very pleasant conversation for an hour, after this woman had told about herself and her adventurous life Down Under, she stood up to go. As she started to pass me her cup, her mouth flew open, the cup dropped, and she fell across our couch and died. Died. Right in our living room. It was the most shocking moment in our lives."

Morgan nodded solemnly.

"God," Paula said.

"Fate sent her to die on the couch in our living room in Germany," Mrs. Morgan said.

Myers began to laugh. "Fate . . . sent . . . her . . . to . . . die . . . in . . . your . . . living . . . room?" he said between gasps.

"Is that funny, sir?" Morgan said. "Do you find that amusing?"

Myers nodded. He kept laughing. He wiped his eyes on his shirtsleeve. "I'm really sorry," he said. "I can't help it. That line *'Fate sent her to die on the couch in our living room in Germany.'* I'm sorry. Then what happened?" he managed to say. "I'd like to know what happened then."

"Mr. Myers, we didn't know what to do," Mrs. Morgan said. "The shock was terrible. Edgar felt for her pulse, but there was no sign of life. And she had begun to change color. Her face and hands were turning *gray.* Edgar went to the phone to call someone. Then he said, 'Open her purse, see if you can find where she's staying.' All the time averting my eyes from

227

the poor thing there on the couch, I took up her purse. Imagine my complete surprise and bewilderment, my utter bewilderment, when the first thing I saw inside was my hundred twenty dollars, still fastened with the paper clip. I was never so astonished."

"And disappointed," Morgan said. "Don't forget that. It was a keen disappointment."

Myers giggled.

"If you were a real writer, as you say you are, Mr. Myers, you would not laugh," Morgan said as he got to his feet. "You would not dare laugh! You would try to understand. You would plumb the depths of that poor soul's heart and try to understand. But you are no writer, sir!"

Myers kept on giggling.

Morgan slammed his fist on the coffee table and the cups rattled in the coasters. "The real story lies right here, in this house, this very living room, and it's time it was told! The real story is *here*, Mr. Myers," Morgan said. He walked up and down over the brilliant wrapping paper that had unrolled and now lay spread across the carpet. He stopped to glare at Myers, who was holding his forehead and shaking with laughter.

"Consider *this* for a possibility, Mr. Myers!" Morgan screamed. *Consider!* A friend—let's call him Mr. X—is friends with . . . with Mr. and Mrs. Y, *as well as* Mr. and Mrs. Z. Mr. and Mrs. Y and Mr. and Mrs. Z do not know each other, unfortunately. I say *unfortunately* because if they *had* known each other this story would not exist because it would never have taken place. Now, Mr. X learns that Mr. and Mrs. Y are going to Germany for a year and need someone to occupy their house during the time they are gone. Mr. and Mrs. Z are looking for suitable accommodations, and Mr. X tells them he knows of just the place. But before Mr. X can put Mr. and Mrs. Z in touch with Mr. and Mrs. Y, the Ys have to leave sooner than expected. Mr. X, being a friend, is left to rent the house at his discretion to anyone, including Mr. and Mrs. Y—I mean Z. Now, Mr. and Mrs. . . . . Z move into the house and bring a cat with them that Mr. and Mrs. Y hear about later in a letter from Mr. X. Mr. and Mrs. Z bring a cat into the house *even though* the terms of the lease have expressly forbidden cats or other animals in the house because of Mrs. Y's asthma. The *real* story, Mr. Myers, lies in the situation I've just described. Mr. and Mrs. Z—I mean Mr. and Mrs. Y's moving into the Zs' house, *invading* the Zs' house, if the truth is to be told. Sleeping in the Zs' bed is one thing, but unlocking the Zs' private closet and using their linen, vandalizing the things found there, that was against the spirit and letter of the lease. And this *same* couple, the Zs, opened boxes of kitchen utensils marked 'Don't Open.' And broke dishes when it was spelled out, *spelled out* in that same lease, that they were not to use the owners', the Zs' *personal*, I emphasize *personal*, possessions.''

Morgan's lips were white. He continued to walk up and down on the paper, stopping every now and then to look at Myers and emit little puffing noises from his lips.

"And the bathroom things, dear—don't forget the bathroom things," Mrs. Morgan said. "It's bad enough using the Zs' blankets and sheets, but when they also get into their *bathroom* things and go through the little private things stored in the *attic*, a line has to be drawn."

"That's the *real* story, Mr. Myers," Morgan said. He tried to fill his pipe. His hands trembled and tobacco spilled onto the carpet. "That's the real story that is waiting to be written."

"And it doesn't need Tolstoy to tell it," Mrs. Morgan said.

"It doesn't need Tolstoy," Morgan said.

Myers laughed. He and Paula got up from the couch at the same time and moved toward the door. "Good night," Myers said merrily.

Morgan was behind him. "If you were a real writer, sir, you would put that story into words and not pussyfoot around with it, either."

Myers just laughed. He touched the doorknob.

"One other thing," Morgan said. "I didn't intend to bring this up, but in light of your behavior here tonight, I want to tell you that I'm missing my two-volume set of *Jazz at the Philharmonic*. Those records are of great sentimental value. I bought them in 1955. And now I insist you tell me what happened to them!"

"In all fairness, Edgar," Mrs. Morgan said as she helped Paula on with her coat, "after you took inventory of the records, you admitted you couldn't recall the last time you had seen those records."

"But I am sure of it now," Morgan said. "I am positive I saw those records just before we left, and now, now I'd like this *writer* to tell me exactly what he knows of their whereabouts. Mr. Myers?"

But Myers was already outdoors, and taking his wife by the hand, he hurried her down the walk to the car. They surprised Buzzy. The dog yelped in what seemed fear and then jumped to the side.

"I insist on *knowing!*" Morgan called. "I am waiting, sir!"

Myers got Paula into the car and started the engine. He looked again at the couple on the porch. Mrs. Morgan waved, and then she and Edgar Morgan went back inside and shut the door.

Myers pulled away from the curb.

"Those people are crazy," Paula said.

Myers patted her hand.

"They were scary," she said.

He did not answer. Her voice seemed to come to him from a great distance. He kept driving. Snow rushed at the windshield. He was silent and watched the road. He was at the very end of a story.

LEO ROSTEN

The Night of the Magi

When Mr. Parkhill noticed that Miss Mitnick, Mr. Bloom, and Mr. Kaplan were absent and heard a mysterious humming beneath the ordinary sounds which preceded the start of a class session, he realized that it was indeed the last meeting of the year and that Christmas was but a few days off.

Every grade in the American Night Preparatory School for Adults each year presented a Christmas gift to its teacher. By now, Mr. Parkhill was quite familiar with the ritual. Several nights ago, there must have been a concerted dunning of those who had not yet contributed to the collection. Now the Gift Committee was probably engaged in last-minute shopping in Mickey Goldstein's Arcade, debating the propriety of a pair of pajamas, examining the color combination of shirts and ties, arguing whether Mr. Parkhill, in his heart of hearts, would prefer fleece-lined slippers to onyx cuff links.

Mr. Parkhill cleared his throat. "We shall concentrate on spelling tonight."

The students smiled knowingly, stealing glances at the three empty chairs, exchanging sly nods and soft chuckles. Mrs. Moskowitz directed a question to Mrs. Tomasic, but Mr. Blattberg's fierce "Shah!" murdered the words on her very lips. Rochelle Goldberg reached for a chocolate, giggling, but swallowed the sound instead of the sweet the moment Mr. Perez shot her a scathing rebuke.

"We shall try to cover—forty words before recess!"

Not one stalwart flinched.

Mr. Parkhill always gave the class a brisk spelling drill during the last session before Christmas: that kept all the conspirators busy; it dampened their excitement over what would soon transpire; it involved no speeches or discussion during which the precious secret might be betrayed; above all, a spelling drill relieved Mr. Parkhill from employing a rash of ruses to conceal his embarrassment. "Is everyone ready?"

A chorus worthy of *Messiah* choraled assent.

"The first word is—'bananas.' "

Murmurs trailed off, smiles expired, as "bananas" sprouted their letters on the arms of the chairs.

" 'Romance' . . ."

Pens scratched and pencils crunched as "romance" joined "bananas."

" 'Fought,' the past tense of 'fight' . . . *'fought.'* " Now all brows tightened (nothing so frustrated the fledglings as the gruesome coupling of *g* and *h*) while the scholars wrestled with "fought."

" 'Groaning' . . ." Mr. Parkhill heard himself sigh. The class seemed incomplete without its stellar student, Miss Mitnick, and bereaved without its unique one, Hyman Kaplan. (Mr. Kaplan had recently announced that Shakespeare's finest moments came in that immortal tale of star-crossed lovers, *A Room in Joliet.*)

" 'Charming' . . . 'horses' . . ." Mr. Parkhill's mind was not really on charming horses. He could not help feeling uneasy as he envisaged what soon would occur. The moment the recess bell rang, the entire class would dash out the door. The committee would be waiting in the corridor. The class would cross-examine them so loudly that Mr. Parkhill would get a fairly good idea of what the present was. And as soon as the bell pealed its surcease, the throng would pour in from the corridor, faces flushed, eyes aglitter, surrounding one member of the committee (the one carrying the Christmas package) to conceal the fateful parcel from their master's view.

The class would come to order with untypical celerity. Then, just as Mr. Parkhill resumed the spelling lesson, the chairman would rise, apologize for interrupting, approach Mr. Parkhill's desk, place the package upon it, and blare out the well-prepared felicitations.

Mr. Parkhill would pretend to be overwhelmed by surprise; he would utter a few halting phrases. His flock would smile, grin, fidget until the bravest among them would exclaim, "Open it!" or "Look inside the present!" Whereupon, Mr. Parkhill would untie the elaborate ribbons, remove the wrapping from the box, lift the top, and—as his students burbled with pleasure—he would pluck the gift from its cradle, exclaiming "It's *beautiful!*" or "I shall certainly put *this* to good use!" or (most popular of all) "It's just what I wanted!"

The class would burst into a squall of applause, to which he would respond with renewed thanks and a stronger counterfeit of spontaneous thanksgiving. (It was not always easy for Mr. Parkhill to carry off the feigned surprise; it was even harder for him to pretend he was bowled over by pleasure: One year the committee, chairmanned by Mr. David Natkowitz, had given him a porcelain nymph—a pixy executing a fandango despite the barometer in her right hand and the thermometer in her left.)

As Mr. Parkhill's remarks concluded, and the class's *Don't mention it!*'s and communal fervor trailed off, the spelling drill would resume and the session would drag on until the final bell.

" 'Accept' . . ." called Mr. Parkhill. "Notice, please, the word is 'accept' . . . not 'except'; be careful everyone; listen to the difference: 'except' . . . 'cucumber' . . ."

And after the final bell rang, the whole class would cry "Merry Christmas! Happy New Year!" and crowd around him with tremendous smiles to ask how he *really* liked the present, advising him that if it wasn't just right in size and color (if the gift was something to wear), or in shape and utility (if something to use), Mr. Parkhill could exchange it! He didn't *have* to abide by the committee's choice. He could exchange the present—for anything! That had been carefully arranged with Mickey Goldstein in person.

This was the ritual, fixed and unchanging, of the session before Christmas.

" 'Nervous' . . . 'goose' . . . 'violets' . . ."

The hand on the wall clock crawled toward eight. Mr. Parkhill tried to keep his eyes away from the seats, so telling in their vacancy, of Miss Mitnick, Mr. Bloom, and Mr. Kaplan. In his mind's eye, he saw the three deputies in the last throes of decision in Mr. Goldstein's Arcade, torn by the competitive attractions of an electric clock, a cane, spats, a "lifetime fountain pen." Mr. Parkhill winced. Twice already had "lifetime" fountain pens been bestowed upon him, once with a "lifetime" propelling pencil to match. Mr. Parkhill had exchanged these indestructible gifts discreetly once for a woolen vest, once for a fine pair of earmuffs. Mr. Parkhill hoped it wouldn't be a fountain pen.

Or a smoking jacket! He had never been able to understand why the committee, in his second semester at the A.N.P.S.A., had decided upon a smoking jacket. Mr. Parkhill did not smoke. He had exchanged it for a pair of fur-lined gloves. (That was when Mr. Goldstein told him that teachers were always changing the Christmas presents their classes gave them: "Why don't those dumbbells maybe ask a teacher some questions in advance, they could get a *hint* what that particular teacher really *wants?*" Mr. Goldstein had been quite indignant about such foolhardiness.)

" 'Pancakes' . . . 'hospital' . . . 'commi—' " In the nick of time, as a dozen apprehensive faces popped up, Mr. Parkhill detoured disaster: " '—*ssion*. Commission'! . . ."

The clock ticked away.

Mr. Parkhill called off " 'Sardine' . . . 'exquisite' . . . 'palace' "—and at long last the bell trilled intermission.

The class stampeded out of the room, Mr. Pinsky well in the lead. Their voices resounded in the corridor and floated through the open door. Nathan P. Nathan was playing a harmonica. Mr. Parkhill began to print "bananas" on the blackboard; he would ask his pupils to correct their own papers after the recess. He tried to shut his ears to the babbling forum outside the door, but the voices chattered like shrill sparrows.

"Hollo, Mitnick!"

"Bloom, what you chose?"

"Ees eet for wear?"

"So what did you *gat*, Keplen? Tell!"

Mr. Parkhill heard Miss Mitnick's "We bought—" instantly squashed by Mr. Kaplan's stern "Mitnick! Don't say! Averybody comm *don* mit your voices. Titcher vill hear soch hollerink. Be soft! Qviet!" Mr. Kaplan was born to command.

"Did you bought a Tsheaffer's Fountain Pan Sat, guaranteet for life, like *I* said?" That was Mrs. Moskowitz. (Poor dear Mrs. Moskowitz; she showed as little imagination in her benefactions as in her homework.)

"Moskovitz, mine *Gott!*" The stentor was Kaplan. "Vhy you don't use a lod spikker?! Cless, lat's go to de odder and fromm de hall!"

The voices of the beginners' grade dwindled as they marched to the "odder and" of the corridor, rather like the chorus in *Aida* (which, in fact, Mr. Nathan was playing, off-key) vanishing into pharaoh's wings.

Mr. Parkhill printed "horses" on the board, then "accept" . . . "except," and he began to practice the murmur: "Thank you . . . all of you . . . It's just what I wanted!" Once he had forgotten to say "It's just what I wanted!" and Miss Helga Pedersen, chairman of the committee that year, had been hounded by her classmates well into the third week of January.

It seemed an hour before the gong summoned the scholars back to their quarters. They poured in en masse, restraining their excitement by straining their expressions, resuming their seats with simulated insipidity.

Mr. Parkhill, printing "cucumber" on the board, did not turn to face his congregation. "Please compare your own spelling with mine—"

Came a heated whispering: "Stand *op*, Mitnick!" That was Mr. Kaplan. "You should stend op, too!"

"The *whole* committee," Mr. Bloom rasped.

Apparently Miss Mitnick, a gazelle choked with embarrassment, could not mobilize the fortitude to "stend op" with her comrades.

"A fine represantitif *you'll* gonna make!" frowned Mr. Kaplan. "You t'ink is for *my* sek I'm eskink? Mitnick, stend *op!*"

"I can't," whinnied Miss Mitnick.

Mr. Parkhill printed "violets."

"Lest call!" barked Mr. Kaplan. "Come op mit me an' Bloom!"

The anguished maiden's eyes were glazing. Even Mr. Nathan's cheerful "Rosie!" fell on paralyzed ears.

"Class . . ." began Mr. Parkhill.

A clarion voice cut through the air. "Podden me, Mr. Pockheel!"

It had come.

"Er—yes?" Mr. Parkhill beheld Messrs. Bloom and Kaplan standing side by side in front of Miss Mitnick's chair. Each was holding one side of a long package, wrapped in green cellophane and tied with great red ribbons. A pair of tiny hands, their owner hidden behind the box, clutched the bottom of the offering.

"De hends is Mitnick," explained Mr. Kaplan.

Not for a second did Mr. Parkhill avert his gaze from the tableau. "Er—yes?"

"Lat go," Mr. Kaplan whispered.

The hands of Mitnick disappeared.

The diminished committee advanced with the parcel. Mr. Kaplan's smile was celestial; Mr. Bloom's nostrils quivered. Together, the staunch duo thrust the package toward Mr. Parkhill's chest as Mr. Kaplan proclaimed "Mr. Pockheel, is mine beeg honor, as chairman fromm de Buyink-an'-Deliverink-to-You-a-Prazent Committee, to prezant you mit dis fine peckitch!"

Mr. Bloom dropped back two paces (it resembled the changing of the guard, so well had it been rehearsed) and stared into space.

Mr. Parkhill stammered, "Oh, *goodness*. Why, thank—" but Mr. Kaplan rode over his words: "Foist, I have to say a few voids!" He half turned to the audience. "Mitnick, *you still got time to join de committee!*"

The maiden was inert.

"She fainted!" cried Mrs. Yanoff.

This was not true.

"She is stage-fried!"

This, despite the solecism, was true.

Mr. Kaplan shook his head in disgust and re-faced Mr. Parkhill,

236

smoothed a paper extracted from his pocket, and read: "To our dear titcher (dat's de beginnink): Ve are stendink on de adge of a beeg holiday. Ufcawss, is all kinds holidays in U.S.: holidays for politic, holidays for religious, an' *plain* holidays. In Fabruary, ve got Judge Vashington's boitday—a *fine* holiday. Also Abram Lincohen's, iven batter. In July comms, netcheral, Fort July, de boitday of America de beauriful. . . . Also ve have Labor Day, Denksgivink (for de Peelgrims), an' for victory in de Voild Vide Var, Armistress Day."

Mr. Parkhill studied his chalk. "Thank—"

"Make an *end* awreddy," growled Mr. Bloom.

Mr. Kaplan scorned impatience at such a moment. "But arond dis time year, ve have a *different* kind holiday, a spacial, movvellous time: Chrissmas. All hover de voild are pipple celebraking. Becauss for som pipple is Chrissmas like for *odder* pipple Chanukah—de most secret holiday fromm de whole bunch."

("'Sacred,' Mr. Kaplan, '*sacred*.'")

"Ven ve valkink don de stritts an' is snow on de floor an' all kinds tarrible cold!" Mr. Kaplan's hand repelled winter's tribulations. "Ven ve see in all de chop vindows dose trees mit rad an' grin laktric lights boinink . . . Ven de time comms for tellink fancy tales abot Sandy Clawss—"

("'*Fairy tales*' . . .")

"—flyink don fromm de Naut Pole on rain-emimals, an' climbink don de jiminies mit stockings for all de lettle kits. Ven ve hear de beauriful t'oughts of de tree Vise Guys, chasink a star on de dasert to Bettelheim."

("*Mister* Kaplan!")

"Ven pipple saying, 'Oh, Mary Chrissmas! Oh, Heppy Noo Yiss! Oh, bast regotts!'—den ve *all* got a varm fillink in de hot, for all humanity vhich should be brodders! Ve know *you* got de fillink, Mr. Pockheel; *I* got de fillink; Caravello, Matsoukas, iven Mitnick"—Mr. Kaplan was not one to let perfidy go unchastised—"got dat fillink!"

"*I* feel my feet dying," muttered Mr. Bloom.

"An' vat do ve call dis fillink?" cried Mr. Kaplan. "De Chrissmas Spirits."

(" 'Spir*it*,' Mr. Kaplan, 'spir—' ")

"*Now* I'll prezant de prazent."

The class leaned forward. Mr. Parkhill straightened his shoulders.

"Because you a foist-cless titcher, Mr. Pockheel, an' ve all oppreciate how you explain de hoddest pots gremmer, spallink, pernonciation, vhich ve know is planty hod to do mit greenhorns, ve all falt you should gat a semple of our—of our"—Mr. Kaplan turned his page over hastily—"Aha! —of our santimental! So in de name of de beginnis' grate of Amarican Night Priparatory School for Edults, I'm prezantink de soprize prazent to our vunderful titcher, lovely Mr. Pockheel!"

(" '*Beloved*,' Mr. Kaplan . . .")

A hush gripped the chamber.

Mr. Parkhill tried to say, "Thank you, Mr. Kaplan . . . Thank you, class . . ." but the phrases seemed so timeworn, so shorn of meaning, they stuck in his throat. Without a word, he untied the big red ribbon, unfolded the green cellophane wrapping, lifted the cover off the package, fumbled with the inner maze of wrapping. He raised the gift from the box. It was a smoking jacket. A black and gold smoking jacket. Black velvet, the lapels a lustrous gold. On the breast pocket, an exotic ideograph sparkled. And a dragon was embroidered all across the front and back; its tongue flickered across the sleeves.

"Horyantal style," Mr. Kaplan confided.

Mr. Parkhill coughed. The room seemed very warm. Mr. Bloom was peering over Mr. Kaplan's shoulder, mopping his bald head and clucking like a rooster. Mrs. Moskowitz sat stupefied. Moist-eyed Olga Tarnova moaned from the depths of one of her many passions.

"Th-thank you," Mr. Parkhill succeeded in stammering. "Thank you—all of you—very much."

Mr. Bloom blared, "Hold it op everyone should see!"

Mr. Kaplan turned on Mr. Bloom. "*I'm* de chairman!"

Rose Mitnick was bleating.

Miss Goldberg cracked a pistachio nut.

"I—I can't tell you how much I—appreciate your kindness." The dragon, Mr. Parkhill noted, had green eyes.

Mr. Kaplan beamed. "So plizz hold op de prazent all should see."

Mr. Parkhill raised high the jacket for all to behold. The symphony of admiring *Oh!*'s and *Ah!*'s was climaxed by Mr. Kaplan's ecstatic "My!"

"It's—beautiful," said Mr. Parkhill.

"Maybe you should toin arond de jecket," suggested Mr. Kaplan.

As Mr. Parkhill revolved the jacket slowly, the dragon writhed in the folds.

"A voik of art!" sang Mr. Pinsky.

"Maybe ve made a mistake?" whispered Hyman Kaplan.

"I beg your pardon?"

"Maybe you don't smoke. Mitnick vorried abot dat. But I sad, 'Uf-cawss a ticher smokes. Not in cless, netcheral. At home. At least a *pipe!*'"

"No, no, you didn't make a mistake. I do—occasionally—smoke. A pipe!" Mr. Parkhill cleared his larynx. "Why—*it's just what I wanted!*"

The class burst into cheers.

"Hooray!" laughed Mr. Trabish.

"I knew it!" boomed Mr. Blattberg, whirling his grandson's tooth.

"Hoorah," growled Gus Matsoukas.

"Bravo!" chimed Miss Caravello.

"In Rossia we song in all the chaurches," droned Olga Tarnova. "On differont day but."

"Vear it in de bast of helt!!" cried Mr. Kaplan.

"Thank you, I will. Class, you have been most generous. Thank you."

"You welcome!" came the congregation's response.

It was over.

Mr. Parkhill started to fold the dragon back into its lair. Mr. Bloom marched to his seat, acknowledging the praises due a connoisseur who had participated in such a choice. But Mr. Kaplan stepped closer to Mr. Parkhill's desk.

"Er—thank you, Mr. Kaplan," said Mr. Parkhill.

The chairman of the committee shuffled his feet and craned his neck and—why, for the first time since Mr. Parkhill had known him, Mr. Kaplan was embarrassed.

"Is anything wrong?" asked Mr. Parkhill anxiously.

Sotto voce, so that no ears but Mr. Parkhill's could hear it, Mr. Kaplan said, "Maybe mine spitch vas too long, or too *formal*. But, Mr. Pockheel, avery void I sad came fromm below mine heart!"

For all the unorthodox English, thought Mr. Parkhill, Mr. Kaplan had spoken like one of the Magi.

HORTENSE CALISHER

A Christmas Carillon

About four weeks before Christmas, Grorley, in combined shame and panic, began to angle for an invitation to somewhere, anywhere, for Christmas Day. By this time, after six months of living alone in the little Waverly Place flat to which he had gone as soon as he and his wife had decided to separate, he had become all too well reacquainted with his own peculiar mechanism in regard to solitude. It was a mechanism that had its roots in the jumbled lack of privacy of an adolescence spent in the dark, four-room apartment to which his parents had removed themselves and three children after his father's bankruptcy in '29. Prior to that, Grorley's childhood had been what was now commonly referred to as Edwardian—in a house where servants and food smells kept their distance until needed, and there were no neurotic social concerns about the abundance of either—a house where there was always plush under the buttocks, a multiplicity of tureens and napery at table, lace on the pillow, and above all that general expectancy of creature comfort and spiritual order which novelists now relegated to the days before 1914.

That it had lasted considerably later, Grorley knew, since this had been the year of his own birth, but although he had been fifteen when they had moved, it was the substantial years before that had faded to fantasy. Even now, when he read or said the word *reality*, his mind reverted to Sunday middays in the apartment house living room, where the smudgy daylight was always diluted by lamps, the cheaply stippled walls menaced the oversize furniture, and he, his father and brother and sister, each a claustro-

241

phobe island of irritation, were a constant menace to one another. Only his mother, struggling alone in the kitchen with the conventions of roast chicken and gravy, had perhaps achieved something of the solitude they all had craved. To Grorley even now, the smell of roasting fowl was the smell of a special kind of Sunday death.

Only once before now had he lived alone, and then too it had been in the Village, not far from where he presently was. After his graduation from City College he had worked a year, to save up for a master's in journalism, and then, salving his conscience with the thought that he had at least paid board at home for that period, he had left his family forever. The following year, dividing his time between small-time newspaper job and classes, living in his twenty-seven-dollar-per-month place off Morton Street, he had savored all the wonders of the single door key opening on the quiet room, of the mulled book and the purring clock, of the smug decision not to answer the phone or to let even the most delightful invader in. Now that he looked back on it, of course, he recalled that the room had rung pretty steadily with the voices of many such who had been admitted, but half the pleasure had been because it had been at his own behest. That had been a happy time, when he had been a gourmet of loneliness, prowling bachelor-style on the edge of society, dipping inward when he chose. Of all the habitations he had had since, that had been the one whose conformations he remembered best, down to the last, worn dimple of brick. When he had house-hunted, last June, he had returned instinctively to the neighborhood of that time. Only a practicality born of superstition had kept him from hunting up the very street, the very house.

He had had over two years of that earlier freedom, although the last third of it had been rather obscured by his courtship of Eunice. Among the girl students of the Village there had been quite a few who, although they dressed like ballerinas and prattled of art like painters' mistresses, drew both their incomes and their morality from good, solid middle-class families back home. Eunice had been the prettiest and most sought after of these, and part of her attraction for some, and certainly for Grorley, had been that she seemed to be, quite honestly, one of those rare girls who were not particularly eager to marry and settle down. Grorley had been so entranced at finding like feelings in a girl—and in such a beautiful one—that he had quite forgotten that in coaxing her out of her "freedom" he was persuading himself out of his own.

He hadn't realized this with any force until the children came, two within the first four years of the marriage. Before that, in the first fusion of love, it had seemed to Grorley that two could indeed live more delightfully alone than one, and added to this had been that wonderful release from jealousy which requited love brings—half the great comfort of the loved one's presence being that, ipso facto, she is with no one else. During this period of happy, though enlarged privacy, Grorley confided to Eunice some, though not all, of his feelings about family life and solitude. He was, he told her, the kind of person who needed to be alone a great deal—although this of course excepted her. But they must never spend their Sundays and holidays frowsting in the house like the rest of the world, sitting there stuffed and droning, with murder in their hearts. They must always have plans laid well in advance, plans which would keep the two of them emotionally limber, so to speak, and *en plein air*. Since these plans were always pleasant—tickets to the Philharmonic, with after-theater suppers, hikes along the Palisades, fishing expeditions to little-known ponds back of the Westchester parkways, whose intricacies Grorley, out of a history of Sunday afternoons, knew as well as certain guides knew Boca Raton—Eunice was quite willing to accede. In time she grew very tactful, almost smug, over Grorley's little idiosyncrasy, and he sometimes heard her on the phone, fending people off. "Not Sunday. Gordon and I have a thing about holidays, you know." By this time, too, they had both decided that, although Grorley would keep his now very respectable desk job at the paper, his real destiny was to "write"; and to Eunice, who respected "imagination" as only the unimaginative can, Grorley's foible was the very proper defect of a noble intelligence.

But with the coming of the children, it was brought home to Grorley that he was face-to-face with one of those major rearrangements of existence for which mere tact would not suffice. Eunice, during her first pregnancy, was as natural and unassuming about it as a man could wish; she went on their Sunday sorties to the very last and maintained their gallant privacy right up to the door of the delivery room. But the child of so natural a mother was bound to be natural too. It contracted odd fevers whenever it wished and frequently on Sundays, became passionately endeared to their most expensive sitter or would have none at all, and in general permeated their lives as only the most powerfully frail of responsibilities can. And when the second one arrived, it did so, it seemed to Grorley, only to egg the other one on.

There came a morning, the Christmas morning of the fourth year, when Grorley, sitting in the odor of baked meat, first admitted that his hydra-headed privacy was no longer a privacy at all. He had created, he saw, his own monster; sex and the devil had had their sport with him, and he was, in a sense that no mere woman would understand, all too heavily "in the family way." Looking at Eunice, still neat, still very pretty, but with her lovely mouth pursed with maternity, her gaze sharp enough for *Kinder* and *Küche*, but abstract apparently for him, he saw that she had gone over to the enemy and was no longer his. Eunice had become "the family" too.

It was as a direct consequence of this that Grorley wrote the book which was his making. Right after that fatal morning, he had engaged a room in a cheap downtown hotel (he and Eunice were living out in Astoria at the time), with the intention, as he explained to Eunice, of writing there after he left the paper, and coming home weekends. He had also warned her that, because of the abrasive effects of family life, it would probably be quite some time before "the springs of reverie"—a phrase he had lifted from Ellen Glasgow—would start churning. His real intention was, of course, to prowl, and for some weeks thereafter he joined the company of those men who could be found, night after night, in places where they could enjoy the freedom of not having gone home where they belonged.

To his surprise, he found, all too quickly, that though his intentions were of the worst, he had somehow lost the moral force to pursue them. He had never been much for continuous strong drink, and that crude savoir faire which was needed for the preliminaries to lechery seemed to have grown creaky with the years. He took to spending odd hours in the newspaper morgue, correlating, in a halfhearted way, certain current affairs that interested him. After some months, he suddenly realized that he had enough material for a book. It found a publisher almost immediately. Since he was much more a child of his period than he knew, he had hit upon exactly that note between disaffection and hope which met response in the breasts of those who regarded themselves as permanent political independents. His book was an instant success with those who thought of themselves as thinking for themselves (if they had only had time for it). Quick to capitalize upon this, Grorley's paper gave him a biweekly column, and he developed a considerable talent for telling men of goodwill, over Wednesday breakfast, the very thing they had been saying to one another at Tuesday-night dinner.

Grorley spent the war years doing this, always careful to keep his column, like his readers, one step behind events. With certain minor changes, he kept, too, that scheme of life which had started him writing, changing only, with affluence, to a more comfortable hotel. In time also, that savoir faire whose loss he had mourned returned to him, and his success at his profession erased any guilts he might otherwise have had—a wider experience, he told himself, being not only necessary to a man of his trade, but almost unavoidable in the practice of it. He often congratulated himself at having achieved, in a country which had almost completely domesticated the male, the perfect pattern for a man of temperament, and at times he became almost insufferable to some of his married men friends, when he dilated on the contrast between his "Continental" way of life and their own. For by then, Grorley had reversed himself—it was his weekends and holidays that were now spent cozily *en famille*. It was pleasant, coming back to the house in Tarrytown on Friday evenings, coming back from the crusades to find Eunice and the whole household decked out, literally and psychologically, for his return. One grew sentimentally fond of children whom one saw only under such conditions—Grorley's Saturdays were now spent, as he himself boasted, "on all fours," in the rejuvenating air of the skating rinks, the museums, the woods, and the zoos. Sundays and holidays he and Eunice often entertained their relatives, and if, as the turkey browned, he had a momentary twinge of his old *mal de famille*, he had but to remember that his hat was, after all, only hung in the hall.

It was only some years after the war that Eunice began to give trouble. Before that, their double ménage had not been particularly unusual—almost all the households of couples their age had been upset in one way or another, and theirs had been more stable than many. During the war years Eunice had had plenty of company for her midweek evenings; all over America women had been managing bravely behind the scenes. But now that families had long since paired off again, Eunice showed a disquieting tendency to want to be out in front.

"No, you'll have to come home for good," she said to Grorley, at the end of their now frequent battles. "I'm tired of being a short-order wife."

"The trouble with you," said Grorley, "is that you've never adjusted to postwar conditions."

"That was your nineteen forty-six column," said Eunice. "If you must quote yourself, pick one a little more up-to-date." Removing a jewel-encrusted slipper toe from the fender, she made a feverish circle of the room, the velvet panniers of her house gown swinging dramatically behind her. She was one of those women who used their charge accounts for retaliation. With each crisis in their deteriorating relationship, Grorley noted gloomily, Eunice's wardrobe had improved.

"Now that the children are getting on," he said, "you ought to have another interest. A hobby."

Eunice made a hissing sound. "Nineteen forty-seven!" she said.

In the weeks after, she made her position clear. Men, she told him, might have provided the interest he suggested, but when a woman had made a vocation of one, it wasn't easy to start making a hobby of several. It was hardly much use swishing out in clouds of Tabu at seven, if one had to be back to feel Georgie's forehead at eleven. Besides, at their age, the only odd men out were likely to be hypochondriacs, or bachelors still dreaming of mother, or very odd men indeed.

"All the others," she said nastily, "are already on somebody else's hearth rug. Or out making the rounds with you." Worst of all, she seemed to have lost her former reverence for Grorley's work. If he'd been a novelist or a poet, she said (she even made use of the sticky word *creative*), there'd have been more excuse for his need to go off into the silence. As it was, she saw no reason for his having to be so broody over analyzing the day's proceedings at the U.N. If he wanted an office, that should take care of things very adequately. But if he did not wish to live *with* her, then he could not go on *living* with her. "Mentally," she said, "you're still in the Village. Maybe you better go back there."

Things were at this pass when Grorley's paper sent him to London, on an assignment that kept him there for several months. He was put up for membership in one or two exclusively masculine clubs, and in their leonine atmosphere his outraged vanity—(*creative* indeed!)—swelled anew. Finally, regrettably near the end of his stay, he met up with a redheaded young woman named Vida, who worked for a junior magazine by day, wrote poetry by night, and had once been in America for three weeks. She and Grorley held hands over the mutual hazards of the "creative" life, and on her lips the word was like a caress. For a woman, too, she was remarkably perceptive about the possessiveness of other women. "Yes, quite," she had said. "Yes, quite."

When she and Grorley made their final adieu in her Chelsea flat, she held him, for just a minute, at arm's length. "I shall be thinking of you over there, in one of those ghastly, what do you call them, *living rooms*, of yours. Everybody matted together, and the floor all over children—like beetles. Poor dear. I should think those living rooms must be the curse of the American family. Poor, poor dear."

On his return home in June, Grorley and Eunice agreed on a six-months' trial separation prior to a divorce. Eunice showed a rather unfeeling calm in the lawyer's office, immediately afterward popped the children in camp, and went off to the Gaspé with friends. Grorley took a sublet on the apartment in Waverly Place. It was furnished in a monastic modern admirably suited to the novel he intended to write, that he had promised Vida to write.

He had always liked summers in town, when the real aficionados of the city took over, and now this summer seemed to him intoxicating, flowing with the peppery currents of his youth. In the daytime his freedom slouched unshaven; in the evenings the streets echoed and banged with life, and the moon made a hot harlequinade of every alley. He revisited the San Remo, Julius's, Chumley's, Jack Delaney's, and all the little Italian bars with back-yard restaurants, his full heart and wallet carrying him quickly into the camaraderie of each. Occasionally he invited home some of the remarkables he met on his rounds—a young Italian bookie, a huge Saint Bernard of a woman who drove a taxi and had once lived on a barge on the East River, an attenuated young couple from Chapel Hill, who were honeymooning at the New School. Now and then a few of his men friends from uptown joined him in a night out. A few of these, in turn, invited him home for the weekend, but although he kept sensibly silent on the subject of their frater-nal jaunts, he detected some animus in the hospitality of their wives.

By October, Grorley was having a certain difficulty with his weekends. His list of bids to the country was momentarily exhausted, and his own ideas had begun to flag. The children, home from camp, had aged suddenly into the gang phase; they tore out to movies and jamborees of their own, were weanable from these only by what Grorley could scrape up in the way of rodeos and football games, and assumed, once the afternoon's treat was over, a faraway look of sufferance. Once or twice, when he took them home, he caught himself hoping that Eunice would ask him in for a drink, a chat that might conceivably lead to dinner, but she was always out, and Mrs. Lederer, the housekeeper, always pulled the children in as if they were packages whose delivery had been delayed, gave him a nasty nod, and shut the door.

For a few weekends he held himself to his desk, trying to work up a sense of dedication over the novel, but there was no doubt that it was going badly. Its best juice had been unwisely expended in long, analytic letters to Vida, and now, in her airmail replies, which bounced steadily and enthusiastically over the Atlantic, it began to seem more her novel than his. The Sunday before Thanksgiving, he made himself embark on a ski train to Pittsfield, working up a comforting sense of urgency over the early rising and the impedimenta to be checked. The crowd on the train was divided between a band of Swiss and German perfectionists who had no conversation, and a horde of young couples, rolling on the slopes like puppies, who had too much. Between them, Grorley's privacy was respected to the point of insult. When he returned that night, he tossed his gear into a corner, where it wilted damply on his landlord's blond rug, made himself a hot toddy—with a spasm of self-pity over his ability to do for himself—and sat down to face his fright. For years, his regular intervals at home had been like the chewed coffee bean that renewed the wine taster's palate. He had lost the background from which to rebel.

Thanksgiving Day was the worst. The day dawned oyster-pale and stayed that way. Grorley slept as late as he could, then went out for a walk. The streets were slack, without the twitch of crowds, and the houses had a tight look of inner concentration. He turned toward the streets which held only shops, and walked uptown as far as Rockefeller Center. The rink was open, with its usual cast of characters—ricocheting children, a satiny, professional twirler from the Ice Show, and several solemn old men who skated upright in some Euclidean absorption of their own. Except for a few couples strolling along in the twin featurelessness of love, the crowd around the rink was typecast too. Here, it told itself, it participated in life; here in this flying spectacle of flag and stone it could not possibly be alone. With set, shy smiles, it glanced sideways at its neighbors, rounded its shoulders to the wind, turned up its collar, and leaned closer to the musical bonfire of the square. Grorley straightened up, turned on his heel, smoothed down his collar, and walked rapidly toward Sixth Avenue. He filled himself full of ham and eggs in one of the quick-order places that had no season, taxied home, downed a drink, swallowed two Seconal tablets, and went to bed.

The next morning, seated at his desk, he took a relieved look at the street. People were hard at their normal grind again; for a while the vacuum was past. But Christmas was not going to catch him alone. He picked up the phone. At the end of the day he was quite heartened. Although he had not yet turned up an invitation for Christmas Day, he had netted himself a cocktail party (which might easily go on to dinner) for two days before, a bid to an eggnog party on New Year's Day, and one weekend toward the middle of December. A lot of people did things impromptu. A phone call now and then would fix him up somehow.

But by Christmas week he was haggard. He had visualized himself as bidden to share, in a pleasantly avuncular capacity, some close friend's family gathering; he had seen himself as indolently and safely centered, but not anchored, in the bright poinsettia of their day. Apparently their vision of him was cast in a harsher mold; they returned his innuendos with little more than a pointed sympathy. Only two propositions had turned up, one from a group of men, alone like himself for one reason or another, who were forming a party at an inn in the Poconos, and one from a waiflike spinster—"Last Christmas was my last one with dear Mother"—who offered to cook dinner for him in her apartment. Shuddering, he turned down both of these. The last thing he wanted to do on that day was to ally himself with *waifs* of any description; on that day he very definitely wanted to be safely inside some cozy family cocoon, looking out at *them*.

Finally, the day before Christmas, he thought of the Meechers. Ted was that blue-ribbon bore, the successful account executive who believed his own slogans, and his wife, a former social worker, matched him in her own field. Out of Ted's sense of what was due his position in the agency and Sybil's sense of duty to the world, they had created a model home in Chappaqua, equipped with four children, two Bedlingtons, a games room, and a part-time pony. Despite this, they were often hard up for company, since most people could seldom be compelled twice to their table, where a guest was the focus of a constant stream of self-congratulation from either end. Moreover, Ted had wormed his way into more than one stag party at

Grorley's, and could hardly refuse a touch. And their Christmas, whatever its other drawbacks, would be a four-color job, on the best stock.

But Ted's voice, plum-smooth when he took the phone from his secretary, turned reedy and doubtful when he heard Grorley's inquiry. "Uh-oh! 'Fraid that puts me on the spot, fella. Yeah. Kind of got it in the neck from Sybil, last time I came home from your place. Yeah. Had a real old-fashioned hassle. Guess I better not risk reminding her just yet. But, say! How about coming up here right now, for the office party?"

Grorley declined, and hung up. Off-campus boy this time of year, that's what I am, he thought. He looked at his mantelpiece crowded with its reminders—greetings from Grace and Bill, Jane and Tom, Peg and Jack, Etcetera and Mrs. Etcetera. On top of the pile was another airmail from Vida, received that morning, picture enclosed. Sans the red in the hair, without the thrush tones of the assenting voice, she looked a little long in the teeth. Her hands and feet, he remembered, were always cold. Somehow or other, looking at the picture, he didn't think that central heating would improve them. "The living room is the curse," she'd said. That's it, he thought; that's it. And this, Vida, is the season of the living room.

He looked down into the street. The Village was all right for the summer, he thought. But now the periphery of the season had changed. In summer, the year spins on a youth-charged axis, and a man's muscles have a spurious oil. But this is the end toward which it spins. Only three hundred days to Christmas. Only a month—a week. And then, every year, the damned day itself, catching him with its holly claws, sounding its platitudes like carillons.

Down at the corner, carols bugled steamily from a mission soup kitchen. There's no escape from it, he thought. Turn on the radio, and its alleluia licks you with tremolo tongue. In every store window flameth house gown, nuzzleth slipper. In all the streets the heavenly shops proclaim. The season has shifted inward, Grorley, and you're on the outside, looking in.

He moved toward the phone, grabbed it, and dialed the number before he remembered that you had to dial the code for Tarrytown. He replaced the receiver. Whatever he had to say, and he wasn't quite sure what, or how, it wasn't for the ears of the kids or the Lederer woman. He jammed on his hat. Better get there first, get inside the door.

Going up to Grand Central in the cab, he pressed his face against the glass. Everything had been taken care of weeks ago—the kids had been sent their two-wheelers, and he had mailed Eunice an extralarge check—one he hadn't sent through the lawyer. But at five o'clock, Fifth Avenue still shone like an enormous blue sugarplum revolving in a tutti-frutti rain of light. Here was the season in all its questionable glory—the hallmarked joy of giving, the good will diamanté. But in the cosmetic air, people raised tinted faces, walked with levitated step.

In the train, he avoided the smoker and chose an uncrowded car up front. At his station, he waited until all the gleaming car muzzles pointed at the train had picked up their loads and gone, then walked through the main street which led to his part of town. All was lighted up here too, with a more intimate, household shine. He passed the pink damp of a butcher's, the bright fuzz of Woolworth's. "Sold out!" said a woman, emerging: " 's try the A & P." He walked on, invisible, his face pressed to the shop window of the world.

At Schlumbohn's Credit Jewelry Corner he paused, feeling for the wallet filled with cash yesterday for the still-not-impossible yes over the phone. This was the sort of store that he and Eunice, people like them, never thought of entering. It sold watches pinned to cards, zircons, musical powder boxes, bracelets clasped with fat ten-carat hearts, raja pearl necklaces and truelove blue-white diamonds. Something for Everybody, it said. He opened the door.

Inside, a magnetic salesgirl nipped him toward her like a pin. He had barely stuttered his wants before he acquired an Add-a-Pearl necklace for Sally, two Genuine Pinseal handbags for his mother-in-law and Mrs. Lederer, and a Stag-horn knife with three blades, a nail file, and a corkscrew for young George. He had left Eunice until last, but with each purchase, a shabby, telephoning day had dropped from him. Dizzy with participation, he surveyed the mottoed store.

"Something . . . something for the wife," he said.

"Our lovely Lifetime Watch, perhaps? Or Something in Silver, for the House?" The clerk tapped her teeth, gauging him.

He leaned closer, understanding suddenly why housewives, encysted in lonely houses, burbled confidences to the grocer, made an audience of the milkman. "We've had a—little tiff."

"Aw-w," said the clerk, adjusting her face. "Now . . . let me see. . . ." She kindled suddenly, raised a sibylline finger, beckoned him farther down the counter, and drew out a tray of gold charms. Rummaging among them with a long, opalescent nail, she passed over minute cocktail shakers, birdcages, tennis rackets, a tiny scroll bearing the words, "If you can see this, you're too darn close," and seized a trinket she held up for view. A large gold shamrock, hung on a chain by a swivel through its middle, it bore the letter *I* on its upper leaf, on its nether one the letter *U*. She reversed it. *L-O-V-E* was engraved across the diameter of the other side. The clerk spun it with her accomplished nail. "See?" she said. "Spin it! Spin it and it says *I LOVE U!*"

"Hmmm . . ." said Grorley, clearing his throat. "Well . . . guess you can't fob some women off with just a diamond bracelet." She tittered dutifully. But, as she handed it to him with his other packages and closed the glass door behind him, he saw her shrug something, laughing, to another clerk. She had seen that he was not Schlumbohn's usual, after all.

As he walked up his own street he felt that he was after all hardly anybody's usual, tonight. It was a pretty street, of no particular architectural striving. Not a competitive street, except sometimes in summer, on the subject of gardens. And, of course, now. In every house the tree was up and lighted, in the window nearest the passerby. Here was his own, with the same blue lights that had lasted, with some tinkering on his part, year after year. Eunice must have had a man in to fix them.

He stopped on the path. A man in. She was pretty, scorned, and—he

253

had cavalierly assumed—miserable. He had taken for granted that his family, in his absence, would have remained reasonably static. They always had. He'd been thinking of himself. Silently, he peeled off another layer of self-knowledge. He still was.

He walked up the steps wondering what kind of man might rise to be introduced, perhaps from his own armchair. One of her faded, footballish resurrections from Ohio State U, perhaps: Gordon, this is Jim Jerk, from home. Or would she hand it to him at once? Would it be: *Dear*, this is Gordon.

The door was unlocked. He closed it softly behind him and stood listening. This was the unmistakable quiet of an empty house—as if the secret respiration of all objects in it had just stopped at his entrance. The only light downstairs was the glowing tree. He went up the stairs.

In the bedroom, the curtains were drawn, the night light on. The bed was piled with an abandoned muddle of silver wrappings, tissue paper, ribbons. He dropped the presents on the bed, tossed his hat after them, let his coat slip down on the familiar chair, and parted the curtains. It had a good view of the river, his house. He stood there, savoring it.

He was still there when a car door slammed and the family came up the path. The Christmas Eve pantomime, of course, held every year at the village hall. Georgie had on one of those white burnooses they always draped the boys in, and Sally, in long dress and coned hat, seemed to be a medieval lady. He saw that this year she had the waist for it. Eunice and Mrs. Lederer walked behind them. He tapped on the glass.

They raised their faces in tableau. The children waved, catcalled, and disappeared through the downstairs door. Mrs. Lederer followed them. Below, Eunice stared upward, in the shine from the tree window. Behind him, he heard that sound made only by children—the noise of bodies falling up a staircase. As they swarmed in on him, she disappeared.

"You shoulda been to the hall," said Georgie, seizing him. "Christmas at King Arthur's court. I was a knight."

"Was it corny!" said Sally, from a distance. She caught sight of herself in a pier glass. "I was Guinevere."

"Had to do some last-minute shopping," said Grorley.

"I saw my bike!" said Georgie. "It's in the cellar."

"Oh . . . Georgie!" said Sally.

"Well, I couldn't help seeing it."

"Over there are some Christmas Eve presents," said Grorley.

"Open now?" they said. He nodded. They fell upon them.

"Gee," said Georgie, looking down at the knife. "Is that neat!" From his tone it was clear that he, at least, was Schlumbohn's usual.

"Oh, Dad!" Sally had the necklace around her neck. She raised her arms artistically above her head, in the fifth position, minced forward, and placed their slender wreath around Grorley's neck. As she hung on him, sacklike, he felt that she saw them both, a tender picture, in some lurking pier glass of her mind.

The door opened, and Eunice came in. She shut it behind her with a "not before the servants" air, and stood looking at him. Her face was blurred at the edges; she hadn't decked herself out for anybody. She looked the way a tired, pretty woman, of a certain age and responsibilities, might look at the hour before dinner, at the moment when age and prettiness tussle for her face, and age momentarily has won.

"Look what I got!" Georgie brandished the knife.

"And mine!" Sally undulated herself. "Mums! Doesn't it just go!" She stopped, looking from father to mother, her face hesitant but shrewd.

"Open yours, Mums. Go on."

"Later," said Eunice. "Right now I think Mrs. Lederer wants you both to help with the chestnuts."

"No fair, no fair," said Georgie. "You saw ours."

"Do what your mother says," said Grorley. The paternal phrase, how it steadied him, was almost a hearthstone under his feet.

"Oh, well," said Eunice, wilting toward the children, as she invariably did when he was stern with them. Opening the package he indicated, she drew out the bauble. Georgie rushed to look at it, awarded it a quick, classifying disinterest, and returned to his knife.

"Oo—I know how to work those! Margie's sister has one," said Sally. She worked it. "If that isn't corny!" she gurgled. Eunice's head was bent over the gift. Sally straightened up, gave her and Grorley a swift, amending glance. "But cute!" she said. She flushed. Then, with one of the lightning changes that were the bane of her thirteen years, she began to cry. "Honestly, it's sweet!" she said.

Grorley looped an arm around her, gave her a squeeze and a kiss. "Now, shoo," he said. "Both of you."

When he turned back to the room, Eunice was looking out the window, chin up, her face not quite averted. Recognizing the posture, he quailed. It was the stance of the possessor of the stellar role—of the nightingale with her heart against the thorn. It was the stance of the woman who demands her scene.

He sighed, rat-tatted his fingers on a tabletop. "Well," he said. "Guess this is the season the corn grows tall."

A small movement of her shoulder. The back of her head to him. Now protocol demanded that he talk, into her silence, dredging his self-abasement until he hit upon some remark which made it possible for her to turn, to rend it, to show it up for the heartless, illogical, tawdry remark that it was. He could repeat a list of the game birds of North America, or a passage from the *Congressional Record*. The effect would be the same.

"Go on," he said, "get it over with. I deserve it. I just want you to know . . . mentally, I'm out of the Village."

She turned, head up, nostrils dilated. Her mouth opened. "Get it ov—!" Breath failed her. But not for long.

Much later, they linked arms in front of the same window. Supper had been eaten, the turkey had been trussed, the children at last persuaded into their beds. That was the consolatory side of family life, Grorley thought—the long, Olympian codas of the emotions were cut short by the niggling detail. Women thought otherwise, of course. In the past, he had himself.

Eunice began clearing off the bed. "What's in those two? Father's and Mother's?"

"Oh Lord. I forgot Father."

"Never mind. I'll look in the white-elephant box." The household phrase—how comfortably it rang. She looked up. "What's in these then?"

"For Mother and Mrs. Lederer. Those leather satchel things. Pinseal."

"Both the same, I'll bet."

He nodded.

Eunice began to laugh. "Oh, Lord. How they'll hate it." She continued to laugh, fondly, until Grorley smirked response. This, too, was familiar. Masculine gifts: the inappropriateness thereof.

But Eunice continued to laugh, steadily, hysterically, clutching her stomach, collapsing into a chair. "It's that hat," she said. "It's that s-specimen of a hat!"

Grorley's hat lay on the bed, where he had flung it. Brazenly dirty, limp denizen of bars, it reared sideways on a crest of tissue paper, one curling red whorl of ribbon around its crown. "L-like something out of Hogarth," she said. *"The R-rounder's Return."*

Grorley forced a smile. "You can buy me another."

"Mmmm . . . for Christmas." She stopped laughing. "You know . . . I think that's what convinced me—your coming back tonight. Knowing you—that complex of yours. Suppose I felt if you meant to stand us through the holidays, you meant to stand us for good."

Grorley coughed, bent to stuff some paper into the wastebasket. In fancy, he was stuffing in a picture too, portrait of Vida, woman of imagination, outdistanced forever by the value of a woman who had none.

Eunice yawned. "Oh . . . I forgot to turn out the tree."

"I'll go down."

"Here, take this along." She piled his arms with crushed paper. In grinning afterthought, she clapped the hat on his head.

* * *

257

He went to the kitchen and emptied his arms in the bin. The kitchen was in chaos, the cookery methods of *alt Wien* demanding that each meal rise like a phoenix, from a flaming muddle belowstairs. Tomorrow, as Mrs. Lederer mellowed with wine, they would hear once again of her grandfather's house, where the coffee was not even *roasted* until the guests' carriages appeared in the driveway.

In the dining room, the table was set in state, from damask to silver nut dishes. Father would sit there. He was teetotal, but anecdotalism signs no pledge. His jousts as purchasing agent for the city of his birth now left both narrator and listener with the impression that he had built it as well. They would hear from Mother too. It was unfortunate that her bit of glory—her grandfather had once attended Grover Cleveland—should have crystallized itself in that one sentence so shifty for false teeth—"Yes, my father was a physician, you know."

Grorley sighed and walked into the living room. He looked out, across the flowing blackness of the river. There to the south, somewhere in that jittering corona of yellow lights, was the apartment. He shuddered pleasurably, thinking of all the waifs in the world tonight. His own safety was too new for altruism; it was only by a paring of luck as thin as this pane of glass that he was safely here—on the inside, looking out.

Behind him, the tree shone—that trompe l'oeil triumphant—yearly symbol of how eternally people had to use the spurious to catch at the real. If there was an angel at the top, then here was the devil at its base—that, at this season, anybody who opened his eyes and ears too wide caught the poor fools, caught himself, hard at it. Home is where the heart . . . the best things in life are . . . spin it and it says *I LOVE U.*

Grorley reached up absently and took off his hat. This is middle age, he thought. Stand still and hear the sound of it, bonging like carillons, the gathering sound of all the platitudes, sternly coming true.

He looked down at the hat in his hand. It was an able hat; not every hat could cock a snook like that one. From now on, he'd need every ally he could muster. Holding it, he bent down and switched off the tree. He was out of the living room and halfway up the stairs, still holding it, before he turned back. Now the house was entirely dark, but he needed no light other than the last red sputter of rebellion in his heart. He crept down, felt along the wall, clasped a remembered hook. Firmly, he hung his hat in the hall. Then he turned and went back up the stairs.

JANE SMILEY

Long Distance

Kirby Christianson is standing under the shower, fiddling with the hot-water spigot and thinking four apparently simultaneous thoughts: that there is never enough hot water in this apartment, that there was always plenty of hot water in Japan, that Mieko will be here in four days, and that he is unable to control Mieko's expectations of him in any way. The thoughts of Mieko are accompanied by a feeling of anxiety as strong as the sensation of the hot water, and he would like the water to flow through him and wash it away. He turns from the shower head and bends backward, so that the stream can pour over his face.

When he shuts off the shower, the phone is ringing. A sense that it has been ringing for a long time—can a mechanical noise have a quality of desperation?—propels him naked and dripping into the living room. He picks up the phone and his caller, as he has suspected, is Mieko. Perhaps he is psychic; perhaps this is only a coincidence; or perhaps no one else has called him in the past week or so.

The connection has a crystalline clarity that tricks him into not allowing for the satellite delay. He is already annoyed after the first hello. Mieko's voice is sharp, high, very Japanese, although she speaks superb English. He says, "Hello, Mieko," and he *sounds* annoyed, as if she calls him too much, although she has only called once to give him her airline information and once to change it. Uncannily attuned to the nuances of his voice, she says, "Oh, Kirby," and falls silent.

Now there will be a flurry of tedious apologies, on both sides. He is tempted to hang up on her, call her back, and blame his telephone—faulty American technology. But he can't be certain that she is at home. So he says, "Hello, Mieko? Hello, Mieko? Hello, Mieko?" more and more loudly, as if her voice were fading. His strategy works. She shouts, "Can you hear me, Kirby? I can hear you, Kirby."

He holds the phone away from his ear. He says, "That's better. Yes, I can hear you now."

"Kirby, I cannot come. I cannot go through with my plan. My father has lung cancer, we learned this morning."

He has never met the father, has seen the mother and the sister only from a distance, at a department store.

"Can you hear me, Kirby?"

"Yes, Mieko. I don't know what to say."

"You don't have to say anything. I have said to my mother that I am happy to stay with her. She is considerably relieved."

"Can you come later, in the spring?"

"My lie was that this Melville seminar I was supposed to attend would be offered just this one time, which was why I had to go now."

"I'm sorry."

"I know that I am only giving up pleasure. I know that my father might die."

As she says this, Kirby is looking out his front window at the snowy roof of the house across the street, and he understands at once from the hopeless tone of her voice that to give up the pleasure that Mieko has promised herself is harder than to die. He understands that in his whole life he has never given up a pleasure that he cherished as much as Mieko cherished this one. He understands that in a just universe the father would rather die alone than steal such a pleasure from his daughter. All these thoughts occur simultaneously and are accompanied by a lifting of the anxiety he felt in the shower. She isn't coming. She is never coming. He is off the hook. He says, "But it's hard for you to give it up, Mieko. It is for me, too. I'm sorry."

The sympathetic tones in his voice wreck her self-control, and she begins to weep. In the five months that Kirby knew Mieko in Japan, and in the calls between them since, she has never shed a tear, hardly ever let herself be caught in a low moment, but now she weeps with absolute abandon, in long, heaving sobs, saying, "Oh, oh, oh," every so often. Once, the sounds fade, as if she has put down the phone, but he does not dare hang up, does not even dare move the phone from one ear to the other. This attentive listening is what he owes to her grief, isn't it? If she had come and he had disappointed her, as he would have, this is how she would have wept in solitude after swallowing her disappointment in front of him. But this is her father's doing, not his. He can give her a little company after all. He presses the phone so hard to his ear that it hurts. The weeping goes on for a long time and he is afraid to speak and interfere with what will certainly be her only opportunity to give way to her feelings. She gives one final wailing "Ohhh" and then begins to cough and choke. Finally she quiets, and then sighs. After a moment of silence, she says, "Kirby, you should not have listened."

"How could I hang up?"

"A Japanese man would have."

"You sound better, if you are back to comparing me with Japanese men."

"I am going to hang up now, Kirby. I am sorry not to come. Good-bye."

"Don't hang up."

"Good-bye."

"Mieko?"

"Good-bye, Kirby."

"Call me! Call me again!" He is not sure that she hears him. He looks at the phone and then puts it on the cradle.

Two hours later he is on the highway. This is, after all, two days before Christmas, and he is on his way to spend the holidays with his two brothers and their wives and children, whom he hasn't seen in years. He has thought little about this visit, beyond buying a few presents. Mieko's coming loomed, imposing and problematic. They had planned to drive out West together—she paid an extra fare so that she could land in Minneapolis and return from San Francisco—and he had looked forward to seeing the mountains again. They had made reservations on a bus that carries tourists into Yellowstone National Park in the winter, to look at the smoky geysers and the wildlife and the snow. The trip would have seemed very American to her. Buffalo and men in cowboy boots and hats. But it seemed very Japanese to him—deep snow, dark pines, sharp mountains.

The storm rolls in suddenly, the way it sometimes does on I-35 in Iowa, startling him out of every thought except alertness. Snow swirls everywhere, blotting out the road, the other cars, sometimes even his own front end. The white of his headlights reflects back at him, so that he seems to be driving into a wall. He can hardly force himself to maintain thirty-five miles an hour, although he knows he must. To stop would be to invite a rear-end collision. And the shoulder of the road is invisible. Only the white line, just beside the left front corner of the car, reveals itself intermittently as the wind blows the snow off the pavement. He ejects the tape he is playing and turns on the radio, to the state weather station. He notices that his hand is shaking. He could be killed. The utter blankness of the snowy whirl gives him a way of imagining what it would be like to be dead. He doesn't like the feeling.

He remembers reading two winters ago about an elderly woman whose son dropped her off at her apartment. She discovered that she had forgotten her key, and with the wind-chill factor at eighty below zero, she froze before she got to the manager's office. The winter before that a kid who broke his legs in a snowmobile accident crawled three miles to the nearest farmhouse, no gloves, only a feed cap on his head.

Twenty below, thirty below—the papers always make a big deal of the temperature. Including wind chill, seventy, a hundred below. Kirby carries a flashlight, a down sleeping bag, a sweatshirt that reads UNIVERSITY OF NEBRASKA, gloves and mittens. His car has new tires, front-wheel drive, and plenty of antifreeze. He has a Thermos of coffee. But the horror stories roll through his mind anyway. A family without boots or mittens struggles two

263

miles to a McDonald's through high winds, blowing snow, thirty below. *Why would they travel in that weather?* Kirby always thinks when he reads the papers, but of course they do. He does. Always has.

A gust takes the car, just for a second, and Kirby grips the wheel more tightly. The same gust twists the enveloping snow aloft and reveals the Clear Lake rest stop. Kirby is tempted to stop, tempted not to. He has, after all, never died before, and he has driven through worse than this. He passes the rest stop. Lots of cars are huddled there; but then, lots of cars are still on the highway. Maybe the storm is letting up.

As soon as he is past the rest stop, he thinks of Mieko, her weeping. She might never weep like that again, even if she heard of his death. The connection in her mind between the two of them, the connection that she allowed to stretch into the future despite all his admonitions and all her resolutions, is broken now. Her weeping was the sound of its breaking. And if he died here, in the next ten minutes, how would she learn of it? His brothers wouldn't contact her, not even if she were still coming, because they didn't know she had planned to come. And if she were ever to call him back, she would get only a disconnect message and would assume that he had moved. He can think of no way that she could hear of his death, even though no one would care more than she would. These thoughts fill him with self-pity, but at least they drive out the catalog of horror: station wagon skids into bridge abutment, two people killed, two paralyzed from the neck down, mother survives unharmed, walks to nearby farmhouse. Kirby weighs the boredom and good fellowship he will encounter sitting out the storm at a truck stop against possible tragedy. Fewer cars are on the road, more are scattered on the median strip. Inertia carries him onward. He is almost to Minnesota, after all, where they really know how to take care of the roads. He will stop at the tourist center and ask about conditions.

But he drives past the tourist center by mistake, lost in thought. He decides to stop in Faribault. But by then the snow seems to be tapering off. Considering the distance he has traveled, Minneapolis isn't far now. He checks the odometer. Only fifty miles or so. An hour and a half away, at this speed. His mind eases over the numbers with customary superhighway confidence, but at once he imagines himself reduced to walking, walking in this storm, with only a flashlight, a Thermos of coffee, a University of Nebraska sweatshirt—and the distance swells to infinity. Were he reduced to his own body, his own power, it might be too far to walk just to find a telephone.

For comfort he calls up images of Japan and southern China, something he often does. These images are the one tangible gift of his travels. So many human eyes have looked upon every scene there for so many aeons that every sight has an arranged quality: a flowering branch in the foreground, a precipitous mountainside in the background, a small bridge between. A path, with two women in red kimonos, that winds up a hillside. A white room with pearly rice-paper walls and a futon on the mat-covered floor, branches of cherry blossoms in a vase in the corner. They seem like postcards, but they are scenes he has actually looked upon: on a three-day trip out of Hong Kong into southern China, with some other teachers from his school on a trip to Kyoto, and at Akira's house. Akira was a fellow teacher at his school who befriended him. His house had four rooms, two Japanese style and two Western style.

He remembers, of course, other scenes of Japan—acres of buses, faces staring at his Westernness, the polite but bored rows of students in his classroom—when he is trying to decide whether to go back there. But these are not fixed, have no power; they are just memories, like memories of bars in Lincoln or the pig houses on his grandfather's farm.

And so, he survives the storm. He pulls into the driveway of Harold's new house, one he has not seen, though it is in a neighborhood he remembers from junior high school. The storm is over. Harold has his snowblower out and is making a path from the driveway to his front door. With the noise and because his back is turned, he is unaware of Kirby's arrival. Kirby stops the car, stretches, and looks at his watch. Seven hours for a four-hour trip. Kirby lifts his shoulders and rotates his head, but does not beep his horn just yet. The fact is that he has frightened himself with the blinding snow, the miles of slick and featureless landscape, thoughts of Japan, and the thousands and thousands of miles between here and there. His car might be a marble that has rolled, only by luck, into a safe corner. He presses his fingers against his eyes and stills his breathing.

Harold turns around, grins, and shuts off the snowblower. It is a Harold identical to the Harold that Kirby has always known. Same bright snowflake ski hat, same bright ski clothing. Harold has spent his whole life skiing and ski jumping. His bushy beard grows up to the hollows of his eyes; and when he leans into the car his mustache is, as always, crusted with ice.

"Hey!" he says. He backs away, and Kirby opens the car door.

"Made it!" Kirby says. That is all he will say about the trip. The last thing he wants to do is start a discussion about near misses. Compared with some of Harold's near misses, this is nothing. In fact, near misses on the highway aren't worth mentioning unless a lot of damage has been done to the car. Kirby knows of near misses that Harold has never dared to describe to anyone besides him, because they show a pure stupidity that even Harold has the sense to be ashamed of.

At dinner, over sweet and savory Nordic fare that Kirby is used to but doesn't much like, the people around the table, his relatives, waver in the smoky candlelight, and Kirby imagines that he can feel the heat of the flames on his face. The other people at the table seem unfamiliar. Leanne, Harold's wife, he has seen only once, at their wedding. She is handsome and self-possessed-looking, but she sits at the corner of the table, like a guest in her own house. Eric sits at the head, and Mary Beth, his wife, jumps up and down to replenish the food. This assumption of primogeniture is a peculiarity of Eric's that has always annoyed Kirby, but even aside from that they have never gotten along. Eric does his best—earnest handshake and smile each time they meet, two newsy letters every year, pictures of the children (known between Harold and Kirby as "the little victims"). Eric has a Ph.D. from Columbia in American history, but he does not teach. He writes for a conservative think tank, articles that appear on the op-ed pages of newspapers and in the think tank's own publications. He specializes in "the family." Kirby and Harold have made countless jokes at Eric's expense. Kirby knows that more will be made this trip, if only in the form of conspiratorial looks, rolling eyes. Eric's hobby—Mary Beth's, too, for they share every-thing—is developing each nuance of his Norwegian heritage into a fully realized ostentation. Mary Beth is always busy, usually baking. That's all Kirby knows about her, and all he cares to know.

Across the table Anna, their older daughter, pale, blue-eyed, cool, seems to be staring at him, but Kirby can hardly see her. He is thinking about Mieko. Kirby looks at his watch. It is very early morning in Osaka. She is probably about to wake up. Her disappointment will have receded hardly a particle, will suck her down as soon as she thuds into conscious-ness. "Oh, oh, oh": he can hear her cries as clearly as if they were still vibrating in the air. He is amazed at having heard such a thing, and he looks carefully at the women around the table. Mieko would be too eager to please here, always looking after Mary Beth and Leanne, trying to divine how she might be helpful. Finally, Mary Beth would speak to her with just a hint of sharpness, and Mieko would be crushed. Her eyes would seek Kirby's for reassurance, and he would have none to give. She would be too little, smaller even than Anna, and her voice would be too high and quick. These thoughts give him such pain that he stares for relief at Kristin, Eric's youngest, age three, who is humming over her dinner. She is round-faced and paunchy, with dark hair cut straight across her forehead and straight around her collar. From time to time she and Leanne exchange merry glances.

Harold is beside him; that, at least, is familiar and good, and it touches Kirby with a pleasant sense of expectation, as if Harold, at any moment, might pass him a comic book or a stick of gum. In fact, Harold does pass him something—an icy cold beer, which cuts the sweetness of the food and seems to adjust all the figures around the table so that they stop wavering.

Of course his eyes open well before daylight, but he dares not move. He is sharing a room with Harold the younger, Eric's son, whose bed is between his and the door. He worries that if he gets up he will stumble around and crash into walls and wake Harold. The digits on the clock beside Harold's bed read 5:37, but when Kirby is quiet he can hear movement elsewhere in the house. When he closes his eyes the footsteps present themselves as a needle and thread, stitching a line through his thoughts. He has just been driving. His arms ache from gripping the wheel. The car slides diagonally across the road, toward the median. It slides and slides, through streams of cars, toward a familiar exit, the Marshalltown exit, off to the left, upward. His eyes open again. The door of the room is open, and Anna is looking in. After a moment she turns and goes away. It is 6:02. Sometime later Leanne passes with Isaac, the baby, in her arms.

Kirby cannot bear to get up and face his brothers and their families. As always, despair presents itself aesthetically. The image of Harold and Leanne's living room, matching plaid wing chairs and couch, a triple row of wooden pegs by the maple front door, seems to Kirby the image of the interior of a coffin. The idea of spending five years, ten years, a lifetime, with such furniture makes him gasp. But his own apartment, armchair facing the television, which sits on a spindly coffee table, is worse. Mary Beth and Eric's place, where he has been twice, is the worst, because it's pretentious; they have antique wooden trunks and high-backed benches painted blue with stenciled flowers in red and white. Everything, everything, they own is blue and white, or white with blue, and Nordic primitive. Now even the Japanese images he calls up are painful. The pearly white Japanese-style room in Akira's house was bitterly cold in the winter, and he spent one night there only half-sleeping, his thighs drawn to his chest, the perimeters of the bed too cold even to touch. His head throbbing, Kirby lies pinned to the bed by impossibility. He literally can't summon up a room, a stick of furniture, that he can bear to think of. Harold the younger rolls over and groans, turning his twelve-year-old face toward Kirby's. His mouth opens and he breathes noisily. It is 6:27.

At breakfast, Leanne sets a bowl of raisin bran before him, and he is struck by the elasticity of her motion. She smiles, so cool and kind that Kirby is suddenly daunted. Ten minutes later, when Anna enters the kitchen in her bathrobe, yawning, he recalls, suddenly, her appearance in the doorway to his room. Fifth grade. Only fifth grade. He can see that now, but the night before, and in the predawn darkness, she had seemed older, more threatening, the way girls get at fourteen and fifteen. "Cereal, sweetie?" Leanne says, and Anna nods, scratching. She sits down without a word and focuses on the back of the Cheerios box. Kirby decides that he was dreaming and puts the incident out of his mind; but, "sweetie"—he would like for Leanne to call him that.

Harold, of course, is at his store, managing the Christmas rush, and the house is less festive in his absence. Eric has sequestered himself in Leanne's sewing room, with his computer, and as soon as Anna stands up from breakfast, Mary Beth begins to arrange the day's kitchen schedule. Kirby rinses his cup and goes into the living room. It is nine in the morning, and the day stretches before him, empty. He walks through the plaid living room to the window, where he regards the outdoor thermometer. It reads four degrees below zero. Moments later it is five degrees below zero. Moments after that he is standing beside Harold's bar, pouring himself a glass of bourbon. He has already drunk it when Anna appears in the doorway, dressed now, and staring at him again. She makes him think of Mieko again—though the child is blond and self-contained, she is Mieko's size. Last evening, when he was thinking of Mieko, he was looking at Anna. He says, attempting jovial warmth, "Good morning, Anna. Why do you keep staring at me?"

She is startled. "I don't. I was looking at the bookshelves."

"But you stared at me last night, at dinner. And you came to the door of my room early this morning. I know because I was awake."

"No, I didn't." But then she softens, and says with eager curiosity, "Are you a socialist?"

While Kirby is trying not to laugh, he hears Mary Beth sing from the kitchen. "Anna? Your brother is going sledding. You want to go?"

Anna turns away before Kirby can answer and mounts the stairs. A "No!" floats, glassy and definite, from the second floor.

Kirby sits down in one of the plaid armchairs and gazes at an arrangement of greenery and shiny red balls and candles that sits on a table behind the couch. He gazes and gazes, contemplating the notion of Eric and Mary Beth discussing his politics and his life. He is offended. He knows that if he were to get up and do something he would stop being offended, but he gets up only to pour himself another drink. It is nearly ten. Books are around everywhere, and Kirby picks one up.

People keep opening doors and coming in, having been elsewhere. Harold comes home for lunch, Leanne and Isaac return from the grocery store and the hardware store, Harold the younger stomps in, covered with snow from sledding, eats a sandwich, and stomps out again. Eric opens the study door, takes a turn through the house, goes back into the study again. He does this three times, each time failing to speak to Kirby, who is sitting quietly. Perhaps he does not see him. He is an old man, Kirby thinks, and his ass has spread considerably in the past four years; he is thirty-six going on fifty, round-shouldered, wearing slacks rather than jeans. What a jerk.

But then Kirby's bad mood twists into him, and he lets his head drop on the back of his chair. What is a man? Kirby thinks. What is a man, what is a man? It is someone, Eric would say, who votes, owns property, has a wife, worries. It is someone, Harold would say, who can chop wood all day and fuck all night, who can lift his twenty-five-pound son above his head on the palm of his hand.

After lunch the men have all vanished again, even Isaac, who is taking a nap. In various rooms the women do things. They make no noise. Harold's house is the house of a wealthy man, Kirby realizes. It is large enough to be silent and neat most of the time, the sort of house Kirby will never own. It is Harold and Eric who are alike now. Only Kirby's being does not extend past his fingertips and toes to family, real estate, reputation.

Sometime in the afternoon, when Kirby is still sitting quietly and his part of the room is shadowed by the movement of the sun to the other side of the house, Kristin comes in from the kitchen, goes straight to the sofa, pulls off one of the cushions, and begins to jump repeatedly from the cushion to the floor. When he says, "Kristin, what are you doing?" she is not startled. She says, "Jumping."

"Do you like to jump?"

She says, "It's a beautiful thing to do," in her matter-of-fact, deep, three-year-old voice. Kirby can't believe she knows what she is saying. She jumps three or four more times and then runs out again.

At dinner she is tired and tiresome. When Eric tells her to eat a bite of her meat (ham cooked with apricots), she looks him right in the face and says, "No."

"One bite," he says. "I mean it."

"No. I mean it." She looks up at him. He puts his napkin on the table and pushes back his chair. In a moment he has swept her through the doorway and up the stairs. She is screaming. A door slams and the scream-ing is muffled. When he comes down and seats himself, carefully laying his napkin over his slacks, Anna says, "It's her body."

The table quiets. Eric says, "What?"

"It's her body."

"What does that mean?"

"She should have control over her own body. Food. Other stuff. I don't know." She has started strong but weakens in the face of her father's glare. Eric inhales sharply, and Kirby cannot restrain himself. He says, "How can you disagree with that? It sounds self-evident to me."

"Does it? The child is three years old. How can she have control over her own body when she doesn't know anything about it? Does she go out without a coat if it's twenty below zero? Does she eat only cookies for three days? Does she wear a diaper until she's five? This is one of those phrases they are using these days. They all mean the same thing."

"What do they mean?" As Kirby speaks, Leanne and Mary Beth look up, no doubt wishing that he had a wife or a girlfriend here to restrain him. Harold looks up, too. He is grinning.

Eric shifts in his chair, uncomfortable, Kirby suddenly realizes, at being predictably stuffy once again. Eric says, "It's Christmas. Let's enjoy it."

Harold says, "Principles are principles, any day of the year."

Eric takes the bait and lets himself say, "The family is constituted for a purpose, which is the sometimes difficult socialization of children. For a certain period of their lives others control them. In early childhood others control their bodies. They are taught to control themselves. Even Freud says that the young barbarian has to be taught to relinquish his feces, sometimes by force.''

"Good Lord, Eric,'' Leanne says.

Eric is red in the face. "Authority is a principle I believe in.'' He looks around the table and then at Anna, openly angry that she has gotten him into this. Across Anna's face flits a look that Kirby has seen before, has seen on Mieko's face, a combination of self-doubt and resentment molded into composure.

"Patriarchy is what you mean,'' Kirby says, realizing from the tone of his own voice that rage has replaced sympathy and, moreover, is about to get the better of him.

"Why not? It works.''

"For some people, at a great cost. Why should daughters be sacrificed to the whims of the father?'' He should stop now. He doesn't. "Just because he put his dick somewhere once or twice.'' The result of too many bourbons too early in the day.

"In my opinion—'' Eric seems not to notice the vulgarity, but Harold, beside Kirby, snorts with pleasure.

"I don't want to talk about this,'' Leanne says. Kirby blushes and falls silent, knowing that he has offended her. It is one of those long holiday meals, and by the time they get up from the table, Kirby feels as if he has been sitting in a dim, candlelit corner most of his life.

There is another ritual—the Christmas Eve unwrapping of presents— and by that time Kirby realizes that he is actively intoxicated and had better watch his tone of voice and his movements. Anna hands out the gifts with a kind of rude bashfulness, and Kirby is surprised at the richness of the array: from Harold he has gotten a cotton turtleneck and a wool sweater, in bright, stylish colors; from Leanne a pair of very fancy gloves; from Isaac three pairs of Ragg wool socks; from Eric's family, as a group, a blue terry-cloth robe and sheepskin slippers. When they open his gifts, he is curious to see what the wrappings reveal: he has bought it all so long before. Almost everything is some gadget available in Japan but not yet in the States. Everyone peers and oohs and aahs. It gives Kirby a headache and a sense of his eyeballs expanding and contracting. Tomorrow night he will be on his way home again, and though he cannot bear to stay here, after all, he cannot bear to leave either.

He drifts toward the stairs, intending to go to bed, but Harold looms before him, grinning and commanding. "Your brain needs some oxygen, brother," he says. Then they are putting on their parkas, and then they are outside, in a cold so sharp that Kirby's nose, the only exposed part of him, stings. Harold strides down the driveway, slightly ahead of him, and Kirby expects him to speak, either for or against Eric, but he doesn't. He only walks. The deep snow is so solidly frozen that it squeaks beneath their boots. The only thing Harold says the whole time they are walking is, "Twenty-two below, not counting the wind chill. Feels good, doesn't it?"

"Feels dangerous," Kirby says.

"It is," Harold says.

The neighborhood is brightly decorated, and the colored lights have their effect on Kirby. For the first time in three Christmases he feels a touch of the mystery that he thinks of as the Christmas spirit. Or maybe it is love for Harold.

Back at the house, everyone has gone to bed except Leanne and Mary Beth, who are drying dishes and putting them away. They are also, Kirby realizes—after Harold strides through the kitchen and up the stairs—arguing, although with smiles and in polite tones. Kirby goes to a cabinet and lingers over getting himself a glass for milk. Mary Beth says, "Kristin will make the connection. She's old enough."

"I can't believe that."

"She saw all the presents being handed out and unwrapped. And Anna will certainly make the connection."

"Anna surely doesn't believe in Santa Claus anymore."

"Unofficially, probably not."

"It's Isaac's first Christmas," Leanne says. "He'll like all the wrappings."

"I wish you'd thought of that before you wrapped the family presents and his Santa presents in the same paper."

"That's a point, too. They're his presents. I don't think Kristin will notice them."

"If they're the only wrapped presents, she will. She notices everything."

Now Leanne turns and gazes at Mary Beth, her hands on her hips. A long silence follows. Leanne flicks a glance at Kirby, who pretends not to notice. Finally she says, "All right, Mary Beth. I'll unwrap them."

"Thank you," Mary Beth says. "I'll finish this, if you want." Kirby goes out of the kitchen and up to his bedroom. The light is already off, and Harold the younger is on his back, snoring.

When he gets up an hour later, too drunk to sleep, Kirby sees Leanne arranging the last of Santa's gifts under the tree. She turns the flash of her glance upon him as he passes through the living room to the kitchen. "Mmm," he says, uncomfortable, "can't sleep."

"Want some cocoa? I always make some before I go to bed."

He stops. "Yeah. Why not? Am I mistaken, or have you been up since about 6:00 A.M.?"

"About that. But I'm always wired at midnight, no matter what."

He follows her into the kitchen, remembering now that they have never conversed and wishing that he had stayed in bed. He has drunk himself stupid. Whatever words he has in him have to be summoned from very far down. He sits at the table. After a minute he puts his chin in his hand. After a long, blank, rather pleasant time, the cocoa is before him, marshmallow and all. He looks at it. When Leanne speaks, Kirby is startled, as if he had forgotten that she was there.

"Tired?" she says.

"Too much to drink."

"I noticed."

"I don't have anything more to say about it."

"I'm not asking."

He takes a sip of his cocoa. He says, "Do you all see much of Eric and family?"

"They came last Christmas. He came by himself in the summer. To a conference on the future of the family."

"And so you have to put up with him, right?"

"Harold has a three-day limit. I don't care."

"I noticed you unwrapped all Isaac's presents."

She shrugs, picks at the sole of her boot. She yawns without covering her mouth, and then says, "Oh, I'm sorry." She smiles warmly, looking right at him. "I am crazy about Kristin. Crazy enough to not chance messing up Christmas for her."

"Today she told me that jumping off a cushion was a beautiful thing to do."

Leanne smiles. "Yesterday she said that it was wonderful of me to give her a napkin. You know, I don't agree with Eric about that body stuff. I think they naturally do what is healthy for them. Somebody did an experiment with one-year-olds, gave them a range of foods to choose from, and they always chose a balanced diet. They also want to be toilet trained sooner or later. I think it's weird the way Eric thinks that every little thing is learned rather than realized."

"That's a nice phrase." He turns his cup handle so that it points away and then back in his direction. Finally he says, "Can I tell you about something?"

"Sure."

"Yesterday a friend of mine called me from Japan, a woman, to say that she couldn't come visit me. Her father has cancer. She had planned to arrive here the day after tomorrow, and we were going to take a trip out West. It isn't important, exactly. I don't know."

Leanne is silent but attentive, picking at the sole of her boot. Now that he has mentioned it, the memory of Mieko's anguish returns to him like a glaring light or a thundering noise, so enormous that he is nearly robbed of the power to speak. He pushes it out. "She can't come now, ever. She probably won't ever call or write me again. And really, this has saved her. She had all sorts of expectations that I couldn't have . . . well, wouldn't

275

have fulfilled, and if she had come she would have been permanently compromised."

"Did you have some kind of affair when you were there?"

"For a few months. She's very pretty. I think she's the prettiest woman I've ever seen. She teaches mathematics at the school where I was teaching. After I had been with Mieko for a few weeks, I realized that no one, maybe in her whole adult life, had asked her how she was, or had put his arm around her shoulders, or had taken care of her in any way. The slightest affection was like a drug she couldn't get enough of."

"What did you feel?"

"I liked her. I really did. I was happy to see her when she came by. But she longed for me more than I have ever longed for anything."

"You were glad to leave."

"I was glad to leave."

"So what's the problem?"

"When she called yesterday, she broke down completely. I listened. I thought it was the least I could do, but now I think that she is compromised. Japanese people are very private. It scares me how much I must have embarrassed her. I look back on the spring and the summer and yesterday's call, and I see that, one by one, I broke down every single one of her strengths, everything she had equipped herself with to live in a Japanese way. I was so careful for a year and a half. I didn't date Japanese women, and I was very distant—but then I was so lonely, and she was so pretty, and I thought, well, she's twenty-seven, and she lives in this sophisticated city, Osaka. But mostly I was lonely."

Leanne gazes across the table in that way of hers, calm and considering. Finally she says, "Eric comes in for a lot of criticism around here. His style's all wrong, for one thing. And he drives Harold the younger and Anna crazy. But I've noticed something about him. He never tries to get something for nothing. I admire that."

Now Kirby looks around the room, at the plants on the windowsill, the hoarfrost on the windowpanes, the fluorescent light harsh on the stainless steel sink, and it seems to him that all at once, now that he realizes it, his life and Mieko's have taken their final form. She is nearly too old to marry, and by the end of her father's cancer and his life she will be much too old. And himself. Himself. Leanne's cool remark has revealed his permanent smallness. He looks at his hands, first his knuckles, then his palms. He says, "It seems so dramatic to say that I will never get over this."

"Does it? To me it seems like saying that what people do is important." And though he looks at her intently, seeking some sort of pardon, she says nothing more, only picks at her boot for a moment or two, and then gets up and puts their cups in the sink. He follows her out of the kitchen, through the living room. She turns out all the lights, so that the house is utterly dark. At the bottom of the stairs, unable to see anything, he stumbles and puts his hand on her arm. She takes it, in a grasp that is dry and cool, and guides it to the banister. Then, soft and fleeting, he feels a disembodied kiss on his cheek.

HEINRICH BÖLL

And There Was the Evening and the Morning. . . .

It was not until noon that he thought of leaving his Christmas presents for Anna in the baggage room at the station; he was glad he had thought of it, for it meant he didn't have to go home immediately. Ever since Anna had stopped speaking to him he was afraid of going home; her silence bore down on him like a tombstone the minute he entered the apartment. He used to look forward to going home, for two years after his wedding day: he loved having supper with Anna, talking to her, and then going to bed; best of all he loved the hour between going to bed and falling asleep. Anna fell asleep earlier than he did because nowadays she was always tired—and he would lie there in the darkness beside her, he could hear her breathing, and from the far end of the street the headlamps of cars now and again threw rays of light onto the ceiling, light that curved down as the cars reached the rise in the street, bands of pale yellow light that made his sleeping wife's profile leap up for a second against the wall; then darkness would fall once more over the room, and all that remained was delicate whorls: the pattern of the curtains drawn on the ceiling by the gas lamp in the street. This was the hour he loved more than any hour of the day, because he could feel the day falling away from him, and he would slide down into sleep as into a bath.

Now he strolled hesitatingly past the baggage counter, and saw his box still there at the back between the red suitcase and the demijohn. The open elevator coming down from the platform was empty, white with snow: it descended like a piece of paper into the gray concrete of the baggage room, and the man who had been operating it walked over and said to the clerk: "Now it really feels like Christmas. It's nice when there's snow for the kids, eh?" The clerk nodded, silently impaled baggage checks on his spike, counted the money in his drawer and looked suspiciously across to Brenig, who had taken his claim check out of his pocket but folded it up and put it back again. This was the third time he had come, the third time he had taken the claim check out and put it back in his pocket again. The clerk's suspicious glances made him uncomfortable; he strolled over to the exit and stood looking out onto the empty station square. He loved the snow, loved the cold; as a boy it had intoxicated him to breathe in the cold clear air, and now he threw away his cigarette and held his face against the wind, which was driving light, profuse snowflakes toward the station. Brenig kept his eyes open, for he liked it when the flakes got caught in his eyelashes, new ones constantly replacing the old which melted and ran down his cheeks in little drops. A girl walked quickly past him, and he saw how her green hat became white with snow while she hurried across the square, but it was only when she was standing at the streetcar stop that he recognized the little red suitcase she was carrying as the one which had stood next to his box in the baggage room.

It was a mistake to get married, thought Brenig; they congratulate you, send you flowers, have stupid telegrams delivered to your door, and then they leave you alone. They ask whether you have thought of everything: of things for the kitchen, from saltshaker to stove, and finally they make sure you even have plenty of soup seasoning on the shelf. They estimate whether you can support a family, but what it means to *be* a family is something nobody tells you. They send flowers, twenty bouquets, and it smells like a funeral; then they throw rice and leave you alone.

A man walked past him, and he could tell the man was drunk, he was singing: "Oh come all ye faithful," but Brenig did not shift the angle of his head so that it was a moment or two before he noticed that the man was carrying a demijohn in his right hand, and he knew the box with his Christmas presents for his wife was now standing all by itself on the top shelf of the baggage room. It contained an umbrella, two books, and a big piano made of mocha chocolate: the white keys were of marzipan, the black ones of dark brittle. The chocolate piano was as big as an encyclopedia, and the girl in the store had said the chocolate would keep for six months.

Maybe I was too young to get married, he thought, maybe I should have waited until Anna became less serious and I became more serious, but actually he knew he was serious enough and that Anna's seriousness was just right. That was what he loved about her. For the sake of the hour before falling asleep he had given up movies and dancing, and hadn't even bothered to meet his friends. At night, when he was lying in bed, he was filled with devoutness, with peace, and he would often repeat the sentence to himself, although he wasn't quite certain of the exact wording: "And God made the earth and the moon, to rule over the day and over the night, to divide the light from the darkness, and God saw that it was good, and there was the evening and the morning." He had meant to look it up in Anna's Bible again to see just how it went, but he always forgot. For God to have created day and night seemed to him every bit as wonderful as the creation of flowers, beasts and man.

He loved this hour before falling asleep more than anything else. But now that Anna had stopped speaking to him her silence lay on him like a weight. If she had only said: "It's colder today. . . ." or "It's going to rain. . . ." it would have put an end to his misery—if she had only said "Yes," or "No, no," or something sillier still, he would be happy, and he would no longer dread going home. But for the space of a few seconds her face would turn to stone, and at these moments he suddenly knew what she would look like as an old woman; he was seized with fear, suddenly saw himself thrust thirty years forward into the future as onto a stony plain, saw himself old too, with the kind of face he had seen on some men: deeply lined with bitterness, strained with suppressed suffering, and tinged to the very nostrils with the light yellow of gall: masks, scattered throughout the everyday world like death's-heads. . . .

Sometimes, although he had only known her for three years, he also knew what she had looked like as a child, he could picture her as a ten-year-old girl, dreaming over a book under the lamplight, grave, her eyes dark under her light lashes, her eyelids flickering above the printed page, her lips parted. . . . Often, when he was sitting opposite her at table, her face would change like the pictures which change when you shake them, and he suddenly knew that she had sat there exactly like that as a child, carefully breaking up her potatoes with her fork and slowly dribbling the gravy over them. . . . The snow had almost stuck his eyelashes together, but he could just make out the number 4 gliding up over the snow as if on sleds.

Maybe I should phone her, he thought, have her come to the phone at Menders; she'd have to speak to me then. The number 4 would be followed immediately by the 7, the last streetcar that evening, but by this time he was bitterly cold and he walked slowly across the square, saw the brightly lighted blue 7 in the distance, stood undecided by the call-box, and looked in a store window where the window dressers were exchanging Santa Clauses and angels for other dummies: ladies in décolleté, their bare shoulders sprinkled with confetti, their wrists festooned with paper streamers. Their escorts, male dummies with graying temples, were being hurriedly placed on barstools, champagne corks scattered on the floor, one dummy was having its wings and curls taken off, and Brenig was surprised how quickly an angel could be turned into a bartender. Mustache, dark wig and a sign swiftly nailed to the wall saying: "New Year's Eve without champagne?"

Here Christmas was over before it had begun. Maybe, he thought, Anna is too young, she was only twenty-one, and while he contemplated his reflection in the store window he noticed the snow had covered his hair like a little crown—the way he used to see it on fence posts—and it struck him that old people were wrong to talk about the gaiety of youth: when you were young, everything was serious and difficult, and nobody helped you, and he was suddenly surprised that he did not hate Anna for her silence, that he didn't wish he had married someone else. The whole vocabulary that people offered you was meaningless: forgiveness, divorce, a fresh start, time the Great Healer—these words were all useless. You had to work it out for yourself, because you were different from other people, and because Anna was different from other people's wives.

The window dressers were deftly nailing masks onto the walls, stringing crackers on a cord: the last number 7 had left long ago, and the box with his presents for Anna was standing all by itself up there on the shelf.

I am twenty-five, he thought, and because of a lie, one little lie, a stupid lie such as millions of men tell every week or every month, I have to endure this punishment; with my eyes staring into the stony future I have to look at Anna crouching like a sphinx on the edge of the stony desert, and at myself, my face yellowed with bitterness, an old man. Oh yes, there would always be plenty of soup seasoning on the kitchen shelf, the saltshaker would always be in its proper place, and he would have been a department head for years and well able to support his family: a stony clan, and never again would he lie in bed and in the hour before falling asleep rejoice in the creation of evening, and offer thanks to God for having created rest from the labors of the day, and he would send the same stupid telegrams to young people when they got married as he had been sent himself. . . .

Other women would have laughed over such a stupid lie about his salary, other women knew that all men lie to their wives: maybe it was a kind of instinctive self-defense, against which they invented their own lies, but Anna's face had turned to stone. There were books about marriage, and he had looked up in these books what you could do when something went wrong with your marriage, but none of the books said anything about a woman who had turned to stone. The books told you how to have children and how not to have children, and they contained a lot of big fine words, but the little words were missing.

The window dressers had finished their work: streamers were hanging over wires that were fastened out of sight, and he saw one of the men disappearing at the back of the store with two angels under his arm, while the second man emptied a bag of confetti over the dummy's bare shoulders and gave a final pat to the sign saying "New Year's Eve without champagne?"

Brenig brushed the snow from his hair, walked back across the square to the station, and when he had taken the claim check from his pocket and smoothed it out for the fourth time he ran quickly as if he hadn't a second to lose. But the baggage room was closed, and there was a sign hanging in front of the grille: "Will be open ten minutes before arrival or departure of a train." Brenig laughed, he laughed for the first time since noon and looked at his box, lying up there on the shelf behind bars as if it were in prison. The departure board was right next to the counter, and he saw the next train would not be arriving for another hour. I can't wait that long, he thought, and at this time of night I won't even be able to get flowers or chocolate, not even a little book, and the last number 7 has gone. For the first time in his life he thought of taking a taxi, and he felt very grown-up, and at the same time a bit foolish, as he ran across the square to the taxi rank.

He sat in the back of the cab, clasping his money: ten marks, the last of his cash, which he had set aside to buy something special for Anna, but he hadn't found anything special, and now he was sitting there clasping his money and watching the meter jump up at short intervals—very short intervals, it seemed to him—ten pfennig at a time, and every time the meter clicked it felt like a stab in the heart, although it only showed two marks eighty. Here I am coming home, with no flowers, no presents, hungry, tired and stupid, and it occurred to him that he could almost certainly have got some chocolate in the waiting room at the station.

The streets were empty, the cab drove almost soundlessly through the snow, and in the lighted windows Brenig could see the Christmas trees glowing in the houses: Christmas, the way he had known it as a child and the way he had felt today, seemed very far away: the important things, the things that mattered, happened independently of the calendar, and in the stony desert Christmas would be like any other day of the year and Easter like a rainy day in November: thirty, forty torn-off calendars, metal holders with shreds of paper, that's all that would be left if you didn't watch out.

He was roused by the driver saying: "Here we are. . . ." Then he was relieved to see that the meter had stopped at three marks forty. He waited impatiently for his change from five marks, and he felt a surge of relief when he saw a light upstairs in the room where Anna's bed stood next to his. He made up his mind never to forget this moment of relief, and as he got out his house key and put it in the door, he experienced that silly feeling again that he had had when he got into the taxi: he felt grown-up, yet at the same time a bit foolish.

In the kitchen the Christmas tree was standing on the table, with presents spread out for him: socks, cigarettes and a new fountain pen, and a gay, colorful calendar which he would be able to hang over his desk in the office. The milk was already in the saucepan on the stove, he had only to light the gas, and there were sandwiches ready for him on the plate—but that was how it had been every evening, even since Anna had stopped speaking to him, and the setting up of the Christmas tree and the laying out of the presents was like the preparing of the sandwiches—a duty, and Anna would always do her duty. He didn't feel like the milk, and the appetizing sandwiches didn't appeal to him either. He went into the little hall and noticed at once that Anna had turned out the light. But the door to the bedroom was open, and without much hope he called softly into the dark rectangle: "Anna, are you asleep?" He waited, for a long time it seemed, as if his question was falling into a deep well, and the dark silence in the dark rectangle of the bedroom door contained everything that was in store for him in thirty, forty years—and when Anna said "No," he thought he must have heard wrong, perhaps it was an illusion, and he went on hurriedly in a louder voice: "I've done such a stupid thing. I checked my presents for you at the station, and when I wanted to pick them up the baggage room was closed, and I didn't want to hang around. Are you angry?"

This time he was sure he had really heard her "No," but he could also hear that this "No" did not come from the corner of the room where their beds had been. Evidently Anna had moved her bed under the window. "It's an umbrella," he said, "two books and a little piano made of chocolate; it's as big as an encyclopedia, the keys are made of marzipan and brittle." He stopped, listened for a reply, nothing came from the dark rectangle, but when he asked: "Are you pleased?" the "Yes" came quicker than the two "No's" had done. . . .

He turned out the light in the kitchen, undressed in the dark and got into bed: through the curtains he could see the Christmas trees in the building across the street, and downstairs there was singing, but he had regained his hour, he had two "No's," and a "Yes," and when a car came up the street the headlamps made Anna's profile leap up out of the darkness for him. . . .

TONI CADE BAMBARA

Christmas Eve at Johnson's Drugs N Goods

I was probably the first to spot them cause I'd been watching the entrance to the store on the lookout for my daddy, knowing that if he didn't show soon, he wouldn't be coming at all. His new family would be expecting him to spend the holidays with them. For the first half of my shift, I'd raced the cleaning cart down the aisles doing a slapdash job on the signs and glass cages, eager to stay in view of the doorway. And look like Johnson's kept getting bigger, swelling, sprawling itself all over the corner lot, just to keep me from the door, to wear me out in the marathon vigil.

In point of fact, Johnson's Drugs N Goods takes up less than one third of the block. But it's laid out funny in crisscross aisles so you get to feeling like a rat in an endless maze. Plus the ceilings are high and the fluorescents a blazing white. And Mrs. Johnson's got these huge signs sectioning off the spaces—TOBACCO   DRUGS   HOUSEWARES, etc.—like it was some big-time department store. The thing is, till the two noisy women came in, it felt like a desert under a blazing sun. Piper in Tobacco even had on shades. The new dude in Drugs looked like he was at the end of a wrong-way telescope. I got to feeling like a nomad with the cleaning cart, trekking across the sands with no end in sight, wandering. The overhead lights creating mirages and racing up my heart till I'd realize that wasn't my daddy in the parking lot, just the poster-board Santa Claus. Or that wasn't my daddy in the entrance way, just the Burma Shave man in a frozen stance. Then I'd tried to make out pictures of Daddy getting off the bus at the

286

terminal, or driving a rented car past the Chamber of Commerce building, or sitting jammed-leg in one of them DC point-o-nine brand-X planes, coming to see me.

By the time the bus pulled into the lot and the two women in their big-city clothes hit the door, I'd decided Daddy was already at the house waiting for me, knowing that for a mirage too, since Johnson's is right across from the railroad and bus terminals and the house is a dollar-sixty cab away. And I know he wouldn't feature going to the house on the off chance of running into Mama. Or even if he escaped that fate, having to sit in the parlor with his hat in his lap while Aunt Harriet looks him up and down grunting, too busy with the latest crossword-puzzle contest to offer the man some supper. And Uncle Henry talking a blue streak bout how he outfoxed the city council or somethin and nary a cold beer in sight for my daddy.

But then the two women came banging into the store and I felt better. Right away the store stopped sprawling, got fixed. And we all got pulled together from our various zones to one focal point—them. Changing up the whole atmosphere of the place fore they even got into the store proper. Before we knew it, we were all smiling, looking halfway like you supposed to on Christmas Eve, even if you do got to work for ol' lady Johnson, who don't give you no slack whatever the holiday.

"What the hell does this mean, Ethel?" the one in the fur coat say, talking loud and fast, yanking on the rails that lead the way into the store. "What are we, cattle? Being herded into the blankety-blank store and in my fur coat," she grumbles, boosting herself up between the rails, swinging her body along like the kids do in the park.

Me and Piper look at each other and smile. Then Piper moves down to the edge of the counter right under the TOBACCO sign so as not to miss nothing. Madeen over in Housewares waved to me to ask what's up and I just shrug. I'm fascinated by the women.

"Look here," the one called Ethel say, drawing the words out lazy slow. "Do you got a token for this sucker?" She's shoving hard against the turnstile folks supposed to exit through. Pushing past and grunting, the turnstile crank cranking like it gonna bust, her Christmas corsage of holly and bells just ajingling and hanging by a thread. Then she gets through and stumbles toward the cigar counter and leans back against it, studying the turnstile hard. It whips back around in place, making scrunching noises like it's been abused.

"You know one thing," she say, dropping her face onto her coat collar so Piper'd know he's being addressed.

"Ma'am?"

"That is one belligerent bad boy, that thing right there."

Piper laughs his prize-winning laugh and starts touching the stacks of gift-wrapped stuff, case the ladies in the market for pipe tobacco or something. Two or three of the customers who'd been falling asleep in the magazines coming to life now, inching forward. Phototropism, I'd call it, if somebody asked me for a word.

The one in the fur coat's coming around now the right way—if you don't count the stiff-elbow rail-walking she was doing—talking about "Oh, my God, I can walk, I can walk, Ethel, praise de lawd."

The two women watching Piper touch the cigars, the humidors, the gift-wrapped boxes. Mostly he's touching himself, cause George Lee Piper love him some George Lee Piper. Can't blame him. Piper be fine.

"You work on commissions, young man?" Fur Coat asking.

"No, ma'am."

The two women look at each other. They look over toward the folks inching forward. They look at me gliding by with the cleaning cart. They look back at each other and shrug.

"So what's his problem?" Ethel says in a stage whisper. "Why he so hot to sell us something?"

"Search me." Fur Coat starts flapping her coat and frisking herself. "You know?" she asking me.

"It's a mystery to me," I say, doing my best to run ol' man Sampson over. He sneaking around trying to jump Madeen in Housewares. And it is a mystery to me how come Piper always so eager to make a sale. You'd think he had half interest in the place. He says it's because it's his job, and after all, the Johnsons are black folks. I guess so, I guess so. Me, I just clean the place and stay busy in case Mrs. J is in the prescription booth, peeking out over the top of the glass.

When I look around again, I see that the readers are suddenly very interested in cigars. They crowding around Ethel and Fur Coat. Piper kinda embarrassed by all the attention, though fine as he is, he oughta be used to it. His expression's cool but his hands give him away, sliding around the counter like he shuffling a deck of slippery cards. Fur Coat nudges Ethel and they bend over to watch the hands, doing these chicken-head jerkings. The readers take up positions just like a director was hollering "Places" at em. Piper, never one to disappoint an audience, starts zipping around these invisible walnut shells. Right away Fur Coat whips out a little red change purse and slaps a dollar bill on the counter. Ethel dips deep into her coat pocket, bending her knees and being real comic, then plunks down some change. Ol' man Sampson tries to boost up on my cleaning cart to see the shells that ain't there.

"Scuse me, Mr. Sampson," I say, speeding the cart up sudden so that quite naturally he falls off, the dirty dog.

Piper is snapping them imaginary shells around like nobody's business, one of the readers leaning over another's shoulder, staring pop-eyed.

"All right now, everybody step back," Ethel announces. She waves the crowd back and pushes up one coat sleeve, lifts her fist into the air and jerks out one stiff finger from the bunch, and damn if the readers don't lift their heads to behold in amazement this wondrous finger.

"That, folks," Fur Coat explains, "is what is known as the indicator finger. The indicator is about to indicate the indicatee."

"Say wha?" Dirty ol' man Sampson decides he'd rather sneak up on Madeen than watch the show.

"What's going on over there?" Miz Della asks me. I spray the watch case and make a big thing of wiping it and ignoring her. But then the new dude in Drugs hollers over the same thing.

"Christmas cheer gone to the head. A coupla vaudevillians," I say. He smiles, and Miz Della says "Ohhh" like I was talking to her.

289

"This one," Ethel says, planting a finger exactly one quarter of an inch from the countertop.

Piper dumb-shows a lift of the shell, turning his face away as though he can't bear to look and find the elusive pea ain't there and he's gonna have to take the ladies' money. Then his eyes swivel around and sneak a peek and widen, lighting up his whole face in a prize-winning grin.

"You got it," he shouts.

The women grab each other by the coat shoulders and jump each other up and down. And I look toward the back cause I know Mrs. J got to be hearing all this carrying-on, and on payday if Mr. J ain't handing out the checks, she's going to give us some long lecture about decorum and what it means to be on board at Johnson's Drugs N Goods. I wheel over to the glass jars and punch bowls, wanting alibi distance just in case. And also to warn Madeen about Sampson gaining on her. He's ducking down behind the coffeepots, walking squat and shameless.

"Pay us our money, young man," Fur Coat is demanding, rapping her knuckles on the counter.

"Yeah, what kind of crooked shell game is you running here in this joint?" say Ethel, finding a good foil character to play.

"We should hate to have to turn the place out, young man."

"It out," echoes Ethel.

The women nod to the crowd and a coupla folks giggle. And Piper tap-taps on the cash register like he shonuff gonna give em they money. I'd rather they turned the place out myself. I want to call my daddy. Only way any of us are going to get home in time to dress for the Christmas dance at the center is for the women to turn it out. Like I say, Piper ain't too clear about the worker's interest versus management's, as the dude in Drugs would say it. So he's light-tapping and quite naturally the cash drawer does not come out. He's yanking some unseen dollar from the not-there drawer and handing it over. Damn if Fur Coat don't snatch it, deal out the bills to herself and her friend and then make a big production out of folding the money flat and jamming it in that little red change purse.

"I wanna thank you," Ethel says, strolling off, swinging her pocket-

290

book so that the crowd got to back up and disperse. Fur Coat spreads her coat and curtsies.

"A pleasure to do business with you ladies," Piper says, tipping his hat, looking kinda disappointed that he didn't sell em something. Tipping his hat the way he tipped the shells, cause you know Mrs. J don't allow no hats indoors. I came to work in slacks one time and she sent me home to change and docked me too. I wear a gele sometimes just to mess her around, and you can tell she trying to figure out if she'll go for it or not. The woman is crazy. Not Uncle Henry–type crazy, but black-property-owner-type crazy. She thinks this is a museum, which is why folks don't hardly come in here to shop. That's OK cause we all get to know each other well. It's not OK cause it's a drag to look busy. If you look like you ain't buckling under a weight of work, Mrs. J will have you count the Band-Aids in the boxes to make sure the company ain't pulling a fast one. The woman crazy.

Now Uncle Henry–type crazy is my kind of crazy. The type crazy to get you a job. He march into the "saloon" as he calls it and tells Leon D that he is not an equal-opportunity employer and that he, Alderman Henry Peoples, is going to put some fire to his ass. So soon's summer comes, me and Madeen got us a job at Leon D. Salon. One of them hushed, funeral-type shops with skinny models parading around for customers corseted and strangling in their seats, huffin and puffin.

Madeen got fired right off on account of the pound of mascara she wears on each lash and them weird dresses she designs for herself (with less than a yard of cloth each if you ask me). I did my best to hang in there so's me and Madeen'd have hang-around money till Johnson started hiring again. But it was hard getting back and forth from the stockroom to this little kitchen to fix the espresso to the showroom. One minute up to your ass in carpet, the next skidding across white linoleum, the next making all this noise on ceramic tile and people looking around at you and all. Was there for two weeks and just about had it licked by stationing different kind of shoes at each place that I could slip into, but then Leon D stumbled over my bedroom slippers one afternoon.

But to hear Uncle Henry tell it, writing about it all to Daddy, I was working at a promising place making a name for myself. And Aunt Harriet listening to Uncle Henry read the letter, looking me up and down and grunting. She know what kind of name it must be, cause my name in the family is Miss Clumsy. Like if you got a glass-top coffee table with doodads on em, or a hurricane lamp sitting on a mantel anywhere near a door I got to come through, or an antique jar you brought all the way from Venice the time you won the crossword puzzle contest—you can rest assure I'll demolish them by and by. I ain't vicious, I'm just clumsy. It's my gawky stage, Mama says. Aunt Harriet cuts her eye at Mama and grunts.

My daddy advised me on the phone not to mention anything to the Johnsons about this gift of mine for disaster or the fact that I worked at Leon D. Salon. No sense the Johnsons calling up there to check on me and come to find I knocked over a perfume display two times in the same day. Like I say—it's a gift. So when I got to clean the glass jars and punch bowls at Johnson's, I take it slow and pay attention. Then I take up my station relaxed in Fabrics, where the worst that can happen is I upset a box of pins.

Mrs. J is in the prescription booth, and she clears her throat real loud. We all look to the back to read the smoke signals. She ain't paying Fur Coat and Ethel no attention. They over in Cosmetics messing with Miz Della's mind and her customers. Mrs. J got her eye on some young teenagers browsing around Jewelry. The other eye on Piper. But this does not mean Piper is supposed to check the kids out. It means Madeen is. You got to know how to read Mrs. J to get along.

She always got one eye on Piper. Tries to make it seem like she don't trust him at the cash register. That may be part of the reason now, now that she's worked up this cover story so in her mind. But we all know why she watches Piper, same reason we all do. Cause Piper is so fine you just can't help yourself. Tall and built up, blue-black and smooth, got the nerve to have dimples, and wears this splayed-out push-broom mustache he's always raking in with three fingers. Got a big butt too that makes you wanna hug the customer that asks for the cartoons Piper keeps behind him, two shelfs down. Mercy. And when it's slow, or when Mrs. J comes bustling over for the count, Piper steps from behind the counter and shows his self. You get to see the whole Piper from the shiny boots to the glistening fro and every inch of him fine. Enough to make you holler.

Miz Della in Cosmetics, a sister who's been passing for years but fooling nobody but herself, she always lollygagging over to Tobacco talking bout are there any new samples of those silver-tipped cigars for women. Piper don't even squander energy to bump her off anymore. She mostly just ain't even there. At first he would get mad when she used to act hinkty and had these white men picking her up at the store. Then he got sorrowful about it all, saying she was a pitiful person. Now that she's going out with the blond chemist back there, he just wiped her off the map. She tries to mess with him, but Piper ain't heard the news she's been born. Sometimes his act slips, though, cause he does take a lot of unnecessary energy to play up to Madeen whenever Miz Della's hanging around. He's not consistent in his attentions, and that spurs Madeen the dress designer to madness. And Piper really oughta put brakes on that, cause Madeen subject to walk in one day in a fishnet dress and no underwear and then what he goin do about that?

Last year on my birthday my daddy got on us about dressing like hussies to attract the boys. Madeen shrugged it off and went about her business. It hurt my feelings. The onliest reason I was wearing that tight sweater and that skimpy skirt was cause I'd been to the roller rink and that's how we dress. But my daddy didn't even listen and I was really hurt. But then later that night, I come through the living room to make some cocoa and he apologized. He lift up from the couch where he always sleeps when he comes to visit, lifted up and whispered it—"Sorry." I could just make him out by the light from the refrigerator.

"Candy," he calls to make sure I heard him. And I don't want to close the fridge door cause I know I'll want to remember this scene, figuring it's going to be the last birthday visit cause he fixin to get married and move outta state.

"Sir?"

He pat the couch and I come on over and just leave the fridge door open so we can see each other. I forgot to put the milk down, so I got this cold milk bottle in my lap, feeling stupid.

"I was a little rough on you earlier," he say, picking something I can't see from my bathrobe. "But you're getting to be a woman now and certain things have to be said. Certain things have to be understood so you can decide what kind of woman you're going to be, ya know?"

"Sir," I nod. I'm thinking Aunt Harriet ought to tell me, but then Aunt Harriet prefers to grunt at folks, reserving words for the damn crossword puzzles. And my mama stay on the road so much with the band, when she do come home for a hot minute all she has to tell me is "My slippers're in the back closet" or "Your poor tired ma'd like some coffee."

He takes my hand and don't even kid me about the milk bottle, just holds my hand for a long time saying nothing, just squeezes it. And I know he feeling bad about moving away and all, but what can he do, he got a life to lead. Just like Mama got her life to lead. Just like I got my life to lead and'll probably leave here myself one day and become an actress or a director. And I know I should tell him it's all right. Sitting there with that milk bottle chilling me through my bathrobe, the light from the refrigerator throwing funny shadows on the wall, I know that years later when I'm in trouble or something, or hear that my daddy died or something like that, I'm going feel real bad that I didn't tell him—it's all right, Daddy, I understand. It ain't like he'd made any promises about making a home for me with him. So it ain't like he's gone back on his word. And if the new wife can't see taking in no half-grown new daughter, hell, I understand that. I can't get the words together, neither can he. So we just squeeze each other's hands. And that'll have to do.

"When I was a young man," he says after while, "there were girls who ran around all made up in sassy clothes. And they were OK to party with, but not the kind you cared for, ya know?" I nod and he pats my hand. But I'm thinking that ain't right, to party with a person you don't care for. How come you can't? I want to ask, but he's talking. And I was raised not to interrupt folk when they talking, especially my daddy. "You and Madeen cause quite a stir down at the barbershop." He tries to laugh it, but it comes out scary. "Got to make up your mind now what kind of woman you're going to be. You know what I'm saying?" I nod and he loosens his grip so I can go make my cocoa.

I'm messing around in the kitchenette feeling dishonest. Things I want to say, I haven't said. I look back over toward the couch and know this picture is going to haunt me later. Going to regret the things left unsaid. Like a coward, like a child maybe. I fix my cocoa and keep my silence, but I do remember to put the milk back and close the refrigerator door.

"Candy?"

"Sir?" I'm standing there in the dark, the fridge door closed now and we can't even see each other.

"It's not about looks anyway," he says, and I hear him settling deep into the couch and pulling up the bedclothes. "And it ain't always about attracting some man either . . . not necessarily."

I'm waiting to hear what it is about, the cup shaking in the saucer and me wanting to ask him all over again how it was when he and Mama first met in Central Park, and how it used to be when they lived in Philly and had me and how it was when the two of them were no longer making any sense together but moved down here anyway and then split up. But I could hear that breathing he does just before the snoring starts. So I hustle on down the hall so I won't be listening for it and can't get to sleep.

All night I'm thinking about this woman I'm going to be. I'll look like Mama but don't wanna be no singer. Was named after Grandma Candestine but don't wanna be no fussy old woman with a bunch of kids. Can't see myself turning into Aunt Harriet either, doing crossword puzzles all day long. I look over at Madeen, all sprawled out in her bed, tangled up in the sheets looking like the alcoholic she trying to be these days, sneaking liquor from Uncle Henry's closet. And I know I don't wanna be stumbling down the street with my boobs out and my dress up and my heels cracking off and all. I write for a whole hour in my diary trying to connect with the future me and trying not to hear my daddy snoring.

* * *

Fur Coat and Ethel in Housewares talking with Madeen. I know they must be cracking on Miz Della, cause I hear Madeen saying something about equal opportunity. We used to say that Mrs. J was an equal-opportunity employer for hiring Miz Della. But then she went and hired real white folks—a blond, crew cut chemist and a pimply-face kid for the stockroom. If you ask me, that's running equal opportunity in the ground. And running the business underground cause don't nobody round here deal with no white chemist. They used to wrinkly old folks grinding up the herbs and bark and telling them very particular things to do and not to do working the roots. So they keep on going to Mama Drear down past the pond or Doc Jessup in back of the barbershop. Don't do a doctor one bit of good to write out a prescription talking about fill it at Johnson's, cause unless it's an emergency folk stay strictly away from a white root worker, especially if he don't tell you what he doing.

Aunt Harriet in here one day when Mama Drear was too sick to counsel and quite naturally she asks the chemist to explain what all he doing back there with the mortar and pestle and the scooper and the scales. And he say something about rules and regulations, the gist of which was mind your business, lady. Aunt Harriet dug down deep into her crossword puzzle words and pitched a natural bitch. Called that man a bunch of choicest names. But the line that got me was—"Medication without explanation is obscene." And what she say that for, we ran that in the ground for days. Infatuation without fraternization is obscene. Insemination without obligation is tyranny. Fornication without contraception is obtuse, and so forth and so on. Madeen's best line came out the night we were watching a TV special about welfare. Sterilization without strangulation and hell's damnation is I-owe-you-one crackers. Look like every situation called for a line like that, and even if it didn't, we made it fit.

Then one Saturday morning we were locked out and we standing around shivering in our sweaters and this old white dude jumps out a pickup truck hysterical, his truck still in gear and backing out the lot. His wife had given their child an overdose of medicine and the kid was out cold. Look like everything he said was grist for the mill.

"She just administered the medicine without even reading the label," he told the chemist, yanking on his jacket so the man couldn't even get out his keys. "She never even considered the fact it might be dangerous, the medicine so old and all." We follow the two down the aisle to the prescription booth, the old white dude talking a mile a minute, saying they tried to keep the kid awake, tried to walk him, but he wouldn't walk. Tried to give him an enema, but he wouldn't stay propped up. Could the chemist suggest something to empty his stomach out and soothe his inflamed ass and what all? And besides he was breathing funny and should he administer mouth-to-mouth resuscitation? The minute he tore out of there and ran down the street to catch up with his truck, we started in.

Administration without consideration is illiterate. Irrigation without resuscitation is evacuation without ambulation is inflammation without information is execution without restitution is. We got downright silly about the whole thing till Mrs. J threatened to fire us all. But we kept it up for a week.

Then the new dude in Drugs who don't never say much stopped the show one afternoon when we were trying to figure out what to call the street riots in the sixties and so forth. He say revolution without transformation is half-assed. Took me a while to ponder that one, a whole day in fact just to work up to it. After while I would listen real hard whenever he opened his mouth, which wasn't often. And I jotted down the titles of the books I'd see him with. And soon's I finish up the stack that's by my bed, I'm hitting the library. He started giving me some of the newspapers he keeps stashed in that blue bag of his we all at first thought was full of funky jockstraps and sneakers. Come to find it's full of carrots and oranges and books and stuff. Madeen say he got a gun in there too. But then Madeen all the time saying something. Like she saying here lately that the chemist's jerking off there behind the poisons and the goopher dust.

The chemist's name is Hubert Tarrly. Madeen tagged him Herbert Tareyton. But the name that stuck was Nazi Youth. Every time I look at him I hear Hitler barking out over the loudspeaker urging the youth to measure up and take over the world. And I can see these stark-eyed gray kids in short

297

pants and suspenders doing jump-ups and scissor kicks and turning they mamas in to the Gestapo for listening to the radio. Chemist looks like he grew up like that, eating knockwurst and beating on Jews, rounding up gypsies, saying *Sieg heil* and shit. Mrs. J said something to him one morning and damn if he didn't click his heels. I like to die. She blushing all over her simple self talking bout that's southern cavalier style. I could smell the gas. I could see the flaming cross too. Nazi Youth and then some. The dude in Drugs started calling him that too, the dude whose name I can never remember. I always wanna say Ali Baba when I talk about him with my girlfriends down at the skating rink or with the older sisters at the arts center. But that ain't right. Either you call a person a name that says what they about or you call em what they call themselves, one or the other.

Now take Fur Coat, for instance. She is clearly about the fur coat. She moving up and down the aisles talking while Ethel in the cloth coat is doing all the work, picking up teapots, checking the price on the dust mops, clicking a bracelet against the punch bowl to see if it ring crystal, hollering to somebody about whether the floor wax need buffing or not. And it's all on account of the fur coat. Her work is something other than that. Like when they were in Cosmetics messing with Miz Della, some white ladies come up talking about what's the latest in face masks. And every time Miz Della pull something out the box, Ethel shake her head and say that brand is crap. Then Fur Coat trots out the surefire recipe for the face mask. What she tells the old white ladies is to whip up some egg white to peaks, pour in some honey, some oil of wintergreen, some oil of eucalyptus, the juice of a lemon and a half a teaspoon of arsenic. Now any fool can figure out what lemon juice do to arsenic, or how honey going make the concoction stick, and what all else the oil of this and that'll do to your face. But Fur Coat in her fur coat make you stand still and listen to this madness. Fur Coat an authority in her fur coat. The fur coat is an act of alchemy in itself, as Aunt Harriet would put it.

Just like my mama in her fur coat, same kind too—Persian lamb, bought hot in some riot or other. Mama's coat was part of the Turn The School Out Outfit. Hardly ever came out of the quilted bag cept for that.

Wasn't for window-shopping, wasn't for going to rehearsal, wasn't for church teas, was for working her show. She'd flip a flap of that coat back over her hip when she strolled into the classroom to get on the teacher's case bout saying something out of the way about black folks. Then she'd pick out the exact plank, exact spot she'd take her stand on, then plant one of them black suede pumps from the I. Miller outlet she used to work at. Then she'd lift her chin arrogant proud to start the rap, and all us kids would lean forward and stare at the cameo brooch visible now on the wide-wale wine plush corduroy dress. Then she'd work her show in her outfit. Bam-bam that black suede pocketbook punctuating the points as Mama ticked off the teacher's offenses. And when she got to the good part, and all us kids would strain up off the benches to hear every word so we could play it out in the school yard, she'd take both fists and brush that fur coat way back past her hips and she'd challenge the teacher to either change up and apologize or meet her for a showdown at a school-board hearing. And of course ol' teacher'd apologize to all us black kids. Then Mama'd let the coat fall back into place and she'd whip around, the coat draping like queen robes, and march herself out. Mama was baad in her fur coat.

I don't know what-all Fur Coat do in her fur coat but I can tell it's hellafyin whatever it all is. They came into Fabrics and stood around a while trying to see what shit they could get into. All they had in their baskets was a teapot and some light bulbs and some doodads from the special gift department, perfume and whatnot. I waited on a few customers wanting braid and balls of macramé twine, nothing where I could show my stuff. Now if somebody wanted some of the silky, juicy cotton stuff I could get into something fancy, yanking off the yards, measuring it doing a shuffle-stick number, nicking it just so, then ripping the hell out the shit. But didn't nobody ask for that. Fur Coat and Ethel kinda finger some bolts and trade private jokes, then they moved onto Drugs.

"We'd like to see the latest in rubberized fashions for men, young man." Fur Coat is doing a super Lady Granville Whitmore the Third number. "If you would." She bows her head, fluttering her lashes.

Me and Madeen start messing around in the shoe-polish section so's not to miss nothing. I kind of favor Fur Coat, on account of she got my mama's coat on, I guess. On the other hand, I like the way Ethel drawl talk like she too tired and bored to go on. I guess I like em both cause they shopping the right way, having fun and all. And they got plenty of style. I wouldn't mind being like that when I am full grown.

The dude in Drugs thinks on the request awhile, sucking in his lips like he wanna talk to himself on the inside. He's looking up and down the counter, pauses at the plastic rain hats, rejects them, then squints hard at Ethel and Fur Coat. Fur Coat plants a well-heeled foot on the shelf with the tampons and pads and sighs. Something about that sigh I don't like. It's real rather than play snooty. The dude in Drugs always looks a little crumbled, a little rough dry, like he jumped straight out the hamper but not quite straight. But he got stuff to him if you listen rather than look. Seems to me ol' Fur Coat is looking. She keeps looking while the dude moves down the aisle behind the counter, ducks down out of sight, reappears and comes back, dumping an armful of boxes on the counter.

"One box of Trojans and one box of Ramses," Ethel announces. "We want to do the comparison test."

"On the premises?" Lady G Fur says, planting a dignified hand on her collarbone.

"Egg-zack-lee."

"In your opinion, young man," Lady G Fur says, staying the arm of the brand tester, "which of the two is the best? Uhmm—the better of the two, that is. In your vast experience as lady-killer and cock hound, which passes the X test?" It's said kinda snotty. Me and Madeen exchange a look and dust around the cans of shoe polish.

"Well," the dude says, picking up a box in each hand, "in my opinion, Trojans have a snappier ring to em." He rattles the box against his ear, then lets Ethel listen. She nods approval. Fur Coat will not be swayed. "On the other hand, Ramses is a smoother smoke. Cooler on the throat. What do you say in your vast experience as—er—"

Ethel is banging down boxes of Kotex cracking up, screaming, "He gotcha. He gotcha that time. Old laundry bag got over on you, Helen."

300

Mrs. J comes out of the prescription booth and hustles her bulk to the counter. Me and Madeen clamp down hard on giggles and I damn near got to climb in with the neutral shoe polish to escape attention. Ethel and Fur Coat don't give a shit, they paying customers, so they just roar. Cept Fur Coat's roar is phony, like she really mad and gonna get even with the dude for not turning out to be a chump. Meanwhile, the dude is standing like a robot, arms out at exactly the same height, elbows crooked just so, boxes displayed between thumb and next finger, the gears in the wrist click, clicking, turning. And not even cracking a smile.

"What's the problem here?" Mrs. J trying not to sound breathless or angry and ain't doing too good a job. She got to say it twice to be heard.

"No problem, Mrs. Johnson," the dude says straight-face. "The customers are buying condoms, I am selling condoms. A sale is being conducted, as is customary in a store."

Mrs. J looks down at the jumble of boxes and covers her mouth. She don't know what to do. I duck down, cause when folks in authority caught in a trick, the first they look for is a scapegoat.

"Well, honey," Ethel says, giving a chummy shove to Mrs. J's shoulder, "what do you think? I've heard that Trojans are ultrasensitive. They use a baby lamb brain, I understand."

"Membrane, dear, membrane," Fur Coat says down her nose. "They remove the intestines of a four-week-old lamb and use the membrane. Tough, resilient, sheer."

"Gotcha," says Ethel. "On the other hand, it is said by folks who should know that Ramses has a better box score."

"Box score," echoes Mrs. J in a daze.

"Box score. You know, honey—no splits, breaks, leaks, seeps."

"Seepage, dear, seepage," says Fur Coat, all nasal.

"Gotcha."

"The solution," says the dude in an almost robot voice, "is to take one small box of each and do the comparison test as you say. A survey. A random sampling of your friends." He says this to Fur Coat, who is not enjoying it all nearly so much as Ethel, who is whooping and hollering.

301

Mrs. J backs off and trots to the prescription booth. Nazi Youth peeks over the glass and mumbles something soothing to Mrs. J. He waves me and Madeen away like he somebody we got to pay some mind.

"We will take one super-duper, jumbo family size of each."

"Family size?" Fur Coat is appalled. "And one more thing, young man," she orders. "Wrap up a petite size for a small-size smart-ass acquaintance of mine. Gift-wrapped, ribbons and all."

It occurs to me that Fur Coat's going to present this to the dude. Right then and there I decide I don't like her. She's not discriminating with her stuff. Up till then I was thinking how much I'd like to trade Aunt Harriet in for either of these two, hang out with them, sit up all night while they drink highballs and talk about men they've known and towns they've been in. I always did want to hang out with women like this and listen to their stories. But they beginning to reveal themselves as not nice people, just cause the dude is rough dry on Christmas Eve. My Uncle Henry all the time telling me they different kinds of folks in the community, but when you boil it right down there's just nice and not nice. Uncle Henry say they folks who'll throw they mamas to the wolves if the fish sandwich big enough. They folks who won't whatever the hot sauce. They folks that're scared, folks that are dumb; folks that have heart and some with heart to spare. That all boils down to nice and not nice if you ask me. It occurs to me that Fur Coat is not nice. Fun, dazzling, witty, but not nice.

"Do you accept Christmas gifts, young man?" Fur Coat asking in icy tones she ain't masking too well.

"No. But I do accept Kwanza presents at the feast."

"Quan . . . hmm . . ."

Fur Coat and Ethel go into a huddle with the stage whispers. "I bet he thinks we don't know beans about Quantas. . . . Don't he know we are the Ebony Jet Set. . . . We never travel to kangaroo land except by . . ."

Fur Coat straightens up and stares at the dude. "Will you accept a whatchamacallit gift from me even though we are not feasting, as it were?"

"If it is given with love and respect, my sister, of course." He was sounding so sincere, it kinda got to Fur Coat.

302

"In that case . . ." She scoops up her bundle and sweeps out the place. Ethel trotting behind hollering, "He gotcha, Helen. Give the boy credit. Maybe we should hire him and do a threesome act." She spun the turnstile round three times for she got into the spin and spun out the store.

"Characters," says Piper on tiptoe, so we all can hear him. He laughs and checks his watch. Madeen slinks over to Tobacco to be in asking distance in case he don't already have a date to the dance. Miz Della's patting some powder on. I'm staring at the door after Fur Coat and Ethel, coming to terms with the fact that my daddy ain't coming. It's gonna be just Uncle Henry and Aunt Harriet this year, with maybe Mama calling on the phone between sets to holler in my ear, asking have I been a good girl, it's been that long since she's taken a good look at me.

"You wanna go to the Kwanza celebrations with me sometime this week or next week, Candy?"

I turn and look at the dude. I can tell my face is falling and right now I don't feel up to doing anything about it. Holidays are depressing. Maybe there's something joyous about this celebration he's talking about. Cause Lord knows Christmas is a drag. The sister who taught me how to wrap a gele asked me was I coming to the celebration down at the Black Arts Center, but I didn't know nothing bout it.

"Look here," I finally say, "would you please get a pencil and paper and write your name down for me. And write that other word down too so I can look it up."

He writes his name down and spins the paper around for me to read. "Obatale."

"Right," he says, spinning it back. "But you can call me Ali Baba if you want to." He was leaning over too far writing out Kwanza for me to see if that was a smile on his face or a smirk. I figure a smile, cause Obatale nice people.

RAY BRADBURY

Bless Me, Father, for I Have Sinned

It was just before midnight on Christmas Eve when Father Mellon woke, having slept for only a few minutes. He had a most peculiar urge to rise, go, and swing wide the front door of his church to let the snow in and then go sit in the confessional to wait.

Wait for what? Who could say? Who might tell? But the urge was so incredibly strong it was not to be denied.

"What's going on here?" he muttered quietly to himself, as he dressed. "I am going mad, am I not? At this hour, who could possibly want or need, and why in blazes should I—"

But dress he did and down he went and opened wide the front door of the church and stood in awe of the great artwork beyond, better than any painting in history, a tapestry of snow weaving in laces and gentling to roofs and shadowing the lamps and putting shawls on the huddled masses of cars waiting to be blessed at the curb. The snow touched the sidewalks and then his eyelids and then his heart. He found himself holding his breath with the fickle beauties and then, turning, the snow following at his back, he went to hide in the confessional.

Damn fool, he thought. Stupid old man. *Out* of here! Back to your bed!

But then he heard it: a sound at the door, and footsteps scraping on the pavestones of the church, and at last the damp rustle of some invader fresh to the other side of the confessional. Father Mellon waited.

"Bless me," a man's voice whispered, "for I have sinned!"

Stunned at the quickness of this asking, Father Mellon could only retort:

"How *could* you know the church would be open and I here?"

"I prayed, Father," was the quiet reply. "God *made* you come open up."

There seemed no answer to this, so the old priest, and what sounded like a hoarse old sinner, sat for a long cold moment as the clock itched on toward midnight, and at last the refugee from darkness repeated:

"*Bless* this sinner, father!"

But in place of the usual unguents and ointments of words, with Christmas hurrying fast through the snow, Father Mellon leaned toward the lattice window and could not help saying:

"It must be a terrible load of sin you carry to have driven you out on such a night on an impossible mission that turned possible only because God heard and pushed me out of bed."

"It *is* a terrible list, Father, as you will find!"

"Then speak, son," said the priest, "before we both freeze—"

"Well, it was this way—" whispered the wintry voice behind the thin paneling. "—Sixty years back—"

"Speak up! Sixty?!" The priest gasped. "That *long* past?"

"Sixty!" And there was a tormented silence.

"Go on," said the priest, ashamed of interrupting.

"Sixty years this week, when I was twelve," said the gray voice, "I Christmas-shopped with my grandmother in a small town back East. We walked both ways. In those days, who had a car? We walked, and coming home with the wrapped gifts, my grandma said something, I've long since forgotten what, and I got mad and ran ahead, away from her. Far off, I could hear her call and then cry, terribly, for me to come back, come back, but I wouldn't. She wailed so, I knew I had hurt her, which made me feel strong and good, so I ran even more, laughing, and beat her to the house and when she came in she was gasping and weeping as if never to stop. I felt ashamed and ran to hide. . . ."

There was a long silence.

The priest prompted, "Is that *it?*"

"The list is long," mourned the voice beyond the thin panel.

"Continue," said the priest, eyes shut.

"I did much the same to my mother, before New Year's. She angered me. I ran. I heard her cry out behind me. I smiled and ran faster. Why? Why, oh God, why?"

The priest had no answer.

"Is that it, then?" he murmured, at last, feeling strangely moved toward the old man beyond.

"One summer day," said the voice, "some bullies beat me. When they were gone, on a bush I saw two butterflies, embraced, lovely. I hated their happiness. I grabbed them in my fist and pulverized them to dust. Oh, Father, the shame!"

The wind blew in the church door at that moment and both of them glanced up to see a Christmas ghost of snow turned about in the door and falling away in drifts of whiteness to scatter on the pavings.

"There's one last terrible thing," said the old man, hidden away with his grief. And then he said:

"When I was thirteen, again in Christmas week, my dog Bo ran away and was lost three days and nights. I loved him more than life itself. He was special and loving and fine. And all of a sudden the beast was gone, and all his beauty with him. I waited. I cried. I waited. I prayed. I shouted under my breath. I knew he would never, never come back! And then, oh, then, that Christmas Eve at two in the morning, with sleet on the sidewalks and icicles on roofs and snow falling, I heard a sound in my sleep and woke to hear him scratching the door! I bounded from bed so fast I almost killed myself! I yanked the door open and there was my miserable dog, shivering, excited, covered with dirty slush. I yelled, pulled him in, slammed the door, fell to my knees, grabbed him and wept. What a gift, what a gift! I called his name over and over, and he wept with me, all whines and agonies of joy. And then I stopped. Do you know what I did then? Can you guess the terrible thing? I beat him. Yes, beat him. With my fists, my hands, my palms, and my fists again, crying: how dare you leave, how dare you run off, how dare you do that to me, how dare you, how dare!? And I beat and beat until I was weak and sobbed and had to stop for I saw what I'd done, and he just stood and took it all as if he knew he deserved it; he had failed my love and now I was failing his, and I pulled off and tears streamed from my eyes, my breath strangled, and I grabbed him again and crushed him to me but this time cried: forgive, oh please, Bo, forgive. I didn't mean it. Oh, Bo, forgive. . . .

"But, oh, Father, he couldn't forgive me. Who was he? A beast, an animal, a dog, my love. And he looked at me with such great dark eyes that it locked my heart and it's been locked forever after with shame. *I could not then forgive myself.* All these years, the memory of my love and how I failed him, and every Christmas since, not the rest of the year, but every Christmas Eve, his ghost comes back, I see the dog, I hear the beating, I know my failure. Oh, God!"

The man fell silent, weeping.

And at last the old priest dared a word: "And that is why you are here?"

"Yes, Father. Isn't it awful. Isn't it terrible?"

The priest could not answer, for tears were streaming down his face, too, and he found himself unaccountably short of breath.

"Will God forgive me, Father?" asked the other.

"Yes."

"Will *you* forgive me, Father?"

"Yes. But let me tell you something now, son. When I was ten, the same things happened. My parents, of course, but then—my dog, the love of *my* life, who ran off and I hated him for leaving me, and when he came back I, too, loved and beat him, then went back to love. Until this night, I have told no one. The shame has stayed put all these years. I have confessed all to my priest-confessor. But *never* that. So—"

There was a pause.

"*So,* Father?"

"Lord, Lord, dear man, God will forgive us. At long last, we have brought it out, dared to say. And I, I will forgive you. But finally—"

The old priest could not go on, for new tears were really pouring down his face now.

The stranger on the other side guessed this and very carefully inquired, "Do you want *my* forgiveness, Father?"

The priest nodded, silently. Perhaps the other felt the shadow of the nod, for he quickly said, "Ah, well. It's *given*."

And they both sat there for a long moment in the dark and another ghost moved to stand in the door, then sank to snow and drifted away.

"Before you go," said the priest. "Come share a glass of wine."

The great clock in the square across from the church struck midnight.

"It's Christmas, Father," said the voice from behind the panel.

"The finest Christmas ever, I think."

"The finest."

The old priest rose and stepped out.

He waited a moment for some stir, some movement from the opposite side of the confessional.

There was no sound.

Frowning, the priest reached out and opened the confessional door and peered into the cubicle.

There was nothing and no one there.

His jaw dropped. Snow moved along the back of his neck.

He put his hand out to feel the darkness.

The place was empty.

Turning, he stared at the entry door and hurried over to look out.

Snow fell in the last tones of far clocks late-sounding the hour. The streets were deserted.

Turning again, he saw the tall mirror that stood in the church entry.

There was an old man, himself, reflected in the cold glass.

Almost without thinking, he raised his hand and made the sign of blessing. The reflection in the mirror did likewise.

Then the old priest, wiping his eyes, turned a last time and went to find the wine.

Outside, Christmas, like the snow, was everywhere.

RON CARLSON

The H Street Sledding Record

The last thing I do every Christmas Eve is go out in the yard and throw the horse manure onto the roof. It is a ritual. After we return from making our attempt at the H Street Sledding Record, and we sit in the kitchen sipping egg nog and listening to Elise recount the sled ride, and Elise then finally goes to bed happily, reluctantly, and we finish placing Elise's presents under the tree and we pin her stocking to the mantel—with care—and Drew brings out two other wrapped boxes which anyone could see are for me, and I slap my forehead having forgotten to get her anything at all for Christmas (except the prizes hidden behind the glider on the front porch), I go into the garage and put on the gloves and then into the yard where I throw the horse manure on the roof.

Drew always uses this occasion to call my mother. They exchange all the Christmas news, but the main purpose of the calls the last few years has been for Drew to stand in the window where she can see me out there lobbing the great turds up into the snow on the roof and describe what I am doing to my mother. The two women take amusement from this. They say things like: "You married him" and "He's your son." I take their responses to my rituals as a kind of fond, subtle support, which it is. Drew had said when she first discovered me throwing the manure on the roof, the Christmas that Elise was four, "You're the only man I've ever known who did that." See: a compliment.

But, now that Elise is eight, Drew has become cautious: "You're fostering her fantasies." I answer: "Kids grow up too soon these days." And then

309

Drew has this: "What do you want her to do, come home from school in tears when she's fifteen? Some kid in her class will have said—*Oh, sure, Santa's reindeer shit on your roof, eh?*" All I can say to Drew then is: "Some kid in her class! Fine! I don't care what he says. I'm her father!"

I have thrown horse manure on our roof for four years now, and I plan to do it every Christmas Eve until my arm gives out. It satisfies me as a homeowner to do so, for the wonderful amber stain that is developing between the swamp cooler and the chimney and is visible all spring-summer-fall as you drive down the hill by our house, and for the way the two rosebushes by the gutter spout have raged into new and profound growth during the milder months. And as a father, it satisfies me as a ritual that keeps my family together.

Drew has said, "You want to create evidence? Let's put out milk and a cookie and then drink the milk and eat a bite out of the cookie."

I looked at her. "Drew," I had said, "I don't like cookies. I never ate a dessert in my life."

And like I said, Drew has been a good sport, even the year I threw one gob short and ran a hideous smear down the kitchen window screen that hovered over all of us until March when I was able to take it down and go to the car wash.

I obtain the manure from my friend Bob, more specifically from his horse, Power, who lives just west of Heber. I drive out there the week before Christmas and retrieve about a bushel. I throw it on the roof a lump at a time, wearing a pair of welding gloves my father gave me.

I put the brake on the sled in 1975 when Drew was pregnant with Elise so we could still make our annual attempt on the H Street Record on Christmas Eve. It was the handle of a broken Louisville Slugger baseball bat, and still had the precise "34" stamped into the bottom. I sawed it off square and drilled and bolted it to the rear of the sled, so that when I pulled back on it, the stump would drag us to a stop. As it turned out, it was one of the two years when there was no snow, so we walked up to Eleventh Avenue and H Street (as we promised: rain or shine), sat on the Flexible Flyer in the middle of the dry street on a starry Christmas Eve, and I held her in my lap. We sat on the sled like two basketball players contesting possession of her belly. We talked a little about what it would be like when she took her leave from the firm and I had her home all day with the baby, and we talked remotely about whether we wanted any more babies, and we talked about the record, which was set on December 24, 1969, the first Christmas of our marriage, when we lived in the neighborhood, on Fifth Avenue in an old barn of a house the total rent on which was seventy-two fifty, honest, and Drew had given me the sled that very night and we had walked out about midnight and been surprised by the blizzard. No wonder we took the sled and walked around the corner up H Street, up, up, up to Eleventh Avenue, and without speaking or knowing what we were doing, opening the door on the second ritual of our marriage, the annual sled ride (the first ritual was the word *condition* and the activities it engendered in our droopy old bed).

At the top we scanned the city blurred in snow, sat on my brand-new Christmas sled, and set off. The sled rode high and effortlessly through the deep snow, and suddenly, as our hearts started and our eyes began to burn against the snowy air, we were going faster than we'd planned. We crossed Tenth Avenue, nearly taking flight in the dip, and then descended in a dark rush: Ninth, Eighth, Seventh, soaring across each avenue, my arms wrapped around Drew like a straitjacket to drag her off with me if a car should cross in front of us on Sixth, Fifth Avenue, Fourth (this all took seconds, do you see?) until a car did turn onto H Street, headed our way, and we veered the new sled sharply, up over the curb, dousing our speed in the snowy yard one house from the corner of Third Avenue. Drew took a real faceful of snow, which she squirmed around and pressed into my neck, saying the words: "Now, that's a record!"

And it was the record: Eleventh to Third, and it stood partly because there had been two Christmas Eves with no snow, partly because of assorted spills brought on by too much speed, too much laughter, sometimes too much caution, and by a light blue Mercedes that crossed Sixth Avenue just in front of us in 1973. And though some years were flops, there was nothing about Christmas that Elise looked forward to as much as our one annual attempt at the H Street Sledding Record.

I think Drew wants another baby. I'm not sure, but I think she wants another child. The signs are so subtle they barely seem to add up, but she says things like, "Remember before Elise went to school?" and "There sure are a lot of women in their mid-thirties having babies." I should ask her. But for some reason, I don't. We talk about everything, *everything*. But I've avoided this topic. I've avoided talking to Drew about this topic because I want another child too badly to have her not want one. I want a little boy to come into the yard on Christmas morning and say: "See, there on the roof! The reindeers were there!" I want another kid to throw horse manure for. I'll wait. It will come up one of these days; I'll find a way to bring it up. Christmas is coming.

Every year on the day after Halloween, I tip the sled out of the rafters in the garage and Elise and I sponge it off, clean the beautiful dark blond wood with furniture polish, enamel the nicked spots on the runner supports with black engine paint, and rub the runners themselves with waxed paper. It is a ritual done on the same plaid blanket in the garage and it takes all afternoon. When we are finished, we lean the sled against the wall, and Elise marches into the house. "OK now," she says to her mother: "Let it snow."

On the first Friday night in December, every year, Elise and Drew and I go buy our tree. This too is ritual. Like those families that bundle up and head for the wilderness so they can trudge through the deep, pristine snow, chop down their own little tree, and drag it, step by step, all the way home, we venture forth in the same spirit. Only we take the old pickup down to South State and find some joker who has thrown up two strings of colored lights around the corner of the parking lot of a burned-out Safeway and is proffering trees to the general public.

There is something magical and sad about this little forest just sprung up across from City Tacos, and Drew and Elise and I wander the wooded paths, waiting for some lopsided piñon to leap into our hearts.

The winter Drew and I became serious, when I was a senior and she was already in her first year at law school, I sold Christmas trees during vacation. I answered a card on a dorm bulletin board and went to work for a guy named Geer, who had cut two thousand squat piñons from the hills east of Cedar City and was selling them from a dirt lot on Redwood Road. Drew's mother invited me to stay with them for the holidays, and it gave me the chance to help Drew make up her mind about me. I would sell trees until midnight with Geer, and then drive back to Drew's and watch every old movie in the world and wrestle with Drew until our faces were mashed blue. I wanted to complicate things wonderfully by having her sleep with me. She wanted to keep the couch cushions between us and think it over. It was a crazy Christmas; we'd steam up the windows in the entire living room, but she never gave in. We did develop the joke about *condition*, which we still use as a code word for desire. And later, I won't say if it was spring or fall, when Drew said to me, "I'd like to see you about this condition," I knew everything was going to be all right, and that we'd spend every Christmas together for the rest of our lives.

One night during that period, I delivered a tree to University Village, the married students' housing off Sunnyside. The woman was waiting for me with the door open as I dragged the pine up the steps to the second floor. She was a girl, really, about twenty, and her son, about three, watched the arrival from behind her. When I had the tree squeezed into the apartment, she asked if I could just hold it for a minute while she found her tree stand. If you ever need to stall for a couple of hours, just say you're looking for your tree stand; I mean the girl was gone for about twenty minutes. I stood and exchanged stares with the kid, who was scared; he didn't understand why some strange man had brought a tree into his home. "Christmas," I told him. "Christmas. Can you say 'Merry Christmas'?" I was an idiot.

When the girl returned with her tree stand, she didn't seem in any hurry to set it up. She came over to me and showed me the tree stand, holding it up for an explanation as to how it worked. Close up the girl's large eyes had an odd look in them, and then I understood it when she leaned through the boughs and kissed me. It was a great move; I had to hand it to her. There I was holding the tree; I couldn't make a move either way. It has never been among my policies to kiss strangers, but I held the kiss and the tree. Something about her eyes. She stepped back with the sweetest look of embarrassment and hope on her pretty face that I'd ever seen. "Just loosen the turnscrews in the side of that stand," I said, finally. "And we can put this tree up."

By the time I had the tree secured, she had returned again with a box of ornaments, lights, junk like that, and I headed for the door. "Thanks," I said. "Merry Christmas."

Her son had caught on by now and was fully involved in unloading the ornaments. The girl looked up at me, and this time I saw it all: her husband coming home in his cap and gown last June, saying, "Thanks for law school, honey, but I met Doris at the Juris-Prudence Ball and I gotta be me. Keep the kid."

The girl said to me, "You could stay and help."

It seemed like two statements to me, and so I answered them separately: "Thank you. But I can't stay; that's the best help. Have a good Christmas."

And I left them there together, decorating that tree; a ritual against the cold.

"How do you like it?" Elise says to me. She has selected a short broad bush which seems to have grown in two directions at once and then given up. She sees the look on my face and says, "If you can't say anything nice, don't say anything at all. Besides, I've already decided: this is the tree for us."

"It's a beautiful tree," Drew says.

"Quasimodo," I whisper to Drew. "This tree's name is Quasimodo."

"No whispering," Elise says from behind us. "What's he saying now, Mom?"

"He said he likes the tree, too."

Elise is not convinced and after a pause she says, "Dad. It's Christmas. Behave yourself."

When we go to pay for the tree, the master of ceremonies is busy negotiating a deal with two kids, a punk couple. The tree man stands with his hands in his change apron and says, "I gotta get thirty-five bucks for that tree." The boy, a skinny kid in a leather jacket, shrugs and says he's only got twenty-eight bucks. His girlfriend, a large person with a bowl haircut and a monstrous black overcoat festooned with buttons, is wailing, "Please! Oh no! Jimmy! Jimmy! I love that tree! I want that tree!" The tree itself stands aside, a noble pine of about twelve feet. Unless these kids live in a gymnasium, they're buying a tree bigger than their needs.

Jimmy retreats to his car, an old Plymouth big as a boat. POLICE RULE is spray-painted across both doors in balloon letters. He returns instantly and opens a handful of coins. "I'll give you thirty-one bucks, fifty-five cents, and my watch." To our surprise, the wily tree man takes the watch to examine it. When I see that, I give Elise four dollars and tell her to give it to Kid Jimmy and say, "Merry Christmas." His girlfriend is still wailing but now a minor refrain of "Oh Jimmy, that tree! Oh Jimmy," etc. I haven't seen a public display of emotion and longing of this magnitude in Salt Lake City, ever. I watch Elise give the boy the money, but instead of saying, "Merry Christmas," I hear her say instead: "Here, Jimmy. Santa says keep your watch."

Jimmy pays for the tree, and his girl—and this is the truth—jumps on him, wrestles him to the ground in gratitude and smothers him for nearly a minute. There have never been people happier about a Christmas tree. We pay quickly and head out before Jimmy or his girlfriend can think to begin thanking us.

On the way home in the truck, I say to Elise, "Santa says keep your watch, eh?"

"Yes, he does," she smiles.

"How old are you, anyway?"

"Eight."

It's an old joke, and Drew finishes it for me: "When he was your age, he was seven."

We will go home and while the two women begin decorating the tree with the artifacts of our many Christmases together, I will thread popcorn onto a long string. It is a ritual I prefer for its uniqueness; the fact that once a year I get to sit and watch the two girls I am related to move about a tree inside our home, while I sit nearby and sew food.

On the morning of the twenty-fourth of December, Elise comes into our bedroom, already dressed for sledding. "Good news," she says. "We've got a shot at the record."

Drew rises from the pillow and peeks out the blind. "It's snowing," she says.

Christmas Eve, we drive back along the snowy avenues, and park on Fifth, as always. "I know," Elise says, hopping out of the car. "You two used to live right over there before you had me and it was a swell place and only cost seventy-two fifty a month, honest."

Drew looks at me and smiles.

"How old are you?" I ask Elise, but she is busy towing the sled away, around the corner, up toward Eleventh Avenue. It is still snowing, petal flakes, teeming by the streetlamps, trying to carry the world away. I take Drew's hand and we walk up the middle of H Street behind our daughter. There is no traffic, but the few cars have packed the tender snow perfectly. It *could* be a record. On Ninth Avenue, Drew stops me in the intersection, the world still as snow, and kisses me. "I love you," she says.

"What a planet," I whisper. "To allow such a thing."

By the time we climb to Eleventh Avenue, Elise is seated on the sled, ready to go. "What are you guys waiting for, Christmas?" she says and then laughs at her own joke. Then she becomes all business: "Listen, Dad, I figure if you stay just a little to the left of the tire tracks we could go all the way. And no wobbling!" She's referring to last year's record attempt, which was extinguished in the Eighth Avenue block when we laughed ourselves into a fatal wobble and ended in a slush heap.

316

We arrange ourselves on the sled, as we have each Christmas Eve for eight years. As I reach my long legs around these two women, I sense their excitement. "It's going to be a record," Elise whispers into the whispering snow.

"Do you think so?" Drew asks. She also feels this could be the night.

"Oh yeah," Elise says. "The conditions are perfect."

"What do you think?" Drew turns to me.

"Well, the conditions are perfect."

When I say *conditions*, Drew leans back and kisses me. So I press: "There's still room on the sled," I say, pointing to the *F* in Flexible Flyer that is visible between Elise's legs. "There's still room for another person."

"Who?" Elise asks.

"Your little brother," Drew says, squeezing my knees.

And that's about all that was said, sitting up there on Eleventh Avenue on Christmas Eve on a sled which is as old as my marriage with a brake that is as old as my daughter. Later tonight I will stand in my yard and throw this year's reindeer droppings on my very own home. I love Christmas.

Now the snow spirals around us softly. I put my arms around my family and lift my feet onto the steering bar. We begin to slip down H Street. We are trying for the record. The conditions, as you know by now, are perfect.

Acknowledgments

"Auggie Wren's Christmas Story" by Paul Auster, copyright © 1990 by Paul Auster. First published in *The New York Times*. Reprinted by permission of The Carol Mann Agency as agent for the author.

"Christmas Eve at Johnson's Drugs N Goods" from *The Sea Birds Are Still Alive* by Toni Cade Bambara. Copyright © 1974, 1976, 1977 by Toni Cade Bambara. Reprinted by permission of Random House, Inc.

"Where You'll Find Me" by Ann Beattie from *Where You'll Find Me*. Copyright © 1986 by Ivory & Pity, Inc. Reprinted by permission of Linden, a division of Simon & Schuster, Inc.

"And There Was the Evening and the Morning. . . ." from *The Stories of Heinrich Böll* by Heinrich Böll, translator, Leila Vennewitz. Translation copyright © 1986 by Leila Vennewitz and the estate of Heinrich Böll. Reprinted by permission of Alfred A. Knopf, Inc.

"The Frozen Fields" by Paul Bowles. Copyright © 1959 by Paul Bowles. Reprinted from *Collected Stories of Paul Bowles* with the permission of Black Sparrow Press.

"Bless Me, Father, for I Have Sinned" from *The Toynbee Convector* by Ray Bradbury, copyright © 1988 by Ray Bradbury is reprinted by permission of Don Congdon Associates, Inc.

"A Christmas Carillon" by Hortense Calisher from *The Collected Stories of Hortense Calisher*. Reprinted by permission of Donadio & Ashworth. Copyright © 1953, 1975 by Hortense Calisher.

"Santa's Children" from *Marcovaldo* by Italo Calvino, copyright © 1963 by Giulio Einaudi editore s.p.a., English translation copyright © 1983 by Harcourt Brace Jovanovich,

319

Inc., and Martin Secker & Warburg, Ltd., reprinted by permission of Harcourt Brace Jovanovich, Inc.

"The H Street Sledding Record" is reprinted from *The News of the World: Stories by Ron Carlson,* by permission of W. W. Norton & Company, Inc. Copyright © 1987 by Ron Carlson.

"Put Yourself in My Shoes" from *Will You Please Be Quiet, Please?* by Raymond Carver is reprinted by permission of Tess Gallagher. Copyright © 1977 by Tess Gallagher.

"The World in a Bowl of Soup: A Christmas Story" by Annie Dillard. Copyright © 1976 by Annie Dillard. Reprinted by permission of Russell & Volkening as agents for the author. Story first appeared in *Harper's Magazine.*

"Xmas" by Thomas M. Disch is reprinted from *Shenandoah:* The Washington and Lee University Review, with the permission of the Editor.

"A Clock Ticks at Christmas" by Patricia Highsmith, copyright © 1985 by Patricia Highsmith, is from her story collection *Mermaids on the Golf Course,* published by William Heinemann Ltd., London, and Penzler Books, New York, and reprinted by permission of Diogenes Verlag AG, Switzerland.

"A Christmas Conspiracy Tale" by Ivan Klíma. English translation copyright © 1985 Reader's International, Inc. Reprinted by permission of Reader's International, Inc.

"Christmas" is an excerpt from *To Kill a Mockingbird* by Harper Lee. Copyright © 1960 by Harper Lee. Reprinted by permission of HarperCollins Publishers.

"Drawing Names" from *Shiloh and Other Stories* by Bobbie Ann Mason. Copyright © 1982 by Bobbie Ann Mason. Reprinted by permission of HarperCollins Publishers.

"The Centerpiece" from *On the River Styx* by Peter Matthiessen. Copyright © 1951, 1957, 1958, 1963, 1978, 1985, 1988, 1989 by Peter Matthiessen. Reprinted by permission of Random House, Inc.

"The Doll" from *The Fanatic Heart* by Edna O'Brien. Copyright © 1984 by Edna O'Brien. Reprinted by permission of Farrar Straus Giroux, Inc.

"Christmas Morning" from *Collected Stories by Frank O'Connor.* Copyright © 1946 by Frank O'Connor. Reprinted by permission of Alfred A. Knopf, Inc. Originally appeared in *The New Yorker.*

"Two of a Kind" from *The Collected Stories of Sean O'Faolain.* Copyright © 1959, 1961 by Sean O'Faolain. By permission of Little, Brown & Company.

THE MASTER GUIDE TO DRAWING ANIME
5-MINUTE CHARACTERS

THE MASTER GUIDE TO DRAWING ANIME
5-MINUTE CHARACTERS

Super-Simple Lessons from the Best-Selling Series

 Get Creative 6

DRAWING WITH Christopher Hart

An imprint of **Get Creative 6**
104 West 27th Street, New York, NY 10001
sixthandspringbooks.com

Editors
LAURA COOKE
MICHELLE BREDESON

Art Director
IRENE LEDWITH

Contributing Artists
AKANE
ANZU
AYAME
AYAME SHIROI
AYASAL
ERO-PINKU
HAIYUN
INMA R.
KAGURA
NACHOZ
SHOUU KUN
SUGAR MIKI
TABBY KINK
TINA FRANCISCO

Chief Executive Officer
CAROLINE KILMER

President
ART JOINNIDES

Chairman
JAY STEIN

Library of Congress Cataloging-in-Publication Data available upon request.

ISBN: 978-1-68462-020-3

Manufactured in China

1 3 5 7 9 10 8 6 4 2

FIRST EDITION

christopherhartbooks.com
facebook.com/CARTOONS.MANGA
youtube.com/user/chrishartbooks

Dedicated to everyone who loves to draw (THAT MEANS YOU!)

Contents

Introduction

The Master Guide to Drawing Anime has been one of my most successful book series. With their popular characters and clear instruction, these books have helped thousands of aspiring artists learn to draw anime. In my newest anime art instruction book, *5-Minute Characters*, I've selected characters from the Master Guide to Drawing Anime series and the very popular *Manga Fashion Bible* that can be accomplished relatively quickly, because they're based on simple techniques that work.

This collection of anime characters shows you how to use templates to draw the heads and bodies so that they look right. You'll also get valuable tips for drawing hairstyles, fashions, and attitudes. And we'll wrap it all up with a great section on drawing characters in simple settings to suggest a story.

You can work your way through the book or pick and choose your favorite characters to draw. Either way, you'll learn new techniques and put them into practice. The sky is the limit!

Drawing the Head in Simple Steps

Anime heads are based on simple shapes, which is one reason they're so appealing and fun to draw. In this chapter, you'll learn how to draw the basic head using a standard template. You'll also turn the head to create accurate side views and 3/4 angles. You can then change the details, like the eyes and expressions, to create a completely different look.

Drawing the Anime-Style Head—The Basics

What is it that gives an anime face its appealing look? The answer lies in its simple shape. With these tips, you can get amazing results.

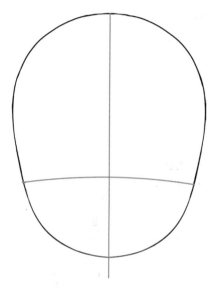

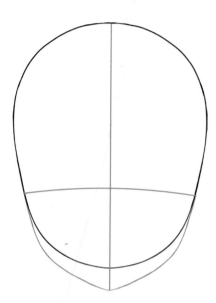

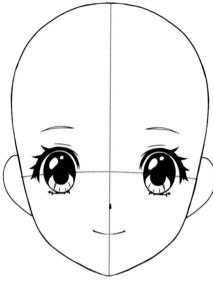

Draw the head shape like a boxy oval. It doesn't have to be perfect (really!).

Once the shape of the head is drawn, modify it by lowering the chin. That's the secret!

Space the eyes far apart. The eyebrows and mouth are drawn with a short line.

PROPORTION TIP

You should be able to draw an equilateral triangle from the eyes to the chin.

Hair is such an important feature for character design. Think about what it says about a character. This cute girl is drawn with simple bangs.

QUICK TIP
Start simple, and add details once the basics are in place.

The interior of the hair is darkened to create depth. For black and white drawings, you can do this with pencil shading.

Drawing the Girl's Head in Five Easy Steps

We're still going to keep it simple, but now we're going to add a few finishing touches for fun. Using the same basic head shape as the character from the previous page, we can create an entirely new character.

The eyes are positioned in the middle of the head, with approximately the same amount of space above and below them.

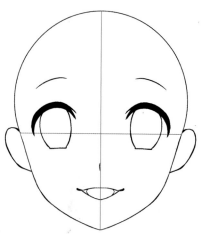

Draw both eyes and ears along the blue, horizontal guideline.

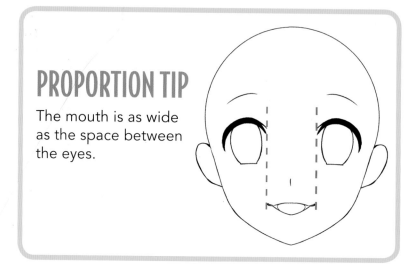

PROPORTION TIP

The mouth is as wide as the space between the eyes.

Hair covers most of the forehead.

The nose only needs a small indication.

Adjust the chin to soften the look.

Indicate an eye shine across the middle of both eyes.

A few curling strands give the hair a casual, lifelike appearance.

When you start with a solid foundation, the rest of the drawing is much easier to complete.

Drawing the Boy's Head in Five Easy Steps

The construction of the boy's head is not as round as the girl's. His jawline is lower and more angular. These simple tricks give the male face a sleeker look. They can be adjusted to create different character types.

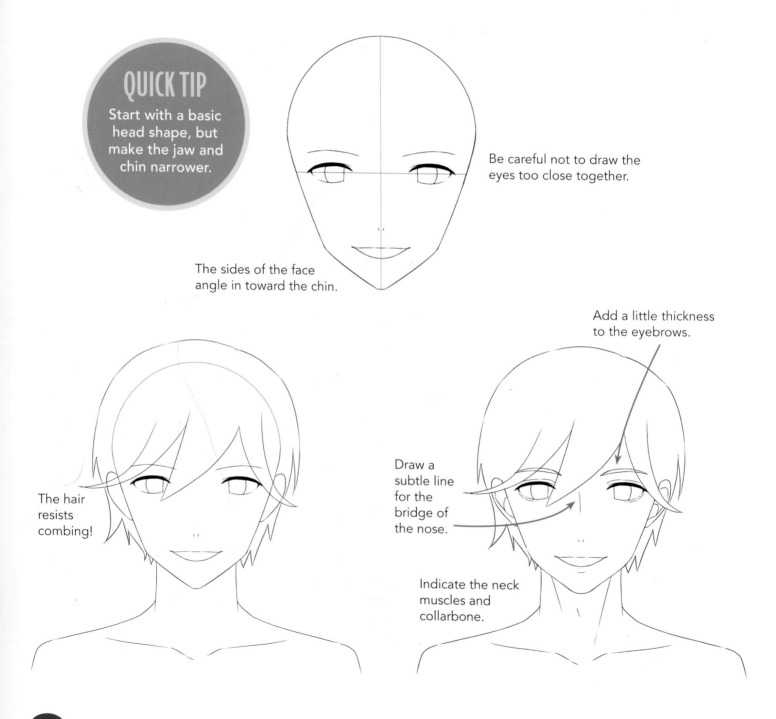

QUICK TIP
Start with a basic head shape, but make the jaw and chin narrower.

Be careful not to draw the eyes too close together.

The sides of the face angle in toward the chin.

The hair resists combing!

Add a little thickness to the eyebrows.

Draw a subtle line for the bridge of the nose.

Indicate the neck muscles and collarbone.

Draw pointed streaks within the hair for an authentic anime look.

Draw small shines at the bottom of the eyeballs.

A few colorful highlights are a good idea, like orange streaks on red hair.

QUICK TIP

Eye shines aren't always white. You can use a bright color instead.

Tips for Drawing the 3/4 Angle

Many beginners have trouble drawing a head at this angle due to a few subtleties inherent to it. By following a few helpful tips, you can master it.

¾ ANGLE—GIRLS

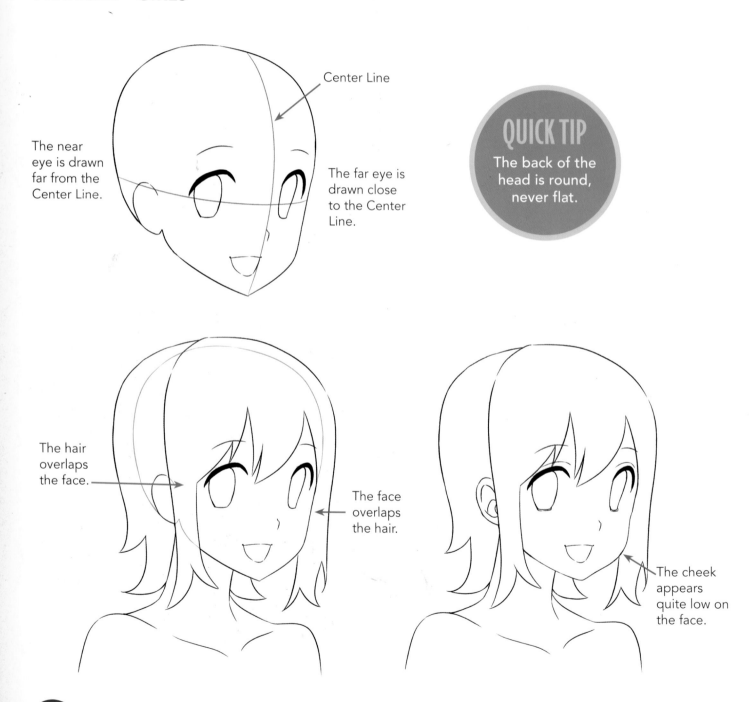

Center Line

The near eye is drawn far from the Center Line.

The far eye is drawn close to the Center Line.

QUICK TIP
The back of the head is round, never flat.

The hair overlaps the face.

The face overlaps the hair.

The cheek appears quite low on the face.

Draw thick strips of hair. This is a popular technique for creating anime hairstyles.

QUICK TIP
Drawing the pupils in the corners of the eyes creates a cute expression.

Draw the "V" collar off to the side, adhering to the ¾ angle.

Add a few blush marks under the eyes.

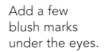

¾ ANGLE—BOYS

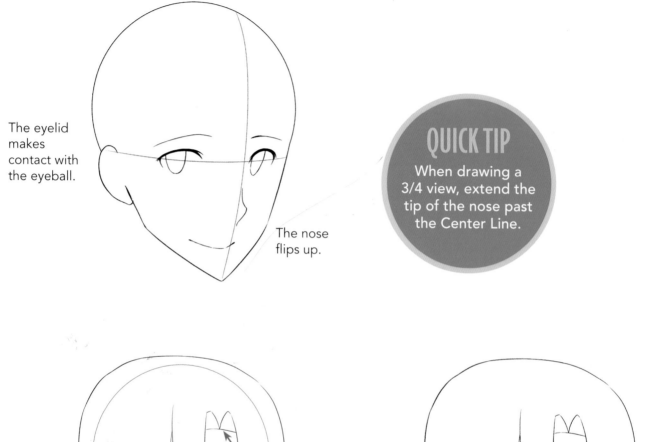

The eyelid makes contact with the eyeball.

The nose flips up.

QUICK TIP
When drawing a 3/4 view, extend the tip of the nose past the Center Line.

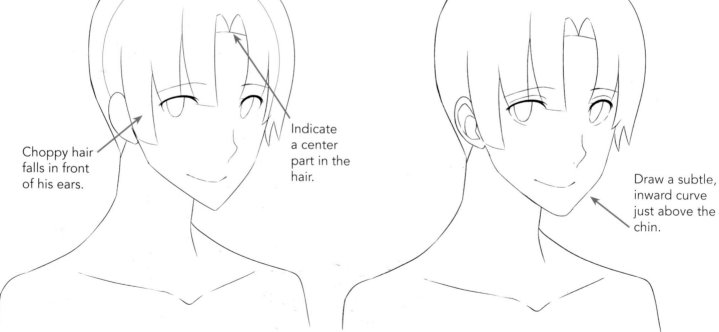

Choppy hair falls in front of his ears.

Indicate a center part in the hair.

Draw a subtle, inward curve just above the chin.

Ear shifts back in a 3/4 view.

QUICK TIP
Draw a boy's hair as if he's two weeks overdue for a haircut.

Leave space between his chin and shoulder.

The hair falls over his eyes, which gives him a casual, friendly look.

Drawing the Side View

The side view looks simple but can be tricky. Not to fear! We're going to add an extra step that will give you all the help you need.

SIDE VIEW—GIRLS

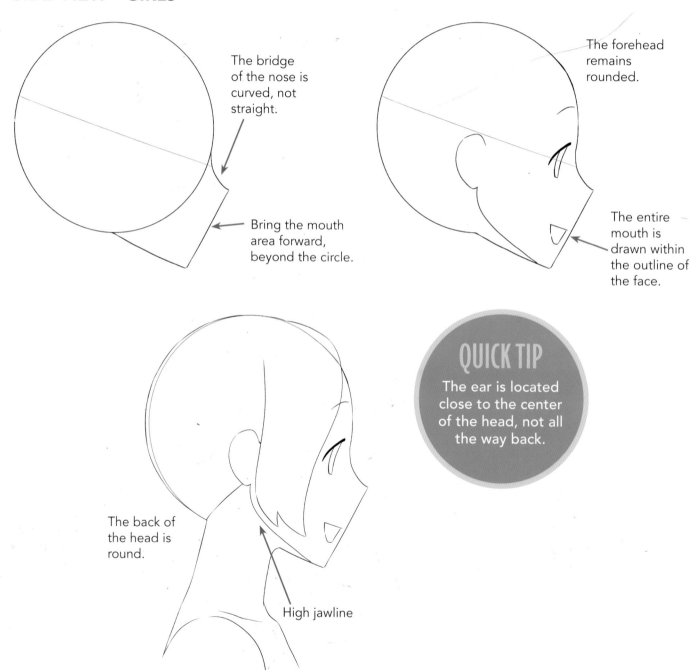

The bridge of the nose is curved, not straight.

Bring the mouth area forward, beyond the circle.

The forehead remains rounded.

The entire mouth is drawn within the outline of the face.

The back of the head is round.

High jawline

QUICK TIP
The ear is located close to the center of the head, not all the way back.

The eyebrow appears short at this angle.

Light crease over the eyelid

The strands of hair converge at the bun.

QUICK TIP
Add shadow under the jaw and on the neck.

The eye is set back from the edge of the face.

SIDE VIEW—BOYS

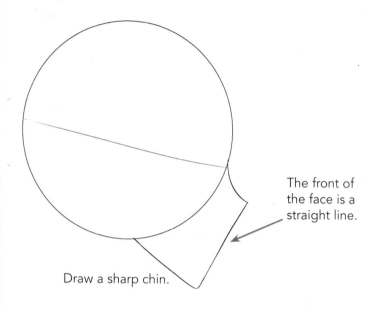

The front of the face is a straight line.

Draw a sharp chin.

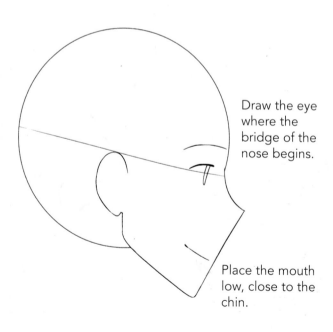

Draw the eye where the bridge of the nose begins.

Place the mouth low, close to the chin.

This popular hairstyle makes the back of the head look higher than it really is.

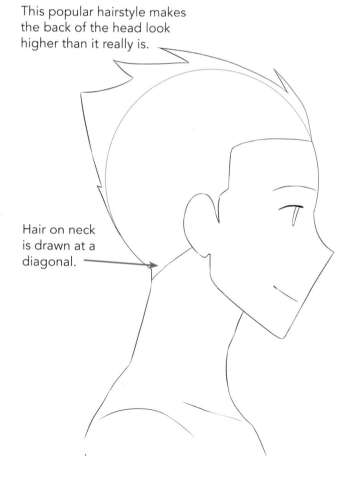

Hair on neck is drawn at a diagonal.

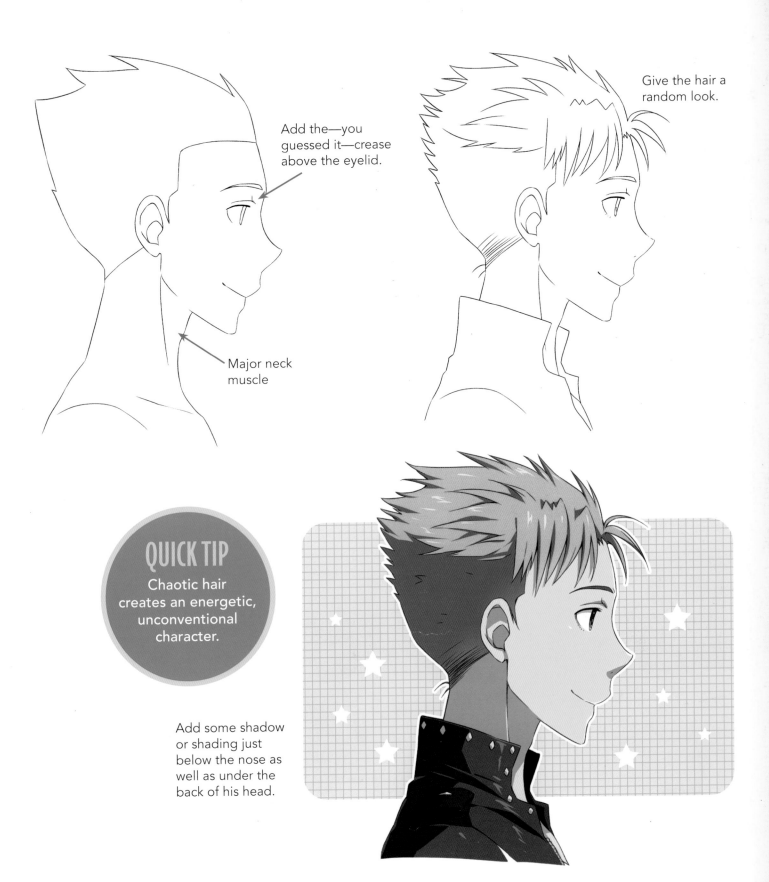

Add the—you
guessed it—crease
above the eyelid.

Major neck
muscle

Give the hair a
random look.

QUICK TIP
Chaotic hair
creates an energetic,
unconventional
character.

Add some shadow
or shading just
below the nose as
well as under the
back of his head.

25

The Preteen Head Step by Step

With preteens, cuteness rules. The eyes are cute. The expression is cute. Even the hair is cute! The upper portion of the head is drawn as a big circle. The lower portion of the head adds only a little mass to the outline. The upper part of the head (forehead) is predominant. That's the key to creating a foundation of cuteness.

PRETEEN GIRL

The eyes are higher on the head than the ears.

The nose and mouth are simplified. But the hair is drawn with more complex line work. The bangs cut straight across.

The upper eyelids are the boldest lines of this image. An important note: The eyelids do not require an abundance of eyelashes in order to be pretty.

A fun hair accessory (the star) adds to the cuteness, as does the playful hair color.

PRETEEN BOY

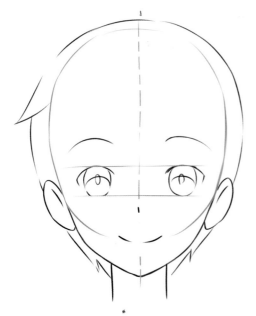

The circle, which represents the top portion of the head, reaches down to the mouth.

Soft ruffles of hair flop over the forehead in a casual manner.

Hair color doesn't have to be realistic. Some artists use pink for girls and blue for boys. But this is only one approach. You aren't locked into using stereotypical male and female color schemes.

Draw high, arching eyebrows.

Attractive Eyes

When drawing eyes, knowing what to draw first helps. Start by drawing the upper and lower eyelids to frame the eyes. With that in place, draw the eyeballs and finish with the details: the eyelashes, eyebrows, and creases of the eyelids.

EYE TEMPLATE: THE FRONT VIEW

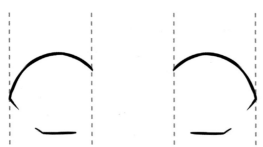

STEP 1

The upper eyelids droop at the ends. The lower eyelids are flatter.

STEP 2

Draw small pupils dead center in the eye and indicate a faint fold above the upper eyelids.

STEP 3

Add random streaks to the iris and a few shines. Draw feathering on the eyelashes.

QUICK TIP

The color of the eyeball is dark on top but fades at the bottom.

SIDE VIEW

Here's where some people find drawing eyes to be tricky. But this diagram should clear things up for you.

STEP 1

In the side view, the eyelids converge to form a point.

STEP 2

The pupil (black dot) is drawn toward the front of the iris.

STEP 3

The eyelashes extend beyond the eyeball.

It's time to add the anime-style shine to the eye. A small shine in the upper left side is all it takes, but you can add more.

Eye Color Variations

Every anime artist knows that the eyes are the most "stand out" feature of the face. Therefore, it's essential to individualize them in order to create an original character. Think about which eye color you envision for your character. Let's take a look at some popular options and techniques.

BLUE-BLACK

The large black pupils meld with the black shadow that falls on the upper eyeball. The bottom has blue fill.

GREEN

The darker green indicates shadow on the top half of the eyes.

BROWN

A thick outline surrounds the eyeballs; the pupils are tiny.

QUICK TIP

Selecting different color eyes for different characters makes it easier to create different identities when you have multiple characters in a scene.

Anime Hairstyles: Stylish & Simple

Once you understand the fundamentals of drawing the head, it's time to have fun with hairstyles! Hair really helps define a character, and changing the hair is an easy way to create a variety of looks and characters. This chapter covers many of the most popular styles for schoolgirls and cool guys, including superlong locks, wild-colored 'dos, perky pigtails, and sleek short cuts.

Popular Hairstyles—Girls

A stylish haircut can help to establish a character's type. For example, cute characters are often drawn with short- or medium-length hair, whereas beautiful characters are frequently given long hair. A hairstyle becomes part of a character's identity.

PIGTAILS (FAMOUS ANIME HAIRSTYLE)

The key to drawing pigtails is to raise them higher than the head.

The part starts at the back of the head.

Hairstyle Tips

Here are a few techniques for drawing hair that you can add to your skill set:

- To make the hair look full, draw the bangs down to the eyes.
- When choosing a hair color, include some lighter and darker shades within a single style.
- Use accessories to add interest to a hairstyle. Barrettes, bows, headbands, and even cat ears can be used to help communicate the character's personality.

Draw the hair in uneven clumps for a natural look.

Add ruffles of hair at the base of each pigtail.

Pigtails curl under for a more lifelike look.

Blend lighter areas of the hair with darker areas.

LONG WITH STRAIGHT BANGS (EXTRA CUTE)

This classic anime cut stays close to the head all around. There are three elements to this style: bangs straight across, long hair down the back, and side strands in front of the ears.

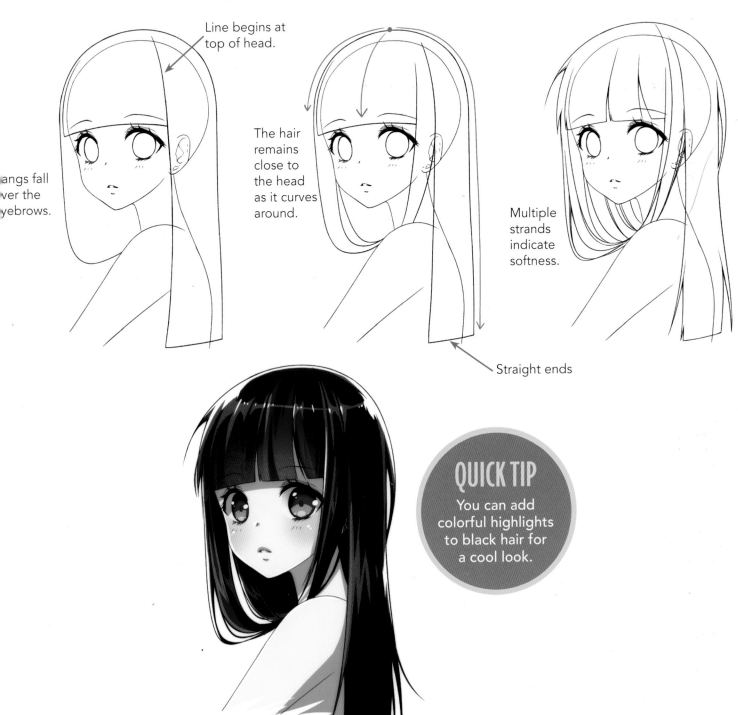

Line begins at top of head.

Bangs fall over the eyebrows.

The hair remains close to the head as it curves around.

Multiple strands indicate softness.

Straight ends

QUICK TIP
You can add colorful highlights to black hair for a cool look.

SUPER-WAVY

A hairstyle full of soft curls creates a captivating look for pretty characters.

Exaggerate the size of the forehead to give more surface area for your hairstyle.

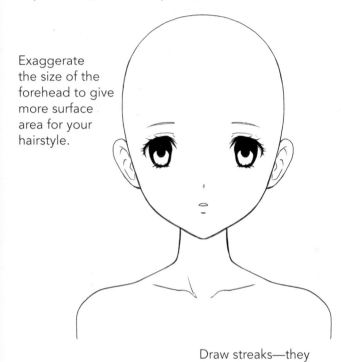

Inner strands overlap the face.

Draw streaks—they show the direction the hair is combed.

Waves begin halfway down the head.

A shadow under the bangs adds depth.

MORE CLASSIC CUTS FOR GIRLS

Use any of these as a starting point for your character drawings.

Short and Sharp
For a slick look, draw a side part.

Braided Ponytail
A ponytail worn over the shoulder is a very popular variation.

Basic Schoolgirl
A headband with a bow indicates a proper student.

QUICK TIP
Note that each face on this page is the same, but the character types appear very different.

Modern Hairstyles–Boys

Creating a cool hairstyle is as important for guy characters as it is for girl characters. If you've been to an anime convention, you know what I mean. Different hair can create a totally different character type.

SIDE BANGS

Side bangs create a character with a little mystery.

Basic hairline

This hairstyle flows in different directions to surround the head.

QUICK TIP

Side bangs can be drawn on male and female anime characters.

A tuft of hair on top breaks up the smooth surface.

Draw jagged bangs.

Hair dips below face.

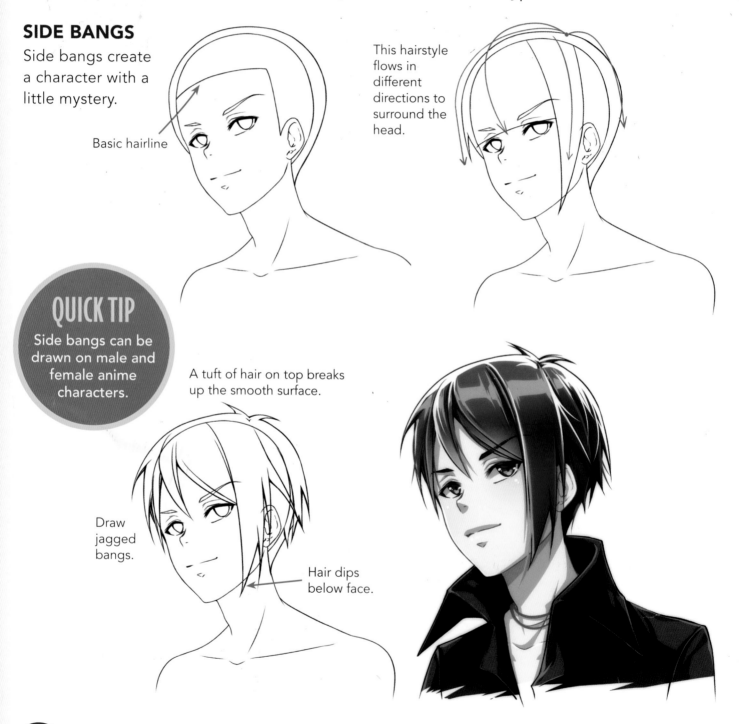

UNCOMBED

All boys look like this just before their mothers yank them back inside and order them to comb their hair. Once it's nice and neat, they send them off to school. Five minutes later, their hair looks nuts again. Not that I would know.

QUICK TIP

By indicating the hairline, you create a good foundation for your hairstyle.

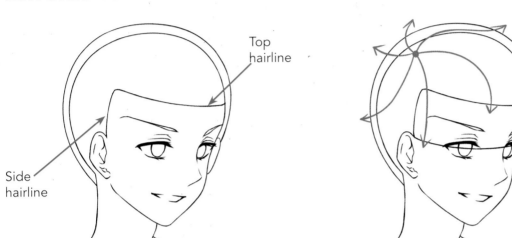

Top hairline

Side hairline

The hair spins out from a central point.

Draw the ruffles to look random and spontaneous.

Draw the hair over most of the forehead.

SHORT (CHOPPED)

Short hair isn't really all that short on most anime characters. It's only shorter than other hairstyles. The hair still falls below the character's eyes. This is a cute cut, similar to the female bob. It's often seen on young characters.

Draw a part down the middle.

Hair is parted along the Center Line.

Sketch the shape of the hairstyle; both sides are drawn at about eye level.

Draw a short rise of the hair at the hairline.

One or two forward-falling strands of hair create a natural look.

MORE CLASSIC CUTS FOR BOYS

Use any of these as a starting point for your character drawings.

QUICK TIP
Some hairstyles don't need a part at all.

Extreme Layering
Draw tufts of hair upon tufts of hair for this highly popular anime look.

Side Sweep
This style is based on a severe sweep to the right, with the hair extending past the head.

Random— No Part
When you draw floppy hair, you don't need a part. The hair surrounds the face.

5-Minute Characters

The Brainy Guy, the Mean Girl, the Star Athlete . . . These engaging characters are staples of the anime genre. Have you always wanted to draw them yourself, but thought it would be too hard? Take your pick from more than 20 authentic characters, all drawn step by step to take the mystery out of character design. We'll focus on just the heads to keep it simple.

General Personality Types

It's safest to keep the character type broad. Don't make it so unique that people can't relate to it. To do this, start by coming up with a broad "umbrella" term to describe your character, such as Hero. Get more specific as you fine-tune the character type (subtype). For example, "Hero" becomes "The Reluctant Hero" or "The Accidental Hero" or "The Hero with a Secret Identity." This conveys a personality to go with the overarching character type.

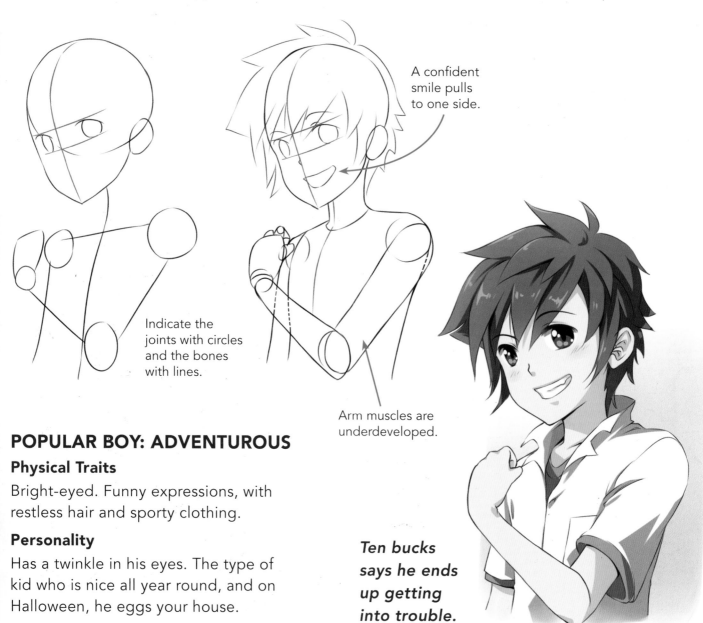

A confident smile pulls to one side.

Indicate the joints with circles and the bones with lines.

Arm muscles are underdeveloped.

POPULAR BOY: ADVENTUROUS

Physical Traits

Bright-eyed. Funny expressions, with restless hair and sporty clothing.

Personality

Has a twinkle in his eyes. The type of kid who is nice all year round, and on Halloween, he eggs your house.

Ten bucks says he ends up getting into trouble.

THE SMART TYPE: CLEVER GIRL

Physical Traits

Slightly downturned eyebrows, which shows a bit of cunning. Conventional hairstyle. The smooth line around the back of her head emphasizes its roundness, which is a cute quality. The sailor suit school uniform gives her a cheerful look.

Personality

Chipper and affable, she's part of a group but remains an individual thinker. Tends to "chibi out" when fuming.

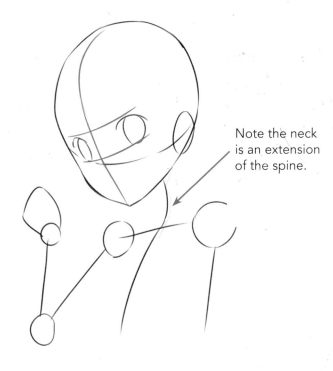

Note the neck is an extension of the spine.

When all looks hopeless, she comes up with answers!

Big eyes are essential. Note the extreme slenderizing of the far eye, due to perspective.

49

THE BULLY: SNEAKY

Physical Traits

This compulsive liar dresses like a "good kid," but it only makes him look slimy! His eyebrows are sharp, and his nose is short and upturned.

Personality

The consummate actor. The only thing that you can count on him to do is stab you in the back—and blame someone else for it.

The sharp chin gives him a harder look.

Coiffed hair shows his narcissism.

A natural poser— and egotist!

THE FEARFUL KID: BULLIED

Physical Traits
Note the thin neck and drooping hair. Nondescript shirt and outfit. He prefers not to stand out.

Personality
Fearful of rejection, afraid of confrontation. A sympathetic character.

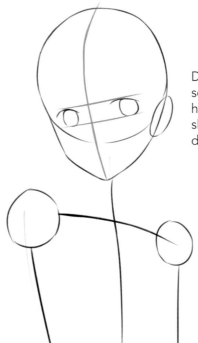

Due to poor self-esteem, head tilts slightly downward.

Raise one shoulder and "droop" the other one.

Tuck chin in, a sign of insecurity.

Someone needs to stand up to the bullies and be his friend.

51

MEAN GIRL: GROUP LEADER

Physical Traits

Show lots of forehead. Give her a bow in her hair to contrast with her sarcastic demeanor. Loud red hair underscores her personality.

Personality

Unlike the sneak, the mean girl has no pretense about who she is. She likes to belittle others, and she likes to be known for it.

Start with a generic head shape.

Her eyebrows always turn slightly downward into a semi-frown.

She always has it in for somebody.

TIMID GIRL: GULLIBLE

Physical Traits

An overall sweet, somewhat childlike look. Big, innocent eyes. Blush added to the face as needed.

Personality

Too trusting. Super honest. When she says she doesn't have today's assignment because her dog ate her homework, that means her dog really did eat her assignment!

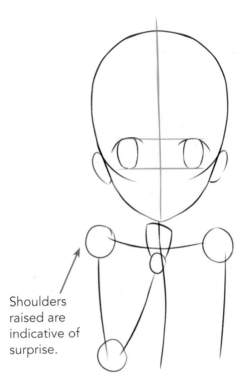

Shoulders raised are indicative of surprise.

"You really have a pet unicorn?"

Symmetrical hair conveys a prim and proper look.

Body language: a delicate hand gesture is effective.

BRAINY GUY: SELF-CONFIDENT

Physical Traits

A subdued smile combined with half-closed eyelids reflect his sarcastic nature. He is small of stature.

Personality

He doesn't need to shout. He can destroy someone with a few caustic observations.

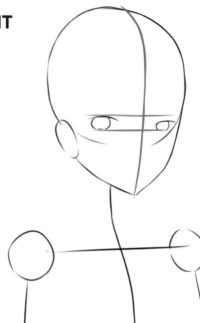

A meek build is a stereotype for brainy characters. Nonetheless, it's a look that works.

Underplay his expression.

He mastered string theory when he was only five years old.

The attire is neat and never flashy.

STUDIOUS GIRL: KNOW-IT-ALL

Physical Traits

Sapping all trendiness from her hairstyle and outfit produces a character who looks older than her years. Her eyes are intense with short and sharp eyebrows.

Personality

She has no hesitation about correcting people. This makes her lots of fun at parties. She has zero sense of humor and never gets a joke or a date. Even her dog finds her annoying!

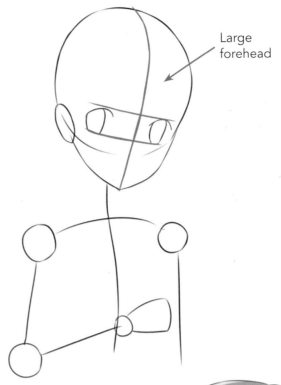

Large forehead

Hair falls forward, following the tilt of the head.

Short, feathered bangs

She secretly wants to be like the cool girls. And the cool girls secretly want to be smart, like her.

Character Types—You Decide!

Here are two appealing character types. You can tweak or change them anywhere along the way to create your own versions.

ROUND FACE TYPE

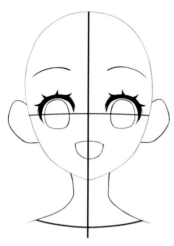

Draw the eyes like this or glamorize them with longer eyelashes.

Pigtails can be drawn medium size, long, or superlong.

Curly pigtails

Minor point at the chin

QUICK TIP

You could turn the expression into a laugh by drawing closed eyes.

The bottom of the face is very round.

COMEDY TYPE

Practical jokers can get big laughs. Unfortunately, they can also get everyone mad at them. Give this character a big expression and pose. Add a humorous outfit that lacks even a hint of fashion sense.

The big pose announces, "I'm here!"

Draw the elbows at the head level.

The arms come up to stretch out the torso.

He has a big smile with the eyes closed. Note the downward eyebrows.

QUICK TIP
An animal hood can be a funny look.

The back muscle adds width to his frame.

He hasn't seen a hairbrush in weeks.

You know the phrase, "coordinating an outfit?" This is the opposite.

HANDSOME TYPE

Idealized features and hair create a dramatic look. It's important to draw them with a slightly bored expression.

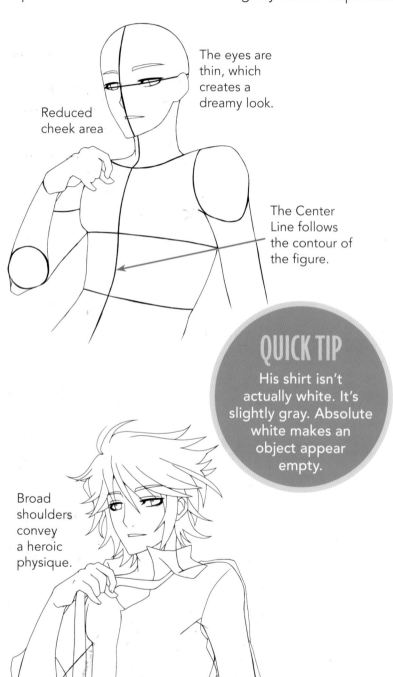

Reduced cheek area

The eyes are thin, which creates a dreamy look.

The Center Line follows the contour of the figure.

The hair brushes back.

QUICK TIP

His shirt isn't actually white. It's slightly gray. Absolute white makes an object appear empty.

Broad shoulders convey a heroic physique.

Add creases to the sleeves and across the front.

GEEKY TYPE

Bright and goofy, with an energetic expression, this is a popular, funny character type. He must have selected that outfit with his eyes closed.

Wide eyes convey an eager look.

QUICK TIP
Young characters are drawn with a simple construction.

Raise the eyebrows when drawing a goofy grin.

A toothy smile is funny.

The flip adds a humorous touch.

Skinny upper body

Dere Character Templates

Use these basic templates for drawing each type of Dere personality. You can also customize them to create your own Dere characters. Now, let's create some comedic dysfunction!

TSUNDERE

The *Tsundre* is the most popular of the Dere girls. Her type acts chilly and antagonistic to the boy she secretly likes, completely confusing him. It's not the best strategy to win a guy's affection. However, she'll occasionally let her guard down and reveal her feelings. But the next moment, she'll return to verbally tormenting him.

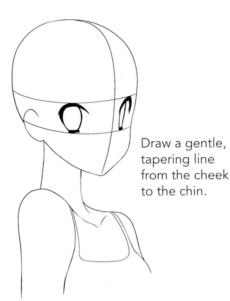

Draw a gentle, tapering line from the cheek to the chin.

This ¾ angle is turned pretty far to the right, so you'll have to draw her far eye very slender.

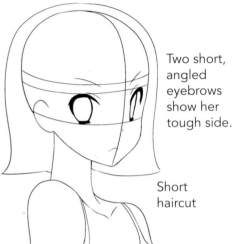

Two short, angled eyebrows show her tough side.

Short haircut

Orange hair for a fiery personality

Hard shell outside, soft on the inside

Define the hair with some floppy layering.

KUUDERE

The *Kuudere* has made an art form of repressing her true feelings. Therefore, it's almost impossible for her to open up to anyone. She hides her feelings so well that even she has a hard time finding them.

The eyeballs are partially covered by the heavy upper eyelids.

The outline of the hair closely follows the shape of the head.

Draw horizontal eyebrows.

The long bangs create a shadow on the forehead.

Ruffle the hair at the bottom.

Draw a slight indication of a nose and mouth.

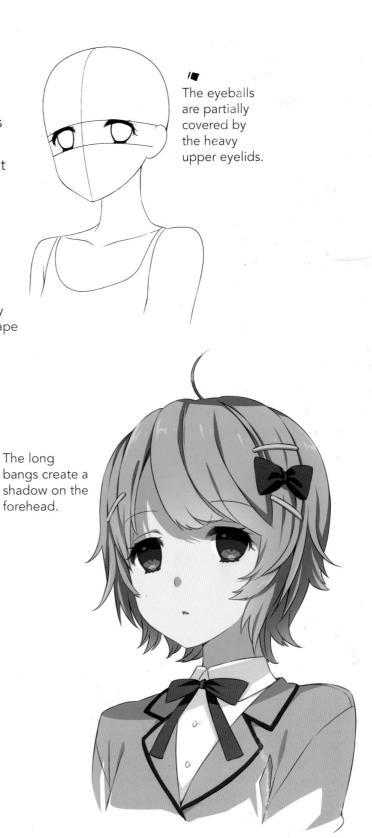

She puts up a wall as a defense.

DANDERE

The *Dandere* is sweet but meek. She'll open up to you, but you've got to invest a lot of time and energy getting to know her. And yet, the Dandere can emerge to become a magnetic character in the same way that a butterfly emerges from its chrysalis.

The eyelids are slightly lowered. It's almost a sad look.

The pigtails wind around and flop over her shoulders.

Draw choppy bangs.

Draw a subtle mouth.

The chin comes to a soft point.

She acts guarded until she knows you.

Color selection underscores the character type. Her outfit is muted, tamping down any emotional exuberance. However, she has brilliant blue eyes, which is a reminder that she's still got a spark of life deep within.

YANDERE

And now we turn to the notorious *Yandere*. This one does not know the meaning of the word *breakup*. If her boyfriend shows interest in another girl, this formerly well-behaved student becomes insanely vengeful. A typical comment to her boyfriend would be, "You can date other people. But you'll be responsible for what happens to them."

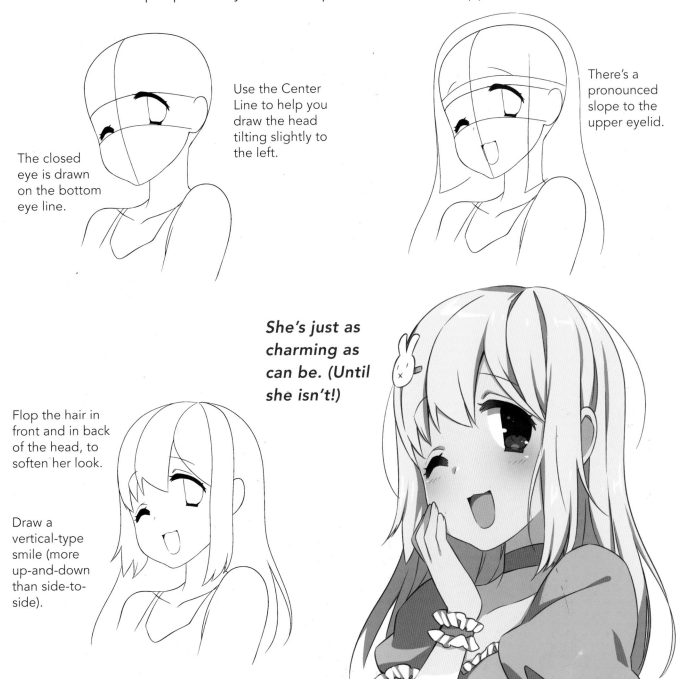

Use the Center Line to help you draw the head tilting slightly to the left.

The closed eye is drawn on the bottom eye line.

There's a pronounced slope to the upper eyelid.

She's just as charming as can be. (Until she isn't!)

Flop the hair in front and in back of the head, to soften her look.

Draw a vertical-type smile (more up-and-down than side-to-side).

Drawing the Body from Simple Templates

If you're a beginning (or even more experienced) artist, you might be intimidated by drawing the body. Don't be! Like we did with drawing the anime head, we will break down the figure into customizable templates that will give you the confidence to draw any character. You'll also learn useful proportions to be able to draw at any angle.

Basic Proportions

The major proportions of the body are indicated by the blue guidelines below. Whether you draw the character small or large, the relative proportions remain the same.

FRONT BODY TEMPLATE

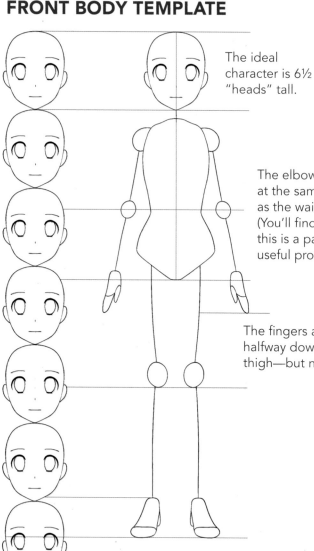

Anime artists begin by drawing the body in segments.

Smooth out the segments to create a flowing, sleek figure.

Leave space between the arms and the body.

Lightly indicate the knee joints.

The ideal character is 6½ "heads" tall.

The elbows appear at the same level as the waistline. (You'll find that this is a particularly useful proportion!)

The fingers are almost halfway down the thigh—but not quite.

The feet are approximately shoulder-width apart.

The steps have paid off. The final drawing is an appealing anime girl in a fun outfit.

To bring the style to another level, try gradating the hair. Gradating means changing one color gradually into another color, as shown where the red shifts to blue at the bottom.

I don't think she's gotten a haircut since she was eleven.

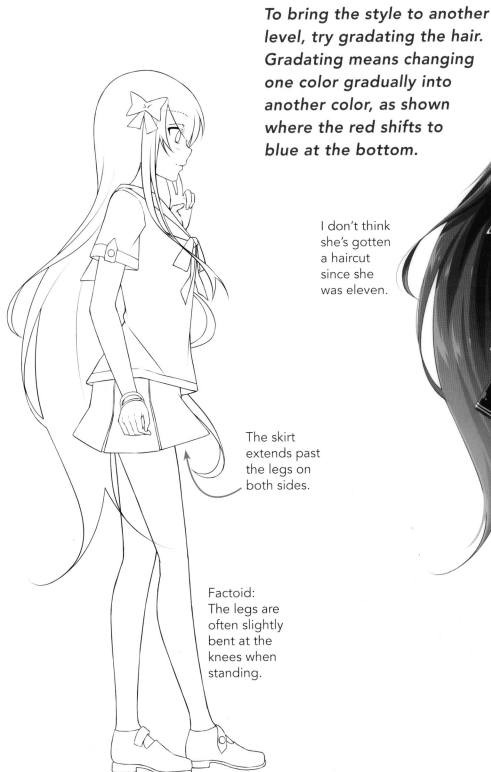

The skirt extends past the legs on both sides.

Factoid: The legs are often slightly bent at the knees when standing.

Basic 360° Schoolgirl Body Template

The blue lines are drawn across the figures to maintain the body proportions of the character as it turns in a complete circle. It's good to practice these yourself. These "measuring points" are located at the following spots:

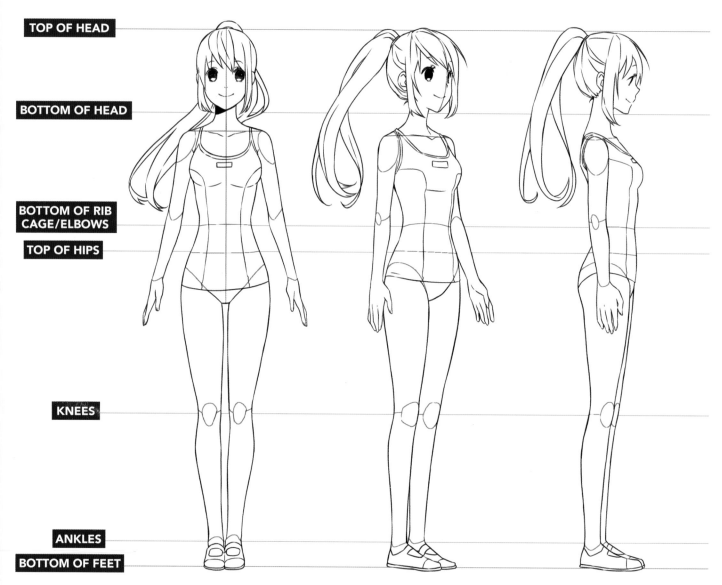

TOP OF HEAD

BOTTOM OF HEAD

BOTTOM OF RIB CAGE/ELBOWS

TOP OF HIPS

KNEES

ANKLES

BOTTOM OF FEET

FRONT
Excellent angle for establishing a character, for funny reaction shots, and for close-ups.

¾ RIGHT
This angle works with everything, especially forced perspective. Good for gestures and fashionable and sitting poses.

RIGHT SIDE
An effective angle for confrontations, this pose can become tiresome if used too frequently.

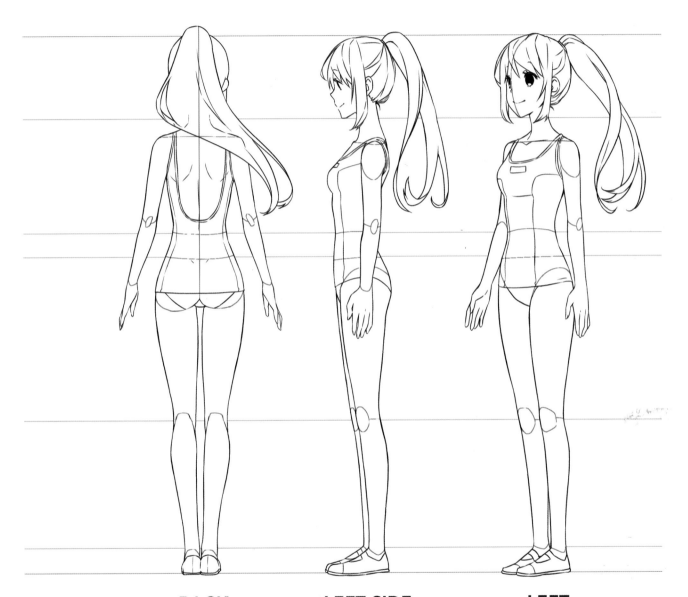

BACK
Infrequently used.

LEFT SIDE
Same as the right-facing side pose.

¾ LEFT
Same as the ¾ right pose.

Boy's Body

One of the most popular boy character types is about 15 years old. He's trim with a medium build and of average height, but he's not the upperclassman, who is tall, lanky, and more stylized. (We'll see examples of that type later in this book.) The upper body of a male character is less flexible than a female's. There's not as much sway between ribcage and hips, therefore, you see a straighter posture. Part of this is due to proportions, since the shoulders are somewhat wider than those usually seen on girl characters.

FRONT VIEW

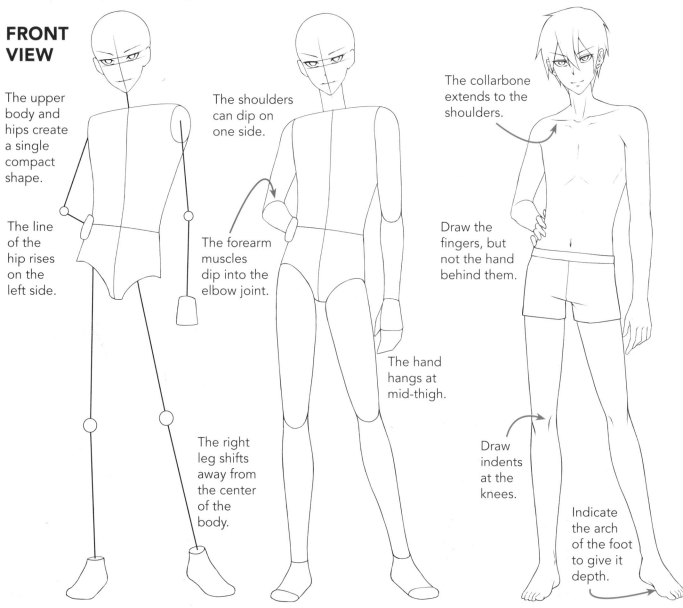

The upper body and hips create a single compact shape.

The line of the hip rises on the left side.

The right leg shifts away from the center of the body.

The shoulders can dip on one side.

The forearm muscles dip into the elbow joint.

The hand hangs at mid-thigh.

The collarbone extends to the shoulders.

Draw the fingers, but not the hand behind them.

Draw indents at the knees.

Indicate the arch of the foot to give it depth.

Creating Contrast with Color

If you like the high-contrast look of manga—drawings in black and white—but you enjoy the color of anime, you can have the best of both worlds by substituting dark colors for black. But you have to know which colors to use. Lighter colors don't look good when darkened, as is the case with a muddy yellow. But colors like a dark red or a dark purple are excellent substitutes for black.

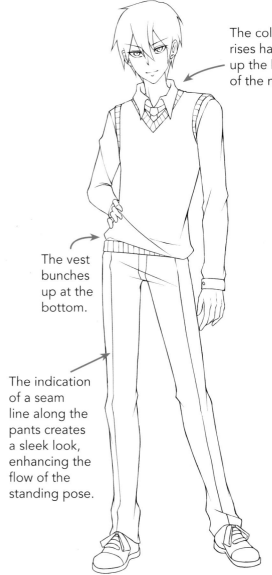

The collar rises halfway up the back of the neck.

The vest bunches up at the bottom.

The indication of a seam line along the pants creates a sleek look, enhancing the flow of the standing pose.

The teen boy can wear a traditional school uniform, like a jacket and tie, or something simpler and sportier, like a sweater vest, long-sleeve shirt, and slacks. Are those athletic shoes allowed by the school dress code? I won't tell if you won't.

SIDE VIEW

High school boys have thin builds, but they still have contours. You can avoid drawing a stiff-looking figure if you try to use curved lines wherever possible. His lower back is not as indented, generally, as a female's lower back, but it still curves inward. On the front, the chest is rounded and juts outward. His neck is set back from the chest.

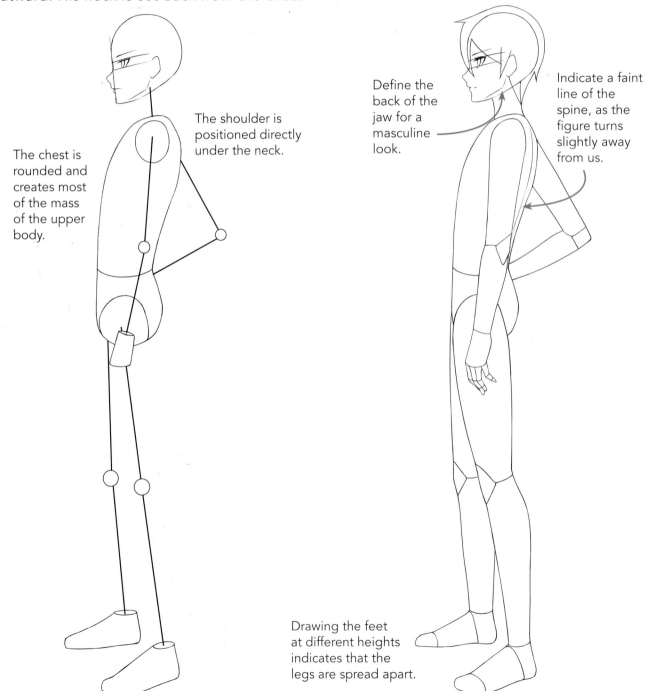

The chest is rounded and creates most of the mass of the upper body.

The shoulder is positioned directly under the neck.

Define the back of the jaw for a masculine look.

Indicate a faint line of the spine, as the figure turns slightly away from us.

Drawing the feet at different heights indicates that the legs are spread apart.

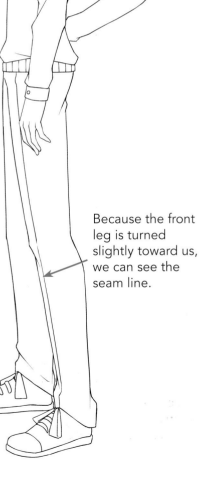

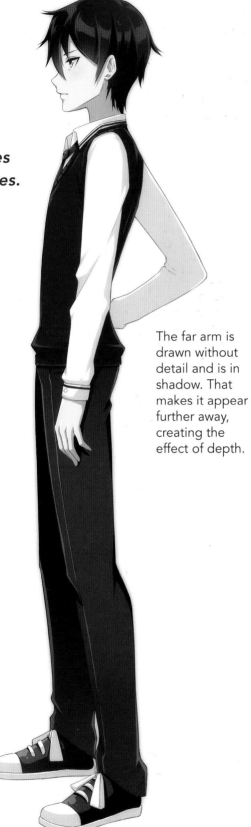

Imperfections make things appear lifelike. A minor bend at the knee and a few creases of clothing is all it takes.

The collar extends forward, past the neck and onto the chest.

The sweater drops below the belt line.

Because the front leg is turned slightly toward us, we can see the seam line.

The far arm is drawn without detail and is in shadow. That makes it appear further away, creating the effect of depth.

Fun & Easy Fashions

There's no easier way to customize a character than with clothing. In this chapter, we'll start with classic schoolgirl and schoolboy uniforms, and then learn ways to change up their looks with variations and authentic accessories, such as shoes, leggings, bags, and scarves. Then, we'll look at different character types and how you can easily convey their personalities through their clothing.

Fashions & Outfits

The next stage in the development of an original character is the outfit. Since the bodies are based on the same template, the clothing is what differentiates one character from another. In other words, your choice of fashions becomes part of the character design. Let's explore some clothing ideas that help create original character types.

USING VARIETY

Many outfits are created from a variety of elements that match well with one another. If they match too closely, there's no contrast. If they are too dissimilar, they won't go well with each other. Strike a balance between the two approaches.

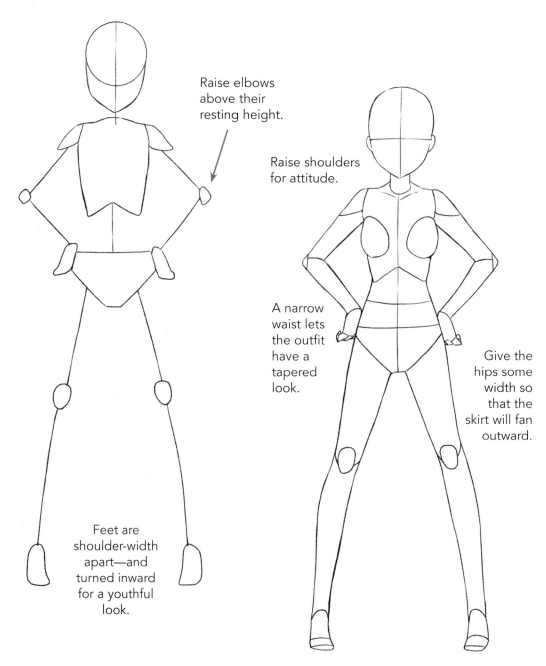

Raise elbows above their resting height.

Raise shoulders for attitude.

A narrow waist lets the outfit have a tapered look.

Give the hips some width so that the skirt will fan outward.

Feet are shoulder-width apart—and turned inward for a youthful look.

ALTERNATING LONG & SHORT CLOTHING

The vest is short, but the shirt underneath is long. The skirt is short, but the leggings are long. Combining short items with long items creates interest. Note the high number of folds in the sleeves. Extra folds are created when a joint is bent, like the arms.

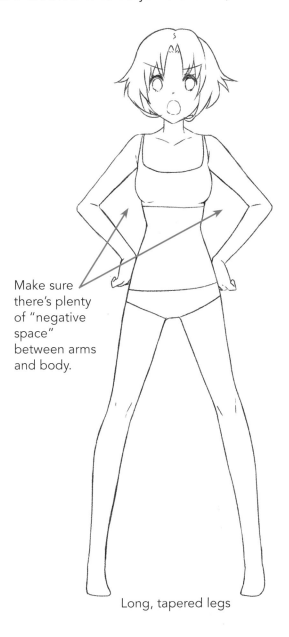

Make sure there's plenty of "negative space" between arms and body.

Long, tapered legs

Schoolgirl Uniform

The schoolgirl uniform is the most popular outfit in all of anime—and a must-know for drawing anime fashions. It's a simple outfit: a jacket, a skirt, and tall socks. Ever wonder why? It's because within the framework of a uniform, there are many different components to choose from. By combining them in specific ways, you can keep the overall appearance of a uniform while infusing it with individuality, as we'll see!

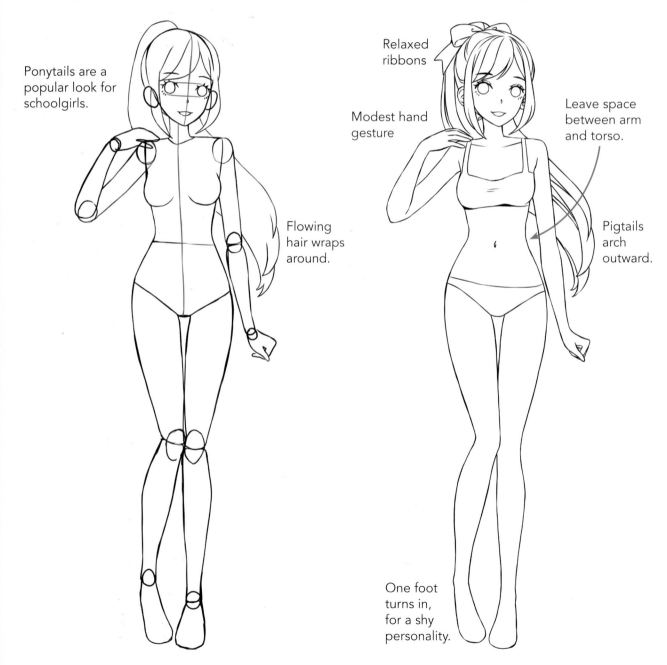

Ponytails are a popular look for schoolgirls.

Flowing hair wraps around.

Relaxed ribbons

Modest hand gesture

Leave space between arm and torso.

Pigtails arch outward.

One foot turns in, for a shy personality.

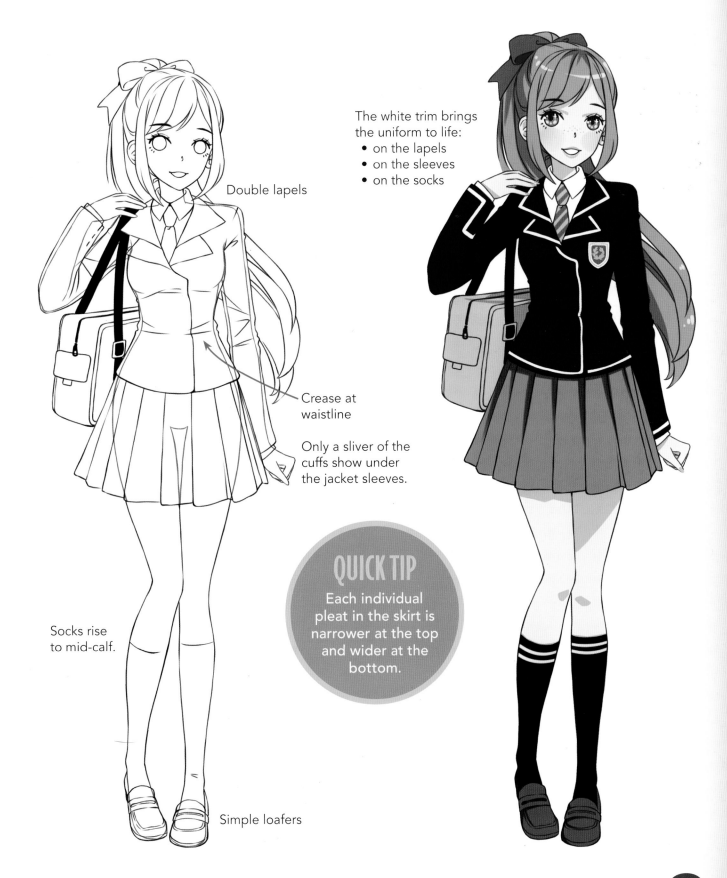

Double lapels

The white trim brings the uniform to life:
- on the lapels
- on the sleeves
- on the socks

Crease at waistline

Only a sliver of the cuffs show under the jacket sleeves.

QUICK TIP
Each individual pleat in the skirt is narrower at the top and wider at the bottom.

Socks rise to mid-calf.

Simple loafers

Fashion Selections for the Basic Schoolgirl

For creating eye-catching characters, you can't beat choosing the right outfit. Clothes enhance a character's attractiveness and help define her personality. It's as much a part of her character design as her facial features or proportions. Although characters may have varied wardrobes, their identities often center on a specific outfit.

VARIETY IN SCHOOL UNIFORMS

The word *uniform* suggests that there is one standard outfit. There isn't. Within the category of school uniforms, you can create a host of appealing fashions mixing and matching mostly traditional (and a few not-so-traditional) items, such as blouses, sweaters, vests, skirts, dresses, jackets, leggings, shoes, and accessories.

Wide, colored collar

Colored trim on sleeve

Knee-length pleated skirt

Sailor Outfit

Narrow cuffs

Form-fitting jacket

Knee-length socks

Two front pleats

High, single-color leggings

Fitted Jacket & Skirt

Double-Breasted Suit

90

Formal collar and tie

Short skirt

Fingerless glove (non-traditional)

Cuffed beneath the elbows

Ruffled trim

Striped leggings (non-traditional)

A tie or scarf is a nice touch added to many school uniforms.

Pleats are well liked by anime fans.

Vest with Short Skirt　　**Low-Waisted Jumper & Leggings**　　**Sweater & Skirt**

SCHOOLGIRL UNIFORM VARIATIONS

1. Button-down sweater

2. Short jacket

3. Plaid pleated skirt

4. Plaid detail

5. Short pleated skirt

6. Button-down Sweater-vest

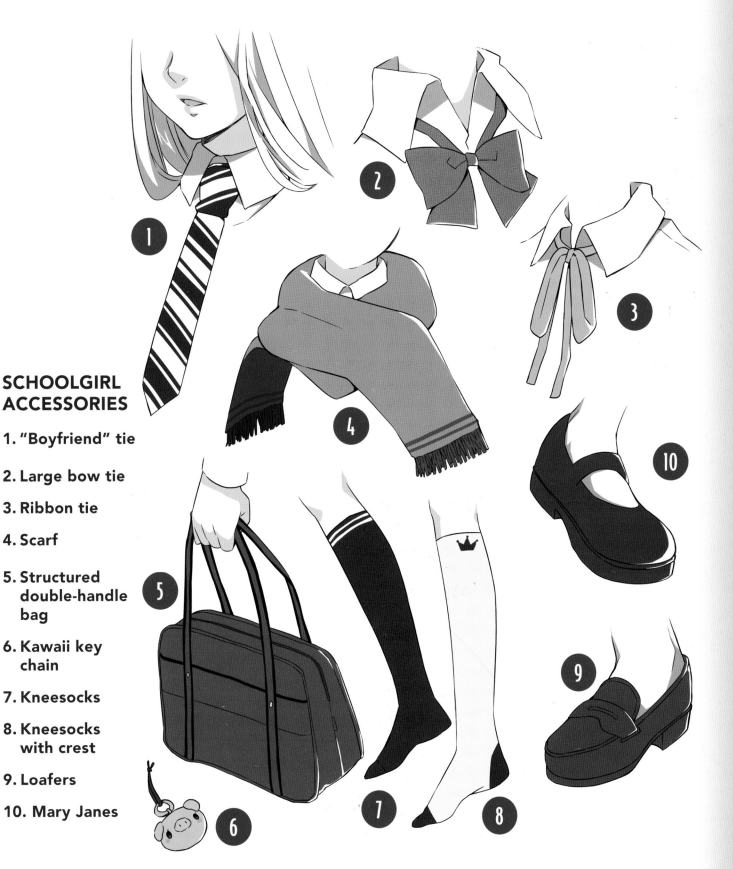

SCHOOLGIRL ACCESSORIES

1. "Boyfriend" tie

2. Large bow tie

3. Ribbon tie

4. Scarf

5. Structured double-handle bag

6. Kawaii key chain

7. Kneesocks

8. Kneesocks with crest

9. Loafers

10. Mary Janes

Clothing and Character Types

Let's look at how personalities can be expressed through various styles of outfits. When creating clothing for your characters, think about how color and details, such as patterns and layers, can be used to create the overall impression.

COOL AND CASUAL

The trick to drawing jeans is to make them look casual and expensive at the same time. How do we do it? We tear them to shreds! Each rip raises the price tag. Unfortunately, this approach doesn't work with everything. I've added numerous nicks to my car, but, curiously, it doesn't seem to have added to its value.

Draw choppy bangs.

Draw pigtails so they can be seen through the arms.

Draw the hands on the widest part of the hips.

The heel of the palm is lower than the fingers.

Knees and feet turn inward for a cute stance.

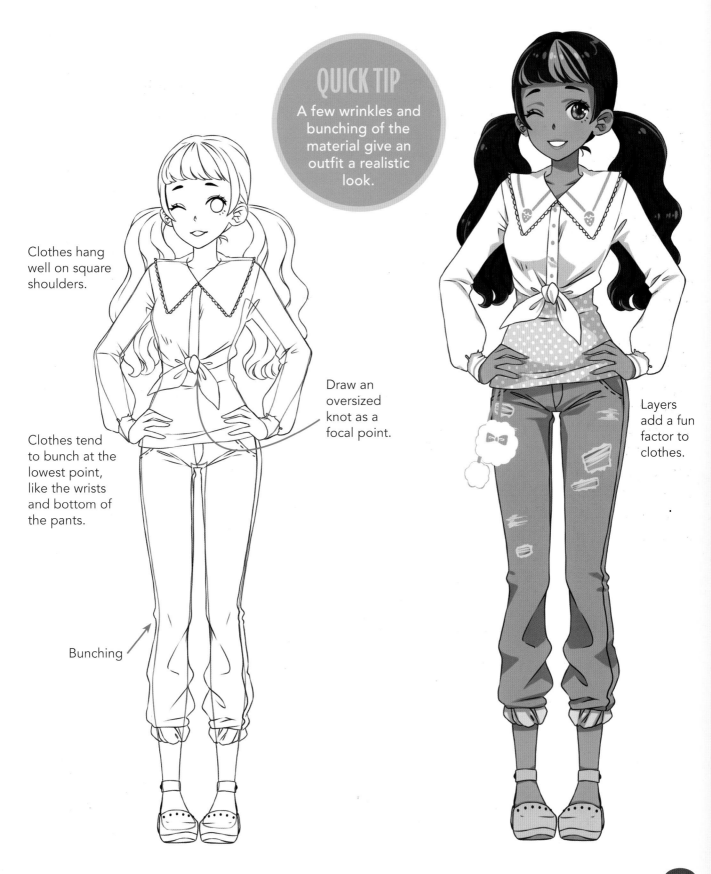

Clothes hang well on square shoulders.

Clothes tend to bunch at the lowest point, like the wrists and bottom of the pants.

Bunching

Draw an oversized knot as a focal point.

Layers add a fun factor to clothes.

INTROVERT

Everyone feels down in the dumps sometimes. I get that way when I try on the pants I wore in college. Her buttoned-up jacket is synonymous with a character that is wrapped up tightly. But a close friend can get her to laugh.

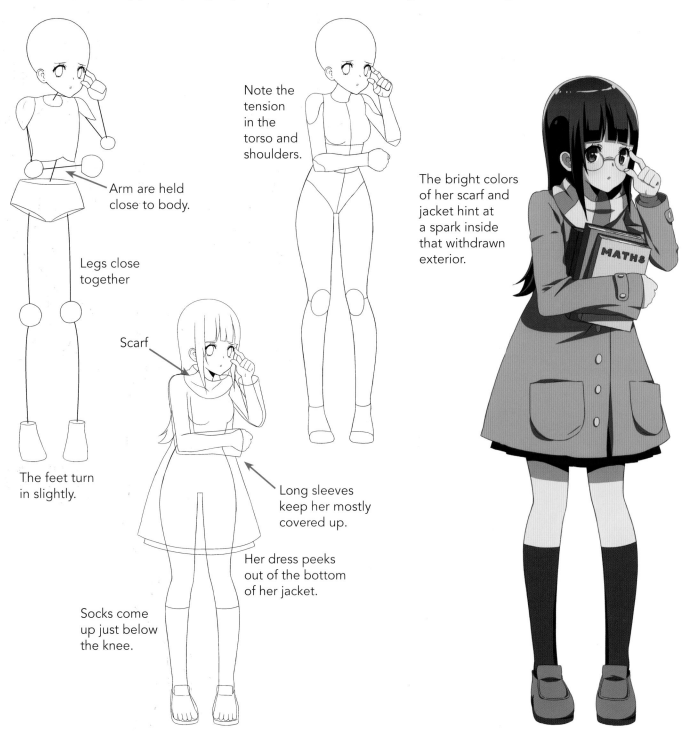

Arm are held close to body.

Legs close together

The feet turn in slightly.

Note the tension in the torso and shoulders.

Scarf

The bright colors of her scarf and jacket hint at a spark inside that withdrawn exterior.

Long sleeves keep her mostly covered up.

Her dress peeks out of the bottom of her jacket.

Socks come up just below the knee.

MATHS

CAREFREE

It's easy to suggest a stylish look. Simply draw one leg bent and resting on the ball of the foot. Then draw the hand (the one on the same side as the bent leg), on the hip. Style is as much an attitude as it is a choice of clothing.

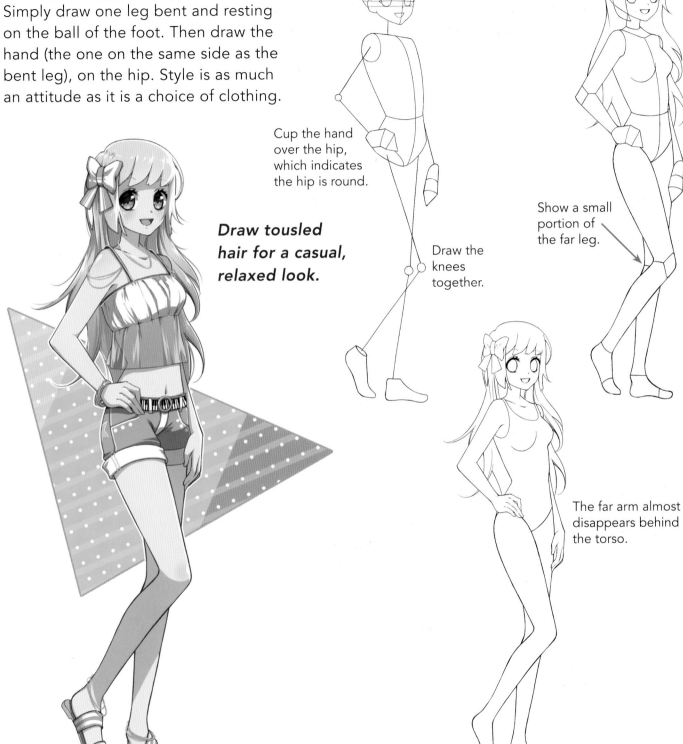

Cup the hand over the hip, which indicates the hip is round.

Draw tousled hair for a casual, relaxed look.

Draw the knees together.

Show a small portion of the far leg.

The far arm almost disappears behind the torso.

MODEST STUDENT

This charming character type suffers from low self-esteem. She doesn't realize that she's a talented artist, so she doesn't show her drawings to anyone. Do you know someone like that?

Her closed pose shows that she finds it hard to relax.

The head tilt adds charm.

She "protects" herself emotionally by keeping her arms in front of herself.

Comfortable sweater

"Plain" skirt

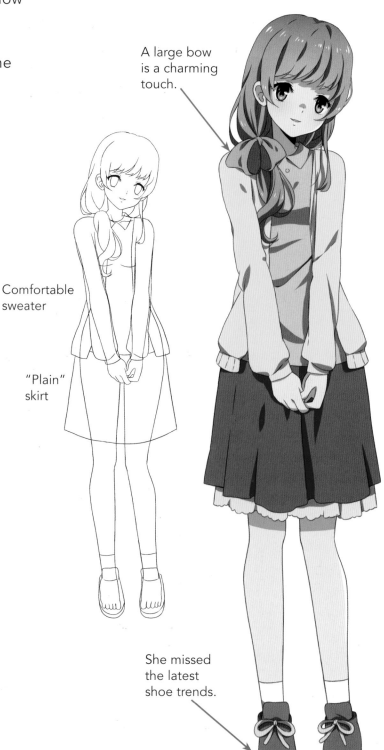

A large bow is a charming touch.

She missed the latest shoe trends.

Schoolboy Clothing

The schoolboy's waking hours are preoccupied with thoughts of girls, food, and cars. Trendy clothes, not so much. He's not going to spend his video game money on them. Generally, everything looks like it could use some ironing. We can boil down his wardrobe to three basic categories: sporty, school clothes, and everything else.

Basic Construction

Sporty

School

Everything Else

VARIATIONS TO MIX & MATCH

1. **Button-down shirt**

2. **Sweatshirt with hood**

3. **Skinny slacks**

4. **Casual shirt**

5. **Showy parka**

6. **Sporty T-shirt**

7. **Cargo pants**

8. **School sweater-vest**

9. **School blazer**

10. **Long-sleeved crewneck**

ACCESSORIES

1. Messenger bag
2. Caps and hats
3. Gloves
4. Eye- or sunglasses
5. Wristband
6. Sneaker types
7. Scarf
8. Headphones
9. Sleek boots
10. Laced boots

TRADITIONAL SCHOOL UNIFORM

You know this type of character. Girls ask *him* to the prom. His clothes contribute to his charisma. He's a popular character in graphic novels and one you'll need in your repertoire.

QUICK TIP
Male anime characters can wear formal outfits, but they wear them in a casual, loose manner.

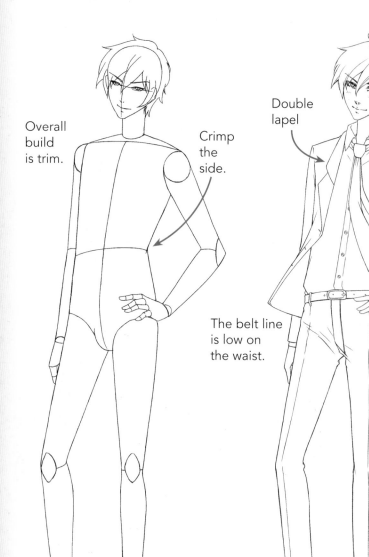

Overall build is trim.

Crimp the side.

Double lapel

Tie and collar are loose.

The belt line is low on the waist.

Use a different color for the jacket interior. This makes the image clearer to read.

On a darker surface, like the pant legs, the seam can be shown with a white highlight.

Pants cover top of the shoe.

The inner line of the foot dictates its direction.

Torso overlaps shoulder.

Wrist bends over knee.

Thigh appears compressed at this angle.

Side foot

Front foot

Loose hood

Opened zipper reveals layer underneath.

Oversized Shoes

The looser the garment, the more folds and creases there are.

SPORTS AND STYLE

The star athletes of anime tend to wear bright, bold colors. The apparel is loose to allow for maximum movement. The shorts and sleeves—if there are any—are usually baggy. That doesn't exactly sound like a recipe for style. But it can be, if you are creative. Let's start by establishing the figure.

Stripes act as a unifying design element. It pulls the entire outfit together.

Long shorts are cut below the knee.

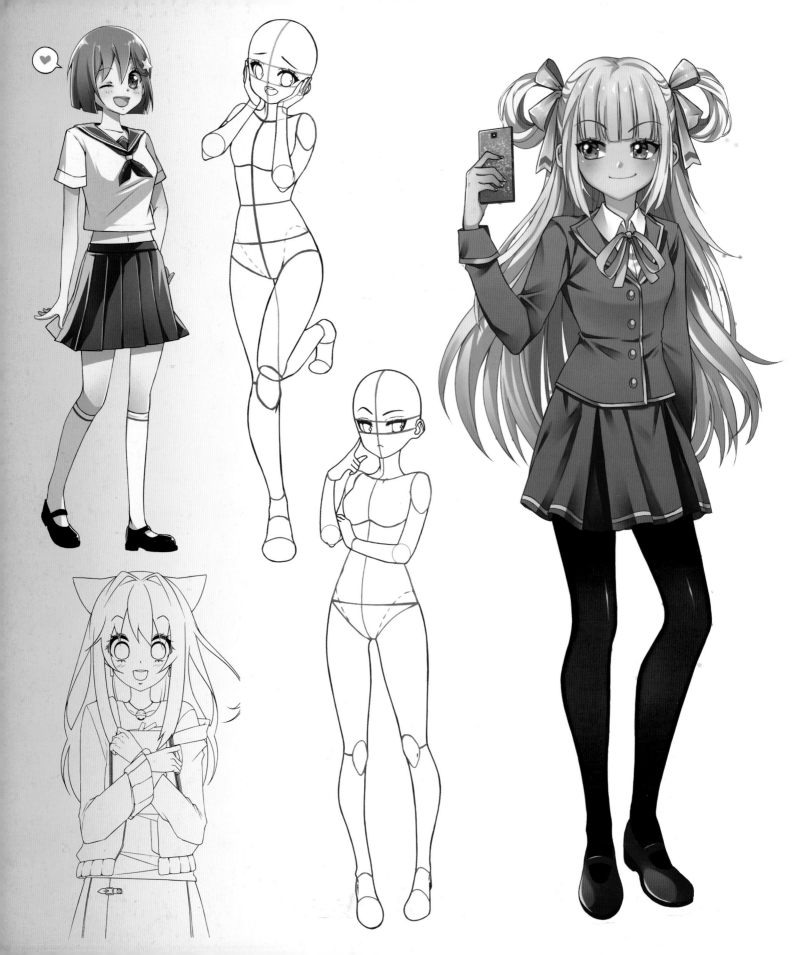

Emotions & Attitudes

Drawing a character's emotions and attitudes is something you can do. We'll break it down into simple steps, and highlight the cues that are key. With the instructions in this section, you'll learn how to indicate your character's mood, or even what they're thinking.

Super-Simplified Expression Chart

Drawing expressions doesn't need to be complicated. The trick is to base them on one or two themes. For example, you can create a stunned look with small eyeballs and a wide-open mouth. If you draw those two things, you'll nail the expression. The rest is merely details.

Super angry

Thinking (note the bead of sweat)

Deadpan (humorous)

Positive reaction

Happy

So sad

QUICK TIP

An expression only requires one or two elements to make it work—so keep it simple!

Apprehensive

Oh, no!

Such good fortune!

On the verge of a huge cry

Stunned

Ugh! I need a nap!

Mannerisms

You can express an attitude simply by adjusting the way your character stands. Here are some examples of popular anime mannerisms of schoolgirls that can be expressed in simple standing poses.

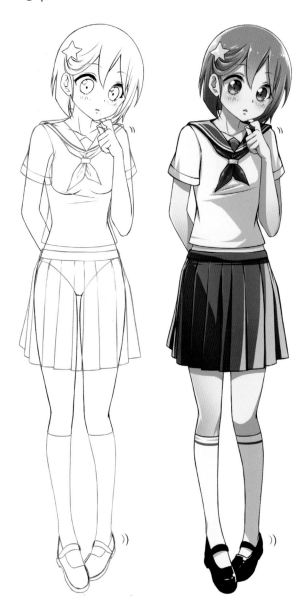

OUTGOING

She has a relaxed, unguarded manner and stands with her arms away from her body.

INNOCENT

This pose mimics the stance of a much younger character. Notice the foot position.

ANXIOUS

She braces herself for the worst. Draw her
elbows close to the body, and bring her hands
together. Note the lifted shoulders.

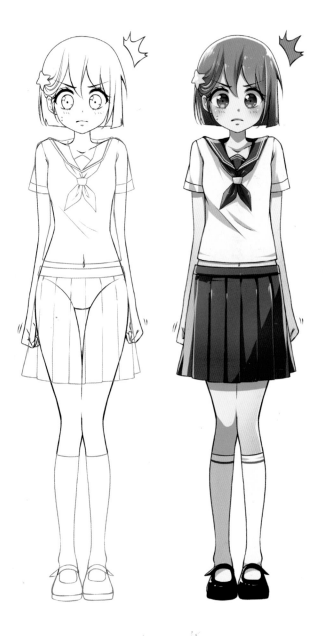

UPSET

She becomes stiff as a board. Her legs
are pressed together, which creates a pose
with total symmetry.

Young Characters, Big Emotions

People sometimes assume that young characters have quiet emotions, but the opposite is true. They have energetic, fun personalities.

OPTIMISTIC

No matter what trouble occurs, this character will find a silver lining. A rainy day? No problem! It's cozier indoors. Lost your purse? The best things in life are free! Sentenced to solitary confinement? Who doesn't need some "alone" time?

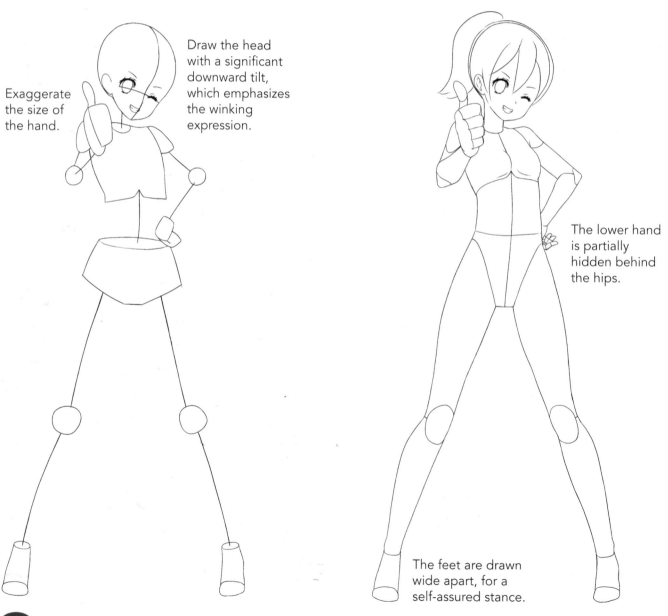

Exaggerate the size of the hand.

Draw the head with a significant downward tilt, which emphasizes the winking expression.

The lower hand is partially hidden behind the hips.

The feet are drawn wide apart, for a self-assured stance.

When the head tilts forward, the ponytail appears to rise in back.

The midsection thins out.

This famous gesture puts viewers in a good mood.

LONELY

Her mom is busy at work. Her dog is at the kennel. And her teddy bear just ran away from home. It makes you want to draw some new characters, just to cheer her up. Notice the withdrawn stance, as if her friends have abandoned her.

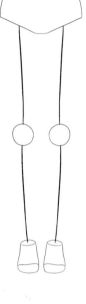

Draw a symmetrical pose.

The hands are drawn at the level of the sternum (the hollow just below the breast bone).

Draw even hips.

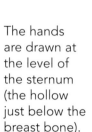

Flowing hair overlaps some of her face, for a spontaneous effect.

Draw the elbows at the level of the waistline.

The thighs are wide at the low end of the hips.

A gentle breeze helps to create a sad scene.

Draw interlaced fingers. If that seems complicated, just draw one hand over the other.

By drawing the feet close together, you create a meek look.

SHOCKED

Surprised is when you see a UFO just outside of your window. *Shocked* is when you've been beamed aboard. Shock is an instant reaction, and the entire body gets involved. There's almost no transition. The character goes from zero to sixty in a split second.

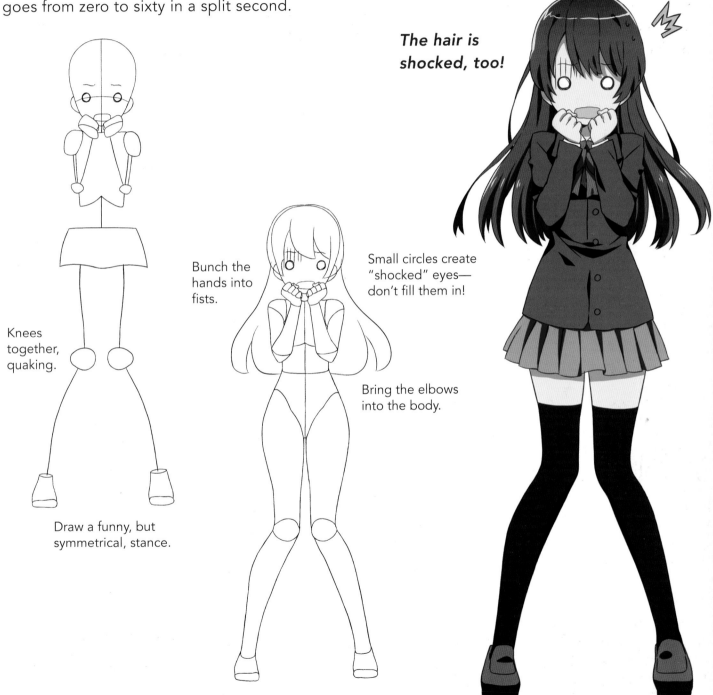

The hair is shocked, too!

Knees together, quaking.

Draw a funny, but symmetrical, stance.

Bunch the hands into fists.

Bring the elbows into the body.

Small circles create "shocked" eyes—don't fill them in!

SOOO MAD!

Can an angry expression get laughs? Yes, if you follow a simple technique. Instead of letting out an explosion of fury, bottle it up. Get your character to fume, but don't let her explode. Look how tightly wrapped this character is.

Someone's going to have to pry those arms loose if they want her to settle down.

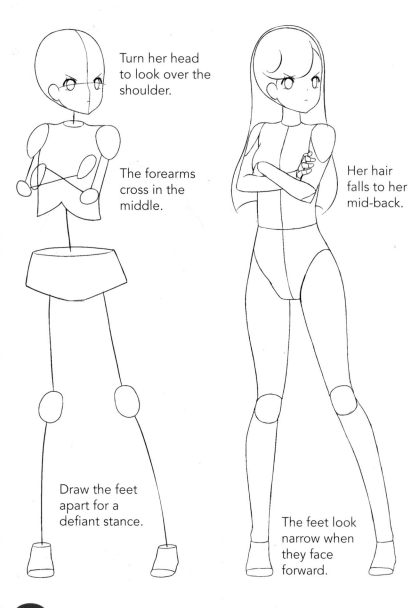

Turn her head to look over the shoulder.

The forearms cross in the middle.

Draw the feet apart for a defiant stance.

Her hair falls to her mid-back.

The feet look narrow when they face forward.

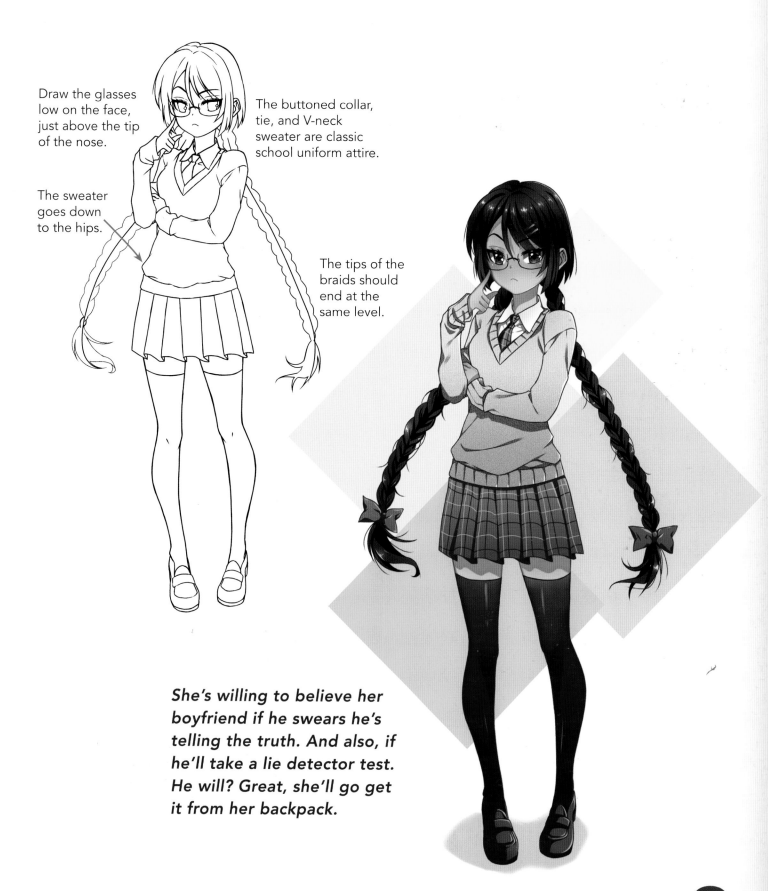

Draw the glasses low on the face, just above the tip of the nose.

The buttoned collar, tie, and V-neck sweater are classic school uniform attire.

The sweater goes down to the hips.

The tips of the braids should end at the same level.

She's willing to believe her boyfriend if he swears he's telling the truth. And also, if he'll take a lie detector test. He will? Great, she'll go get it from her backpack.

INFATUATED

She's only known him for two seconds, and she's already planning to send out wedding invitations. It's natural for anime characters to fall head over heels. The infatuation stage lasts a couple of weeks, followed by the "discovery of his faults" stage, followed closely by the "I will improve you" stage, followed inevitably by the "I'm outta here" stage.

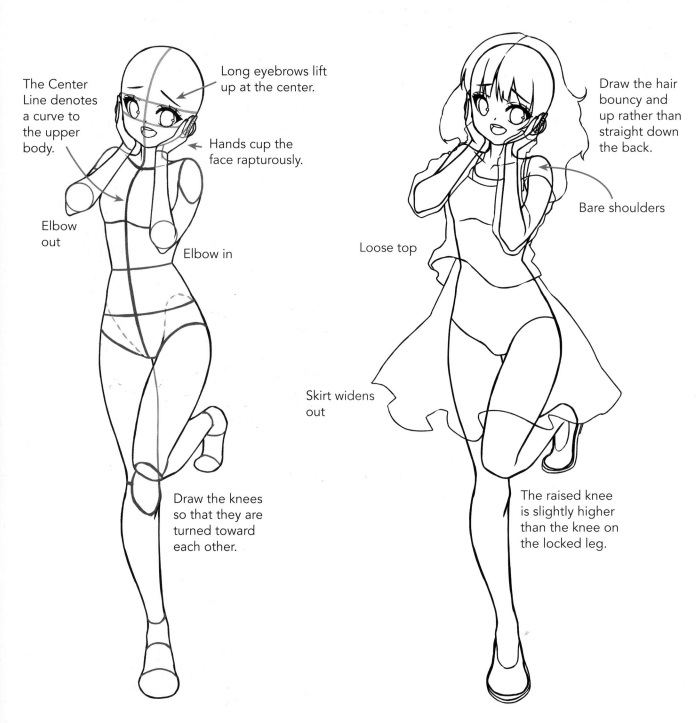

The Center Line denotes a curve to the upper body.

Long eyebrows lift up at the center.

Hands cup the face rapturously.

Elbow out

Elbow in

Draw the knees so that they are turned toward each other.

Draw the hair bouncy and up rather than straight down the back.

Bare shoulders

Loose top

Skirt widens out

The raised knee is slightly higher than the knee on the locked leg.

The sleeves cover the top of the hands.

A few wrinkles along the side of the blouse make the material look soft.

This is her "He's perfect!" squeal. What do you want to bet that he's not?

STUCK UP

If being self-absorbed is a stage she's going through, then she's going through it very, very slowly. Every day starts out with a thorough search across social media to see if anyone mentioned her name. If not, she can always review previous posts. It makes such good reading!

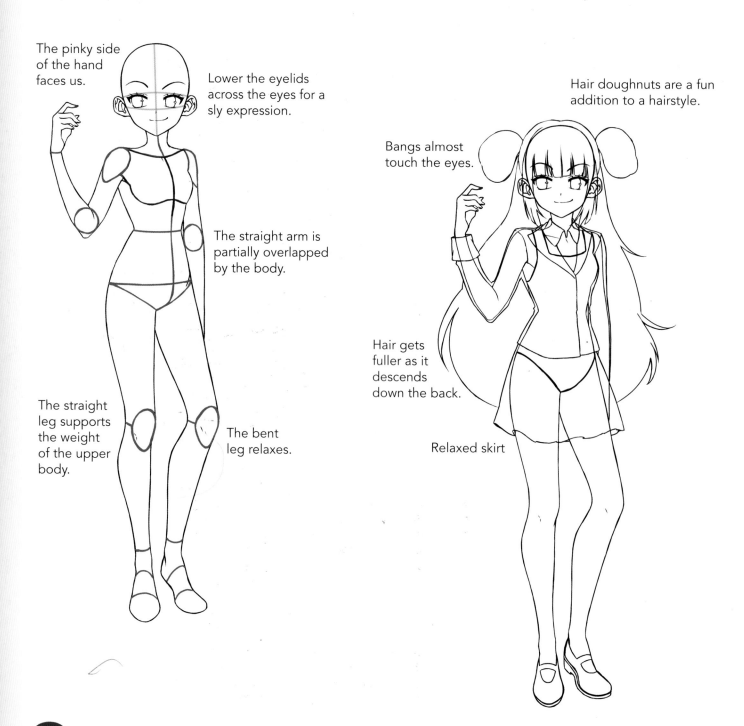

The pinky side of the hand faces us.

Lower the eyelids across the eyes for a sly expression.

The straight arm is partially overlapped by the body.

The straight leg supports the weight of the upper body.

The bent leg relaxes.

Hair doughnuts are a fun addition to a hairstyle.

Bangs almost touch the eyes.

Hair gets fuller as it descends down the back.

Relaxed skirt

Don't look now but he's going to need an ice pack for that shiner. "What shiner?" you might ask. Wait a moment and you'll see.

FAKE MARTIAL ARTS MASTER

The pseudo martial arts master wears what he thinks makes him look like an eleventh-degree black belt, even though there are only ten degrees. The outfit needs to look like something he purchased from a catalog. It shouldn't look official, just pretentious. I still can't figure out what those mesh sleeves are for!

His limbs are going in all different directions— "Mr. Coordination."

His torso curves inward— a sign of weakness.

Broad expressions work well in comedy. One eye winces. The mouth opens wide. And the hair reacts to his being hit on the head.

For this character to work to its fullest comedic effect, give him two chibi friends laughing at him!

Please don't teach me that move!

THE WEEKEND ATHLETE

She bats lefty. Or righty. She can't remember which. But it doesn't matter, she always belts the ball for a hit but also breaks a car window in the process. Her jersey is a sweatshirt, and her cleats are basketball shoes. And get a look at those carnival stripes on her cap. The hair is roughed up a bit.

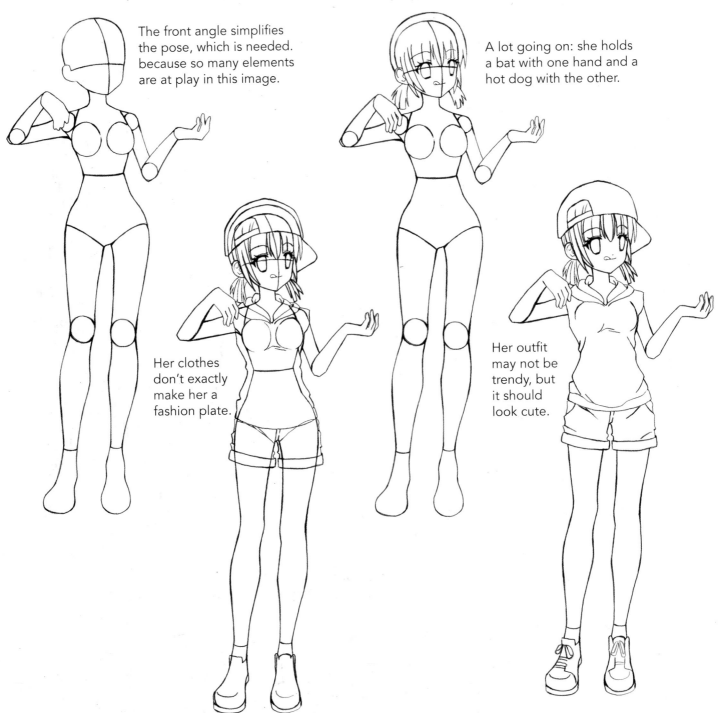

The front angle simplifies the pose, which is needed. because so many elements are at play in this image.

A lot going on: she holds a bat with one hand and a hot dog with the other.

Her clothes don't exactly make her a fashion plate.

Her outfit may not be trendy, but it should look cute.

130

She may only weigh 105 pounds, but all of it goes into her swing.

Creating Special Moments

The best drawings are about something. They capture a character, or characters, in important moments. In this chapter, you'll get the steps to drawing characters in key moments that grab the audience's attention. We'll even draw a few couples. It may take you five minutes to draw each character, but it's worth the extra effort to take your anime to the next level.

ALMOST A KISS

Characters in love are often cautious. That's because of the obstacles that have been put in the way of their romance. Those obstacles could be parents, an ex, or obligations. Adding such impediments creates depth.

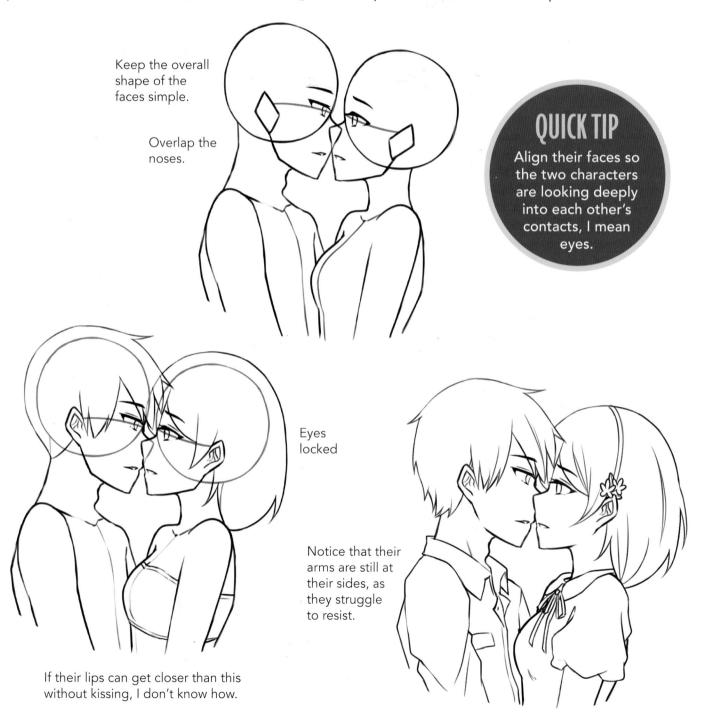

Keep the overall shape of the faces simple.

Overlap the noses.

QUICK TIP
Align their faces so the two characters are looking deeply into each other's contacts, I mean eyes.

Eyes locked

Notice that their arms are still at their sides, as they struggle to resist.

If their lips can get closer than this without kissing, I don't know how.

The most important part of this scene is the moment before the moment. In other words, it's the tension that grabs the audience's interest. Will they kiss or won't they? What do you think? (I think so, too.)

Pet Lovers

Pets are great icebreakers. While the two characters strike up a conversation about their pets, we begin to realize that the dogs set this up! Position the characters close to one another, but leave just enough space between them to keep the scene from looking cramped.

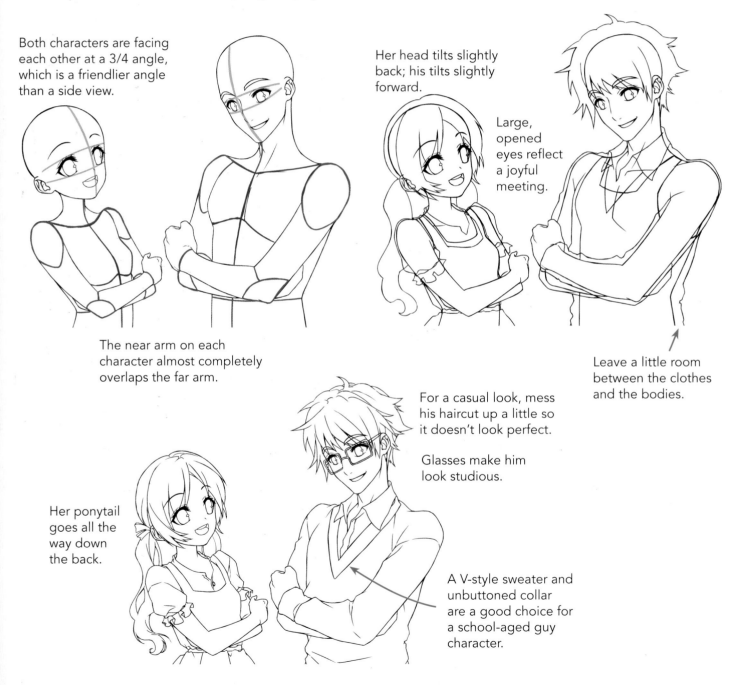

Both characters are facing each other at a 3/4 angle, which is a friendlier angle than a side view.

Her head tilts slightly back; his tilts slightly forward.

Large, opened eyes reflect a joyful meeting.

The near arm on each character almost completely overlaps the far arm.

Leave a little room between the clothes and the bodies.

For a casual look, mess his haircut up a little so it doesn't look perfect.

Glasses make him look studious.

Her ponytail goes all the way down the back.

A V-style sweater and unbuttoned collar are a good choice for a school-aged guy character.

The dogs will be funnier if they aren't perfectly behaved.

The girl is doing the talking and the boy is doing the listening. Conversations flow smoother if the characters appear to take turns.

The Comfort of Home

When your friends have let you down, and you've got no one else to turn to, you can always rely on your pal with the floppy ears for unconditional love. Home is where you find your room, your dog, and a big bag of caramel corn hidden in the back of the pantry.

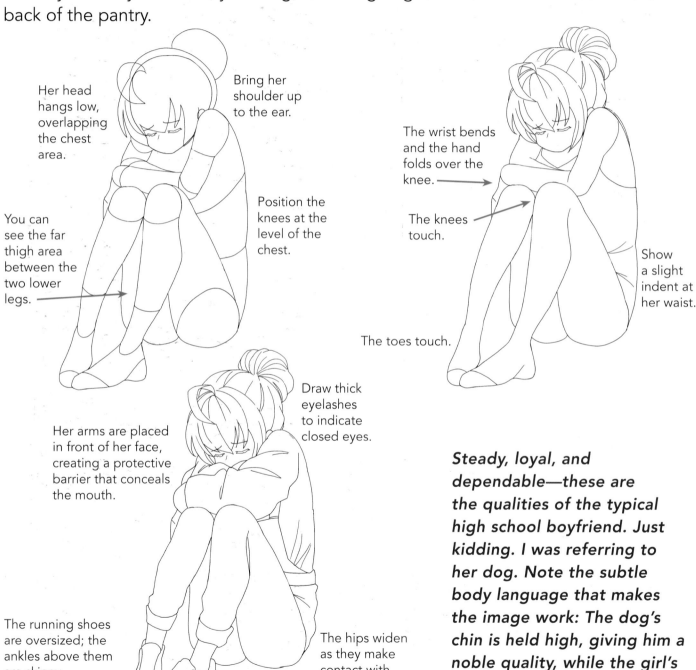

Her head hangs low, overlapping the chest area.

Bring her shoulder up to the ear.

You can see the far thigh area between the two lower legs.

Position the knees at the level of the chest.

The wrist bends and the hand folds over the knee.

The knees touch.

Show a slight indent at her waist.

The toes touch.

Draw thick eyelashes to indicate closed eyes.

Her arms are placed in front of her face, creating a protective barrier that conceals the mouth.

The running shoes are oversized; the ankles above them are skinny.

The hips widen as they make contact with the floor.

Steady, loyal, and dependable—these are the qualities of the typical high school boyfriend. Just kidding. I was referring to her dog. Note the subtle body language that makes the image work: The dog's chin is held high, giving him a noble quality, while the girl's head is low, showing sorrow.

Uninvited Guests

In the mystery genre, characters are thrust into suspenseful situations where they must use their wits to save themselves. The genre also features some uninvited guests. Fortunately, they're easier to get rid of than some relatives.

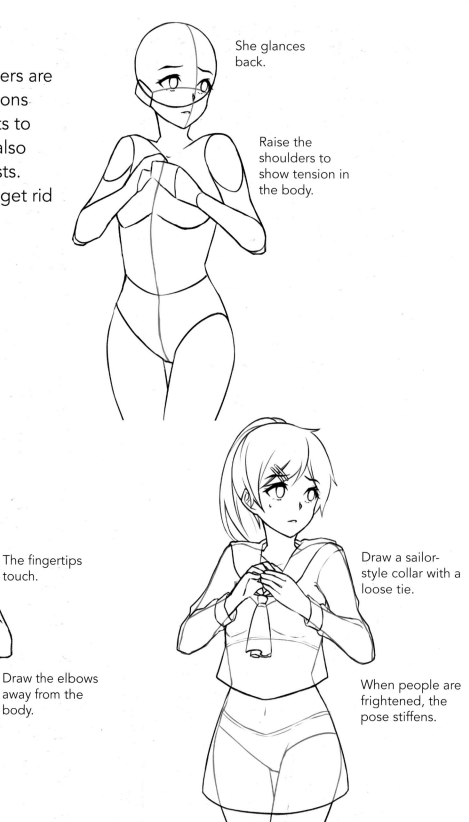

She glances back.

Raise the shoulders to show tension in the body.

Draw the ponytail on the left side.

The fingertips touch.

Draw the elbows away from the body.

Draw a sailor-style collar with a loose tie.

When people are frightened, the pose stiffens.

Looks like she has a new friend.

Daydreamers

A whimsical scene can put a smile on your face without going for big laughs. At moments like these, characters explore their lives with a cheerful curiosity.

Draw both characters facing straight ahead, without eye contact.

His hands disappear behind his head.

Her hair fans out on the grass.

His body stretches out, straightening his outline.

Her legs meet at the knees, and then widen out.

Draw her toes pointing toward each other, for a cute pose.

Draw his feet pointing up, with the soles partially visible.

Draw a ruffled hemline.

Make his clothes look slightly rumpled.

Here, our couple is involved in a deep, existential conversation, which will momentarily be interrupted by the boy's comment, "Want to get pizza?" The mystery of life, thrown under the bus for a slice of pepperoni.

Index